This book is dedicated to Angelo and Yolanda Tosone

This book is a work of fiction.

**I've bent the space time
continuum to
serve my will and taken huge
liberties with the laws of physics
and nature.
Enjoy!**

PARADOX I.N. TIME

by Lauren DuChateau

Chapter 1

September 2016 AD

Buffalo, New York

Just time separates life and hope from death.

I slid to a halt on the polished floor in front of the secretary's desk. "Holly, call a code blue," I said. No time for please or thank you. Then I sprinted back toward the hospital room. My long brown curls waved frantically behind me as I ran. This patient couldn't die.

I needed answers—long sought after answers about my past—and this could be my first real lead.

She had to live.

"Lydia—call a code?" Holly asked, bouncing upright in her chair, sputtering mid-sip on her coffee.

"Yeah, code blue," I hollered over my shoulder as I ran. "I need help in Room Four-thirty-four. Jane Doe just smiled at me, nice as can be, and then went out on me." My voice sounded strangely disembodied, echoing down the long, horseshoe-shaped intensive care unit, bouncing off the white-on-white walls. Hospital codes were always surreal, making time shift into slow motion.

In the patient's room, alarms rang, joining into one piercing, adrenaline-inducing shriek in my head. My clumsy fingers felt numb as I scrambled to get a back board under her. *Get a grip, Lydia,* I told myself. *Only novices get nervous during codes.*

I started chest compressions and the ventilator pumped lifesaving oxygen into the patient's lungs. The outdated ABC algorithm—*A* for airway, *B* for breathing…repeated in my head for some reason. I took a deep breath, but the familiar smells of alcohol and clean linen that usually helped in these situations weren't working. *Remain calm. You'll be more efficient.*

My mind raced. *Could this woman be linked to my past?* She didn't look important—she was so small, fragile, and still, covered with only a thin, white sheet. She seemed to fade into the bed, her silvery hair barely contrasting with the clinical white pillowcase. Dozens of tubes and wires snaked from her to all different points around the room.

Her eyes were now closed, but the memory of them open and staring still haunted me. Could it have been my imagination? No, I'd definitely seen that familiar hue of violet reflected in her eyes—the same unique color as mine. They were a soft brown, but if you looked closely, you could see violet flecks. It was the first time I'd ever seen anyone with eyes exactly like mine.

The code was announced overhead and then repeated.

A million questions I couldn't ask swirled around in my head. I teetered on the precipice of something big. After years of fruitless searching for my biological parents, I finally had a clue. Hairs stood up on the back of my neck—it had been like looking into a mirror. *This woman must hold the answers,* I thought, pushing on her chest. *She can't die.*

With a resounding crack, the large glass breakaway doors swung in, and other members of the team poured into the room.

"What do we have, Lydia?" Chris asked, her eyes flashing from the patient to the numbers and rhythms on the alarm monitor over the bed.

Someone thankfully pressed the monitor's silence button. Its repetitious sound had been jangling my already frayed nerves. "A Jane Doe," I recited to the nurse practitioner in auto-mode, "admitted half an hour ago from the E.R. She's temping at one hundred and four degrees, septic from two large arm lacerations. Heart rate, thirty-four. She just started bradying down two minutes ago."

And is on her way to cardiac standstill and death, I thought. *Please don't die. I need to talk to you.* I fought back tears of frustration.

Mark from Respiratory grabbed an Ambu-bag, hooked it to her E.T. tube and gave it a squeeze. His movements snapped me back to the moment.

"Let's check a heart rhythm," Chris called out. "Asystole, let's give her some EPI. Hang a normal saline wide open. Resume chest compressions."

Chest compressions resumed before Chris even finished her sentence.

"EPI here," voices called, coming at me from all sides. Hands were everywhere, handing syringes and IVs into the room from the code cart. I repressed a hysterical smile. Fleeting thoughts of a heavy metal singer being levitated above a mosh pit flashed through my mind. *This is how the human mind deals with extreme stress, that's all. I'm normal.*

"EPI in," I said, still holding the IV line I'd just injected into. My hands shook as I watched the monitor, trying to be hopeful. Two minutes crawled by. This had to work.

"Someone grab the Zoll in case we have to pace her," Chris said. "Stop compressions. Let's see a rhythm. Any family, Lydia?"

"No, she's a Jane Doe. No history is available. No advanced directives."

How are we supposed to treat this woman without any background history? Does she have any allergies? Does she even want us to do this?

"Asystole," Chris said. "Her heart's stopped. Another EPI, continue compressions."

Great, the patient's lips are blue, I thought. Why did people wait so long to get medical attention? I hated this part of my job; I'd seen it before way too many times. Untreated infections, given enough time, inevitably spread into the bloodstream, causing sepsis and then multi-organ failure.

Why didn't she go to the hospital for her infected arm wounds? What could have possibly taken precedence?

The rest of the code faded into a blur. Like a robot, I performed my tasks without error. It was a hopeless dance we were all doing. *Best I go on autopilot now.*

I looked up to note the time of death thirty minutes later, when the nurse practitioner told everyone to stop. Tears misted my eyes, making it difficult to see the defeated look on the team's faces as they trickled out of the room.

I turned off the monitor over the bed. Any hope of talking to the woman had just died with her. I only wanted answers to one or two questions—was that asking too much? I'd waited so long for any kind of an answer to the mystery surrounding my adoption.

Even after spending six years as a registered nurse in the intensive care unit, this part of my job still always made my heart heavy. I hated losing a patient and that helpless feeling as they slipped away.

Still, I loved working in the health field. I'd even gone back to school to become a doctor. Physics, organic chemistry, molecular biology, Latin, and calculus. It had been fantastic. *Then there was Scott*, I thought with a sigh.

Amazing how one little man—well, he hadn't been *that* little—could get me so off-track. I guess it's happened to the best of us: Eve, Cleopatra, Juliet, and Bonnie of the duo Bonnie and Clyde. On the bright side, I hadn't died in a volley of gunfire
yet—and at least I'd finished my premed degree before Scott had cheated on me.

A bunch of empty promises, two years, and one broken heart later, here I was, thirty and single. Why were men such stupid whiners, anyway?

I was still in the room with the dead woman, feeling sad and defeated. Letting out a sigh, I leaned back against the sink. The pressure on my lower back felt good. Being tall did have its drawbacks—and at one inch shy of six feet tall, my back did sometimes ache at work. I needed a minute to catch my breath and calm down, then I'd wrap the patient for the morgue.

I rested my head to one side, closed my eyes, and pressed my temple against the cool glass. Why couldn't I meet a real man? One who never whined, even if bamboo splinters were shoved under his fingernails.

I tried to conjure up a mental image of my perfect man, even with the bamboo splinters being shoved under his nails. My dream man said, *I don't care what you do to me— just let the girl go. I love her with all my manly heart.* His bulging muscles strained under a thin sheen of the sweetest-smelling sweat that you could ever imagine. You know, that manly-smelling sweat that would never fall under the heading of "body odor." Instead, it fell squarely under the me-Tarzan-you-Jane heading. *Okay, back to reality,* I thought. *Besides, there just aren't any real men like that anymore.*

I stooped over to clean the room. Empty packets and syringes lay everywhere, evidence of the frenzied activity that had taken place. Stillness permeated the room. There were no alarms blaring or people shouting. Strange how only minutes could separate life and hope from death.

Grabbing a washcloth, I willed myself to focus on the person in front of me, remembering her when she was still alive. Gently wiping the wrinkled face, I reached out my hand to open the woman's eyes. *Just one more time.*

What if I'd imagined everything? A chill ran down my spine, and I hesitated.

What was the big deal, anyway? I wrapped dead people on a regular basis. But this time, it was different. Those eyes had looked just like mine.

My adoptive mother, Anita, had always said my eyes were a part of my special beauty. As a little girl, I would always ask her what my real mother had been like. She would just smile and say she didn't know—but added that she must have been a beautiful princess. That would make me giggle and forget to ask more questions.

When I got older, I learned that Father Tom had been the only one to see my real mother and father. He told me he'd only seen them once—when they'd left me at the church as a tiny baby. They'd said my name was Lydia, but he hadn't been able to understand anything else in their language.

No one had seen them since. Father Tom said bad people had been chasing them, and that other strange things happened in town that day. He'd called the police, but he feared the worst for my biological parents.

Being a typical, curious teen, I'd asked him why he was so afraid for my parents.

He'd simply answered, "Because no parent would leave such a precious angel without having a life-or-death reason."

My adoptive parents were the only parents I'd known. But ever since Father Tom had told me that story, I'd been burning with curiosity to find out who my biological parents were, and the need to know them had become more powerful as time passed.

Pulling myself back to the present, I wondered how old the woman had been. I tucked her shoulder-length silver hair behind both of her ears and smoothed it down. Gingerly, I lifted the woman's wrist up and looked at her name band. It read:

Date of Birth: 1900

Impossible. This woman had been over one hundred years old.

"Lydia," Erin called from around the curtain.

I jumped, letting out a tiny shriek.

"Do you need help wrapping her up?"

"You just scared me to death. Yes…thanks, I'd appreciate it." I had to get a grip on myself. My heart suddenly felt like it had been switched with that of a hummingbird.

"No problem. I'm all caught up," Erin said as she pulled the curtain open and quickly shut it again, entering the room. "Poor thing, huh? You couldn't find any family on her?"

"Nope, no one." I tried not to let any emotion leak in my voice, but it didn't matter. I couldn't fool Erin; she knew me too well. We'd been friends, both at work and outside of work, for four years now.

Erin was a smart, pretty girl with enviably straight, blonde hair that did everything it was told, unlike my brown mess. She was thin, not too tall, not too short; she was just right. She also knew how to keep a secret, which was a good thing, because she knew a lot of mine.

"Maybe because her family is dead," I said.

"What do you mean? How do you know that?" Erin stared as she leaned in closer to the body, as if looking for clues she'd missed.

"According to her name band, she was born in nineteen hundred," I explained. "She looks pretty good for someone over a hundred years old."

Erin grabbed the lady's wrist. "Hang on—she's a Jane Doe, right?"

"Yeah, unfortunately." I looked at the woman's still face and closed eyes.

"That's why then," Erin gently laid the woman's wrist back onto the bed. "Hospital admissions must have entered "nineteen hundred" precisely *because* she's a Jane Doe. The system just needs a birth date, *any* birth date, in order to function. Lydia, are you okay?"

"I'm just a little freaked out right now." I opened drawers and began to bag up the woman's clothes and possessions. "Right before she died, I got a good look at her eyes, and they were the same color as mine. Now I'm fighting with myself, because I have this ridiculous urge to open her eyes back up and take one more look at them. All I wanted was to ask her a few questions. I know it's selfish of me, since she certainly didn't want or mean to die. But I'm telling you, they were exactly like mine."

Erin came over and put an arm over my shoulder. "Look, Lydia, I know how badly you want to find your biological parents, but this isn't the way. Stick with what you're already doing—the internet and agencies."

She was right. I was being silly; the woman *was* just a Jane Doe. Still, I couldn't let it go. "You're probably right. But would you take one little peek at her eyes and tell me what you think? If I'm right, what are the chances of them being like that?"

"You mean the lady you thought was a hundred and sixteen?" Erin said with her head tilted down, looking up at me with a skeptical expression. "Besides, there's nothing you can do about it now, anyway."

This made me smile. "You're right. I'm being obsessive, so I'll stop. Enough is enough." I pulled more of the woman's clothes out of the bottom drawer. *It's always like this*, my thoughts said, bombarding me. After thirty years, I was used to having zero control of my subconscious.

"What, no 'Yellow Bird' serenade?" Paula asked, sticking her head into the room.

"Not funny, Paula," I replied in a low monotone. I put some of the clothes on the bedside table because the bag was almost full. I couldn't believe she'd just brought that up.

"Oh come on, I'm just joking with you. Are you okay? Need any help from your momma bird?"

"No, Erin's helping me. Thanks, though."

"You got it," Paula said, using one hand to pull the curtain shut, and the other to stifle her giggles.

Leave it to Paula to find a weak spot and hold onto it like a tenacious terrier. Paula, of course, hadn't forgotten the whole "Yellow Bird" glitch she'd happily discovered while training me for the unit. She was a talented lady, and was great at finding my sore spots—if only to exploit them for her own hilarity.

"Don't pay any attention to her," Erin said, stooping to pick up wrappers on the floor.

"I know. She's harmless enough." I mentally redirected myself in an attempt to put a positive spin on my newest thought spree. Was it so odd for a new recruit, fresh in the unit, to get the hiccups and start humming "Yellow Bird" during a crisis? Paula wasn't the one who'd been dealing with the whole "Yellow Bird" anomaly since she was eight years old.

"What the hell did she mean by a 'Yellow Bird' serenade, anyway?" Erin asked in a protective tone.

Resigned to telling the story to yet another person, I set the bag of clothes onto the table and began my memorized version. "When I was eight, my dad brought me to the university where he worked. He taught Greek there, and my mom taught Roman history."

"The same college they're at now—UB, right?" Erin asked, tugging at three IV lines.

"Yeah. Spring session had just finished, and my dad needed to get some things out of his office."

"You know, I'm jealous you know so many languages," Erin interrupted. "I wish *my* parents were professors."

Die-hard academics that they were, my dad had always spoken to my sisters and me in Greek, while my mom spoke to us in Italian. "Don't be *too* jealous," I said, remembering. "It was really confusing when we were little, but now I'm glad they took the time to make me multilingual."

"How many languages *do* you speak?" Erin asked.

"Let me finish. Remember 'Yellow Bird'?"

"Oh yeah, I'm sorry. Go ahead." Erin's voice was soft, and most of her concentration was devoted to the hopelessly tangled IV lines.

"Anyway, I got tired of watching my dad shuffle through papers and ran out to a small pond, just outside his office, to feed the ducks. My dad hollered for me to be careful and said that he'd be out in two minutes.

"That's really all I remember, other than hearing ambulance doors slamming shut and being terrified. Then I heard that song in the emergency room:

> *Yellow bird, up high in*
> *banana tree*
> *Yellow bird, you sit all alone*
> *like me.*
> *You can fly away in the sky*
> *away.*"

My tuneless rendition of the song faded out.

"Oh my God, Lydia—you could have died." Erin stopped fumbling with the snarl of tubing for a second.

"I know. But all I got were the hiccups. Three straight days of the hiccups."

Erin laughed. "What did you do?"

"There was nothing I *could* do, just hiccup. The doctors said it was from the water in my lungs. Whatever, it's just a small blip in my history. I'm fine now, except for the teensy, annoying remnant Paula keeps ribbing me about. Oh yeah, and an ungodly fear of any deep water. Swimming is *definitely* not one of my strong points."

"What remnant?" Erin asked. "I haven't noticed any remnants." She stepped on the floor pedal of the trash can and threw the tangled mess of IV lines away.

"Well…sometimes, when I get really scared, I can hear 'Yellow Bird' playing in my head. Then I start to hiccup. It's no big deal, I suppose—maybe I just really like that song. But it hasn't happened for a long time."

As I jammed another handful of clothes into the already bulging bag, I suddenly noticed something peculiar. I pulled a garment back out of the bag and examined it. *Strange*, I thought. *It looks like it's hundreds of years old.* I held the garment up so that Erin could see it. "Take a look at this," I said. "Is this supposed to be a shirt?"

"Weird. Talk about old-fashioned." Erin smoothed her hand over the blouse. "Maybe she really *was* a hundred and sixteen. This looks like some kind of ancient tunic."

Intrigued, I gingerly lifted another piece of clothing back out of the bag. It was similar to the other one—roughly textured and made of all-natural fabric. My curiosity piqued, I pulled out a cream-colored garment which looked like a veil.

"Do you think she worked at Medieval Times or something? Look at these bizarre clothes." I held up a long, gown-like garment with frayed hems.

"Way not in style, and that's putting it mildly," Erin said, looking as puzzled as I was.

"These are like the clothes in some of the books I've found in my mom and dad's study. How weird."

"Yeah, unless you just jumped out of a Leonardo da Vinci painting. But I guess we'll never know."

"Yeah, that mystery died with her." I sighed.

"All right now, no backtracking," Erin said. "You finish packing her stuff, and I'll get the shroud. Be right back." Erin zipped out of the room.

Inspired, I hummed a tune from Vivaldi's *Four Seasons* and bent over to look into the drawer. *Let's see what else we have in here,* I mused. *Oh my god, look at these shoes.* They were plain brown leather and looked absolutely primitive. As I turned the shoes over to see if there was any writing on the soles, I heard something shift inside one of them.

I reached into the shoe and pulled out an ornate pin. It was slightly larger than my palm and featured an inset stone. As I studied it, I could see that it was probably made of real gold. Intricately fashioned, the pin's body twisted into a pattern that reminded me of a double helix. Thin, repeating horizontal bars glittered with infinitesimally small golden beads. The beads seemed to be randomly interspersed, scattered accents. The delicate crafting gave the pin an overall look of fine cloth turned to gold.

Poor woman, I thought to myself. I held in my hand what may have been her only valuable in the world—and there wasn't even anyone I could give it to.

Looking closer at the stone, its quality seemed incongruous with the rest of the pin. It was a drab matte gray color, about the size of my thumbnail. The stone's lack of luster was puzzling. I rubbed my finger over it, thinking that maybe it just needed to be buffed.

The stone grew warm under my touch, and I felt a tingling charge go through my fingers and up my arm.

Eyes wide, I froze where I stood. An unknown force locked me rigidly in place. I tried to drop the pin, but I couldn't. My hair began to move, and the weight of it shifted off my shoulders. Cool air poured down the nape of my neck.

What's happening to me?

I tried to turn my head but could only move my eyes. I looked hard to the left and then to the right. The strain of moving my eyes made the sockets hurt, and little silver fireflies swam around in my vision. I could see my hair floating straight out, all around my head. Each brown curl had taken on a life of its own.

I tried to scream for Erin, but I couldn't. There wasn't any air in my lungs or even in the room, for that matter.

It's the damn pin, I thought. *It's electrocuting me!* Why did I have to grab everything like a child? *I should have been more careful.* And I'd actually been feeling sorry for the old woman.

Reality was shutting down. I kept trying to let go of the pin. *If I could just drop it,* I thought. The room blurred, and an ungodly humming sound hammered into my ears. My legs gave way, but instead of falling, I felt myself snatched upward into the air.

I saw a bird's-eye view of the room getting smaller at an amazing rate, and what looked like the code blue going off once more. I heard the familiar calypso strains of "Yellow Bird."

Then there was nothing but blackness.

Chapter 2

September 384 BC

Etruria

(Known as the Italian province of Tuscany in present times)

Time stood still for a moment.

Time stood still for a moment. A Tyrrhenian Sea breeze, warm for September, carried through the open terrace and feathered over Nortia's body. Closing her eyes, she reclined like a goddess on the bench. Then the moment was gone.

After six years of marriage, she was now with child. What would she do without a husband? It wasn't fair. Why did she have to be a widow, trying to raise a baby by herself?

How kind the Gods could be—and yet, how cruel at the same time.

Nortia laid her hand on her stomach. She knew that she should be happy. This baby was her first, and she had waited a long time to be a mother. Her heart should be singing from the joy of it.

Ati walked up and touched Nortia's sun-warmed hair. She ran her fingers down the length of one of her spiral brown curls, as she'd done thousands of times before. Pulling the lock straight, she then let it go, watching it bounce back up into a tight curl.

Nortia looked up at her mother and smiled, reassured by her caring touch. She shaded her eyes with one hand as the sun glinted off Ati's shoulder-length silver hair. At barely five feet tall, her mother was diminutive in size—but not in spirit or intellect. In her moment of self-pity, Nortia had forgotten that she could count on her for support.

"Your eyes are speaking to me," Ati said.

Of course, her mother saw past Nortia's calm facade and knew something was wrong. Ati was a soothsayer. She continued to gaze into Nortia's eyes for almost a minute before she spoke again. "You have an important task ahead of you. Our family line has been long, and the women are predestined. They have been given many trials, but also many gifts. Our line is one with great promise."

With that said, Ati walked away, leaving Nortia to deal with her thoughts once more.

Nortia didn't know why, but ever since she'd been with child, her thoughts had been disturbed. Something she couldn't control was affecting them. Blaming it on her husband's death wasn't working, because it had begun to happen weeks before he died.

Had it only been forty-one days since Forte died on his way to battle? A familiar pain washed over her. For six years, he had been a good husband and protector. It had been an arranged marriage and a mutually beneficial match. When her father died, her husband dutifully took his place running their large villa in Populonia.

Nortia rose from the bench and walked to the long wall overlooking the sea. The gaps between the stone pillars supporting the wall allowed the wind to mold her tunic against her still-slender body. With a deep breath, she took in the marine scent and leaned against the wall, elbows resting on the weather-roughened stone.

Guilt washed over her, for she'd never even loved her husband. Yes, she missed him, and her heart hurt for her lost friend, but she'd never loved him as a lover. That love belonged to another: Antoni, her personal guard.

She looked out over the water, appreciating the gift of beauty the spellbinding sea gave her, which was different every single day. The waves were a brilliant, transparent blue without the slightest hint of green, grouping into peaceful, hypnotic rows. They were like an army of trapped ancient mariners—trying to rise, one by one, only able to pull their backs out of the troughs before having to rest once more.

Nortia listened to the steady collapse of waves against the shore, absently rubbing the golden pin fastened to the red mantle over her tunic. The pin felt strangely warm to her touch. That odd sensation broke through the charm the ocean had on her. Had it always felt this way?

Her thoughts narrowed in on the pin that had been passed down through generations on the maternal side of her family. It featured a single inset stone, not a polished gem or even something that seemed to have any value. The gem looked like a worthless rock compared to the otherwise flawless workmanship of the pin, and this always puzzled Nortia.

Once she asked her mother about the mysterious story surrounding the stone. Ati had only told her what she had learned from her mother, explaining that much of the tale had been lost through the generations.

"The stone's name is 'Hemisatres,'" Ati had said, "named after the God of time and necessity. It's very powerful, worth much more than any of the finest polished gems. An unfulfilled prophecy surrounds it—about two girl children being born who will ride the four quarters of the sky. These girls will unleash the powers of the stone, the only defense against a deadly evil—a darkness that could ripple through the celestial and terrestrial quarters that hold our world together. Failure would mean the annihilation of humankind."

The first time Ati told her the story, Nortia had been in awe of the importance of her ancestry, but she also thought it was just another one of those tales about miracles and prophecies that had been embellished over the generations. They were fun to hear and retell, but they never came true. Now when she recalled the prophecy surrounding the pin, it sent a chill through her.

"Are you well, my lady?" asked Antoni.

Nortia startled and turned from her spot at the wall toward Antoni's voice. Quickly recovering, she smiled as she watched her loyal protector and childhood friend approach her. His height distributed his muscles evenly, lending a certain fluid leanness to his muscled frame. Antoni's build hinted to the perfect balance between strength and agility that he possessed.

His straight dark brown hair was cut right across the back of his neck. Long bangs swept to either side, which alternately lifted and settled in the sea breeze. His face was smooth and tanned, and it reflected the usual seriousness with which he took his duty.

Antoni, like his father before him, and as far back as any of them could remember, were all personal guards for nobility—specifically, the maternal line of Nortia's family.

He strode toward her, his concerned expression only making him even more handsome to her. She found her secret love for Antoni unbearable when his blue eyes picked up the reflection from the sea.

"I'm fine," she answered, adding an extra-long sigh. It was no wonder she hadn't heard him approach. Even with his slight limp, his sandals barely made any noise as he walked over the crushed-coral walkway. A twinge of guilt nagged her as she recalled how Antoni acquired his injury.

When Nortia was eight and Antoni was twelve, Nortia had been playing with a group of children in a field of grass above the sea. All the children were running about, enjoying the warm early spring day. She had strayed from the group, as well as the watchful eye of her mother and Antoni's father.

Her antics had taken her too close to the edge of the seaside cliff. As the ground crumbled away beneath her feet, she wasn't able to stop herself from toppling over. Too terrified to yell for help, she had somehow managed to stop her fall by grabbing onto a rock jutting out from the cliff's side.

Only moments passed, but they seemed like an eternity to a small, frightened girl. Antoni leaned over the edge and immediately saw what had happened. Unable to pull her up from where she hung without sending her plummeting down thirty feet, he climbed down beneath her and pushed her up over the top, out of harm's way.

The moment she was safe, the small ledge beneath Antoni gave way. He had sacrificed himself for her.

Antoni healed, months after the fall. Nortia was only allowed to see him a few times after the injury. She didn't know what was wrong with him, but he didn't look like he was getting any better.

Finally, feverish and near death, he told her not to be sad—that he would rather be dead than have an injury that would leave him unable to fulfill his inherited duty as her guard.

At that moment, she fell in love with him. Nortia, as young as she was, knew she had to get her father to help him.

Nortia's father recognized that he had this young man to thank for his daughter's life, and went with Nortia to see Antoni. Nortia could tell from her father's expression that it pained him to see Antoni wasting away on the pallet in such pitiful condition. Her father leaned down and whispered something into Antoni's ear.

On the short ride back to the villa, Nortia sat in front of her father in the saddle. During their trip, she asked her father what he had said to Antoni.

"Don't worry, little one. He will get better now," her father told her, patting her on the head. "I promised him his rightful place in the guard as a reward for his bravery. To do that, he will have to get well and train hard. Only when Antoni is properly trained will he be allowed to guard what I prize most—you, my daughter. If he needs help because of any physical shortages, additional guards will be provided to assist him in his important duty."

Her father had been right. Antoni's health and strength returned at a miraculous rate. Nortia rarely, if ever, saw Antoni after that day. She tried to put herself in places where she would run into him, as any young girl in love would do—but their paths just didn't cross. It was as if they lived in two different worlds.

Antoni trained for years, until no soldier could best him. All injuries and signs of that fateful day faded under his rigorous training. The faint limp that remained was her only reminder that it had even happened at all.

When she turned sixteen, Antoni took his rightful place as her guard. No longer a lovestruck young girl, she was promised to Forte. They were to wed on her eighteenth birthday. The choice of who she married was not her own. But who she loved, that *was* her choice—and her joyous and painful secret.

"Are you well, my lady?" repeated Antoni.

"I am well. I am merely thinking about the banquet tonight and wondering if my stomach will calm before it begins." But in truth, her heart wasn't into the banquet any more than her stomach was. In her heart, she didn't feel like celebrating the harvest.

She considered telling Antoni about the pin and its strange warmth, but dismissed that idea. Even though Nortia wanted to talk with him about it, she knew how protective Antoni was. He might rip the pin from her chest and grind the heirloom under his heel if he thought for a moment that it might harm her.

Finally, she said, "I think I'll go in and rest before the feast tonight." With that, she excused herself.

Cool air washed over her as she entered the villa, and her eyes adjusted to the new lighting. A sea breeze flowed around her, through the halls, and out through the arched openings—its coolness pooling into a wide, central courtyard. The courtyard was planted with a pleasing balance of tall, thin trees and smaller, branching fig trees, as well as shrubs and colorful flowers. Benches were scattered about, in seemingly unplanned, private spots.

Truly relieved to be out of the direct afternoon sun, Nortia descended the stairs and wove her way through the courtyard to the hall, opposite the first floor entrance. She didn't realize how warm she'd been until she stopped to take her sandals off. As her feet touched the cool stone floor, chills spread throughout her body. After she padded into her chamber and lay down, she spent the next hour trying unsuccessfully to rid herself of her troubled thoughts.

While waiting for sleep to claim her, Nortia stared at the painted murals on the stone walls, masterful renderings of Etruscan life. Her eyes went from picture to picture. Some showed trees laden with fruit and planted fields, while others displayed musicians surrounded by dancers in festive dress. Scenes which delighted and comforted her as a child now made her wonder if soon they would be all that was left of her people.

So many things had changed. Because of her family's wealth from iron smelting, they had been spared from the worst of the attacks by the Romans, Greeks, and Gauls. It wouldn't be much longer before the rapid destruction of their way of life would reach even their high-class walls.

Her husband, Forte, had lost his life on the way to defend the temple in Pyrgi from the Greeks. Receiving word that the temple was to be attacked by Dionysius the Elder, he had left for the territory of Caere, along with many of their soldiers.

They were attacked not far into their journey, and they never reached their destination. All of them were dead now, except for a few remaining survivors. Trying to push these thoughts from her mind, Nortia felt the sun's heat leaving her body as she drifted off into a troubled sleep.

~~~

Nortia felt a hand on her arm and woke with a start. She heard her mother's voice calming her as she opened her eyes, willing them to focus.

"There, there," Ati said, patting her arm. "Do you feel better, dear? You must have been very tired. Are you feeling well?"

"Yes, Mother, I'm feeling much better, now that I've rested. Have the guests begun to arrive for the celebration banquet?"

"Yes." Raising her eyebrows, Ati leaned in and peered into Nortia's eyes. "Is there something you're not telling me?"

"No," Nortia lied.

"It's time to get ready for tonight's feast." Ati continued to look at her daughter.

Nortia could tell Ati was worried and knew something wasn't right. Over the years, her mother had learned to listen to her feelings of foreboding. That was Ati's gift. If she really watched what was going on around her, she would receive signs. They weren't elaborate, merely vague suggestions or extra insight into what was happening. The more Ati watched and listened, the clearer the omens became.

"When I was young," Ati said, "I thought I was born without a gift, and that has never happened with the women of this family. When I was twenty-three years old, I finally learned to slow down and really watch and listen, so that the signs could come.

"I was thankful for even that small gift. It has saved me and my loved ones many times, forewarning me of storms, fires, and even deaths. Yes, sometimes the details evade me, but the early warning of danger usually gives me just enough time to turn the outcome into a more favorable one."

"But, Mother, you know I already know this."

"Yes, but I'm telling you again for two reasons. First, you are of an age where your gift should already be known to you, and it's not. Heed my words: Do not ignore even the most subtle sign. Take care, and do not waste your gift.

"The other reason," Ati continued, "is that I'm beginning to feel very unsettled about things that may concern you. Now is not the time to talk. But after the banquet, we must do so."

"Yes, after the banquet." Nortia knew there was no sense in arguing. Ati must be seeing omens. She wouldn't stop questioning her until she'd made sense of them. She must tell her mother about the pin and her troubled thoughts. But it could at least wait until after she'd eaten.

After Ati left the room, Nortia cleaned up in the wash basin and dressed for the banquet. She put on a festive purple tunic made of a light pleated material, which was heavily embroidered on the edges. The garment came down to her feet, which were adorned in finely decorated leather sandals, crisscrossing up her lower legs. Over her tunic, she put on a blue mantle with wide, multicolored bands, fastening it with the pin.

As she closed the pin on the cloth, she felt the warmth radiating from it again. As she tried to let go of it, she found that she couldn't. Panicked, she attempted to call out to Antoni, who was standing guard just outside the entrance to her chamber—but her mouth simply opened, and she couldn't even make a sound.

Spellbound, she sat down heavily onto her pallet. Faint scenes flashed like lightning in her head, faster and faster, giving her a rush of sensations. Nortia shook her head to break free of the trance, but she couldn't do it.

The warmth from the pin wasn't only in her hand. It moved up her arm, through her chest, and spread to her neck. The scenes were faded, but every so often, she recognized one: a baby, a stone, a farmhouse, Antoni, or her and Ati running together.

Suddenly, a dozen dark, cloaked figures on huge mounts appeared in her visions, bearing down upon her. Terrified, she began to gasp for air. As the visions continued to flash before her, she tried once again to call out to Antoni. More and more scenes appeared, some repeating over and over: her home, Ati, Antoni and her running together, a farmhouse, a baby.

The pin fell to her pallet, and the warmth abruptly left her. An icy feeling took its place, making her blood run cold with sudden awareness: the baby that appeared in the visions was hers.

She sank back onto the pallet, letting out a soft gasp, the first sound she was able to make. Then everything went dark.

~~~

Nortia awoke to the heavy pounding of running feet. Antoni's loud voice penetrated the haze in her head.

"Nortia, are you unwell?" Antoni yelled. "Wake up!"

Nortia tried to open her eyes when she heard Antoni's shouting. Then she felt her mother's warm touch.

"Antoni, what happened?" Ati asked. "Has she fallen? Was she attacked?"

Nortia felt her mother cradle her head in her arms and stopped trying to open her eyes. They were just too heavy.

"I don't know what happened!" Antoni answered, still shouting. "I was standing just outside her chamber when I suddenly heard a small, strange sound coming from Nortia. When I rushed into the chamber, I found her like this. I don't know who's to blame for what has happened to her—or they would already be lying at your feet, slain."

Nortia felt Ati's small hands touching her, searching for injuries. She wanted to open her eyes, but she couldn't. Ati's breath on her cheek began to mingle with her own.

"Take heart, Antoni," Ati said. "You haven't failed Nortia. It seems that no great harm befell her. No one is lurking about here or in the halls, so you may send the guards back to their usual posts. She could be having momentary weakness because of the child she carries."

"Yes, my lady."

Nortia heard Antoni's reply and his retreating footfalls. She wished Antoni was holding her instead of her mother. A damp cloth on her forehead pulled her back to awareness. Ati sat beside her, patting her hand.

Nortia drew in a few deep breaths. "What happened?" she asked in a wavering voice. She felt as though she had just risen from a long slumber.

"Go slow, my child—just lie there. You have had a momentary weakness and were unable to stand. Please tell me what's going on—I know that something is very wrong." Ati's face looked anxious.

Nortia sat up suddenly. Her head spun as she remembered the terrifying scenes. Trembling, she began to tell Ati about the pin's strange warmth and what she had seen. "I merely touched the pin while dressing, and the visions appeared. I couldn't stop them from coming. I tried, but I couldn't take my hand away from the pin. The scenes changed so fast, I could only see very few of them. There were dark, cloaked riders, horrible and terrifying, that thundered down upon us as we fled. They rode vicious-looking mounts with bared teeth that snapped in the air, nothing like our horses—and they were also an enormous size, unlike anything I've ever seen.

"Death shone in the eyes of the riders, and their leader was a pale woman who was almost beautiful in a cold, cruel way. I could feel our fear as we ran—you, Antoni, and I were all there." Nortia hesitated, out of breath. "I don't want to think of this anymore. It frightens me. I must stop." Tears streamed down her face.

Still sitting on the edge of the pallet, Ati took both of Nortia's hands, trying to steady her. When Nortia looked into her mother's eyes, it was like looking into her own.

"You must tell me more, child," Ati said. "What else did you see? Tell me everything. It's time to be brave."

Nortia struggled to regain control, willing herself to breathe more slowly. After a few moments, she reluctantly continued. "All was dark. I could make out the shore and waves near our home as we ran toward them. The sea looked angry, and the waves glowed red. They rose up to great heights, trying to reach the sky.

"Then the scenes changed, and they weren't as frightening. I saw a farmhouse. It seemed safe. We were all there: you, Antoni, myself and…" She stopped to catch her breath. "…and a child," she said softly. "*My* child."

Ati sat down beside Nortia, looking jarred. "Now I am sure we aren't safe here any longer. These visions are to be heeded, not simply feared. The pin has been with our family for a long time. It warns us in order to keep us safe. It is telling us to flee this place in order to protect the child. I know this is difficult for you, daughter—but did you sense these visions would begin to unfold soon?"

Nortia couldn't find her voice as fear gripped her again. She looked up at Ati through her tears, hating her answer. "Yes…soon."

Her thoughts haunted her. Did her mother mean they must leave their home? Where would they go? How would they eat? Who would protect them? Nortia stared down at the pin as if it were a venomous snake.

Antoni appeared in the doorway. Confronted with their tears, he backed quickly into the dimness of the hallway and resumed his post beside the door.

~~~

That evening at the banquet went by like a dream for Nortia. She'd managed, solely because of hunger, to collect herself enough to attend the event. Sitting on a pillow beside her mother, she tried unsuccessfully to enjoy what she ate, even though the meal was incredible. The tantalizing smells that came from the five huge tables should have been enough to seduce her—but it was no use.

Two tables were laden with figs, hazelnuts, olives, and every kind of fruit imaginable, with mounds of grapes artfully arranged in each of the eight corners. One table was ornately set with black urns, some filled with wine, and others with delicate oils. There were lightly spiced cakes, stacked and drizzled with so much honey that it dripped down onto the brightly colored cloth adorning the table. The last two tables were stacked with fresh seafood of every variety—fish, shellfish, and crustacean—all heaped into small mountains on huge platters.

The food tasted delicious, but she just couldn't enjoy it.

Rich iron merchants and land owners introduced themselves, extending their condolences regarding her deceased husband. Others conveyed their wishes for a profitable harvest for their villa. Nortia found she was barely able to converse with any of them, and she was thankful that her mother did most of the talking, explaining that Nortia didn't feel well this evening.

Double pipe and lyre music filled the air. Dancers, dressed in bright colors, whirled about around the low tables, boosting everyone's spirits—everyone, that is, except for Nortia. She had agreed with her mother that they must tell Antoni about the pin after the feast, as well as the danger they both knew was coming. Once he knew, they could make a plan.

~~~

After the guests departed, Nortia and Ati sat with Antoni on one of the benches and told him of the impending danger.

Antoni looked at the two women, trying to digest what they had just told him. *Leave tomorrow? Just the three of us?* They were supposed to flee to some farmhouse in a vision, but neither woman knew where it was or how to get there. This was madness. Yes, he was a fierce warrior—but alone, he stood little chance of protecting them against this kind of evil—wherever it was they were actually going.

Antoni knew of Ati's gift with visions, but she had never before asked to leave the safety of their home without guards. All of this had to do with the pin that Nortia wore. Should he really believe that a bit of gold—just jewelry the day before—now had some kind of power to give Nortia visions?

"Please, Antoni," Ati said. "You must listen to me. The signs are ominous. We *must* leave tomorrow—and your protection is needed."

Antoni stood to his full height before speaking. "If you say we must go, then I must heed your request. But your safety is also my duty, so we will bring guards with us."

"That's not possible," Ati replied.

Antoni couldn't believe the woman's stubbornness and lost his patience. "Why not? Why do both of you insist on making me solely responsible for your lives, or the Gods forbid, your deaths?"

"Nortia saw only you in the visions," Ati said, as if it needed no more explanation.

"You both told me we will be facing a dozen enemies on giant, charging steeds, led by a woman who looks like she's from the underworld. Yet I alone am to face them? Certainly you haven't thought this through."

Nortia looked at Antoni. "Please, Antoni, I know this sounds like the ranting of women who have lost their sanity, but we need you to aid us. You are in all the visions as our protector. I fear for my unborn child. Whoever these evil people are, they are coming for me and the baby. We must heed the pin's warning before it is too late. Who are we to question the gift of forewarning? Not only have I seen the visions, but my mother has also been getting signs. Surely both of us are not wrong."

Antoni thought of Ati, who was a soothsayer. Her visions were true, and she had saved people before. Only last winter, the children of one of the house guards escaped death because of her timely warning.

Ati's visions had started days before the children were in harm's way, but she waited until they became clearer. Once Ati was sure whom the visions were about, she walked up to a house guard, one she had never spoken directly to before, and made him leave his post to check his home. The guard did as he was told.

When he returned to his post two days later, he said he arrived home just in time to pull his two sons, eight and ten years old, from their burning home. His wife had been away tending his sick mother that day. The boys, who were usually responsible when they were left alone, had begun to play with the fire in the hearth, accidentally setting fire to the home.

When the guard arrived, he found his sons huddled together in one corner of the home, and he was able to rescue them in time.

Maybe it would be foolish not to heed the visions, Antoni thought. They could leave for a short time, and if nothing came to pass, they could come back. His indecision as well as his lack of options made him feel frustrated and angry. Nortia's husband, if he were still alive, would have had his head for even contemplating putting both women in such danger. He also didn't like the idea of blindly following omens.

Antoni considered the possibilities, eventually realizing that he didn't have a choice. If he didn't willingly offer his aid, they would leave without him. Then he would be forced to follow them, anyway.

After one last look at the resolve on the two women's faces, he relented. "I will do as you wish," he said through gritted teeth.

Chapter 3

September 384 BC

Etruria

(One mile from the villa in Populonia)

Their timing was bad.

Night fell as the riders reached the top of the hill. Charontes saw the ocean in the distance, many miles ahead. Weak starlight reflected off the restless sea, insignificant shards of light barely able to penetrate the ominous black clouds.

"I told you our stone would show us the way," Vanth hissed to the immense, cloaked warrior beside her. "We will stop here for the night and continue on in the morning. That way, we will arrive under the cover of night. Tomorrow, we will simply kill her and anyone who tries to stop us—then take their half of the stone." She casually shrugged her shoulder and tilted her head.

Charontes's horse reared up, impatient from the delay. The small bronze medallions adorning its breastplate and reins clinked together. "As you wish, Vanth." Charontes's toneless voice was so deep that it sounded bottomless.

He didn't want to cross her, on this day or on any other day. Her fury could rival the female demon of death that was her namesake. Vanth was evil through and through, with a heart as cold as a snow-covered peak. She'd said the stone knew where and when to find its other half, and she'd been right.

The prophecy was now unfolding.

His eyes narrowed as he signaled the other riders to dismount. Two of the men had already dismounted, setting their spears to the side. With shields hooked over their left forearms, they drew their short swords and circled, slashing at each other in a lethal, familiar dance. They were ruthless.

These Riders of the Reunity, the last of their kind, had worshiped the prophecy of the stone for over five hundred years. They encompassed generations of warriors trained for two objectives: to kill and to find the other half of the stone. When Vanth's stone reunited with its other half, they would claim the four quarters of the sky. Then, the Chosen One, a priestess of the Reunity, would walk through time at will and pillage as she chose. Then godlike invincibility and wealth beyond their imaginations would be theirs for the taking.

Vanth had come to him weeks ago, and told him she was with child—the child of the prophecy. She'd said the stone had awakened, and they must find its other half before the child was born. It was the beginning of the end of the prophecy.

At first, he had been stunned by the news, but now his mind raced. What about that night he and Vanth had been together? Was that when she had conceived? Charontes tried to crush the horrible thought. Vanth didn't care who she lay with; he was only one of many. He wasn't the father.

He forced his thoughts from the foul path they had taken. His men, like the ones before them, had prepared for the coming of the Chosen One for hundreds of years. When Vanth spoke, they'd been ready.

The day after her shocking news, they armed themselves and left for the coast. It had been a long ride to this seaside land from the mountains they called home. Their half of the stone had shown Vanth the way.

Charontes swung down from his horse, took two long strides, and grabbed one of the fighting men. With one enormous hand, he lifted him up and held him out from his body, as if the large man weighed nothing. Charontes's arm and chest muscles bulged. The man's sword struck harmlessly off his bronze breastplate as he shook him. Growling at the dangling man, he threw him down in front of him and kicked him.

Charontes turned, and his face was a storm of rage. The other man paled and quickly put the point of his sword down.

"Save your strength for tomorrow, fools," he said, straightening up to his full six-foot-six-inch height. He loomed over the other Riders.

The Riders of the Reunity were all large men. Over the generations, they'd been selected, even bred, to enhance their height and strength. All were a head and a half over most men. Still, none were as large as Charontes—not even close. His massive chest, armored with a gleaming bronze cuirass made him look even larger. The cuirass itself, a work of art, sculpted into a perfect imitation of the muscles it fit over. A round shield hung from his left forearm, and a rectangular bronze armguard, fastened with leather straps, adorned his upper arm. Tiered strips of linen encircled his waist and fell to his knees, just brushing the tops of the bronze greaves that protected his shins.

His shoulder-length brown hair swirled in the raw, sea wind as he bellowed, "For five hundred years, our kind has waited. Only eleven warriors remain—and you two chance to make that ten. Nothing can go wrong tomorrow. We must be successful."

The men, not wanting to be within his powerful reach, backed up a few steps. He glared at them, daring any to defy him. The Rider on the ground snarled curses and struggled to

rise to his feet. This only earned him another kick from
Charontes's huge foot.

Charontes walked back to tend to his horse. Deftly
avoiding his black stallion's snapping teeth, he removed the
bridle and tethered him. Just like the warriors, their horses
were raised never knowing kindness, or even a caress.

Charontes felt Vanth's eyes boring into him. He was
weary and didn't feel like fighting with her, too. Reluctantly,
he turned toward her.

She vaulted off her horse. Black, wavy hair fell
perfectly over a slender shoulder. Her jaw pushed forward,
pulling her lips into a tight, straight line. "Can't you control
the men?" she shrieked.

"They are tired and impatient," Charontes growled.
"They've waited a very long time for this."

Vanth flashed him a dangerous look.

He just turned his back to her and walked down the
hill, where the men had begun building the fires. Hungry and
tired, he felt glad that they had calmed down so quickly.
Several of the men went off to hunt game, while others
tended to the horses.

These fierce men grouped together only to complete tasks. They didn't need each other for companionship—only for survival. When the work was complete, they chose to sit alone, scattered about the different fires for warmth. There wasn't much talking among them, only a few curses when they got in each other's way.

Making his way off to one side of the encampment, Charontes built a small fire for himself. He wanted to be alone to plan for tomorrow and think about the prophecy. The ride here had put him in constant, close proximity to Vanth and all the men, and it had tried his patience to its breaking point.

Life for him had been devoid of love and friendship. He'd barely left his mother's breast when he was sent away to train, having been bred for the honor of being a Rider of the Reunity. Charontes knew no other way of life. He had been taught that feelings made warriors vulnerable, like weak links in a chain. A warrior must be impervious to them in order to survive. Feelings like hunger, love, pain, and fatigue weren't considered safe, and they had all been driven out of him long ago.

"Kill or be killed, if necessary, in pursuit of the stone" was his only

mantra, and he liked it that way. He was his own man—remorseless and

friendless—and was only part of the group for the sole purpose of uniting the stones and reaping his reward.

He was not unfamiliar with brief and necessary physical love as a release, and he knew how to satisfy a woman, but only as a means to an end. In this harsh world, he had himself to worry about and that was enough. He would always be this way.

An hour later, he sat by his fire, chewing on a large piece of boar. The boar had tasted much better three days ago, but he hadn't caught any fresh game since they'd stopped, so he opted to finish the last of the meat he had with him.

He purposely overcooked and charred the meat in an attempt to rid it of the nasty smell. The end result was a dry, thoroughly foul hunk of meat. However, he didn't care; he just chewed harder.

His wish to be alone this evening would not come true. As soon as he began eating, Vanth came to his fire. As was typical of Vanth, she didn't ask to join

him; she just sat down, uninvited. Her cloak swirled, as if

alive, swallowing her whole as she sat, making her look like a

black lump. Under her hood, her face glowed a ghostly white,

making it appear as though her head was floating by itself in

the darkness. She was fiendish, and Charontes found it

difficult to look into her eyes.

Why had he lain with her?

"I can barely wait for tomorrow," Vanth said. Without

asking, she helped herself to his meat. "The faint images I am

getting from the stone have led us this close. Now that I've

had a taste of its power, I want more." Licking the grease

from the side of her mouth, she chewed. "I crave it," she said,

smoothing one finger over the stone in her golden bracelet,

like someone possessed. "Bearing this child is a waste of my

time. I should be the Chosen One. I am here, and I am strong.

What purpose could a useless child have? I don't even *want* a

child. I hope it dies—then the stone will have to use *me* as its

Chosen One."

Charontes sat there, unable to reply in the face of such

depravity. Uncaring as he was, his blood ran cold when she

spoke in such a terrible way about the child growing within her.

Vanth violently spat out the meat she'd been chewing. Charontes could only wonder if it was the meat's bad flavor or if her mouth was filled with its own rancid venom.

Dragging the arm of her cloak across her face to mop up the spittle, Vanth stood, leaning close to Charontes to whisper into his ear. He tried not to cringe as her hot, revolting breath scalded his neck.

"The child is mine to do with as I wish," she hissed. "That means the power of the stones will be mine, too." With a swoosh of her cloak, she left.

Charontes's appetite deserted him. He banked the fire and lay down, using his cloak as both a bed and a blanket. He pulled the cloak tightly around him to ward off the chafing wind, but sleep eluded him. Sounds from the other men, restlessly preparing for sleep, drifted around him. A small scuffle over who would be posted as sentry was quickly settled.

From where he lay, Charontes could see the sleepless Vanth. She stood on the hill, arms folded, staring toward the sea. She'd been the only one talking during the meal—and now he knew all too well that her thoughts were murderous ones.

As he drifted off to sleep, the image of her eyes still haunted him. They were the eyes of a mad woman. How had he not noticed it before?

~~~

After a sleepless night, Charontes ate a small, cold breakfast just before sunrise. His fire had gone out, and he had no way to heat the food. After breakfast, he and the other Riders put on their armor and gathered their weapons. Mounting their horses, they rode toward the sea.

Chapter 4

July 1481 AD

Firenze

(Known also as the Italian city of Florence)

Time can be the kindest and cruelest of masters.

I opened my eyes to a blur, and my head felt as though it had been axed in two. A steady *thump, thump, thump* amplified my headache. Something crushed the air out of my lungs with each sound. I struggled to draw in a breath and got half a lungful of hot, stale air.

As I became more aware of things around me, I felt the sun warming my back. I tried to raise my head and open my eyes, but they refused to focus. Drawing in another breath, I forced myself to use any of my senses that would cooperate. My face was pressed into some kind of fabric. My next partial breath pulled a heavenly scent through the cloth—an intoxicating, thick, spicy, clean scent with a familiar, but not unpleasant tang to it. I tried to breathe in more of it.

An earthquake jolted me to the side.

My mouth now uncovered, I gulped in pure, fresh air, which brought lucidity along with it. My eyes finally began to focus—I was moving, above the ground. With great effort, I lifted my head and looked around—I could see trees, grass, and other recognizable things. My body lay over some sort of moving shelf or couch. As I looked down, I saw the bottom of the couch's sandals. *Sandals?* I shook my head and willed my eyes to focus. *Yep, sandals. Oh no, someone is carrying me over his shoulder.* It was someone male—someone huge.

I squeezed my eyes shut.

What's happening to me? my brain screamed as my vocal cords refused to work. The last thing I remembered was the code in the ICU. Although I was reassured to see the sleeve of my white scrubs out of the corner of my eye, my mind still reeled.

What on earth is going on?

I remembered the code, the woman dying, me cleaning the room—and then nothing. This wasn't the hospital, I was sure of that. I lifted my head as high as possible and could see grass, trees, and flowers bouncing by. Birds swooped in around me, chirping excitedly. I could feel the sun and the breeze. *Why am I outside?*

It was hopeless; I couldn't remember anything else. I looked down at the backside of whatever, or rather, *whoever* was carrying me.

Nice.

My gaze trailed down his legs. The backs of his thighs were impossibly muscled. *I'm not going off onto one of my tangents,* I reprimanded myself. *Not while suffering from oxygen deprivation.*

I tried to redirect my thoughts. Maybe what was happening was like one of the silly romance novels I loved. I'd suffered some kind of glancing blow to the head that had left me totally dependent on a sandaled couch man.

Of course, I wouldn't be permanently injured—just long enough so that he would have to care for me until we fell in love. A permanent injury would ruin everything. I wouldn't be able to bear him an heir and a spare.

Eureka, that's it, I thought. *Couch-man-cabana-boy is just a dream.*

Reaching down, I pinched him. *Nothing.* Barely getting any skin the first time, I tried again. This time, I pinched harder and grabbed as much skin as I could. It elicited a low, rumbling grunt out of the couch man.

I wasn't dreaming. My stomach clenched into a knot, and I knew I was going to vomit. I was really scared and wanted down—*now.*

I kicked my legs up and down, pushing with all my might on the heavily muscled shoulder. Nothing happened except for one of the freak's fourteen triceps started to dig more painfully into my abdomen. *Is the circus in town? Who is this guy carrying me, anyway—Sampson?*

I struggled some more and was rewarded with my scrub top flipping down over my head. *Great, now I can't see.* I stopped flailing and closed my eyes. *I might as well,* I thought. *Everything's whirling and I can't see anything, anyway*. My head throbbed from the blood pooling down into it.

Maybe Sampson would get tired soon and put me down. I put my ear onto his back. He wasn't even breathing hard and didn't feel at all sweaty. I moved past fear, and into the anger zone. *Why won't he talk to me? Just put me down, and explain what's going on.*

Having rested a bit since my last futile outburst, I focused all my strength on speaking. The words finally rushed out in a screeching shout. "Put me down!"

Thump, thump, thump. The hulk just kept plodding away.

"Okay, buddy—you asked for it. *Help! Help! Rape! Fire!* Someone please help me, anybody!"

There was nothing but silence. Even the birds had stopped chirping.

I laid my aching head down and tears of frustration slipped out. It hurt so bad, I didn't even care anymore. I just wanted to sleep. Maybe Sampson was taking me to the emergency room. Via—I don't know—Greece or something.

That's it, I thought. *I must have passed out during the code from all the excitement, and now an orderly is taking me to be treated. But what kind of orderly wears sandals, anyway?* I'd have to remind him of the open-toe policy here at the hospital.

"Hello, Mr. Sampson, sir. Excuse me—could you please put me down?"

There was no response.

Maybe he's deaf.

That's very plausible, I answered my own thought sarcastically. *A deaf, Grecian, rogue orderly*. I sniffled as I felt Gigundo shift me a little on his shoulder and pick up his pace.

Something inside of me just snapped. "Put me down, damn you!" I screamed and pounded my fists into his back, like a toddler having a temper tantrum.

Suddenly, Sampson stopped.

Aha, that showed him. Feeling merciful, I stopped thrashing him.

But he didn't put me down or stop for very long—he just effortlessly shifted my 140 pounds to his other shoulder.

Oh, God help me, he's one of those Schwarzenegger Terminators. He would keep going and going, then turn into liquid metal and kill everyone I knew to get to me. *Well, he could kill my ex, Scott. That would be okay. That was stupid. What am I thinking? He already has me, anyway.*

I heard a door open and the Terminator advanced forward. Through the small opening my scrub top afforded me, I could see a planked floor with straw on it.

"What's the matter with you?" I yelled. "Answer me. Why won't you put me down, you abomination?" My voice was hoarse from screaming. I struggled some more, but I could feel myself weakening.

The giant hunched as he climbed some stairs, straightened, and walked a few more feet forward. I heard another door opening. Hands went under both of my arms and I was pulled backwards. My scrub top slid down from over my head, followed by my unruly curls.

I stared straight at him.

He held me level with his face, his arms extended straight out in front of him so that my body and legs just dangled in the air. Speechless, I looked into the biggest, blackest eyes I'd ever seen. Black on black. Irises like shiny onyxes that his pupils got lost in. They weren't red, though; that shot down my Terminator theory.

Sampson was looking right into my eyes, and he was perfect—just like a giant, bronzed, exquisitely proportioned statue. If his face had been missing the masculine, rugged bone structure, I could have even called him beautiful. A museum showpiece. A hunk of Michelangelo's marble come to life.

A big hunk.

He had to be seven feet tall. Waves of brown hair fell about his face, twining just above his shoulders in a way that suggested movement when there was none. As I watched his thick lashes lower over those ebony eyes, I guessed his age to be about thirty-two or thirty-three.

I closed my mouth and swallowed hard. A little squishy noise was audible. *No, I could* definitely *call him beautiful.*

Sampson just kept staring at me in an incredulous way, as if he hadn't known I'd been on his back.

I broke the spell with a screeching yell. "Put me down, you freak!" I pulled my dangling legs up and began kicking him in the abdomen. My kicks just bounced right off his armor.

"I don't know what kind of sideshow you escaped from, but if you don't put me down, I swear I'm going to press charges, damn it. In fact, I *am* pressing charges." Blood pounded in my temples and my heart beat like it was coming out of my chest.

My captor remained unfazed. He just held me at arm's length and stared at me as if I were from Mars.

"I come in peace, you asshole," I sobbed in more subdued tones, my bravado spent. One or two more halfhearted kicks to his breastplate did absolutely nothing.

Then he spoke four words in a language I didn't understand. His voice came out in a low, rumbling growl, and he did not look happy. After plunking me down onto the floor, he stepped out of the room, slamming the door behind him.

I stuck my tongue out at the closed door, then curled up on the floor and trembled, putting my aching head into my hands. Even though I'd used all my strength, I had still been helpless against him. Closing my eyes, I tried to slow my breathing. I didn't want to look around, as I was scared of what I might see. God only knew what surrounded me. Maybe there were newspaper clippings of his previous murders and giant moths pinned to the walls. The sound of the door being locked echoed around the room.

What's going on? I thought in panic. *Breathe in and out, in and out.* I willed myself to calm down. What had he said? It had sounded a little bit like Greek, with some weird clicking noise between two of the words. Could it be a dialect of Greek or Italian I'd never heard before? Maybe it was a remote, old dialect—or maybe just Greek for "Fe Fi Fo Fum."

The defiant thoughts helped bolster my courage enough to look around. A bed, chair, and a small chest sat about the ten-by-twelve-foot room. A single, covered window decorated one wall.

I hurried to the window and lifted the cloth, only to find bars on the outside of the hazy, paned glass. I opened the pane and grabbed the bars—but they held solid. The ornate iron design prevented me from slipping my body between them.

I turned to the door. The giant abomination had locked it, but I tried to open it, anyway. Nothing, not even a jingle. Backing up, I gauged my distance, lowered my shoulder, and prepared to ram the door. *It always works on television*, I told myself.

I ran fast, painfully slamming my shoulder against the solid wood.

Ow. Bad idea.

Rubbing my shoulder, I returned to the window to look for help. A moderately sized clearing lay below my room. Trees and scrub brush began about fifty feet from the house. I saw no people or other houses.

My head pounded. I felt dizzy and sat down on the bed. My fingers located a large, tender lump on my head. I must have hit my head pretty hard to have a knot that size. *If I only had an ice pack,* I thought.

How had this day gone so wrong? Where was I, and how long had I been passed out? It was still daylight out—but was this even the same day? I hadn't recognized any of the scenery. At least, it didn't look like any place in Buffalo that I'd ever visited.

I curled up into a ball on the furthest side of the bed and faced the door, utterly defenseless and too tired to cry. I closed my eyes, praying that the spinning in my head would stop.

Chapter 5

September 384 BC

Etruria

Time seemed to be slipping away.

Nortia paced her room. Finally, they were almost done with their preparations to leave. The previous day had been quite difficult for the three of them.

Antoni had to lie to the head of the villa guard, making up a story about an extended trip to the clifftop city of Volterra to visit family. When the guard protested, Antoni was forced to elaborate even further, saying that hired guards would be joining them shortly after their departure.

Then there was her mother. Ati had been in and out of Nortia's chambers throughout the day, speaking about the evil coming in increasingly agitated tones.

With trembling fingers, Nortia lit a small torch to brighten her chamber in the darkness. They would leave at dawn. She looked at the small bundle of possessions she had gathered to take with her, now unsure of her choices. Should she take something for the baby? Where would they be going? Would they be safe?

She needed more strength to bear all that was happening. *Why now?* Nortia had waited so long for this child. She was twenty-four, and most women had already had three or four children by that age. This should have been a joyous and peaceful time for her and her husband as they excitedly awaited the birth of their child. She now knew that would never happen.

Her insides lurched. She shouldn't have told anyone about the pin and her visions. Then they could have stayed in their own home, warm and safe. She had been a fool to tell anyone, and it had been selfish. Now the people she cared for most could be in great danger.

Blinking back hot tears of frustration, she hugged herself. Then an idea began to take hold.

She would get rid of the pin.

It was the cause of all this pain, and how she hated it as a result. She would tear it from her breast and throw it into the sea. Why hadn't she thought of this sooner?

Nortia peeked out the doorway of her chambers. Antoni wasn't at his usual post—he was probably still seeing to the details of their trip. Even though he was otherwise occupied, he would still be close by, so she knew she must be stealthy. As she ran from her chambers, she remembered to hug the walls, chafing at the way her tunic made noise when it swished against the stones.

After she made her way outside, she brazenly strode to the waiting horses—but she didn't feel as confident as her actions made her appear. Surely this was the right—no, the *only* choice she had—even if it meant leaving everything she had so carefully readied behind. She must get to the ocean.

Nortia steadied herself, and without a word to the guard, grabbed the horse's reins from his hands, mounted, and turned toward the sea. Her horse took several hopping jumps to one side, startled and skittish. She fought for her seat, as well as control of the animal.

Her horse took several more leaps, then it began to respond. Nortia leaned forward, urging her mount on. Crouched over the horse's neck, she felt its speed gather until it was running flat out.

~~~

Antoni heard shouts from the guard and ran outside. Ati followed, somehow managing to almost keep up with him.

"What happened?" Antoni asked the guard, trying to make some sense of the confusion.

The guard blurted out, "She came up to me quickly and didn't say a word. I thought the three of you would be leaving together, but she took the horse and rode off."

"*And you let her go?*" Antoni yelled. "What were you thinking? Which way did she go?"

"By the Gods, man, speak up," Ati shouted. "Which way?"

The guard, his eyes cast downward, pointed to the sea.

There Antoni saw a silhouetted rider in front of the angry backdrop of the sea. The once-calm surf roiled, and waves pulled up to impossible heights before crashing back down. The sky was just beginning to get light, and the moon remained a sliver on the horizon. Dawn's smoldering red glow cast over the wave tops, setting them aflame.

All eyes shifted to the north. In the distance, the outline of twelve riders headed toward Nortia, moving at an incredible speed. Their horse's necks were stretched in line with their running bodies. The riders' dark cloaks, barely visible against the darker side of the sky, whipped in the wind.

Without hesitation, Antoni mounted his horse, followed by Ati on hers. He spurred his horse in the direction he'd last seen Nortia and pulled ahead of Ati, who struggled to keep up.

What is Nortia doing? The wind tore at his face. The sound of sharp hooves hitting the ground in rapid succession echoed in his ears. The rhythm was as fast as the pounding of his heart.

He knew he must make it to Nortia before the riders did. The visions were coming true—the dark riders, the churning ocean—all of it. He couldn't believe it was happening. Why hadn't he heeded the warnings? They should have left sooner; he couldn't vanquish all these riders alone.

Twisting around in the saddle to see behind him, he bounced on his horse's back. Were any of the guards following him? He snatched a glimpse of horses twirling around as they were being mounted. This reassured him until he saw Ati, about twenty horse lengths behind him. He waved his hand, signaling for her to fall back, but Ati's horse never changed stride.

He reached the sand, still some distance behind Nortia, and called out to her. The wind whipped the words from his mouth.

Nortia pulled furiously on the reins. Her horse sat back on its haunches and slid to a halt, spraying up sand. With the forward momentum, Nortia swung off the horse's back and hit the sand running.

What is she doing? She'll hurt herself and the child.

Antoni shouted her name, over and over. His horse lost its footing in the deep sand, so he flung himself to the ground and ran toward her. He could hear hoofbeats behind him.

His legs pumped desperately as his old injury jabbed like a hot dagger in his thigh. Reaching Nortia at the water's edge, he seized her arm and spun her around.

She clawed at the pin on her chest.

"What are you doing?" he shouted into her face. "Have you gone mad, woman?"

"I must stop it!" she screamed, her eyes wild, glowing violet. "We must be rid of this evil."

Out of breath, Ati grabbed both of them with a strength that belied her age. "We must run!" she yelled as she tried to pull them away. "They are upon us—the dark ones."

Antoni looked up. The first of the dark riders, a woman, bore down on them, her cold eyes emanating death. It was too late.

Next to him, Nortia still frantically pulled at the pin, her fingers brushing over the stone. Suddenly, she relaxed as she looked into Antoni's eyes, then at her mother.

The savage, murderous woman raised her sword above her head. Her mouth opened wide in a demonic shriek. She leaned in for the kill, her arm coming down in a lethal arc.

Sand sprayed into the air as her horse miraculously balked, skidding to a stop. The sword aimed at Nortia's head cut through the air.

Sick at heart, Antoni lunged at Ati and Nortia to get them down.

Time seemed to slow down. Nortia's hair floated in midair.

The Rider's sword swiped a hunk of her hair, narrowly missing the mark.

Nortia, eyes impossibly wide, stared at Ati.

Antoni collided with both of them, his arms wrapping tightly around their bodies. As the lady demon's furious howl rang in his ears, Antoni shot upward at an unimaginable speed into the thinning air. An intense, crushing sound pressed into his ears.

He couldn't see or feel Nortia or her mother. Uselessly, he flailed his arms, straining every muscle to reach into the darkness. Suddenly, he couldn't move or feel his own body. Even his breathing stopped.

I must be dead, he thought.

Chapter 6

September 384 BC

Etruria

Time was no longer on their side.

While Vanth let out her blood-curdling shriek, Charontes rode up next to her and watched in shock as the intended victims disappeared.

Vanth closed her mouth. "Curse them," she screamed. Rage took hold of her face, contorting it. Her eyes became dangerous, glowing slits. With the charge left in the air, strands of her curled, black hair lifted off her back and swirled in the wind. She beat the horse's neck. "You stupid beast! I could have had her."

Charontes grabbed her hand as it swung down, stopping another vicious blow to the horse.

Vanth snatched it away from him. "Take your hands off me! Don't you ever touch me, you vile man."

Charontes just blinked. He knew better than to show her any signs of fear. "You were not always so repulsed. I remember someone, who looked a lot like you, asking me to put my hands *on* them."

Vanth glared at him and rode a few feet away.

He breathed a sigh of relief at her small retreat. She was taking this better than he had expected. She had been so close to having her hands on the other half of the stone. The woman from Vanth's visions had stood within her reach—then just vanished into midair. *Damn her.*

He knew Vanth could feel the stone's absence—she had told him as much. The stone possessed her, somehow. Even now, her hands clenched and unclenched, as if they missed holding the lost stone.

Charontes heard the thunder of hooves above the crashing of the enraged surf as the rest of the riders piled up behind Vanth. Their horses were breathing hard, squealing and snapping. This would not brighten her mood.

"Back away, you fools. You're too close and *too late*," she shrieked, scalding them all with one of her demonic looks.

The salt spray had soaked through her black cloak, making it cling to her body. Charontes kept his eye on her, as she was unpredictable. Especially when she was angry.

As Vanth tugged at her hood, her horse side-stepped wildly from all the excitement, and she struggled to keep her seat.

The dark warriors grumbled and swung their horses around, wisely riding just out of her reach.

Used to her tantrums, Charontes brought his mount in closer. He needed some answers, and she could sulk later. "What sort of demons are we chasing? Our task will be impossible if they can merely vanish each time we get near them."

"She is not a demon—and I will make her bleed. The power of the stone allows her to move through time and escape us. Fortunately for her, the stone protects her unborn.

It may also give her visions, just as our half does." She smiled a poisonous smile. "It's only a matter of time until we follow her. She will not escape me." Vanth flushed, and her milky-white neck streaked with crimson from a new wave of anger.

Chapter 7

July 1481 AD

Firenze

Held hostage by time.

I opened my eyes. The light of a lone candle flickered beside the bed. Turning to look at the light, pain shot through my head. Everything came rushing back.

I was still in the middle of a nightmare.

A lit candle? Who brought that in? I can't believe I slept through someone coming into the room.

I suddenly felt cold and my skin crawled. *That huge pervert must have been watching me while I slept. Why candles? Maybe he doesn't want a traceable electric bill in his name.*

Still dizzy, I got up slowly from the bed. There were a few wall sconces. I took the candle and lit the others with it. With the room much brighter, I looked around. The smell of candles burning filled the small room.

The floors were planked with rough wood, and straw was strewn about. The unevenly textured walls didn't have any electric sockets or phone jacks. The heavy wooden bed was very tall, and was placed in the middle of the room. Under the bed were some drawers.

Maybe my kidnapper forgot his gun or chainsaw. I tried opening the drawers, but they wouldn't budge. Other than the bed, there was a chair, a small stool, and a chest. I tried opening the chest, but it was locked, just like everything else.

As I looked out the window again, I could still barely see anything in the dark, maybe only ten feet around the house—and once again, there wasn't anyone to call out to for help.

I heard the lock on the door turn and dove behind the bed. *Way to go, Braveheart. He'll never find you back here.*

"I mean you no harm," a soft female voice said. The voice sounded friendly, and it spoke in heavily accented, proper Italian.

Getting up on my knees, I peeked over the high bed.

"My lady, my name is Amelia. I won't hurt you."

I could see the candlelit outline of Amelia's face. She had the face of an angel. Wisps of hair escaped from her head scarf and formed a halo of dark brown ringlets. Finally, someone who could help me.

I stared at what she wore, momentarily unable to speak. She looked like she was dressed to go to a Renaissance fair, except it was eerie how authentic her costume looked. The trim, ties, and shoes looked like the real McCoy. Prickles went up the back of my neck.

She stared at what I wore, too.

"I have brought you something to eat," Amelia said, "and something for after you eat, my lady." She smiled and set the tray on the bed.

Her shape was hidden under long skirts, but she was a slight girl who looked to be about seventeen or eighteen years old. She turned abruptly and headed back out the door.

I panicked. "No, don't leave," I called to her in Italian. "Please, help me." I tried to get off my knees, but my legs were stiff. I'd just pushed myself to a standing position when Amelia walked back through the door.

She set a pot on the floor next to the door. "For later, my lady, for..." she curtsied, glancing at the pot.

I was baffled. "Listen, I appreciate you thinking about me, but I'm not hungry. I want to leave now." I began to walk toward the door.

Amelia put up her hand. "Stop, my lady. Go no farther."

I stopped. There was something in the girl's tone. "Look, I'm not your lady, and I'm asking nicely this time. I want to leave now."

"This is not possible, my lady." The girl's head was down, but she was definitely blocking the door on purpose.

"Why are you blocking my way out? Where are we, and why are you speaking Italian? I want to leave—I never asked to come here."

"I know," Amelia replied in a quiet voice, "and yet, it's not my place to answer all your questions."

"Fine," I said in an imperious tone while walking toward her, "then it is not your place to stand in my way, either. Move out of my way." I was much taller than the girl, and if I had to, I would *shove* her out of my way.

"Please, I beg you, do not try to pass. If you leave this room, he will just catch you and put you back." She lowered her eyes from mine. "And then, I will be punished for certain."

I stopped, midstride. "What are you talking about? Who'll punish you? Who's putting me back in the room, Sampson? Where on earth am I?"

Amelia backed out of the door and whispered through the crack, "Firenze." The door shut, and the lock clicked into place.

I ran to the door and pounded my fists on it. "Come back, Amelia!" I cried. "Please help me! I've been kidnapped.

You must help. Please just call 716-555-3241. It's my father's house, and he'll come and help. You don't have to do anything

else—just call!"

I turned and leaned back against the door. Letting my head fall back, I looked up at the plaster ceiling. That wasn't going to work—the girl had that look of fear in her eyes. I'd seen it before in the eyes of a patient's family members, when their loved one hovered on the brink of death.

How come I don't feel more afraid? If they were going to rape or kill me, they probably would have done it by now. I hoped so, anyway. Whatever. No sense obsessing about it. It wasn't like I had any practice at being kidnapped. Maybe there was an algorithm for being kidnapped, and I had missed the memo. Either way, I knew I needed a plan.

My stomach growled, and it felt like a long time since I'd last eaten. The empty pinch of hunger was something I wasn't used to, and my throat was dry and sore from thirst. I should eat to keep up my strength. Then at the first opportunity for escape, I would be strong enough to get away.

I turned my attention to the tray on the bed. There was wine in a decanter, and a small loaf of bread on a piece of linen. A silver-gray plate contained a bunch of grapes, a piece of cheese, and a hunk of meat—from an animal of unknown origin. No utensils. That's good, because otherwise I would have been forced to stick Sampson in the eye with a fork the next time I saw him.

I sniffed the wine. What did poison smell like, anyway? I was so thirsty, I really had no choice but to drink it. Taking a small sip, I found that it tasted okay, just watered down. *Good, I have to keep my wits about me.* I took a few bigger gulps, and the alcohol burned my dry throat.

Breaking off a big hunk of bread, I filled it with some cheese. *It must be hard to poison bread or cheese,* I thought. Poisoning bread would make it all mushy, and poisoning cheese would take too much planning ahead. The bread was coarse-grained and delicious, as was the cheese.

The meat smelled fresh and slightly spicy, but I didn't dare try it. It seemed to be the most likely portion of the meal to be poisoned. Instead, I popped some grapes in my mouth and mused while chewing. If it weren't for the fact that I was imprisoned and possibly eating poisoned food, the meal would have been thoroughly enjoyable.

While eating, I tried to ignore the growing problem of my full bladder. Now it was imperative that I took care of it. There was only the single door in the room. *Maybe I should pound on it to let them know I have to relieve myself.* If they took me out of the room to use the bathroom, I could find out more information. But I could also draw negative attention to myself. I was torn about what to do.

Nature eventually won out, and I walked up to pound on the door, my foot accidentally kicking the pot Amelia had brought in. My mind played back what Amelia had said earlier. "For later, my lady, for…" I looked at it in horror, as realization suddenly dawned. They expected me to relieve myself, right in the middle of the room, in a pot.

Great, this was going from bad to worse. First kidnapped, and now forced to defecate or eliminate in a pot. What kind of weirdos were they, anyway? I pounded on the door and shouted, "I have to use the bathroom!"

I waited a minute and then hollered again, "Listen, I have to use the bathroom. Now. This isn't fair, you jerks.

Either you let me use the bathroom, or I'm going to pee in this pot." *There. That should bring them to their senses.*

Another minute went by with no response from my captors. If I didn't go in the pot, my choices were limited to going on the floor. Although they deserved the mess, I couldn't bring myself to do something so foul.

It was all probably part of the torture; they were trying to wear me down until I was a just a shell of who I'd formerly been. That way, they could overpower me easily, bending me to their evil will. I'd seen enough of it in my dad's *Missing in Action* Chuck Norris movies.

"Don't say I didn't warn you!" I shouted in the loudest voice I could muster with a full bladder. "Well, here goes nothing." *Great, no toilet paper.* That's okay, I wasn't going to let it bother me. I wasn't falling into any of their little dehumanizing traps. I would do just fine without it. *Bastards.*

With that behind me, I was able to refocus on my dilemma. The food and drink had helped clear my head; now maybe I could begin to figure out this puzzle with the limited information that I had. They didn't speak English, or at least they hadn't yet. One was speaking Italian and the other, some Latin-Greek sort of language.

I was never more grateful than now that my parents had given me so many valuable language skills. Amelia had said "Firenze," which was Italian for "Florence." That just wasn't possible. I couldn't have been unconscious for that long. Could I? Well, Sampson surely couldn't have boarded a plane, or any other mass transit, armored up and with an unconscious person. There would have been questions.

I pondered my situation for a good part of an hour until a twinge of my former headache returned. Still, I wasn't any closer to figuring out where I was, or why I'd been kidnapped. Why would anyone want me? I wasn't special in any way—I was just plain, old me. Average really, nothing outstanding.

I fought back the fear that kept trying to get hold of me. I was tired. Tired of being in this room, tired of being afraid, just tired. I crawled under the thin blanket on the bed. Picking the same spot as before, I wrapped the blanket around me, wishing it was a force field—or at least a rabbit hole I could tumble down.

I awoke to bright sunlight and ran to the window. For a considerable distance, all I could see were trees. It wasn't a thick forest, but one interspersed with scrub brush. From my vantage point, I could just barely make out fields in the distance. I must have missed them when I was looking out of the window yesterday evening.

Tall, thin, dark green trees edged the fields. I squinted through the thick glass. Were those people in the fields? I couldn't tell, as they were too far away. It made sense, though, that people should be working in the fields—and where there were people, there would be help—and cell phones.

I could call my dad. I wouldn't be able to tell him where I was, because there weren't any roads or distinguishing landmarks. There weren't any telephone poles or lines, and there wasn't a car in sight. When I thought about it, there wasn't even a driveway going up to the house.

I looked directly down, and could see the path that led away from the house. It disappeared with a curve into the tree line. Maybe I was in Amish land or Quaker country. That made sense; Sampson could have driven me to Pennsylvania. The Pennsylvania border was only an hour and a half from Buffalo.

As unlikely as it seemed, it was possible. Harrison Ford had been stuck here, too, in that movie, *Witness.* He'd made the best of it, building barns and riding in carriages. That even explained the lack of electricity and bathrooms. I eyed the pot by the door, hating the thought of using it again. But if I didn't, things were going to get messy.

How do people live this way? I didn't want to have a full bladder, on top of whatever torture my kidnappers had in store for me. I imagined wetting myself while on the torture rack. *Better to just get it over with before anyone comes into the room.*

Feeling better, I decided it was time to take matters into my own hands. As soon as someone opened that door, I was going to shove them out of the way and run out. Hopefully it wouldn't be Sampson—he wouldn't be too easy to shove. If it were Amelia, it would be far easier. I'd try not to hurt her, because it seemed like she was merely following orders—and she was just as afraid as I was.

I positioned myself beside the door. When it opened, I'd be right there. I'd kick the door the rest of the way open, throwing whoever had their hand on the door off balance. To distract them, I'd let out a loud yell, and then I could hopefully run past them.

I waited. *What if they kill me for trying to escape?* I wasn't going to think about that now. Better to plan for what to do next after I was already out of the room. First, the stairs. Judging from the simplicity of my room, the house probably didn't have an intricate floor plan. I should be able to find the front door easily. Once out the door, I'd run as fast as I could toward the fields, where there was help.

Stiffness crept up my legs, and my lower back knotted from waiting in one position too long. I wanted to take one more look out the window to see if I could see people in the fields, but I didn't dare move. A small trickle of sweat dripped down my temple. I raised my hand to wipe it away.

The door began to open.

I kicked hard, pushing the door open the rest of the way.

Poor Amelia fell into the room, spilling the tray she was carrying on one hand. I heard the loud crashing of plates.

Bolting through the door, I forgot to scream.

The stairs were right ahead of me. My shoulder bounced off the wall as I rounded them, taking three stairs at a time. Amelia yelled, and I was making an ungodly clamor. But freedom lay just outside.

I sprinted for the front door. Fumbling with the strange latch, my fingers refused to cooperate. *Come on—to have gotten this far and then not be able to open the door?* What seemed like minutes ticked by. I made a squeal of frustration in my throat. *Open, please!*

At that instant, I heard heavy footfalls and what sounded like a roar. Sampson was on to me.

I clawed at the latch, and the door finally burst open. I was free. Sweet air hit my face as I ran outside. I ran like I'd never run before—for my very life.

Chapter 8

September 1480 AD

Firenze

Time became their ally.

Antoni awoke with the sun beating on his face. Lips cracked and dry, he put his hand to his head, groaned, then rolled over. It felt like a morning after he had drunk too much wine.

Suddenly, the warrior in him came to his senses. He leaped to his feet, grabbed his shield, and drew his sword, all in one fluid motion. *The dark riders are upon us,* he thought anxiously, bracing himself for battle.

Nothing happened.

Bewildered, he looked about. A quiet peacefulness permeated the air around him. It was daytime, and their horses were gone. Nortia and Ati were lying at his feet. Ati still clutched onto her daughter's arm.

He knelt down beside them. "Awaken." Worried, he gently shook their shoulders. The women began to stir. Like him, they groaned and grabbed their heads, but then they became still again. He must wake them; the dark riders would be back.

He stood up and looked around again. The pain in his head made him wince. Where were his guards? They had been right behind them. Where was the ocean—and how had they gotten inland? Puzzled, he began searching the ground for hoofprints.

What is happening?

He knelt again beside the women to tend to them. His gaze was drawn to Nortia's sleeping face—her long, whisper-soft dark lashes lay against her flawless skin. Her hair was a riot of shining brown curls that radiated from her head like thirsty roots. How he loved her. A familiar weight settled on his chest, and his throat tightened.

Stealing the moment, he stretched out his hand and caressed her cheek, a liberty he wouldn't have dared to take if she had been awake. It was a small gesture, but one he had longed to do for years. Her cheek was so smooth and soft. As he touched her, he took in a deep breath and closed his eyes. Happy memories washed over him: Nortia playing as a child, dancing about and laughing, then growing into a beautiful young woman.

At twenty-eight, he'd spent most of his life watching her, and he had no regrets. Many of the guards had wives and children, but he'd chosen not to take that path. How could he? Each day, he would have had to gaze on the woman he really loved while being married to someone else. It would have been too much for him. When Nortia married, it had nearly killed him. His life was devoted entirely to her, and that would have to be enough.

Ati was the first to speak. "Antoni, where are they?" she croaked.

Antoni snatched his hand back. "I don't know. When I awoke, it was daytime, and we were just lying here."

"Where *are* we?" Ati struggled, but she managed to sit up and look around. "Where's the ocean? Have we been captured?" She put her head into her hands.

"I think not," he replied, unable to answer any of her other questions. When she was more awake, he hoped the wise woman would be able to explain what had happened— and why they weren't all dead.

"Oh, Nortia," Ati cried, bending over Nortia's prostrate form. "Nortia...Nortia, awaken."

Nortia made a small noise, and her eyes fluttered open. "Am I dead?" Her voice was barely a whisper.

"No…you are well," Ati answered happily.

Nortia fought her way into a sitting position, blinked her eyes a few times in protest to the bright light, then squeezed them shut. "Is it daytime again?"

"It is day, Nortia, and we must take cover." Antoni's heart went out to her, as she'd never seemed so fragile. He longed to take her in his arms and carry her to safety—if only he knew where that might be. The riders probably thought them such easy marks that they went to the villa first to loot it before returning to finish them off.

He helped Ati to her feet, then turned to Nortia and helped her stand. She swayed, and his arms wrapped protectively around her. For a fleeting but glorious moment, he was holding her. Antoni savored the way her body felt pressed to his, and the flowery smell of her hair. He felt Ati's gaze upon him.

"Antoni is right. We must make haste," Ati said, brushing some lingering sand from her tunic. "Do you recognize anything, Antoni?"

"No. The horses are gone, too—most likely back to the villa. We should try to make our way toward there, keeping hidden until we know it's safe." He tried to sound confident, but he really had no idea which way to head first. "Ati, do you sense a right or wrong way to go? I looked for hoofprints leading away, but I couldn't find any."

"No, I'm not feeling anything about where we are, or which way we should go. Nothing here is familiar except, of course, the sun. Maybe we should walk in the opposite direction of where it has risen to find the sea again."

Antoni thought that it was as wise a plan as any, and nodded his assent to Ati. He began assisting Nortia in that direction.

"No, this way," Nortia pulled her arm from his grasp and pointed toward the rising sun.

"What do you think, Ati?" Antoni asked, looking at the disheveled woman for confirmation. Her silver hair, now adorned with small twigs and bits of leaves, stuck out at all different angles.

"Nortia, is that what Hemisatres is telling you to do?" Ati asked.

Nortia shrugged, "I don't know, I think so. It just seems right."

Antoni tried to control his growing frustration and anxiety. "Ladies, we must decide now. We are easy prey standing here, like a nest of baby birds waiting to be picked off, one by one. Let us at least take cover until we decide."

"It's this way," Nortia said, still pointing east.

"We've come this far trusting the stone, and it would be foolish not to listen to it now," Ati said. "It has already saved us once." She straightened her back with resolve.

Antoni knew she was right. If they had stayed at the villa, they would already be dead. What was left of their villa guard after Forte's failed journey would not have been enough to protect them against that murderous band of riders.

"Make haste." He ushered the women forward, in the direction Nortia had pointed, alternatively supporting them as best he could. "Please, go quickly," he added, expecting to be attacked at any moment.

They walked a short while, taking great care to use whatever foliage they could find as cover. They came to the edge of a clearing and stopped. Antoni was ever alert for signs of the dark riders.

Ahead, there was a stone house. Not wanting to go out into the open, they waited while Antoni assessed the strangely built house. He didn't recognize the structure, and that surprised him. He knew all the houses and buildings around the villa.

Nortia gasped and grabbed onto Ati. "It's the farmhouse, the one from my visions," she said.

They advanced a few steps into the clearing, forgetting the danger for a moment. The three of them just stood there, staring at the house. Antoni had never seen a house like this before.

It had two levels and walls made from large tan stones with smooth, rounded edges. Each stone was no larger than a foot and varied slightly in color and size. The roof came to a low pitch in the middle and was covered in curved pieces of reddish terracotta. Small windows were covered with what looked like iron spears, bent into various designs.

"What is the meaning of this?" Antoni asked. "You know this strange building, Nortia?"

"This is the farmhouse from my visions," Nortia said again, which didn't seem to help.

Antoni still stared at the house. It had such an odd look to it. His gaze shifted to the surrounding hills and landmarks. None were familiar. They definitely were not on their land. How was that possible?

"Antoni, should we go to the farmhouse and speak with the people inside?" Ati asked.

"What if they try to slay us?" Antoni replied. "What if they're demons? I don't have any guards to protect you, so it would be only my sword between us and whoever is in that home." He was using a desperate tone, and he knew it—he was not accustomed to not being listened to.

As if in reply to his last statement, the door to the farmhouse opened, and a woman slowly walked out. A short way down the trodden path, she stopped. She was older, and her youthful beauty had faded. Standing there, she looked tired, gaunt, and not the least bit threatening.

Antoni raised his shield and drew his sword, just in case.

Long white hair lay in a single thick braid down her back. She was oddly dressed in a long blue tunic that tightened along her arms and above her waist. Long pieces of leather were woven and crisscrossed down her arms, and over other parts of the tunic. Antoni thought they looked like sandal straps. The straps gathered loose material close to her body in certain places, emphasizing her slenderness.

She looked directly at the three of them. Antoni held his breath and waited for her next move.

Her faced bloomed into a relieved smile. Then, in a weary but clear voice, she spoke. "My name is Patrizia. I have been waiting for you."

The three of them exchanged baffled looks at each other.

"What has happened to our villa?" Antoni asked the woman. "How is it that you know us, when we have never seen you before?" He had tried to sound loud and accusing, but what sounded like fear feathered the edges of his voice.

"I will answer all your questions and more. Please, come inside—and we will talk." When she spoke, her Etruscan tongue had an odd accent.

Antoni turned to Ati and Nortia, hoping that they had begun to figure out the puzzling turn of events—but the blank look on both of their faces told him that wasn't the case.

"Are we to believe that you are alone?" Antoni asked the woman. Every muscle in his body was rigid, and he hadn't budged from his fighting stance.

"Aside from the servants, I am alone," Patrizia answered. "You have my word that I will not harm you."

Nortia giggled.

"Nortia, by the Gods, this is *not* funny," Antoni hissed at her, momentarily forgetting his place.

"The visions were of this farmhouse," Ati said. "We were to go there to be safe. I don't understand what has happened to our villa, but we will go in and see what this kind woman has to say. It will be the quickest way to find out what has happened."

"Hopefully she is kind enough to leave our heads attached," Antoni mumbled under his breath.

Patrizia had already turned and started walking back toward the house. Ati, Nortia, and Antoni followed.

Chapter 9

September 384 BC

Etruria

Too many times, death is victorious.

Charontes cautiously watched as the villa guards came to an abrupt stop a few paces from him and Vanth. He placed his hand on his sword, prepared to use it if needed. The rest of the Reunity Riders sat on their horses behind them.

Looking around, the guards seemed momentarily confused about the lack of signs that there had been a struggle, as well as the absence of the trio they had come to defend. One of the guards rode a few strides ahead of the rest and then hesitated. He addressed Charontes. "Where have you taken Nortia and her mother?"

Before Charontes could reply, Vanth grinned evilly and asked the guard, "Is that fear that makes your voice unsteady? I don't think you need to worry about where I took her. Instead, you should worry about how many of your guards can escape death before I'm done with them."

Vanth dismounted and pulled her short sword from her pack. The wind blew her hair into a swarm of lashing black tentacles, and she started to advance on the villa guards. With quick hand motions, she signaled for half the Riders to circle around the guardsmen and for the rest to dismount.

Charontes remained on his horse, close enough to see the sweat beaded on the lead guardsman's forehead. It was apparent that there was to be no more talking. The lead guardsman waved to the two guards in the rear to ride for reinforcements—a hopeless maneuver that Charontes knew the flanked Riders had expected.

The two escaping villa guards were violently and immediately cut down.

The lead villa guard turned forward to see the now dismounted Riders nearly upon them. "Remain mounted for the advantage, men—we are twice their number!" he shouted. "Stick together and show no mercy, as they will do the same. We will make them deliver Nortia to us."

The guardsman lined up in a practiced formation to fend off both frontal and rear attacks.

Emitting a deep chuckle and slowly drawing her second sword, Vanth stared up at the lead guard, who was now only yards away. "Don't worry about the Riders behind you. They are only there to stop your inevitable retreat. You must understand that I am the one who will be slaying you. I can't have people who defend the lovely Nortia just strolling about, now can I?"

With a show of remarkable athleticism, Vanth dashed forward with unbelievable speed and leaped high into the air. In one swift motion, she brought her two blades in an upward crisscrossed arc over the surprised lead guardsman's raised sword, neatly lopping off his head. Before the head hit the ground, she was upon the next guard, cutting him down with a ruthless stab to the abdomen.

Although it was an impressive show for a woman with child, as Charontes watched her frenetic attack, he felt nothing but disdain for her. If she kept up at this rate, he may not even have to dirty his blade.

With Vanth so engaged, he motioned for the Riders to separate, indicating that they would not be taking any prisoners. Bored, he parried one guardsman's attacking blade, and in one fluid motion, he brought his sword down in a large overhead swing, cleaving his opponent nearly in half.

Vanth was now surrounded by the twisted bodies of dead guardsmen. Their anguished death masks only fueled her rage. "Where did she go?" Vanth screamed as she planted a kick into the throat of another attacker, sending him sprawling to the sand. "Nortia—at least now I know her name."

All she needed was one quick breath, and she pivoted to meet an already-wounded guardsman's arcing swing of desperation at her head. Vanth easily ducked the blade, but the Rider behind her had no time to react to the overreaching blow.

Charontes was already in motion to the Rider's side. He raised his arm, which was encrusted in special armor. There was a loud, metallic clang as it struck his intercepting arm guard. Even with the arm guard, a large gash in his arm ran with bright red blood. But he would heal, and the Rider still had his head attached.

Vanth grinned and lunged. That overreach would cost the villa guard his life. She eagerly dug both of her swords into his chest, then twisted the blades free, spraying both Charontes and herself with blood.

The smell of death was pungent. Bowels were sliced open and the tangy taste of blood hung in the air. Charontes watched Vanth wipe the crimson from her blade, then survey the scene. All of the guardsmen, save one, had been killed. She watched the single, distant guardsman fleeing, and it brought a scowl to her blood-spattered face.

Once the fighting was over, as if nothing had happened, Vanth finished what she was saying to Charontes. "We'll go a short distance from here, just off their land, and wait for a sign from our stone." A strange high-pitched noise, which Charontes eventually recognized as a laugh, began somewhere deep inside her and erupted from her mouth. "It will show me—the when, where, and how to find its other half."

He couldn't avoid looking into her eyes, no matter how hard he tried. They were aflame with a maniacal violet fire. Squinting at the disgusting sight, he rumbled deep in his throat, emitting a feral growl. The woman grew more difficult to understand, making less and less sense every time she spoke. He thought she may be approaching madness, and he knew she would have to be watched.

In the meantime, blood ran freely down his arm. He cleaned his blade on a dead guardsman's tunic and made his way toward the water to tend to the wound.

Chapter 10

July 1481 AD

Firenze

Time for me to fly…

My feet had wings. I ran in the direction of the fields at top speed. Cool, damp air hit my face and rushed by my ears. All those hours on the treadmill were finally paying off.

When I reached the thicket, trees whipped at my arms and legs as I ran by. Underbrush wrapped around me, slowing me down and dragging me backwards. I ran harder, listening for any sounds behind me that would indicate I was being followed—but I heard nothing. Still, I dared not look back.

I must be much lighter and faster than that Sampson man. He had to be pushing three hundred pounds, and even more with that armor.

Run, Lydia. Run.

I leveled off my sprint some. The fields I'd seen from the window were far away, and I had to last the distance. My adrenaline was pumping, and it felt great to be out of that cell of a room.

I burst out of the far tree line, running…running. *No fences, good.* I wasn't going to be able to do hurdles, too. I ran through a cut field that smelled like straw, and aimed myself down one of the crooked furrows. It would be faster.

Thank God I wore my sneakers to work the other day and not my clogs, I thought. *Too bad my white scrubs will stand out like a sore thumb, but there's nothing I can do about that now.* This was the most direct route to people. I stumbled over a giant clod of dirt, and just barely avoided falling.

Watch where you're going, I reprimanded myself. *Your life depends on it. I* checked my pace once more and chanced a glance behind me. *Where is he?* It didn't seem right. *How come no one is chasing me? Is this some kind of trick?*

I had no choice but to keep on going. Sweat poured down my face and pieces of hair stuck to my skin. I felt disgustingly grubby. *How long has it been since I've showered?*

Run, Lydia.

I passed through the long, thin green trees I'd seen out the window, looking up at one as I sped by. To my surprise, I realized that they were Lombardi poplars. *Those don't grow in Buffalo*, I puzzled. I had seen them before in Tuscany, when I'd gone on a trip to Italy with my mom. It had been enchanting at the time to see the trees dotting the countryside, which I recognized from famous Renaissance paintings.

Overwhelming dread clenched my wildly beating heart, then sunk like a lead weight into my stomach as reality began to set in. The poplars…Italian-speaking maids who said you were in Firenze…a very Tuscan-looking countryside…

I was in Italy.

I ran on into another cut field. What was happening? Why did they want me? Was it just random?

I looked around wildly. Where the hell were all the people I'd seen in the fields? Or rather, I'd *thought* I'd seen. I needed them to be there. I could barely breathe, and my lungs were on fire. I couldn't run much farther.

As I started up a hill, I was forced to slow down even more. It was steep enough that I couldn't see anything past the top. As my original adrenaline rush began to dwindle, I put my head down and tapped into the last reserves of endurance I had left. Maybe there were people on the other side. *Please, please let there be people.*

At the top of the hill, I fell to my knees. I had to rest— I couldn't go any farther, and my breath came in ragged gasps. In the near distance was a city. The prominent building was unmistakable.

It was Florence.

I could see the Duomo's green, white and pink marble shining in the sunlight. The huge dome dwarfed the other structures beside it. It reminded me of the trip with my mom, and tears began to blur my vision. *No, I won't cry now.*

I could see people down there. At least now, I knew where I was. I didn't know how I'd gotten here, but I was free. The city looked different from what I remembered; if it wasn't for the Duomo, I wouldn't have recognized it at all. The buildings were cramped together, and there was a huge medieval-looking wall around the city.

Wait a minute, I don't remember there being a wall. Mom and I had stayed there for five glorious days, and by the time we'd left, I'd been pretty familiar with the layout of the city. To the west was the Arno River. Yes, this was Florence. I could even see the Basilica of Santa Maria Novella, so I must be north of the city.

Trying to take in all the sights in at once, my eyes went back to the wall. It had to be twenty feet tall, and there were huge towers spaced at regular intervals along it. *This is really weird.* I just stared, trying to figure it all out. Then I felt the cold chill of realization race through me once more, and my blood turned to ice in my overheated body. I finally remembered where I'd seen the wall before—in museum paintings.

There *had* been a wall around Florence at one time, hundreds of years ago. I closed my eyes, my heart racing anew, blood pounding in the sides of my neck. What on earth was going on? I was somehow in Florence, hundreds of years ago? From my spot on the hill, I frantically looked around again for evidence to disprove my newest and most ridiculous theory ever.

Where are the cars and honking horns?

More detail sprang out at me. In the distance, I saw a horse-drawn cart which was filled with straw, approaching an opening in the wall. People were walking about, far enough away that they looked small. Still, I could see that some of them were dressed in robe-like garments, and others were wearing pants and long shirts. A few were carrying huge bundles of sticks or straw on their backs. A person on horseback rode past the cart and through the wall at a canter.

A rivulet of sweat trickled into one of my eyes, breaking me out of my trance. Somehow, I'd time traveled. *How can I even be thinking that? I don't believe in time travel.*

In physics class, I'd been interested in some of Einstein's theories, but they'd all come to the same conclusion: it wasn't possible to go faster than the speed of light. As this was one of the key variables in all the equations, time travel was considered to be impossible.

My eyes narrowed. This was Sampson's fault. Somehow he was behind all this.

As if my thoughts had somehow conjured him, I heard the heavy hoofbeats of a lone rider's horse. I turned around, and my jaw dropped at the visage. This was the first time I had a really good look at him—the whole picture. Sampson, or whatever his name was, galloped toward me at full tilt.

Clumps of churned-up earth flew into the air from each stride of his horse's enormous hooves. He looked like a Greek god, or an armored warrior from the movie, *Gladiator.* Swords were strapped to his side.

He was heading straight for me—and he looked pissed.

I ran. It was futile, as he was almost upon me—but I ran toward the wall, anyway. If someone saw me, maybe they would help. Flying down the side of the hill, I aimed toward the opening in the wall. I ran faster than humanly possible because of the steepness of the hill. My thigh muscles screamed.

I closed in on the city—so close now that I smelled the pungent odor of refuse.

Then suddenly, I ran on only air.

> *Yellow bird, up high in*
>
> *banana tree*
>
> *Yellow bird, you sit all alone*
>
> *like me*
>
> *You can fly away, in the sky*
>
> *away.*

He scooped me off the ground and plunked me onto the front of his horse. The horse hopped and snorted to a halt. I was held down, sitting sideways securely in front of Sampson—encircled by an arm made of steel.

"Let go of me, you jerk," I yelled. *Hiccup.* "What's your problem?" *Hiccup.* You let me go, *now*. Help, Help!" I screamed out in Italian, kicking my feet and pounding his arm with my fists. I desperately hoped one of the people by the wall would hear me.

Then I had a horrible thought. *Even if they do hear me, they would be hundreds of years too early to help.*

Sampson wore bronze armor on his upper left arm and chest, and it hurt my hands when I hit him. Panicked thoughts skittered through my brain. My childhood dreams of knights in shining armor ran through my head as I remembered the prophetic saying: *Be careful what you wish for.* Obviously, I had not been careful enough. In fact, tragically careless.

Hiccup. Damn it. Couldn't anything in my life go right? Kidnapped by a barbarian, disastrously thrown back through time, and so stressed out I had the hiccups. To top it off, that infernal song wouldn't stop playing in my head.

"Let me go," I yelled.

He didn't. He hadn't even heard me. He just turned his horse around and headed back the way he'd come.

Who was I kidding? No one was going to help me. Even if they tried, what could they do? Why was this happening to me? How had hundreds of years disappeared?

Where was everyone I loved? How would I get back? He must know how to get me back to my time.

I looked up into his face. He looked very angry. *Hiccup.* Why did he have to be so handsome? His dark hair waved proudly about his shoulders. A nicely cut jawline, set in a stubbornly determined manner, did nothing to detract from his good looks. His skin was clear, dark, and richly tanned.

The sun was beating down on both of us, and the smell of him swirled around me in the breeze. It was an intoxicating, masculine, outdoorsy scent, with a hint of leather.

I must be crazy. This man kidnapped me, and all I could do was sniff him and moon over him like a starstruck teen. I needed to talk to him and ask him what was happening. Beg him to put me back in my own time. Maybe he was a wizard or a magician…or something. Apparently, lots of things I thought weren't possible actually *were*.

I tried speaking slowly to him in Italian again, but there was no response. I didn't know French, but it was worth a try. "Parlez-vous Français?" *Weren't some of these people*

like Normans or something way back when? Oh, I can't
remember.

Everything I knew about history, or at least
remembered, was from romance novels—and now even that
lay in a tangled heap in my brain. History in school had been
next to useless—they'd just kept teaching us about the
Revolutionary War, over and over again. My parents would
have been scandalized if they had known.

No response to the French. Maybe he can only
communicate in monosyllabic grunts when he's away from a
television remote. Oh yeah, I forgot—in Paleolithic times,
there was *no television.*

So let's see, that leaves Greek and my sparse Latin
vocabulary for languages to try.

"Are you a big, stupid man?" I asked in Greek, using a
voice I usually reserved for two-year-old children and very
small puppies. Then I tried it in Latin. "Are you a man, big
and stupid?" I wasn't sure if the "stupid" part translated
correctly. "You know, bigamus, stupidus?" I added in
English, more to bolster my courage and cheer myself up than
anything else.

Sampson pulled the horse to a halt. Jet black eyes looked down at me.

I stopped breathing.

He wrapped his arm farther around me, gently grasping the back of my head with his hand. His fingers touched my scalp and wove through my curls. He tilted my head up and stared into my eyes, as if thinking about his next move.

Great, I was just starting to get used to the size of him, and now he's going to snap my neck and crush my skull.

Five heart-stopping seconds later, I saw one corner of his mouth tip upward in what must have been amusement. He lowered his mouth toward mine, tightened his grip around my body, and pressed his lips to mine.

I whirled in a cascade of feeling. He was kissing me.

I should stop him, I thought—but his kiss felt ever-so-gentle and feather-light. Not the kind you'd expect from a barbarian. As his lips brushed over mine, I spiraled into ecstasy.

Hiccup. I pulled my mouth away, coming to my senses. Until then, I'd been frozen in one position, paralyzed by the sudden unexpectedness of his advance.

"Stop that!" I shouted in Greek. "I never asked you to kiss me, you giant brute!"

I reached up to slap him, but he was too quick. He simply lowered the hand he had on my head to deflect the blow. His arm came to rest over my arms, holding them down.

"I hate you!" I yelled in his face, squirming in my seat. I turned my head and made a show of wiping my mouth off on my shoulder.

He just looked at me with the same upward tilt of his lip. He nudged the horse into a slow canter and headed back toward the house. I was at a loss over what to do next.

~~~

As we approached the farmhouse, I got a chance to see it from the front. It was two stories high, made of stone, and it looked rather plain. The roof was peaked and made of red tile. I could see that all the windows had iron bars over them. *A handy feature for a kidnapper's house,* I thought.

As my captor moved to dismount, his sun-heated breastplate touched my bare arm, burning it. I pulled my arm back quickly. He mumbled something low in his throat, touching my arm gently—a gesture that could have only been an apology.

Why would my kidnapper apologize to me? As if this situation could get any stranger.

He jumped down from the horse. Why did he have on such light armor? It looked like it was from ancient Greek or Roman times. We were in Italy, but not during that time period. I didn't know a lot about Roman history, but I'd learned some during my trip to Florence.

My *Frommer's Travel Guide* had said the Duomo was built sometime in the twelve hundreds or thirteen hundreds. So why the Spartan outfit? He even had on a three-tiered skirt and shin guards, just like Gerard Butler in that movie, *300.*

Eureka, that's it! When I got back to my time, I would sell the movie rights to my time travel story for millions. Of course, there would be a clause that Gerard Butler would have to play my abductor, and I would play the heroine. I'd run to work every day, and I'd do it for free.

Sampson grabbed me and put me over his shoulder. Ripped from my reverie, I yelled, "Damn! Can't a girl in shock even have a nice dream? I hate to break this to you, but I *do* have legs, you know. Why do you insist on carrying me everywhere? My legs are going to atrophy and become all shriveled up—then you'll have to kidnap a fresh, new specimen."

He didn't respond.

I kicked my legs wildly in the air. "Jerk."

~~~

Upstairs, he set me gently onto the bed in my room. "Are you happy now, you damned Neanderthal?" I spoke Greek to him, but peppered it with some English words that didn't translate, especially the profanity. It didn't matter—it all went over his head, anyway.

He just stood there, looking at me with those penetrating black eyes. Defiant, I stared back at him, purposely squinting my eyes and scrunching my eyebrows in an attempt to convey the sort of angry and displeased look that would be universal.

However, after that kiss, it was hard to glare at him. Some baser instinct made me want to sigh and throw myself into his arms. For some reason, I wasn't as afraid of him as I should be. *Such a gorgeous man. Maybe I'm dreaming.* I thought about pinching myself a couple hundred times.

It occurred to me that I could simply be in a coma back at my unit. If all the men were this good-looking in comas, I should have tried giving myself severe head injuries long ago.

The muscles bunched under the tanned, smooth skin of his legs as he shifted his weight.

My face reddened. I realized my gaze had traveled down a lot lower than it should have. He'd caught me looking at him, of course—I could tell by the glimmer in his eyes. My head jerked up when he began to speak.

"I don't make the same mistake twice." His voice was a deep, velvety growl.

I understood him. He'd spoken in an exotic-sounding, Greek-like language, but somehow, I'd understood him. Not every word, but since he'd finally said more than three words, I could piece together the meaning.

So if I knew what *he* was saying, then he knew what *I* was saying. Suddenly, I was furious with him again, and let loose a tirade of Greek. "What's happening? Are you a wizard? Who are you, and why do you have me here? I demand to be released now."

Completely ignoring me, he stepped out of the room and closed the door behind him, locking it. I couldn't believe he'd just walked out without saying a word.

"You incredible jerk! Why won't you answer me? Come back, you coward—you yellow-bellied, giant tree-trunk of a man! What, are you scared to face a *girl?*"

The door immediately swung open and I was crushed against his armor. It wasn't possible for someone his size to move that fast. Covering my shriek of outrage with his mouth, he kissed me roughly. I tried to pull away, but he had the back of my head in his palm. I couldn't get away. He lifted me up, carrying me a few steps until my back was pressed against the wall, never releasing my mouth.

Gentling the kiss, his lips and tongue caressed over my mouth hungrily. He pushed his body against me, pinning me to the wall so that my feet weren't even touching the floor. The armor was a new feel for me, and I started to melt. *This can't actually be happening.*

His mouth demanded that I kiss him back. I couldn't help myself—I was unable to think of anything else but him. We molded together as if we had been made for each other. I could feel him holding back, barely controlling himself.

It felt so good, but it had to stop. I didn't want to be in this house, kidnapped and held against my will. I kicked my feet. He pressed into me, seducing me, letting me feel the weight of him. Deliberately, he drew the kiss to a close by pulling my upper lip into his mouth. Lowering me to the floor, he walked out of the room.

This time, I was speechless.

Trembling, I lay down on the bed. What was I doing? I had to get a hold of myself. What was wrong with me? I had actually smooched with my abductor. *Who does that?*

Overwhelmed, I tried to push it all out of my mind for a moment. Heart racing, I lay there with my eyes closed, trying to calm myself. Eventually, I noticed I smelled horrible. My body was still sweaty from running all over the countryside. *Yeah, under the Tuscan sun.*

The stupid joke made me grimace, or was it the smell under my arms? I really needed to wash. Maybe cavemen were attracted to that sort of thing—wild, sweaty pheromones. That could be why Sampson kissed me.

There was a gentle knock at the door.

"Come in," I called out. "It's locked from the outside, anyway. What would you like me to do, open it for you?" I figured the light knock must be the girl, Amelia, so I spoke in Italian. I couldn't help being sarcastic—I was feeling extremely discouraged after my failed escape attempt, and just a little ashamed of my disgraceful behavior with Sampson. *Why should I be nice to Amelia, anyway?* She was in cahoots, for the most part, with Sampson.

The girl timidly poked her head through.

I smiled when I noticed she had immediately released her grip of the door handle. That broke the ice for me. "Come in. I'm not going to hurt you," I said, feeling exasperated and a little more than uncharitable.

"Begging your pardon, my lady. I've brought your meal and some water to wash with."

My spirits were heartened some by the thought of being able to wash, even if it was only in a basin full of water.

"I've also brought you some clothes. They aren't like yours, but I hope you will find them serviceable." Amelia went back out of the room and brought in the clothes. She kept a wary eye on my position on the bed.

I purposely didn't move. "Thank you, Amelia. I want to apologize for frightening you this morning, but you understand that I had to try to get away."

"Yes, I understand." Amelia wouldn't look directly at me.

I should try to be nice to Amelia, I thought. *I desperately need information, and she might know something useful to me.* The more I knew, the better my chances were of either escaping this house or managing to somehow get back to my own time. I had to get her to stay in the room longer.

"Would you be able to help me with these clothes? I'm not familiar with this style. What year were these made?"

"What year? I'm not sure. Last year, I think."

"What year was that?" I asked. "I'm afraid I'm not very good at remembering numbers." I was unable to think of any other excuse.

Looking at me as if I were stupid, Amelia said, "The year of our Lord fourteen eighty, of course."

"Of course. Yes, silly me, it must have slipped my mind." I groaned inwardly at how stupid I must sound to the girl. So it was now 1481. I had suspected that I'd been swept into the past, but to hear someone confirm it so nonchalantly was mind-boggling.

The year 1481—that meant Leonardo da Vinci was alive. Yes, he was alive now. I'd read about him in a book I'd bought in Milan. One of the stops on our trip had been to see *The Last Supper*. After viewing the fresco, my mom and I had stopped in an adjacent gift shop, and I'd been the typical inspired tourist.

Amelia stood there staring at me. "You wanted help with your clothes, my lady?"

"Oh…yes. Would you be able to come back after I've eaten and washed?" I needed time to absorb this new information. If Amelia came back, I would have another opportunity to ask questions, and some time to think up how to phrase them.

Amelia didn't look happy about it but shrugged her shoulders and said yes.

I couldn't blame her. The poor girl probably thought I was scheming another escape.

~~~

While I ate, I decided that I should try to find out more about Sampson from Amelia, like maybe his name. I'd grown tired of making up new, hulking names. I tried to think of ways to trick the girl into answering my questions, but I wasn't very good at it.

All I could come up with were sad little ploys that even a young girl would be able to see through, such as, "Amelia, would you ask…what's his name, you know, the hulking Goliath who has all of us shaking in our shoes?" Then Amelia would obediently supply the answer. "Yeah, him. Would you ask him to come up here?"

Well, I'd have to try it, anyway.

I thought about Sampson's delicious kisses and got hot all over. It made me feel guilty to admit that I liked them, even to myself. Shouldn't I be frightened of him? There was something about the way he acted, almost as if he were protecting me. It made me fairly certain that he didn't want to hurt me.

Perfect, I've plunged over the edge of sanity now. It wasn't bad enough that a silly song played over and over in my head, and bouts of uncontrollable hiccups attacked at random. Like a sponge for every psychosis, now I suffered from an all-new affliction—Stockholm Syndrome. I was falling in love with my abductor. What was the cure for that? Escape?

Trying not to think about it, I dipped a thin linen cloth into the cool water and wiped it gently over my skin. Stripping down to my undershirt and panties, I washed the rest of my body as best as I could. I'd clean my underclothes later, when I was sure to have privacy.

I rearranged the clothes Amelia left for me on the bed, then took a good look at them. Just touching them made the hairs stand up on the back of my neck. Honest to goodness clothes from the fourteen hundreds. I'd actually time traveled.

I didn't know the names of all the clothes, but remembered some terminology from my most reliable source of historical information so far—romance novels. I laid out a thin off-white linen shift, or *chemise*. It looked like a cotton slip, but longer. There was a long brown skirt and a cream-colored long-sleeved shirt. The shirt looked like it would go down to my knees.

I picked up my sneakers and set them by the bed. At least for now, I'd keep my own shoes. Hopefully no one decided to burn me at the stake for my Nikes. The skirt was so long, nobody would be able to see them, anyway. But I didn't plan on staying here and could pretty accurately anticipate the need for my runners in the near future.

The near future—when would that be, exactly? This time travel stuff could get really confusing.

I needed to run away again, that much was sure. But to where? I didn't know. It didn't matter what time I was in; I was tired of being a prisoner, and I wanted to be free. Information was the key. After I found out as much as possible, I would make my escape back to my own time.

Someone knocked softly on the door.

"Come in," I said.

Amelia entered once again, keeping a cautious eye on me. Without wasting any time, she began to help me dress. It became apparent that Amelia had done this before, whereas I found it awkward to be dressed by someone else.

Unsure how to approach the whole line of questioning, I figured it was now or never. "So, Amelia, are you a prisoner here, too?"

"No." Amelia looked at me strangely.

"Then why do you stay here if you are afraid of…I'm sorry, what is the big man's name?"

"I call him 'sir,'" Amelia answered. "I really shouldn't be answering any questions. Let me help you dress, please."

Tears threatened to flow, but I was able to ward them off. It was so nice to finally talk to someone, even if they were unwilling to answer me. "It's just that I'm afraid, and if I only knew a little more, maybe I wouldn't be so frightened. I don't know who else to ask. Sir Giant Man won't answer any of my questions."

Amelia giggled at my "sir slur." That encouraged me some, and it made her seem more approachable. "I don't want to get you in trouble, but if you answer a few simple questions, surely that would be okay, wouldn't it?"

"I shouldn't stay long in here. He will notice," Amelia said, adjusting my shirt from the back. Very quietly, she asked, "What do you want to know? I don't want you to be frightened."

"Thank you, Amelia. I appreciate your kindness more than you'll ever know. Where are we? I mean, I know we are near Firenze, but whose house is this?"

"We are in my mistress's house, and on her land—but she is dead now." Amelia looked terribly sad after she'd said the words.

My heart went out to her. "He killed her and took over the house?" I asked.

"No, she was sick for a long time. He didn't kill her, but he tried to stop the evil one who did."

"So he moved into her house. Then what happened?" I tried to ask open-ended questions to keep Amelia talking and get as much information as I could.

I could tell I didn't have long. My line of questioning had hit a spot which instantly increased the poor girl's agitated state. So young and so terrorized, she looked ready to bolt out of the room at any moment.

"No, no, you are misunderstanding everything. I don't know exactly what's happening. We were all fine until last year. Then those people came, my mistress got sick, then everything went wrong." Fresh tears shone in her eyes. She looked like a person on the edge of a nervous breakdown.

"Who came? What went wrong?" I asked, taking her small hand to comfort her and hopefully discourage her from fleeing.

"I don't know what's happening. All I know is if *she* comes back, Franco promised that we would leave here." Her hand trembled in mine.

"She...*who?*" I asked.

"*Her!* The one who killed my mistress—the evil one. If she comes back, Franco will take me, that same hour, that same minute, just as he promised. Listen to me...it isn't the big man you need to fear...it's *her*." Amelia's look of dread was unmistakable as she turned for the door.

"Calm down. Please don't leave me like this. I'm even more frightened now than before you answered my questions. Who's Franco? Will he help me, too?"

"I'm sorry, my lady. I don't know why they are keeping you, and I don't know how to help you. Franco works here with me, but he isn't a warrior. If he and I leave here, we have no one and no place to go. I don't know what to do. The big one has been here for weeks, but he hasn't hurt anyone. I don't think he's evil like the others, but he was with them."

"I don't understand. *Who* is evil? How many people live here now? Are evil people coming here?" Panic crept through me.

"I really don't know, my lady…it's the truth. I don't speak their language. All I know is the evil ones left and haven't been back since. I can't say any more. I've been in here too long as it is, and he'll know. I must go now—I promise to try to help you if I can. I will talk to Franco." Amelia quickly left the room.

I didn't know what to make of the new information. I felt some small relief that Amelia wanted to help me and would talk to Franco. But he wasn't a warrior, which meant he probably wouldn't stand a chance against Sampson.

I looked down at the clothes I wore, which wrapped around me in voluminous layers, unlike my scrubs. However, they were surprisingly comfortable. *This is crazy*, I thought. *I'm in Renaissance Florence, dressed like a Florentine, after catapulting through time. Evil people are all over, somewhere—and, oh yeah, my only ally is a maid who is scared silly.*

Resolutely, I laced up my running shoes. The *Wide World of Sports* theme song played softly somewhere in my subconscious. *The thrill of victory and the agony of defeat.* I didn't have many choices. I could stay here and pee into a chamber pot, waiting for an evil woman to kill me—or I could try to escape again.

I wished there was some way to ask Sampson about getting back to my own time. So far, he had been less than helpful in the information department. Should I stay and try to learn more, or leave immediately and take my chances?

It would probably be dangerous for a single woman in these times. Where could I run? To the city? That seemed risky, although the evil people returning at some unknown time didn't sound very promising, either.

I'd almost made it last time. If I had kept running, I would have been through the gates of the city. Once I got past the gates, Sampson would have a hard time barreling down the crowded streets on his huge horse. I, on the other hand, would be able to slip in and out of small alleys and side streets.

So how do I escape again? Sir I-Don't-Make-the-Same-Mistake-Twice must have taken some sort of precautions. I'd have to be sly this time—or maybe not. Maybe the last thing anyone would suspect would be for me to try to escape in exactly the same way.

I'd eaten as much of my lunch as I could to keep up my strength. It was only about one-thirty or so, and they'd never expect it. Amelia would bring me an evening meal, and I'd make my break then. I'd eat the rest of the bread, cheese, and fruit that was left over from lunch, which would hopefully tide me over until tomorrow. Then, the same drill.

Poor Amelia—I felt bad about betraying her, but I'd have to ambush her again.

Oh well. Nothing personal.

Chapter 11

September 1480 AD

Firenze

It was time to be brave.

Antoni entered the home first. Shield up and sword drawn, he stepped gingerly onto the rushes which lay over the entire floor. They made dry, cracking noises as he walked over them. Alert for treachery, he checked the house, examining every shadow and recess, upstairs and down, before he motioned for the women to follow.

If the dark riders hid within, he would die defending his ladies. It might be a futile effort, but in such a small space, he could wreak havoc before falling to his adversaries.

Finished searching for danger, Antoni took time to really look around the lower level. There were three rooms, and all of them seemed small and confining. *Poor woman, how does she live this way?* He was familiar with poorer quarters, of course, but had grown accustomed to the open courtyards and wide, breezy halls of the villa.

Odd pieces of cloth and iron crafted into patterns that hung on the windows, probably for decorative purposes. He tried to admire their artistry, but even their beauty didn't change his initial opinion of the home. It made him feel closed in like a captive.

There were furnishings, chests, tables, and chairs. The hair prickled on the nape of his neck. Something felt very different. In fact, *everything* was different. Patrizia sat on a well-worn chair, which she must have sat in often, and watched them with an interested, patient gaze. It seemed that she was waiting for them to calm down and adjust to their surroundings.

Satisfied with his cursory examination, he chose to stand beside the already-seated Ati. His curiosity flared like a flame burning too bright, and he wanted Patrizia to start explaining everything. Antoni stared at her with a watchful eye, but for some reason felt he could trust her. Either way he wouldn't let his guard down, even though she didn't seem to mean them any immediate harm.

Nortia stood in the entrance of the house and hadn't moved the entire time. As she looked around, she appeared to be overwhelmed and unable to react.

Ati also saw her distress and signaled for Antoni to bring Nortia in to sit down. Keeping his sword by his side, Antoni put his shield by the chair and went out to get Nortia. After he had retrieved her, he led her to sit down next to the other women.

Once seated, Nortia took a deep breath, closed her eyes slowly, then opened them again. Unable to fully relax, Antoni preferred to remain standing and ever on guard.

"What I am to tell you will be difficult to understand and to bear," Patrizia began. "I am somewhat certain that you can stay here safely for a while. At least until the birth of the child—this much I know. I will tell you some of the tale today, but as days pass, I will tell you more. I have nothing to hide, but you must acquire this knowledge only a small amount at a time. Learning too much too quickly could needlessly hurt, worry, and frighten you. First, tell me your names."

"I am Ati, this is my daughter, Nortia, and our guard, Antoni," Ati answered in barely a whisper. She spoke their names and was silent once more.

How did Patrizia know that Nortia is with child? Or that we hadn't been safe once but are safe now? Antoni had many questions, so many that he was unable to ask any. He also remained silent.

Patrizia, as if she could hear his thoughts, went on. "I will answer all your questions in time." She pointed at the pin on Nortia's chest and asked, "Tell me, Ati, what do you know of the stone Hemisatres?"

Initially, Ati seemed startled. She looked at the pin, then back at Patrizia. But then she answered the question, as if spellbound, reciting what sounded to Antoni like a memorized version. "The stone is named after the God of time and necessity. We know it is very powerful and there is an unfulfilled prophecy surrounding it. The prophecy tells of two female children who can ride the four quarters of the sky.

It is also said that they will unleash the powers of the stone, the only defense against a deadly evil. If they fail, humankind will be no more."

As soon as Ati spoke the words, Antoni had a sick feeling in his stomach. He looked at Nortia. She returned his gaze, but there was an emptiness behind her eyes. She didn't seem to grasp what was being said. Antoni had seen this look before in the eyes of soldiers who had seen too many battles and too much death.

"What you have said is true," Patrizia continued, "but much of the prophecy seems to have been lost through the generations. Time, as you will learn, is not important; cycles are. Cycles are like waves in the ocean. Good and evil will cycle in groupings of saecula, as your people say, or what we also know as 'life spans.' You need but look to see them." Patrizia paused to catch her breath and went on.

"What is important is that good and evil will inevitably rise and fall. The rise and fall we cannot control, but the outcomes can be shaped and diverted. The direction can go toward good *or* evil. It has always been that way.

"I will tell you some more, then give you time to understand and accept what I have said. Please understand that you must do this first before you can be told everything."

Antoni found his tongue. "You will tell us how to find the villa—that would be most helpful." His tone sounded unfair in the light of how helpful Patrizia seemed to be, but he was afraid.

"Your villa still stands," Patrizia answered patiently, "but it's not here in this time. It is exactly the way you left it, some twenty-three saecula ago. You will learn that this span of time is also known as almost nineteen hundred years."

"Why is it there?" Antoni was utterly confused. "Not at *what* time?" *What is she talking about?*

"As it is said in the prophecy, you have ridden the four quarters of the sky. I call it 'time jumping.' The stone allowed you to do this. Hemisatres is one half of a whole, and will protect and guide the unborn child of the prophecy. That's why you are here."

Antoni rolled his eyes. The woman was out of her senses. "What of the dark riders? Why do they hunt us?" He used great effort to control the pitch of his voice. He needed to remain practical in the midst of the old woman's rantings.

"All in good time," Patrizia said, offering Antoni a small smile. "I will tell you what you need to know, all in good time."

"How is it," Ati asked, "that you know about us, the child, the stone, and the riders—and yet, we know so little?"

Patrizia gave her a reassuring look. "You must trust me. I'm here to help you. I can promise that what is happening will become much clearer to you in time. I welcome you three into my home. It isn't much, but you will be safe here for a while. Upstairs there are three rooms that you may use. The stairs are difficult for me now, and I am already accustomed to sleeping down here. Will you stay?"

Antoni didn't like the idea of staying with a complete stranger, but what other choice did they have? He looked to Ati for approval, or at least some sort of guidance. She just put her head down and shook it slowly, shrugging her shoulders upward. She didn't seem to know what to do, either.

He couldn't believe how one day could make such a difference in their vulnerability. How had he let it go this far? He didn't believe any of the "riding the four quarters of the sky" talk. Still, he couldn't explain what was happening, or even figure out a way to get them back to their villa.

He turned to Nortia, who seemed distant and closed off. Still wearing the pin on her mantle, it hung down at an odd angle, as the fabric around it had ripped. Every so often, she would look down at it and stare, then look away at nothing. Antoni hoped she was just tired. *A good rest maybe, and she will be back to her old self,* he thought.

"You have our gratitude for taking us in," Ati finally answered, speaking for all three of them. "We will stay and listen to what you have to tell us. We appreciate your hospitality and guidance."

"It's nothing," Patrizia said. "I'm glad you've decided to stay."

The dark hairs on Antoni's arms stood up, and for a moment, he felt that the woman had known all along that they would accept her invitation.

Patrizia called out in a language foreign to Antoni, and two servants came into the house—a young man with black hair of about nineteen or twenty, and a pretty brunette girl. The girl seemed a few years younger than the man, maybe around eighteen years old. They must have been making themselves scarce, tending to chores outside. Antoni guessed that the girl helped with cooking and cleaning inside, and the young man tended to the garden and beasts outside.

Patrizia spoke with the girl, pointing to the three of them, and then upstairs. Then she quietly addressed the young man. During her conversation, she motioned toward outside, and then the kitchen. Antoni couldn't understand what was being said, but got the gist of her meaning.

The kind tone Patrizia used with the servants helped him relax a notch more. He'd always found that the way a person treated their servants was a good indicator of their inner character.

Ati held out her hand to Nortia, who obediently rose and came to her. Ati followed the young maid, who was politely indicating the way upstairs. Antoni fell into line behind them. He noticed that the servants had been trying not to stare. If he thought the servants were dressed strangely, then they must surely think the same way about the three of them.

"Thank you for taking us to the room. You are most kind." Ati spoke to the girl in her native language.

Antoni watched her exaggerate her body language in order to be understood. It was slightly humorous because Ati was so small, but it seemed to work. The girl smiled, handed Ati and him some cloths, then pointed to the filled water basin in the room.

"I will be right out, Antoni. I'm going to help Nortia wash and lay her down. She, like all of us, has had a trying day."

"I will be here, as always, guarding you both," he answered.

After a few minutes, Ati slipped back out of the room, smoothing her straight, silver hair. It settled neatly in a straight line, just at her shoulders. "We will need to think of a way for you to also get some rest. You can't guard us day and night without resting." She put her hand on his shoulder in a motherly way.

"Yes, but for now, I will watch so you both may refresh yourselves. Once you are awake, I will rest."

Ati agreed and went to her room.

Antoni sat outside guarding both doors. He thought about what Patrizia had said. *Twenty-three saecula.* Was he to believe they had really advanced that far? The house and the way these people dressed were different. But why was this happening? It was too strange. There must be some other explanation.

He knew the stone was powerful, and he'd certainly heard the prophecy recited enough times. The idea that they were actually *part* of the prophecy was a little more than he could think about right now.

Nortia's unborn child was one of the children in the prophecy? Was that what Patrizia meant? Maybe Patrizia was just old and made up stories, but he would have to find out more. How did she know of the stone? Taking a resigned breath, he suspected deep in his heart that Patrizia was telling the truth. For him, that truth was just too much to accept.

Nortia wasn't taking this very well. Hopefully, as Patrizia explained things, learning more would help Nortia.

Antoni wondered about their fate. Did Patrizia know what it was? He would have to ask her more questions.

Lying back against the wall, he enjoyed a moment of rest—but he dared not close his eyes. There wasn't anything he could do until he knew more. His head hurt. Sitting still, he touched a finger and thumb to his eyes to fight off sleep.

As he sat outside the ladies' doors, his eyes kept drooping. The ache in his head had lessened somewhat, but it would not go away. *What else can go wrong?* He cursed himself for being led into this chain of events. He just hoped that he could get the ladies back to the villa—wherever *that* may be.

He tried to replay the events of the last day in his mind, hoping that some sense would come of it. His mind drifted back to when they were on the beach, just before the riders were upon them. He remembered a great upward movement and then the feeling of being separated from his body. Was that why Patrizia called it "time *jumping*?"

Antoni felt frightened. Patrizia's tale about their villa still being there a long time ago didn't make any sense. He didn't feel as if he had gone anywhere. Maybe Ati could make sense of this—she was the wise one. He would just continue doing what he knew, protecting Nortia and Ati.

Nortia and Ati slept for a few hours, then Ati approached Antoni.

"Take your rest now," Ati said. "We'll be fine."

"I will rest through dinner," he said. "Wake me when you have finished, then I will eat." Eager to close his eyes, he hoped that maybe the ache in his head would finally go away.

~~~

Ati went into Nortia's room to bring her down for dinner. The rich, fatty smell of the cooking wafted through the house. Nortia looked directly at Ati and smiled. She seemed to feel much better.

"What do you think of all that has happened?" Ati asked her.

"What do you mean, Mother?" Nortia asked, plucking at the fabric of her tunic.

"What Patrizia told us," Ati said, beginning to get impatient.

"I'm not sure what she meant." Nortia faltered as she spoke. "She said the stone protected us. If Hemisatres is so powerful, why didn't it just get rid of the dark riders on the beach?"

"I don't know. Maybe that would not have been best for us. If we are to believe Patrizia, we have come through many saecula and are now in a different time. All that is happening may be centered around the child you are carrying."

Ati stopped herself from saying anything more. Nortia looked so rested and happy, and she didn't want to ruin it.

"Let's go downstairs for dinner and talk with Patrizia," Ati said, changing the subject. "If we know more, maybe it won't be so frightening." She took Nortia's arm and led her down the stairs.

Dinner was delightful. Ati hadn't eaten since the night before, but her appetite and headache had improved greatly with rest. It didn't matter that a few of the dishes were ones she'd never seen before.

The main course, a large fowl, proved to be savory. The vegetables were familiar and cooked with a sweet fruit sauce over them. Nortia looked like she was enjoying the meal, trying a small sample from every dish put on the table.

After dinner, fruits and sweets were brought out.

"These sweets have a wonderful taste," Ati said. "What are they made from?"

"Almond nuts, ground into a paste, then sweetened," Patrizia answered. "It's called 'marzipan.'" Patrizia sounded pleased that her guests were enjoying the food.

"The meal tasted very good—thank you," Nortia managed to say. It was all she'd said throughout dinner.

Ati saw Patrizia's sympathetic smile toward Nortia, and ached to undo all that had happened. She took a deep breath, searching for the courage to ask Patrizia more questions. It wasn't that she was afraid of her—she was afraid of her answers.

"We really are twenty-three saecula ahead in life?" Ati finally asked.

"Yes, you three have time jumped," Patrizia said gently.

"I know I have asked you this already, but how is it you know so much about us?" Ati pressed.

"I also am not from this time," Patrizia explained. "I have been put here to help the child, and all those who are in our line."

"The child that Nortia is carrying?" Ati asked.

"Yes, she is a child of the prophecy," Patrizia said.

Nortia made a small gasp, and Ati tried to console her.

"Nortia, it will be fine—please try to stay calm. We should know more about Patrizia and what has happened before letting any talk upset us." She hoped that Nortia would understand what she implied, because she didn't want to insult Patrizia.

"I'm not upset, Mother. I'm just surprised that my child is to be a girl."

Ati couldn't believe it. Nortia was just told that she would give birth to the child of the prophecy and all she'd gotten out of the conversation was that her baby was a girl.

A disturbing thought suddenly crossed Ati's mind. *Where has my daughter gone?*

Ati could see her sitting there, but it wasn't her daughter. Instead, it was a shell of what she'd once been.

Maybe the stone was affecting her mind, or the jump through time had changed her.

She caught herself thinking that the time jump had actually happened. Realizing everything all at once, she finally believed what Patrizia was telling them. "Patrizia, what are we to do now?" Ati asked. "And how are we to get back?"

"I don't know if you'll ever get back to your time. We'll talk more each
day—it's for your own good. Learning slowly will make all these unbelievable occurrences easier to accept. Trust that I will tell you everything you need to know, and that, for now, you are safe. Tonight you should just rest, and let your minds take ease."

Somewhat mollified, Ati thanked Patrizia again for dinner and beckoned Nortia to follow her upstairs. Patrizia was right about one thing—she and Nortia needed more rest. She felt bad about waking Antoni, but she knew he would be very agitated if she didn't. Then next time, he wouldn't trust her to wake him, and consequently, he would *never* get any rest.

Antoni woke with a start, still holding his sword. Ati took a prudent, large step backward. "We will rest now. Go get something to eat," she said. "Your vigilance is appreciated. Tonight it may be best for you to sleep in the hall. That way, you can sleep and guard. Surely now that you've rested some, you will wake up if someone tries to come up the stairs." It wasn't the best solution, but maybe Antoni would agree to it.

"The windows have bars on them," he said, "but I want to make sure they're secure. Then I will go and eat. Later on, when I'm tired, I will sleep as you've suggested, guarding the stairs and hall."

Chapter 12

Fall Through Spring

1480-1481 AD

Time had mellowed them.

Antoni grew accustomed to staying at Patrizia's. More at ease, he relaxed his vigilance some, even leaving his sword by the stairs every now and then.

Nortia was healthy, but he noticed that her strange detachment to reality persisted. Everyone accepted her behavior as her way of dealing with the enormity of what was going on.

Days turned into weeks and summer waned. Antoni began to feel safe at the farmhouse. Patrizia, as promised, took care of their every need. She'd sent the two servants to Firenze to purchase materials from which several outfits had been made for each of them.

Antoni had been greatly disappointed when Patrizia discouraged him from accompanying the two young people into the city. She explained it was best to let the servants go instead. Having people from this time go to the city would avoid interference with the anticipated flow of the future.

She stressed that if they changed the future too much, they may put themselves at a disadvantage. Any changes people from the past made who shouldn't naturally be here could cause the future to unfold differently—making it much harder for her to help them.

Unlike Ati, who accepted that they were no longer in their own time, Antoni found it very difficult to believe. Their days were filled with lessons that revealed amazing new things—and these revelations only aggravated him more.

Over the months, Patrizia patiently taught the three of them a new calendar, and many other new ways of thinking and doing things. He couldn't help but to argue and fight every new bit of information Patrizia told them, and he was always on the lookout for mistakes or evidence that she was lying.

Eventually, he began to realize that there was no other explanation, and disbelief gradually turned into acceptance. The new household items, advanced farming equipment, clothes, different foods, and altered language all pointed to one simple truth—they actually *were* in an advanced time.

Nortia behaved politely during the lessons she chose to attend, but Antoni didn't think she listened to any details. It didn't matter, anyway. Even if she fully understood everything, they would be no safer or better off. He felt thankful that Nortia's distant attitude spared her from harsh reality.

Nortia still wore the pin, albeit against her will. Antoni had witnessed her protestations, but Ati insisted she wear it all the time, even when sleeping. Although displeased, Nortia confided to him that she only wore it because Patrizia said it would protect the unborn child and warn them if the dark riders were close.

Antoni tried to make the best of a bad situation. When it had still been warm, his days consisted mostly of following

Nortia during her frequent walks. She would go for long strolls through the woods and pastures surrounding the farmhouse. He watched over her, but also tried to give her enough room to enjoy what little freedom she had left.

~~~

Weeks turned into months, and the child grew within Nortia. Patrizia's lessons and tale also developed in their depth and complexity. Little by little, she painstakingly taught them many things she knew. As they sat around the table, she tried to boost their comprehension by giving them simple lessons in what she called "technology," as well as mathematics and even some basic physics.

It was all too much, too quick. Antoni didn't think they were stupid, but the amount of knowledge and intelligence needed to fully understand her lessons was enormous. It would take even the brightest person years of higher learning to grasp it all, and this was apparently something that Patrizia had accomplished—even though she was a woman.

The weather turned cold when Patrizia got to the story of her past. Antoni could follow a simple outline, now that he had learned more history and more about the future. Still, there were many details that neither he nor Ati would ever understand.

What Patrizia told them was amazing. The chain of events leading up to their arrival in 1480 had actually spanned many millennia.

"I was born in the year twenty-four-forty AD," she said, pointing to the spot on the timeline they'd used for studying. "Technology was very advanced from what it is now. We even had machines that did the thinking for people, the ones I've told you about before, called 'computers.'

"In my time, great scientists devoted their lives to making these computers smaller and more powerful. Some of the computers were so small that they couldn't even be seen. These small ones were made by other computers, programmed by people. We called the science 'nanotechnology,' and both of my parents were doctors in the field. It was a time of fantastic discoveries.

"The technology itself had been around for hundreds of years, but combining nanotechnology with human physiology for social and medical benefits was a rapidly expanding science. New applications were being discovered and perfected all the time.

"The combined science was called 'implantable nanotechnology,' or I.N. for short. The machines they were making were small enough to be placed inside people to help them think. Some even cured their diseases.

"When I was growing up, learning came easy to me. Soon, I'd passed the other students. My increased rate of learning helped me graduate with a doctorate in nanotechnology by the age of twenty. I desperately wanted to follow in my parents' footsteps and design the tiny machines. It was the way of the future.

"Almost every simple item we used to hold in our hands, like the math calculators and the telephones I talked about, were turning into implantable nanotechnology.

"People no longer held the telephones because of I.N. Microscopic receivers were implanted or put into their bodies, then connected to a worldwide network. The same procedure was followed with computers, the machines that helped people think. Whole computers could be placed internally. They were made of materials that the body wouldn't reject, and they were so small that the tiny insertion wound would easily heal.

"We were all working toward a day when these tiny microprocessors, or computers, would allow all communication, learning, current events, and other available information to become accessible internally, through our thoughts. I.N. was every scientist's dream come true. The breakthrough technology made it an exciting time to be alive.

"I'm sorry, I can see by the looks on your faces that I've probably said too much. I get excited talking about it, and I feel like I'm back in my own time." The gleam in Patrizia's eyes began to fade. "I will return to the more pertinent parts of the story. In my twenty-first year, my mother became pregnant. At forty years old, it was rather unexpected.

"At the beginning of the pregnancy, the stone appeared. My mom said it just appeared on the counter in the kitchen. It was a plain, gray sphere. Not much to look at, but she felt compelled to pick it up. When she did, it grew warm in her hands, and images flashed in her head. She told my father and me that they were frightening visions of horrible future events—scenes she would never forget.

"My mother showed us the stone, but no amount of coercion would get her to tell us exactly what horrible visions she'd seen. I begged my mother to let me have it to do research on. Reluctantly, she gave it to me to take to the lab. Later, I found out why she hesitated—it was because she already knew what I would discover."

"What?" Antoni asked. "What was it? Was it Hemisatres?"

"Not exactly," Patrizia said. "But I'll get to that. In one month of testing the stone, I discovered very little. Experimenting on it proved to be nearly impossible because it had some sort of defense mechanism built into it. I did discover that it wasn't a stone after all, but a magnet—and I was elated to also find out that it contained nanotechnology. Most importantly, I.N. technology.

"Unable to get any other information out of the magnet itself, I resorted to speculation. Since it had a built-in defense system, I theorized that it functioned independently as a self-contained, complete, and very advanced microprocessor."

Antoni stared at Patrizia with a look of complete incomprehension. A quick glance in Ati's direction told him that, thankfully, he was not alone. Frustrated, he ran his fingers through his dark brown hair. Nortia had dozed off on one of the larger chairs in the main room a while ago.

"That's enough for today," Patrizia said, chuckling. "I can see that we have a bit of remediation ahead of us."

~~~

It took weeks for Antoni to get used to the idea that Patrizia had come from the distant future. Antoni could see that Ati also struggled with the idea. They besieged Patrizia with questions, not understanding all her answers. Frustrated and overwhelmed with disbelief, Antoni even stopped talking to her for a week—but her kindness and honesty finally brought him around. As hard as he tried, Antoni couldn't disprove anything she'd said.

Patrizia took the time to actually show them some marvels of the future, like how to turn saltwater into fresh water. She also drew more pictures of the machines from the future—chariots that didn't use horses to move, and even ones that flew through the air. These revelations were astounding to Antoni, and more importantly, were the proof that he desperately needed. Somehow Patrizia managed to convince him and Ati that she was telling the truth before moving on to the next part of her tale.

They had just finished dinner and retired to the main room. It was dark outside and raining hard. The rain made a soothing sound as it hit and sluiced down over the roof tiles. Antoni watched Nortia curl up on the biggest chair, trying to tuck her legs up with her large belly in the way. Antoni hoped they would be safe here until the child arrived, as Patrizia had said.

"Patrizia, what happened with the magnet?" Ati asked. "We will let you finish your story—please accept my apology for my disbelief." She gave Antoni a hard look.

Antoni nodded, "Yes, I also apologize—it was rude of me. I am ready to know more."

Patrizia leaned back into her worn chair and pulled her long white braid out from behind her back. She coughed to clear her throat. "We kept the magnet at our house when I wasn't testing it. One day, about a month and a half after it had arrived, it became activated. My mother again felt compelled to pick it up. She said that the familiar warmth radiated into her hands and the images flashed before her once more.

"These images were very vivid, and even more terrifying to her than before. She was too distraught to share all of it with us, but what she said filled my father and me with fear." Patrizia went on to explain that, similar to their experience, her family had also chosen to flee.

"My mother said the magnet, as I suspected, was an advanced microprocessor from the future named Satres. One of its main functions was to enable its user to move through time. It had shown her scenes of indescribable destruction, and what looked like millions of people dying.

"She said she was to have twins, and the magnet was programmed to only speak with certain chosen descendants, or 'receivers.' There were complications when the magnet had left the future—and it had arrived too soon, before the birth of the chosen children. The messages it gave her, instead of the children, were brief—but it stressed that she must heed them, or all would be lost.

"It could supply her with one-way information, but it can't answer any questions. The reason it was able to communicate with her at all was because she had DNA similar to the two receivers.

"As she spoke, my mother looked like she was in a trance. Her voice sounded strange, and it became clear to us she was being used as a sort of mouthpiece or speaker to give the magnet a voice.

"She continued reciting, saying that the magnet had been sent through time by our future descendants as a last, desperate effort to save themselves. In their haste, some minor miscalculations in the programming had occurred, and some calculations hadn't finished running. It wasn't funny, but in the future, they literally had 'run out of time.'

"Errors were discovered immediately before the magnet's time jump, but by then, it was too late to fix them. There were miscalculations in *when* Satres would arrive, and in its choice of receivers, meaning the twins. These errors made its choice of backup and subsequent receivers also slightly flawed. Since the magnet had arrived too soon, it was necessary that our family immediately leave twenty-four-sixty-one in order to compensate for the miscalculations.

"Over the last month and a half, it had run an almost-infinite number of possible outcome computations, and creating a closed timeline curve was the only way Satres could correct the mistakes that would be made in the future. It was drastic, but according to the magnet, the paradox its arrival would create would leave all of us dead.

"Since we were ancestors of Satres's creators, it wouldn't bode well for them if we died. My mother said the magnet self-programmed in the closed timeline, or protective loop in time, and would conduct the journey for us. Then she woke from the trance.

"My mother wasn't the type of woman who would make anything up or imagine things. In fact, she was just the opposite. My father and I never questioned what she'd said—we believed her. We knew we had to listen to the magnet and also knew that we may be headed for another land—and possibly, another time."

Antoni leaned in closer to hear Patrizia, as her voice seemed to be growing weaker. He was on edge—he knew exactly how Patrizia's father must have felt. He looked at Nortia to see if the part of the story about the flashing scenes had upset her, but she was dozing peacefully in her chair. Across from him, Ati's back was straight as an arrow, and she was looking intently at Patrizia.

"We all agreed to heed Satres's warning," Patrizia continued, "and put our trust in it. Not knowing what to expect, my wonderful father tried to prepare us for our unknown futures. He traded many of our possessions for pieces of gold and other timeless valuables, which we sewed into our clothing.

"The preparation took less than two days, and my mother grew increasingly distressed, begging us to hurry. When I look back now—or forward, whichever it is—I see that it was a time of great uncertainty, requiring us to take a great leap of faith.

"The dawn of the third day after the images began to appear, my mother became frantic. She began shouting that we were all going to die, and we must go now. We rushed about to get dressed. The traveling clothes my father had readied were as nondescript and basic as he could find. He'd tried to stay with low-key neutral colors and nothing too trendy.

"Once we were dressed, my mother picked up Satres and told us to hold onto her tightly. I put my arms around her and hugged her with all my strength. I felt overwhelmed that I may lose her. My father put his arms around both of us, and in an instant, everything as we knew it changed."

Patrizia's tale sounded improbable. If Antoni hadn't experienced time travel firsthand, he would have never believed her. Even after he'd accepted the fact that he had actually time traveled, he still could hardly believe the rest of her story.

Patrizia had been wise to only tell them small bits at each sitting, letting a few days pass before continuing on with new information. It gave him time to learn what new concepts he could, and then sift through the all-too-unsettling facts.

"What happened?" Antoni asked, excited. "Where were you?" He touched the hilt of his sword.

"When we awoke, we had no idea where we were," Patrizia said. "We walked to a village that was nearby. As soon as we saw it, we knew we'd gone back in time. How far back? We didn't know. The houses were huts with thick, bundled grass on them, and they were very primitive.

"My mother cried. She had to get it out of her system. Later, when we had time to talk, we all agreed on one thing— our situation in the time we had come from must have been very dire for this extreme time change, and Satres must have saved our lives, as well as the lives of the unborn children.

"We, of course, were unable to speak the language. When we approached the first hut, a nearly naked man came out, armed with a huge spear. My father stepped in front of us, doing the best he could to communicate using hand gestures. He tried to pantomime that we were from far away and had been robbed.

"More armed men and some women began to come out of the other huts nearby. We were really afraid. My father's hand signals weren't working, so in desperation, he showed the man a gold piece he had.

"Some things never change," Patrizia said, smiling. "The gold worked. The man my father showed it to was the only one to see it. The other villagers weren't close enough yet. Once the man saw the piece of gold, he thought for a moment. Then he let out a joyous shout of recognition, welcoming us as if he knew who we were.

"He took us into his hut, and let us stay there. During the short time we were with him, we learned that his name was Latimus. Lucky for us, he was a young warrior who was striving to make his fortune so he could take a wife.

"We didn't have to stay with him long. My father was smart, and he had more gold. Because of Latimus's bought sponsorship, we all managed to learn enough of the language to ask to stay in the village. A few more pieces of gold, and we had our own land and home. It wasn't much, but we were safe and together."

"What time were you in?" Ati asked.

"You weren't attacked by anyone?" Antoni interrupted. "Who were these people?" The story of her father's bravery amazed him.

"I will tell you the rest over the next few days."
Patrizia sighed and coughed, then paused to catch her breath.
"I wish I didn't have to tell you this, but I must finish telling
you everything very soon. The birth of Nortia's child nears,
and I am not well. I fear we don't have much time left."

Antoni put his head into his hands, running his fingers
through his hair. "What else will go wrong?"

"You aren't well?" Ati sounded terribly alarmed.

Now that Antoni looked at Patrizia, he could see that
she looked pale and extremely tired. He hadn't really noticed
her condition before and felt ashamed to have been so selfish.
Patrizia had spent months teaching them and trying to help. In
caring for them, she'd worn herself down.

"Don't blame yourself, Antoni," Patrizia said.

"I do. It was dishonorable of me not to think of you."
He wondered how she always knew his thoughts.

"I'm getting old," Patrizia said. "I just need to rest and
recuperate."

Antoni looked at her, and Patrizia smiled. He'd spent
many months learning to believe in Patrizia. Now, as he
looked into her eyes, he knew she was lying. She wasn't

going to get better with rest. But he didn't say anything—he just pulled Patrizia a little bit closer to the fire.

Ati brought her something warm to drink.

Antoni pondered this new information. What else could he do? He couldn't even help Ati and Nortia, so how could he help this woman?

Chapter 13

Spring 383 BC

Etruria

Time was at a standstill.

They'd been waiting forever. Charontes sat on the
ground, his back against a tree, eating a piece of roasted hare.
He licked his greasy fingers between each bite. It had been a
long, cold winter, but he and his men were used to waiting.

Last fall, the other half of the stone had slipped
through their fingers. Getting as close as they had to it had
encouraged them, and it made this winter of waiting more
bearable.

He got up to get more to eat. Still hungry, his first portion had tasted delectable—hares stuffed with shoots of early onions and other spring herbs, then roasted over the fire. The juices from the onions mixed with the meat as it slowly cooked and flavored it, making the meat exquisitely tender at the same time.

At least there had been enough food and fresh water to last through the winter. Since the night they killed the villa guards, they'd remained hidden in rocky outcroppings which formed natural caves, just one day's march from the villa.

He sat back down under the same tree, blowing on his food as it burned his fingers. He had lots of time to think, and unfortunately, most of his thoughts were not good. Throughout her pregnancy, Vanth had continued her uncaring attitude. She never seemed excited about her unborn child or even spoke fondly of it. If it weren't for her swollen belly, no one would have even known she was going to be a mother.

Months before the child was born, she'd sent three of his guards home to bring back two servants. The servant women were to help with the birthing and care of the child. *Maybe it's for the best*, he thought. *Better for a young innocent to stay clear of its mother's poisonous ways for as long as possible—lest it become like her.*

In the beginning of their long wait, it was nearly impossible to tolerate being around Vanth. She would rant and rave continuously, frustrated and unable to understand why their half of the stone had grown silent just as they were so close to their prize. Her violent outbursts eventually turned into a sustained, stony silence.

It was midwinter when she finally shared her thoughts with Charontes.

"I've been thinking about what's happening, and why we're still here," she began, not sounding the least bit apologetic for any of her impossible behavior. "My half of the stone will remain silent until my child is born. It has stopped us from following them until then. Once the chosen children are born, the stones will be stronger, each more capable of finding its other half. It will also help us because the two children will be about the same age."

"*Children?*" Charontes asked, confused. "There are *two* children chosen by the stone? I thought your child was the child of the prophecy—is this no longer true?"

"Yes, you fool," Vanth spat back at him. "There are two children, and my child *is* the child of the prophecy. The one we are chasing is also with child, but she is only the favored child of their stone—the stone which we will soon have. So, she is of no importance...especially since we will kill them all."

The way she'd casually admitted the existence of another child, even its gender, made Charontes certain that Vanth had known about the other child all along. She must have seen her in the visions from her stone, but shrewdly told no one. Why would she? Vanth probably figured that she'd be rid of the other woman, as well as the child she carried, long before anyone was the wiser.

His nostrils flared in disgust. *Just look at her*, he thought. *Even now she is loathe to admit it.* She had to be wildly jealous of losing her exclusivity as the mother of the chosen child—so she called him a fool, then brushed it off with a shrug and a you-should-already-know-what-I'm-talking-about attitude.

Well, he wasn't a fool—and he knew exactly how manipulative she could be. Vanth was the kind of woman who could have looked a god in the eyes and lied right to their face. However, he didn't bother asking any more questions, and let Vanth continue with her explanation.

"If both children are born before we resume chasing them, there is no chance of error. If we had followed them that night at the sea, we may have ended up close to *when* they were, but not exactly. Then the children could have been different ages, possibly giving one an advantage over the other.

"Each moment that passes between time journeys must slightly change the outcome of the journey. So you see, our stone is protecting us by waiting until it can precisely locate the other stone. I think this will be after my child is born." Vanth, done talking, turned on the ball of her foot and stomped off.

Charontes presumed she left in order to irritably await the birth of her child. He didn't care how she felt any longer. After he thought about what she'd said, it really didn't make much sense—but if it made her stop her tantrums, she could believe whatever she wanted.

Chapter 14

July 1481 AD

Firenze

Sometimes we stumble, and sometimes we fall.

It was early evening and still light out when I heard the tentative knock at the door. Crouched and ready, I didn't answer because Amelia would know I was right beside the door. The door cracked open.

I kicked it exactly like I'd done before and ran past the startled Amelia.

"Oh no. Please don't do this again!" Amelia shouted as she struggled to balance the tray in her hands.

Already halfway down the stairs, I yelled, "Sorry, my friend!" It was all I could manage to say. This was actually working the second time. I reached the door and shot outside, my skirt flying. As I picked up speed, I thought about how angry Sampson would be—and I ran faster.

It would be more personal this time. I was making him look really stupid. He'd said he didn't make the same mistake twice, and this definitely proved him wrong. *I'd better make it through the city wall this time.*

I ran past the poplars and through the fields, adjusting my speed to conserve energy. Unbelievably, no one was following me yet, so I paced myself.

He probably had to put all his armor on and get his horse, or whatever barbarians do to get ready to chase and capture people. You know, the normal barbarian lag time. This time, however, I would use it to my advantage. I wouldn't waste any time by standing in one place and gawking at an ancient city from the past. This time, I would keep running.

I'd just crested the hill before the city when I heard the hoofbeats. They were beating almost as fast as my heart. I hurtled down the hill toward the opening in the crenellated city wall.

There wasn't anyone around the opening, and I didn't know what I would say to someone, anyway. Something like, "Hey, can you help me? I've traveled through time, and now Sampson is trying to capture and abduct me again. Yeah, him—the huge, angry man with the giant sword aimed at your head." Somehow, I instinctively knew that Sampson wouldn't hesitate to hew down anyone I enlisted to help me.

I kept running. My lungs were burning again, and my legs felt like jelly. I didn't dare look behind me. From the sound of the hooves, I thought I would just make it. I ran toward the tower with the arched opening, which loomed at least fifty feet over my head. I aimed myself at the opening.

I was in.

Cool, damp darkness surrounded me as I ran through the tower. Then it was light again. *I made it to the other side,* I thought. *Now which way should I run?* I turned down the first open street. The tall, tightly-packed buildings threw a blanket of shadows everywhere. I didn't hear hoofbeats anymore.

I turned down another side street, then another, randomly weaving my way deeper into the city. There wasn't time to figure out where I was—I just had to lose the damned barbarian chasing me. Unable to keep up the same grueling pace any longer, I slowed to a jog. Even though I neared exhaustion, I kept on going.

The gathering dusk darkened the inner streets as if it were the middle of the night. Turning down an even gloomier side street, I ran right into someone. Spent and unable to stop my momentum, we both slammed into the ground.

I tried to get up, but I couldn't find my footing. I heard cursing in Italian. Someone hauled me off the person I'd been entangled with and stood me back onto my feet.

Still wheezing for breath, I stared at two pissed-off-looking Renaissance men. A third one had me by the back my shirt.

"Oh, thank God! Can you help me? There is this crazy, bad man chasing me." As I spoke, I tried to shrug my way out of the man's grasp.

He just held on tighter. The two other men were still staring at me.

I realized I must be quite sweaty and disheveled. My hair was tangled into a wild brown mass, sticking out everywhere. Without thinking, I began to hysterically blurt everything out. "Really, there is a barbarian with a sword who's chasing me. I don't know how to get home. I'm just a nurse, and I didn't hurt anyone. I don't understand why all of this is happening to me. Please, you must help me. I'm all alone here." I sobbed uncontrollably.

"She's crazy," I heard one of the men say.

"She may be crazy, but she's beautiful," said the man holding my shirt. He grabbed me tighter and held me from behind, wrapping one arm around my neck.

"Yes, very beautiful," the third man said. He grabbed the front of my skirt and began to lift it up.

I couldn't believe it. They thought I was crazy—and now they were going to try to rape me. This day just couldn't get any worse.

"I'm not crazy!" I yelled, kicking up at the man lifting up my skirt, hitting him squarely in the chest. He grunted in pain, but he didn't let go of my skirt. I tried with all my might to extract myself from the viselike grip the other man had on me.

"Shh, pretty one, we won't hurt you," the man holding my skirt said, fumbling with his pants. "You will like this." He looked at the third man. "Hold up her leg and then you can have her after me."

I kicked and kicked. Putting my feet on the ground, I pushed as hard as I could. Leverage worked in my favor, because I was taller than the man holding me. He stumbled backwards, trying to catch his balance.

Then I lost track of which man was which, as there were all these hands clawing at me, trying to subdue me. I heard my skirt rip and felt disgusting hands on my legs. I kicked my one free leg upward and pushed against the wall of the building with all my strength.

The man who held me got knocked off balance, and we began to fall. He twisted at the last second and fell on top of me. My left leg turned at an odd angle, and I heard it snap when we hit the ground. I screamed as white-hot, searing pain shot up through me.

"Be still, you she-devil!" one of the men screamed. I heard feet scuffling on the ground and felt hands all over me. Someone grabbed my hair and slammed my head down hard into the ground.

The last thing I heard were hoofbeats, echoing in the narrow side street.

~~~

I must be dead, I thought. *Correction, I wish I were dead.* My leg throbbed so terribly, I couldn't bear it. I tried to open my eyes, but the light made my head feel like a train ran over it.

I heard someone shout in what sounded like Greek. "You help her now."

I felt small hands touching me all over—and I groaned from the unbearable pain. A small voice whispered in my ear in Italian. "Try to take a few sips of my mistress's medicine. It will help with the pain."

Amelia? I thought. *What happened?* I tried to remember and struggled to get up. Large, gentle hands held me down.

"Hurry up and give her that—I must fix her leg," I heard a deep voice say in Greek. I opened my eyes and saw a blurry image of Amelia hovering in front of my face.

"Drink this now. It will help you. Lie still—you're hurting yourself." Amelia looked so worried that I obeyed.

Soon I felt a warmth go through my body, and the pain began to subside. As I lost contact with reality, I felt a large, rough hand smooth over my forehead.

"It will be okay, my beautiful one," the Greek voice said. "I will take care of you."

He thinks I'm beautiful? I thought in surprise. Then there was blackness.

~~~

He just stared at her face. It had enchanted him from the first time he'd ever seen it. She was just so beautiful. Brown curls softly caressed the outer edges of her face and fell over her fresh and flawless skin. Her face no longer gave evidence of the pain she'd felt. Something the servant girl gave her had taken away the pain.

Charontes wasn't happy that she'd been hurt, but he relished that he could touch her freely now. He ran his finger along her cheek. His large hand, so calloused and scarred, stood out in stark contrast against her loveliness.

He felt drawn to her, but he didn't know why. Why should he care if she lived or died? He'd never cared about those things before. Protecting Vanth was his duty as a Rider of the Reunity. He had slept with Vanth simply because she'd asked him

to—but he certainly had never loved her. Now after what she'd done to him, he loathed the woman.

Charontes thought about how he felt when he'd seen those men attacking the girl. She was so innocent and helpless compared to Vanth. He was enraged beyond control, unable to think straight. As he raced toward them, he drew his sword, ready to kill. Even though the men dropped her when they saw him and tried to escape, none of them made it. All three fell to his sword. He could have killed them twice for hurting her.

Charontes had spent his whole life as a warrior, and these new feelings made him frustrated and angry. He should just leave her alone now.

Straightening the bone back into her leg had not been easy on her. He'd fixed similar wounds on injured warriors, but never on a woman. Fortunately, the bone had slid back from where it was poking through the skin and stayed firmly in place. There had been little bleeding.

Charontes hoped she wouldn't grow hot and sicken. What was he thinking? What had come over him? Why did he feel so responsible for her? Her wound was tended to, and the servant girl would give her the potion to help with the pain. He should just leave her to her fate now.

As he laid his hand on her forehead, she moaned softly, and he felt a stirring deep inside. That helped to ease his anger and confusion. It must be only lust he felt for this woman. He tried valiantly to convince himself that was what these feelings were.

Her eyes flickered open, focused on nothing, then closed again.

She'd shown such bravery by running from him. He found it inconceivable that someone would so blatantly disobey him. Not just once, but twice—then mock him to his face on top of it. He'd just had to kiss her.

He'd understood most of her Greek, but he hadn't answered her—mostly because he didn't have any answers to her questions.

However, he had many lingering questions. Who was she? When he found her unconscious in the woods, she had a pin in her hand. Charontes recognized the stone in it—it was exactly like the one in Vanth's bracelet. It was the other half of the stone, the one they'd all been looking for. How had the girl come by it?

He had the pin now, hidden somewhere safe. When she was better, maybe she would be able to help him. She must be important, somehow. He didn't know how she fit in, but he would find out. For now, he had to wait—and waiting was something he was very good at.

Chapter 15

Spring 1481 AD

Firenze

Time is of the essence.

As spring unfurled its first petals, Ati found she could do nothing to help Patrizia's worsening condition. Bravely though, Patrizia continued to teach them and finish her story. Ati noticed that even Antoni had stopped arguing and questioning her. As it was, Patrizia could only manage to sit up and talk with them for a few hours each day. Then her voice would falter, and she would lose her breath. If she continued talking after that, her body would be racked with spasms of coughing that forced her to rest.

Ati did her best to tend to her and Nortia. She made Patrizia as comfortable as possible, bringing her warm drinks with honey that the servant girl, Amelia, had taught her to make.

Lately, when Patrizia was in a lot of pain and the honey didn't ease her coughing, she would ask for her medicine. She said it was made from the poppies that grew around the farmhouse. Ati had never seen this before, but it helped Patrizia's coughing and took away the pain so she could sleep.

Nortia, just weeks away from giving birth, still hadn't recovered from the shock of their time travel. She remained quiet and distant. Ati wondered if she would ever be the same again—something in her mind had just given way. She worried about Nortia's condition, but seeing her and talking to her each day would have to be enough.

It was evening, and Ati sat at the table after dinner. Both she and Antoni stared at Patrizia expectantly. Tonight she would finish her story, and Ati was filled to the bursting point with unanswered questions. She could tell by the way Antoni looked at Patrizia that he felt the same way. He'd been the first to finish his meal. Nortia stayed behind at the table, playing with her napkin.

"Patrizia, are you well enough tonight to tell us more?" Ati prompted when the sweets and nuts were laid on the table.

"Yes, I'm able." She took a minute to clear her throat and started where she'd left off before. "Once we had a home, we began to feel safe and established. My father and I tried to figure out *when* we were. We reached the amazing conclusion that we were, more than certainly, sometime after 1,100 BC—possibly the tenth century BC.

"As we got a better grasp of the language and events, there were certain things that tipped us off. The use of iron to make tools and weapons was becoming commonplace. This, we knew from history, should have occurred sometime around the tenth century BC. Therefore, we knew we were close in our estimation—but were never entirely sure of the exact date. Their calendar couldn't help, because it primarily centered around events in their own history. This left nothing even remotely similar to compare it with."

"Patrizia, did you ever find out *where* you were?" Antoni asked. "What was the name of the village?"

Patrizia sipped her drink and nodded. "Yes, we did. Once we had a rough idea of *when* we were, we set out to find *where* we were." She laughed softly, then coughed. "That's quite a mouthful, isn't it? We ventured out of our village some, and then began to recognize some of the bigger landmarks. Certain large mountains, and the lie of the sea in relation to the land. We realized that we were still in the same area of Italy, or Etruria, as you know it, that we had come from in twenty-four-sixty-one AD."

"Did Satres help you at all?" Ati asked. "Did your mother have any more visions?" She wondered how they'd ever managed in such a primitive time, and why Patrizia was here now in this time period. It was so confusing, but she didn't want to tire Patrizia with too many questions.

"No, Satres had remained inactive since our jump through time, and we took this to mean we were safe. We missed where we came from terribly, but we were happy to be together and alive. Because of the gold we had brought with us, we lived comfortably and were even wealthy."

"Did Satres turn back on after your mother had the children, the Chosen Ones?" Ati was so curious. Even though she knew she shouldn't be asking the poor woman more questions, they just kept popping out of her.

"Not exactly, well, not right away, anyway," Patrizia continued. "When my mother went into labor, I was terrified. We didn't have any medicines or the kind of help we were used to. Her age was also a factor. Thankfully, everything went smoothly, and two identical girls were born.

"As my sisters grew, it became apparent that they were identical in looks alone. Their personalities were like night and day. Elena was sweet and radiated goodness. Diana was the opposite. From when she was a small child, her moods were dark, and her demeanor sour. She always got into trouble, then blamed it on Elena. As we grew up, it was a struggle to have two sisters who were so different. I loved them both—but Elena had my heart.

"My poor mother was haunted for years by the visions she'd been afraid to mention to us. She finally confessed this to me, just days before the twins' sixteenth birthday. She pulled me aside and told me that the magnet had us jump through time exactly when it did in order to create a closed timeline curve."

"This story is hurting my head, Patrizia," Antoni said, sounding exasperated. "What is the curve again, and why should it matter? Did we learn this already?"

Ati could see that Antoni was barely able to contain himself. He kept squirming and shifting in his chair, like he usually did when Patrizia went beyond his understanding.

"Simply put, Antoni, it's a protective loop in time. This curve protected the future from any new paradoxes popping up. It averted the original mission from failing and also provided a way to correct the problem of the twins being inappropriate receivers.

"It was logical to have two human receivers for the magnet instead of one, and it was also a safeguard. That way, in case something happened to one of them, the other could carry on. That was one of the reasons the twins, Elena and Diana, were originally chosen—their identical DNA made programming quicker and easier.

"Unfortunately, basic human nature was overlooked, and the fact that the chosen children were identical twins made that oversight in Satres's programming apparent."

"Well, that explains it fully for me, thank you," Antoni said sarcastically.

"Antoni, Patrizia is trying her best," Ati said, trying to get him to relax so Patrizia could draw her lesson to a close. "We will let her try to finish—she is getting tired. If we don't understand everything that she says, that's fine. We will still know more than we did before she told us her story. She's trying to help us—and some of the details she's shared with us may save our lives."

"My apologies, Patrizia," Antoni mumbled. "Please tell us more—I will hold my peace."

"What else did Satres tell your mother?" Ati prompted gently, sensing that Patrizia had lost her place in the story.

"My mother said that Satres predicted long ago that one daughter would become evil. At first, she'd tried not to believe what she'd heard. She was their mother, and she loved them, good or evil. The magnet had shown her that on their sixteenth birthday, the twins were to connect with it as receivers and inherit its power to travel anywhere—and *anywhen.*

"The twins' opposite nature, a paradox in itself, could only be fixed by creating the closed timeline curve. This would allow for simple rewrites of history, anywhere inside the curve, but prevent paradoxes from occurring outside of the loop. The future after twenty-four-sixty-one would be protected from change until it could be fixed by one of the Chosen Ones.

"When Satres was sent to us originally from our own future dying world, it had been done in great haste. When Satres later computed the paradox that the twins' polar personalities would create, it was unable to prevent it *because* the girls were identical. It couldn't reprogram and deselect one of the twins' DNA, because unavoidably, the other twin would be deselected. If Satres went to the wrong twin, all would be lost."

"So why didn't Satres just time jump to another time and one of the other Chosen Ones?" Antoni asked.

"That's a really good question," Patrizia answered, "and one I've tried very hard to answer with my research. There were many times I'd wished the magnet would have just disappeared from our lives. I think that no matter where or who the magnet goes to, these problems instantly occur for the receivers. Most likely, this is because we are not meant to have that kind of power. Life already has countless choices and possible outcomes—but once someone is in possession of the magnet, these become more than limitless. The magnet is probably saving each of the receivers for upcoming attempts at saving the future, in case we fail."

"Are you tiring, Patrizia?" Ati asked as she gave Antoni a stony look.

He just shrugged at her, then sat back in his chair.

"A little," Patrizia answered, "but I will try to finish this part." She took a deep breath and continued. "I found it hard to believe what my mother told me about the twins. Diana was naughty and not that fun to be around, but never evil. My mother agreed but said that once one of them possessed the power of the stone, that power could corrupt them.

"I'd never seen my mother look so sad. She said that was why we had to go back so far into the past. After it was already sent, Satres had time to do a probability forecast using available historical data of the twins' personalities, taken from their lives without the magnet's involvement. You have to remember that the twins had lived whole lives and had died, long before the magnet was even created.

"From the data, it concluded that if they grew up in the twenty-four hundreds with Satres, Diana would have gotten the stone. Diana's dark side could not have withstood the corruption."

"What *proof* did it actually have?" Antoni shouted. "You all just blindly believed a rock!"

All Ati could do was rest a quieting hand on Antoni's arm to calm him. She knew he wasn't trying to argue—he was just being protective.

"This wasn't just a guess, Antoni," Patrizia said patiently, "it was science. The almost-infinite number of possible outcomes and probabilities the computer ran made predicting the future a mathematical solution—which, even in twenty-four-sixty-one, was almost never incorrect. If Satres had the time before it was sent to run the computations, we may have been spared. The twins would have never been chosen. But fate must have played a part in this, too.

"That night, my mother and I told my father what we knew. He flew into a rage, screaming that the magnet wasn't going to ruin our lives anymore. He threatened to take the magnet and cut it in half, then give each twin one piece of it. 'A balance in power,' as he called it.

"Diana and Elena must have heard his shouts, because they came running into the room in time to hear what Father was saying about cutting the magnet. Diana yelled terrible things—it was as if she'd turned into another person. She shocked us all by saying that the only reason she still lived at home was because she'd been waiting for her sixteenth birthday. She said she hated us all and couldn't wait to get the magnet so she could get out of this time.

"Diana said that she wouldn't let Father ruin everything she'd waited for. Then she grabbed my poor Father and tried to wrestle the magnet from his hands. Elena and I jumped in to stop her, and somehow, we pulled her off him. My mother was crying and Father screamed for Diana to get out of his house. He handed me Satres to hold, then turned toward Diana.

"As soon as he put the magnet in my hand, hundreds of images started flashing in my head. There were so many that a person couldn't recall them at will. I stood there in the room, frozen, unable to call out to my family. Then I moved upward into the air exceptionally fast. The next thing I remembered was waking up here, inside this house—Satres had jumped me to this time."

"So you have the magnet?" Antoni asked.

Ati thought his voice sounded pitifully hopeful.

"No," Patrizia said, her head drooping. "It didn't stay with me. It just sent me here and then disappeared. I never saw my family again."

"Oh, how terrible!" Ati said. "You must have been so frightened and sad."

"Initially, I was. I didn't have any idea what was going on, but over the years, I recalled many of the images. Now I know that they were special pictures, meant to be remembered, images that Satres had programmed into my mind. Whenever I need them, they come back to me.

"Some were pictures of this house we are in now and of the man who used to own it, Atillio. He found me right after my time jump and took me in. I knew I was where the magnet wanted me to be, but at first, I didn't know why.

"I grew to love Atillio, and we married. I told him everything, and he tried really hard to believe me. I also tried to prepare him for the visits we would be getting, the ones I'd seen in the pictures the magnet gave me. I believed that I'd figured out why the magnet put me here.

"In the images, I was always at this house—but different visitors would approach my door, and I would greet them. When the first visitors really did begin to show up, they were confused, scared, and desperately in need of my help. That's when I started to understand what Satres must have done.

"When my father threatened to cut it in half, Satres's self-defense programs must have activated. It calculated the outcomes and repercussions that being cut in half would cause, then acted upon them. I believe Satres put me here as a home base to help other time jumpers."

"Like us," Ati said.

"Yes, like you three," Patrizia said, nodding.

"It doesn't make sense," Antoni said, "when Satres could just jump to another Chosen One."

"Well, I'm *not* a Chosen One. Satres can function independently except when a Chosen One has it—but after being cut in half, its capabilities would be significantly impaired."

"I still don't understand everything, and I know now that I never will." Patrizia's voice was low and a little hoarse. "All I can tell you is that our brains don't work like computers. We're not able to do millions of calculations in seconds. Believe me, I've struggled with the same question over the years—and the only answer I've come up with is the one I've already told you. It must be in Satres's programming to not give up on its receivers until they are dead.

"It may be saving receivers, each for their own chance at redeeming the future. What I do know is that, no matter where or whom the magnet goes to, these problems instantly occur for the receivers."

"So the visitors you've had…were they other Chosen Ones?" Ati asked in a small voice. "Do you already know if we are to…to fail?" She couldn't bring herself to say the word "die."

"No, I don't know if your Chosen One fails," Patrizia answered. "I could never be that cruel to not tell you that. Honestly, there are things I know now that haven't happened yet—things that I can't tell you about." Patrizia looked very sad and tired.

"What about your husband?" Antoni asked. "Where is he?"

"My wonderful husband got a sudden fever and died, only six months after we married. He never even had a chance to meet a time jumper." Patrizia sounded so forlorn after she finished this part of her story.

When Ati looked at her, she could sense a void deep in Patrizia's heart. It must have been hard, after all those years, not being able to be with the ones you loved—and even worse, knowing that almost everyone you cared about had been dead for over a thousand years.

"Don't fret for me, Ati," Patrizia said, intuitive as always. "The way I see it is that my family hasn't been born yet. That is held in the future—and hopefully, the creation of the timeline curve hasn't changed things too much. I had thirty-seven wonderful years with my family then, and I must protect that. I do admit, early on, there were times I fancied that my family would come to this time. Maybe Father hadn't cut the magnet, or if he had and Diana were to die, then maybe Elena would get both halves of the magnet. But it just didn't come to pass.

"Other than helping other time jumpers, I've spent the last thirty years finishing my thesis on Satres and the closed timeline curve. Having experienced its power and effects firsthand helped me greatly in my understanding of it. Other time jumpers have also explained things to me.

"I want you to know that the pages are here." Patrizia had raised her voice oddly, so it carried through the whole downstairs. "They are extremely detailed and written in a language from the future. You won't be able to use them now—but someday, and I already know this, they'll be useful to someone."

~~~

Later that night, Ati paced—sleep had eluded her. She went downstairs to check on Patrizia and covered her with a blanket. She looked so frail. Ati had only ever seen one or two women as old as she was.

Patrizia had asked for her medicine and was now sleeping peacefully. Ati walked back upstairs, stepping over Antoni again. He was awake, but he looked as if he'd been asleep only moments ago. After all these months, he'd never given up his post at the top of the stairs.

She gave him a smile, then went into her room. As she sat on her bed, her head reeled as she tried for the hundredth time to piece together Patrizia's tale. She snuggled deeper into her bed, warm under a blanket filled with goose feathers. Her mind drifted.

Only the occasional sound from the animals outside or Antoni in the hallway made it through to her room. Her thoughts shifted to Antoni and Nortia, and a surge of pity for them welled up in her heart.

She knew Antoni loved Nortia as much as a man could love a woman. She'd watched his love for Nortia take hold and grow since their childhood—but they were born to different stations in life, and that couldn't be changed.

Nortia had loved her husband, but their marriage had been more of a dutiful, arranged relationship—not the kind of love that, when that person walks into the room, you feel your heart miss a beat just because they're there.

Ati sighed as her eyes grew heavy, sleep nearly claiming her. Thinking of Nortia and Antoni's walks made her smile. Maybe now that everything was so different, they could at least find comfort in each other. She knew her thoughts were wrong—Nortia carried Forte's child. Still, Ati allowed her dreamy thoughts to continue. *Why not?* She was just a silly woman, anyway, and no one cared what she thought. It wouldn't exactly be a betrayal—would it? Nortia's husband had died over 1,800 years ago. Everyone they knew was dead. Who was to say that Nortia and Antoni couldn't be together?

Ati drifted toward sleep, smiling. Her dream began with Antoni taking Nortia into his arms and kissing her. Was this a dream—or a vision? She wondered with her last vestige of wakefulness. As the forbidden embrace that held the elusive key to their secret prison faded in her mind.

Chapter 16

April 8, 1481 AD

Firenze

Nature chose its time.

Antoni, who had been nervously practicing swordplay for the last few hours, made his way back into the farmhouse. The sharp decrease in noise was his cue that the birth had taken place.

"Everything is fine," Ati assured him. "Nortia and the baby are well."

"The baby is a girl, as Patrizia had predicted?" Antoni asked. He almost hoped that the woman had been wrong.

Then maybe some of her other predictions wouldn't come to pass.

"Yes, it's a girl." Ati's tone told Antoni that she knew why he'd asked the question. "Nortia doesn't know what to name the baby yet, but she is thinking about it. They are both resting—you may see them, if you'd like."

Antoni had mixed feelings. He was pleased that the baby was healthy—but how he wished the child was his. That longing only intensified as he looked at the baby for the first time. Why was life so unfair? Antoni yearned, as he had many times in the past, to be of noble birth, not the son of a guard. Not for fortune or recognition—but for Nortia.

He walked into the warm room and smelled the faint tang of blood in the damp, heavy air. The sunset sent shafts of light through one small window. Rays grabbing their last chance at brilliance fell directly onto the sleeping mother and child, illuminating the edges and angles of their bodies. Small bits of dust, suddenly visible, swirled in the air.

The scene before him looked magical. The memory of it would stay vivid and unchanged for as long as he lived.

~~~

Antoni couldn't believe how quickly Nortia regained her strength. After four weeks, if the baby weren't there as proof, no one would have ever known she'd been pregnant. The baby had plumped up, and her fine brown hair was just long enough to show the promise of a tight curl, just like her mother's.

Antoni wanted to hold the child, but he hadn't yet. Since he was not used to handling babies, he hadn't asked to do so. He did, however, get close enough to look at her features, and noticed that her eyes were the same color as her mother's and grandmother's—that soft brown, flecked with violet.

The weather was warm enough again for their walks to resume. Often, Nortia brought the baby out with them, but sometimes they went by themselves.

They set out in the late morning, just the two of them, side by side. Spring was in full bloom, and the trees were just starting their warm weather displays. Antoni tried to get used to walking alongside Nortia instead of behind her. A week earlier, she had timidly requested for him to walk next to her. The first few days they set out together, Ati had stared at them as they left the farmhouse—but her looks were oddly not disapproving.

Neither one of them talked today—they just walked. Nortia seemed to be as deep in thought as he was. Antoni mulled over how strange it was for the three of them and realized that Ati must also understand this. Rules that usually bound them, such as social standing, no longer seemed to be set in stone or able to dictate their current actions. How could they? All their vows and promises had been made to people who now were dust. Their sense of duty was centered around people who were not even in existence in their current time.

Should they live the remainder of their lives as if they would be restored to their usual time? Antoni didn't think they would ever return to their old lives, so why should he continue to act as if they would? He wasn't even sure that he wanted to go back now. He felt much closer to Nortia here— sometimes he even forgot that she and the baby weren't his.

"Antoni," Nortia said, breaking the silence and taking him totally off guard. "I've loved you, too. When you were injured and chose death if you could not be by my side, I knew then that I loved you."

Antoni stopped walking and turned to face her. He couldn't believe her declaration. They had both been thinking about nearly the same thing. His head, so recently full of thoughts, and now he was at a loss for words.

"A woman's life isn't her own," Nortia said, looking down and slowly shaking her head. Her beautiful brown curls swirled at her elbows. "The decisions weren't mine. If they had been, my choices would have been different. Now we are two souls lost in time, bound only to each other and those we love."

Antoni took her hand, stunned by her revelation and unexpected lucidity. There was nothing more for him to say. He kissed her on the forehead and breathed in the scent of her sun-warmed skin.

They finished their walk slowly. Antoni didn't want their time together to end.

~~~

Weary, Ati sat down in a chair beside Patrizia's bed. The poor woman was so ill now that she could hardly remain sitting upright for more than a minute or two—just long enough to take a few sips of water or broth.

Patrizia had been in and out of delirium for the last two weeks. She looked painfully thin and worn. *What a brave lady,* Ati thought. *She must have been ailing even before we arrived.* When Patrizia said she was relieved to see the three of them that first day, she probably had feared she wouldn't live long enough to even meet them. *Unless this wasn't the first time she had met them.*

Ati had been up with her since dawn. She'd signaled to the servant girl, Amelia, that she would take care of Lydia so she could get some rest. She felt an attachment to Patrizia. After hours of putting cooling cloths on her that morning, Patrizia's fever finally broke. At least now, Ati could rest a bit. Tucking an errant lock of her silver hair behind an ear, she leaned her head back, her eyes burning as they began to close.

The house was quiet, enveloped in a late-morning stillness. The baby slept, and Nortia and Antoni were out for a walk. The only sounds in the room were the small, rasping noises Patrizia made with each breath. Ati, unable to reopen her eyes, was almost asleep when Patrizia's hand touched her arm.

"Do you need something, Patrizia?" Ati's heart thumped wildly in her chest, like it always did when she was awoken from a light sleep.

"Yes, I need to tell you something that I should have said much sooner. I haven't been able to think clearly, nor have I felt well enough until today to say it. I don't want to frighten you or Antoni, but the time has come. It could already be too late." Patrizia winced, then paused for a minute to catch her breath.

Ati gave her a sip of her drink and laid her white-crowned head gently back on the pillow.

"The dark riders that were chasing you are a deadly threat, especially to the baby. They call themselves the 'Riders of the Reunity.' Their sole reason for existence is to unite the two halves of the magnet. Their leader, Vanth, is a direct descendant of my sister, Diana, albeit a distant one.

"Long ago, her line twisted and followed the path of evil. They don't care who they kill and will stop at nothing to have Satres, the united magnet, in their possession. Now that the child has been born, you are no longer safe here."

"We could give them Hemisatres," Ati said. "Surely our lives are worth more than this stone."

"If only that would work," Patrizia said in a low voice. "They would still kill all of you. As long as the child is able to use the magnet, they will not allow her remain alive."

"Certainly they won't be able to find us here," Ati said. "We are so hidden. We're not even in the same time as them."

"Unfortunately, that isn't a problem," Patrizia said. "Hemisatres will increase in strength with the birth of the Chosen One, as will their stone. Both magnets will be better able to find their other half because of this. It is only a matter of time now before they find us. I'm not able to go with you, but you three must take Hemisatres and leave—the sooner the better, so the Riders don't get too close. Group together, and make sure you're holding onto each other tightly—then you will be inside the same charge and will all go to the same spot in time. Hemisatres will protect you—you must trust it."

Ati felt a familiar sense of panic rise up inside her. Suddenly, she realized how secure she'd come to feel at the farmhouse. She started to ask another question, but Patrizia put up a shaky hand, stopping her. It didn't appear that Patrizia was finished talking—she seemed to just need a moment to let her pain subside.

Ati felt like crying. There wasn't anything she could do to help Patrizia, and she was wasting away right in front of her. "We can't just leave you here," Ati said, too distressed to remain silent.

Patrizia managed a small smile, "You must—my life is nearly finished. My purpose will have also come to an end once I've guided the child safely to the next spot in time. You need to tell Antoni and Nortia what I just told you and act on it immediately. Don't let the Riders get any closer. The closer they get, the easier it will be for them to find you."

A spasm of coughing racked her body. Ati waited, praying Patrizia would be able to catch her breath. Finally, her breathing became more even.

"Ati, I have tried to think of a simple way to explain wormholes in time, and the space-time continuum to all of you, but have repeatedly been left frustrated. Last week, I had an idea that I think may work. I hope my mind will stay clear long enough to share this explanation with you. It's crucial that I'm understood. Once you fully comprehend what you are up against, you will heed my words.

"Think of it this way. When a time jumper goes through time, it's similar to pushing into an unbreakable bubble. As the jumper goes through it, they stretch it, creating an indentation which gradually becomes an unbroken hole in the bubble. The hole they've created closes in on itself, behind them. This leaves only a residue, or a faint trail of disturbance. It is this trail that the magnets can follow. The more time that passes, the fainter the trail becomes.

"Time is growing short, Ati. I see you understand what I've just said. Now please remember this—it's what I've been teaching you all along. When the magnet was whole, it made time follow a never-ending circle, the closed timeline curve. It did this by sending me and my family back to the tenth century BC. The circle was protective, and it prevented paradoxes in the future, outside of the loop, by leaving the future intact. It's allowing our line another chance to fulfill our destiny—but it is fragile. Paradoxes can still be created within the circle. Small parts of the timeline can be and unavoidably *will* be written over—but main events such as births and whole lives must occur.

"If the Riders are successful in killing the child, it will create a paradox, and the loop will be broken. Like all of us, her survival is responsible for the continuation of our line. Think, Ati—the baby's history has already happened once, and I'm living proof of that. I'm a descendant of her future generations.

"Her life must happen again. Small rewrites will occur, which will be factored in by the magnet. These are contained by the closed timeline curve. Her life must not be erased, or the future will be irrevocably changed."

Patrizia's face had a grayish cast to it, and a fine sheen of sweat had developed from the effort of speaking. She stopped talking and tried to shift her body to the side a bit.

Ati could tell she was in a lot of pain. Maybe if she helped her sit up higher, Patrizia would be able to breathe easier. Ati felt helpless, desperate for something, anything that would ease the woman's suffering. She found two folded blankets and placed them behind her back so they would give her something firmer to lean on. She opened Patrizia's medicine, but Patrizia put up her hand again to stop her.

"My head needs to remain clear. I have only a few more things to tell you, but they are important." Patrizia took a shallow breath, and her color improved ever so slightly. "When time looped back on itself, it, in essence, doubled time. The baby is not only a *descendant* of my sister Elena— she is also an *ancestor* of Elena, as well as mine. Because she is a chosen receiver, the child is at a greater risk than the others in our line.

"With her aid, Satres must be made whole again. This way the sickness called a virus, that destroys man in the future, outside of the closed time curve, can be stopped. This shows clearly how fragile the loop is, and why it must be protected. The baby has become central—her death would alter our history."

Ati was having a difficult time taking in all this information. She'd thought she understood everything before. Now, she wasn't sure of anything anymore. *Loops in time? Riders coming through bubbles?* It all seemed so surreal. She wanted to put her head into her hands and weep, but Patrizia was looking at her with eyes that pleaded for some sort of confirmation of understanding.

"I never knew there was so much to it," Ati said. "I do see what you mean, but I need some time to think. I know you are weak, but I have one question. If you aren't able to answer, I understand. I have always wondered about the gifts our women have. Do you know about them? Are you able to tell me?"

Patrizia's eyes were almost closed, and her voice was barely above a whisper. "Time doubled over itself when my family was sent back. The women born after Elena and Diana have been rewritten slightly, always with a bit extra added to them. That's why all the women born to the two lines have special gifts. However, I never understood why this didn't happen to the men. Maybe it did, but it just wasn't realized by the individual."

"Nortia doesn't have a gift, either," Ati said.

"She will—you all do." Weakened from talking, Patrizia lapsed into a deep sleep.

Tears began to stream down Ati's face. She realized that she may never hear the sound of Patrizia's voice again. A feeling of urgency, fueled by more than just the woman's words, took hold of her. Once again, the house was quiet. That earlier tranquility was now transformed into an ominous silence laced with danger. She hoped Nortia and Antoni would be back soon.

Ati agonized over the decision, but in the end, she saw no other way. Nortia and Antoni would have to take the baby and go where Hemisatres deemed they go. She would stay here with Patrizia. Patrizia was family, too, and she couldn't leave her alone to die. In her heart, she knew this was the right thing to do. She also sensed it. It would be difficult to explain to Nortia and Antoni, and she wasn't sure yet how she would convince them to leave her. They would just have to understand.

Chapter 17

May 383 BC

Etruria

Good has a nemesis, every time.

Throughout the rest of her pregnancy, Vanth became slightly easier to deal with, but she still acted spiteful and was miserable to be around. Charontes did his best to explain to the men what was happening, giving them a much simpler version of what Vanth had told him. Most of them understood right away, and they were heartened by the explanation. Even though they were accustomed to having blind faith in the stone and its prophecy, they seemed relieved to have a solid reason for the prolonged wait.

It had been five weeks since the birth of the child, and Charontes began to doubt Vanth's previous explanation for the stone's delay. Her child seemed to be ordinary. He had checked two days ago while Vanth was off washing. She cried, relieved herself, and made tiny bubbles come out of her mouth, just like a normal baby.

When he looked at the tiny black-haired babe, Charontes had felt a twinge of paternal warming in his heart. He immediately rationalized that it must be pity, not affection, that he felt.

Sitting on a rocky outcropping, he looked up at the glimmering stars, wondering. Why did this child look so much like every other he'd seen? It didn't look like a chosen *anything*—not special at all. What if that snake of a woman had lied about everything? He thought about her accuracy predicting where the other half of the stone, and the woman, Nortia, would be. No, she knew too much to have made it all up. She must be getting help from her stone, just as she said. He would give it a few more days—they had already waited this long.

He got up stiffly. It was spring, but still cold at night. Before lying down, he added some kindling and extra wood to the dwindling fire.

The baby began to cry. Charontes made an exasperated noise through his nose. That baby *never* stopped crying. The men had taken to sleeping farther and farther away from the encampment just to get some peace. He looked at Vanth at a nearby fire. She didn't care—she didn't even stop eating to glance at her child. He knew she heard her crying.

"You know, I've decided to name the baby Aidyl," she called over to him in between bites.

It didn't surprise him that she was a terrible mother. All she ever thought about were the stones—and herself.

"Why bother naming her?" he shot back. "You're never even with her."

"Well, the nursemaids have to call her *something*, now don't they?" Vanth tipped her head to one side and flashed her characteristic evil smile. The firelight carved deep shadows in her face.

~~~

It was predawn when Vanth awoke him. An excited, maniacal light gleamed in her eyes. "The stone is warm again," she said. "Soon it will be time. We'll go to the same spot on the shore where the three of them disappeared. There we'll wait for the stone to guide us."

"Is it good to travel so soon after the birth?" Charontes asked, thinking about the baby being so young and fragile. He knew that Vanth would think he was worried about her instead of the child. But in his mind, the child of the prophecy should be protected from harm.

"I'm fine," Vanth answered predictably and selfishly. "It's been five weeks."

"I meant the *child*," Charontes pressed, braving her wrath just for his own satisfaction.

Vanth's eyes clouded over with the realization of what Charontes had done. She'd fallen into a trap he'd laid for his own enjoyment. "Aidyl is *my* child!" she shrieked, waking the whole camp. "*I* will see to her needs."

Aidyl, startled awake by the noise, began to wail in the background.

He brought himself up onto one elbow. Vanth, in her fury, didn't even hear the baby—she just stood there glaring down at him. He could hear the soft murmuring from the servant women as Aidyl continued to wail.

Charontes stood up, towering over her. He glared right back into her face. "Yes, anyone can see that," he growled. At the same time, he didn't understand why her lack of mothering skills should provoke him so.

Charontes's height and menacing aura didn't intimidate Vanth in the least. "Look, you stupid mountain of a man, I don't care *what* you think about how I'm raising my child!" she shouted. "I'm simply telling you that we're leaving today. Get your men ready!"

Angry, he turned from her and walked to the edge of the encampment to relieve himself. He didn't think it was right to bring a small infant on such a dangerous journey. What was wrong with him? Why would he worry about Aidyl's safety so much?

He thought back to that night many months ago, when they were still at their mountain home. It had been a moment of indiscretion, one hour of carnal pleasure. He didn't love

Vanth, or even like her for that matter—but he was a man, and he'd been unable to escape her seduction that night. She'd never come to him before that night…or since.

He tried to fight of the rising paternal feelings that threatened to take hold of him. The way he figured it, the timing was about right. *Don't be such a fool*, he chided himself. Knowing Vanth, she probably had a different man each night, maybe even more. Who knew for sure who the father of that child was? He willed himself not to think about it anymore and turned back toward the camp. They had a long ride ahead of them that day.

~~~

They reached the beach uneventfully. Charontes could hear Vanth chuckling a bit to herself. She looked nervous and jittery. Aidyl cried loudly and made hungry sucking sounds on her fists. Two of the Riders had been taking turns carrying the baby so the nursemaids could concentrate on controlling their mounts.

"Take care of that baby," Vanth yelled at the nursemaids. She looked at Charontes. "They are so incompetent," she complained.

He just shrugged. She'd been a horrible mother all along, and time hadn't made her any better. If it were at all possible, she actually grew *less* nurturing as the baby got older. He didn't like it, but it didn't directly concern him.

"The stone is getting even warmer. I think it's time now." Vanth held her arm out to show him the bracelet as she spoke. "In the visions, I have seen us all in a tight line, side by side on our horses. Our legs are touching the person beside us. We all must be touching for the stone to move us."

He wasn't too sure about the stone moving all fourteen horses, but he would do what Vanth said. He'd trained his whole life to find the other half of the stone.

Chapter 18

July 1481 AD

Firenze

It's never too late for a first time.

Lydia was burning up. Charontes knew her name because Amelia had told him. Well, gestured it to him. While caring for Lydia, the servant girl pointed at her, said her name, then pointed at herself, and said her own name. Then Amelia had pointed at him, indicating that he should introduce himself.

He'd just grunted. She was a serving girl, and she didn't need to know his name. Initially, he'd given Amelia free rein to cleanse Lydia's wound and change the bandages.

However, he'd made her stop four days after the attack because Lydia became hot. All the handling of the wound must not have been good for it. The servant girl protested, but he didn't understand her language, so he just waited. Each time Amelia tried to touch the wound, he'd made her stop.

After two days of that, Amelia had become extremely agitated. Finally, she held up one finger and looked at him pleadingly, so he allowed her to remove the bandage from Lydia's upper leg and leave it off. All that remained were the four sticks he'd placed lengthwise around her thigh, tied with cloth strips at even intervals to hold the leg steady. Those would have to stay on.

When Amelia had taken the bandages off on the sixth day after the injury, the leg had looked painfully swollen and bulged out around the tied areas. The wound itself was grotesque—bright red and swollen where the bone had originally broken through the skin.

Amelia had pointed to that spot, then crossed herself, making praying gestures. She'd looked to the heavens for help and raised her voice, becoming so distressed that he relinquished and let her continue with her ministrations. He figured it couldn't make Lydia any worse.

It was late evening, and he touched Lydia's forehead. Her skin felt like it was on fire, and it seemed like she was going to die. Between the potion Amelia was giving her and the sickness, Lydia had never even woken up. He needed her to live. Somehow, she'd found the pin containing the other half of the stone and used it. He needed her to show him how to use it so he could go after Vanth. There was no way he was going to be left behind when there was so much at stake.

When he'd first brought Lydia back to the house, he'd taken the pin and tried to make it work for him. Desperate, he'd tried everything—rubbing the stone, talking to it, and even trying to heat it up—but that had only earned him burned fingers. He had to find a way to follow Vanth, and he realized that Lydia may be one of the few people who could help him. He wasn't about to let that evil bitch, Vanth, get away with what she did to him. He didn't know exactly how Lydia fit into everything, but he knew she was a large part of the answer.

Realizing he actually wanted Lydia to live was a revelation. Even though it was selfishly motivated, it was still a new feeling for him. She was extremely brave and very beautiful. There was just something about her, as if he already knew her.

Amelia dribbled more pain potion down Lydia's throat and added a fresh, hot cloth to the wound. Lydia looked pale and thin, and she was lying very still. There were dark rings around her eyes. The heat was drying her up, robbing her of her vitality. Amelia also looked exhausted—she'd been tending to her day and night.

She got up and stirred the pot of boiling water that she was soaking the cloths in. When she'd first made it, she'd encouraged Charontes to dip his finger in it and taste the water. It had been salty, like the sea. Now she replaced the cooled cloth on Lydia's leg with a hot new one. Lydia moaned when it touched her skin, then settled back down.

The night grew late, and Amelia moved slower and slower. He knew she had barely slept in days, so he gestured for her to go away and sleep. Amelia widened her eyes and vehemently shook her head. He stepped in between her and

Lydia to communicate that he was taking over, then began taking off the cooled strip and replacing it with a new one.

Clumsy at first, he realized that he was simply too large for some of the tasks that women did. Amelia stepped in front of him and shook her head no again—but he just picked her up and set her aside. He then repeated his gestures of "go" and "sleep."

She actually smiled at him, for once—but he didn't return her smile. Too many years of not smiling had made it a habit for him. Showing emotions meant showing weakness.

Amelia went upstairs, and he felt relieved to be left alone with Lydia. It was quiet in the house since there was only himself, Lydia, and Amelia inside. The other servant, Franco, made himself scarce. He slept in the barn with the animals, did his chores, and didn't cause any problems. Amelia would go out to talk to Franco when she got milk or eggs, but he didn't see any harm in that. He needed the help around the house because he didn't know anything about running one. Protecting a house, yes. Anyway, what did he care if the servants talked to each other?

He laid another steaming cloth on Lydia's wound. She stirred again uncomfortably and made low whimpering sounds. Suddenly, he felt unsure. *Maybe I should get Amelia,* he thought. What was he thinking? He couldn't tend to a sick woman—he was a warrior. Then Lydia took a deep breath and settled into sleep again. She looked terribly quiet for a moment, and he was scared for her life—her breaths seemed so small.

What was it about this woman? Why was he so drawn to her? Was it destiny, fate, or both? He'd lived his whole life not caring about anyone. Now all that had changed. This woman mattered to him, and there was someone else, too—Aidyl. They could be the reason he was changing inside. Maybe it was both of them.

Suddenly, people other than him were important. He'd already lost one of them, but he'd fix that. Vanth would pay. In the meantime, he didn't want to lose this one, too.

Hours passed as he diligently changed the cloths when they cooled.

~~~

Charontes awoke with his forehead lightly touching Lydia's arm. He lifted his head and watched her as she slept peacefully. As he trailed his fingers down her temple and over one cheek, he noticed that she felt much cooler and that some of the paleness had left her face.

When he lifted the now-cooled cloth from her wound, a tan, blood-tinged liquid streamed out of the spot where the bone had broken through the skin. The vile poison that had made her hot was now leaving her body. He closed his eyes—and for the first time in his life, he thanked the Gods.

Chapter 19

May 1481 AD

Firenze

There is always time.

When Antoni and Nortia returned to the farmhouse after their walk, Ati rushed out to meet them, distraught. After informing them that Patrizia was faring much worse, Ati told them everything that she had communicated to her. "We must leave now," she concluded.

Antoni's stomach wrenched. He paced back and forth, shouting. "Why leave? We have been safe here. Why should we go? Just because this old woman says we have to? Maybe she is just tired of having us in her home."

"So far," Ati said, "that *old woman* has kept us safe—her and Hemisatres. Why stop listening to her and the magnet now? Patrizia said the Riders are coming, and it's foolish not to heed her warning."

"What, would you have the infant travel?" Antoni asked incredulously. "The baby is but six weeks old. We don't know where we're going, and it's not safe. What if we end up in harm's way because we listened to a stone?"

"Patrizia told me the magnet will keep the baby safe because she is the Chosen One," Ati said. "We must listen to her and to Hemisatres. There is no other choice."

"So, what exactly do you suggest we do?" Antoni asked. He couldn't believe that Nortia just listened passively to their conversation and didn't say anything. She was acting like a mere spectator to reality. He felt like shaking her.

"I think you should take Nortia and the baby, then go wherever Hemisatres leads you. Give it a chance to protect you. Hold onto each other, and let Nortia rub the magnet. Wherever it takes you will be a safer place."

"Just Nortia, me, and the baby?" Antoni asked. "What about you? You will be going with us, won't you?"

"No, I must stay here and take care of Patrizia. I sense that it's the right thing to do."

"Mother, *no!*" Nortia cried, finally out of her trance, "You *must* come with us. I won't be apart from you."

Antoni fumed, beside himself with anxiety. "How can I protect everyone, if we don't remain together? I cannot be in two places at once. I won't let this happen—I won't let that stone pull us apart."

"Why can't you see that it's already decided?" Ati asked. "This is our fate. It isn't up to you or me, Antoni." Ati grabbed onto a rail beside the door with a trembling hand to hold herself up. "We must do what Hemisatres tells us. Once again, we must put all our trust in the magnet. You must agree that if it hadn't been for Hemisatres, we already would be dead. If it's not meant to be, then you will not go anywhere—but it's time to try. We are in grave danger, but I sense the magnet will protect us. You must flee the Riders...*now!*" Ati's usual soothing voice was now a shout.

"We must flee—but what about you, Mother? Nortia said through tears. "What about Patrizia?"

"She is too ill, and I will not leave her alone. She is family, and I cannot abandon her."

"But you would abandon *us?*" Antoni said, using guilt as a weapon. It wasn't an honorable tack, but he'd do just about anything to get her to change her mind.

"That's not fair," Ati replied. "I'm not abandoning you. You're making this impossibly difficult for me. I know you will take care of Nortia and the baby. Don't you think my heart is tearing from this? This is my duty—I sense it. I must stay and take care of Patrizia. I'm compelled to stay, and I feel it's the right thing to do."

Nortia touched Antoni's hand and looked up into his face. "I fear my mother and Patrizia are right. Hemisatres has felt warm for the last two days. I couldn't bring myself to tell anyone, since everything is so...so perfect here." Ashamed, she looked down at the ground.

Antoni saw the red bloom of embarrassment in her cheeks.

"I want my baby to be safe," Nortia continued, "but she is no longer safe here."

Antoni couldn't believe this was happening again. Anger seethed in him. They were never left with safe choices. Although he believed in the gifts of the women, he instinctively needed to rely on only the tangible. It terrified him to have to listen to their visions. After being separated and thrust into yet another unknown, dangerous situation, he knew that he couldn't possibly protect both women and the baby. There seemed to be no other choice, and he couldn't stand the thought of it.

This new situation seemed eerily similar to the last time. What would the consequences have been if Hemisatres *hadn't* helped them? They would have all been killed. He could still see the look in their leader's eyes—murderous evil, through and through.

"We will do as you say, Ati," he answered, his voice low and resigned. "We will listen to Patrizia and put our faith in Hemisatres. I don't think anything will happen—but it's hard to believe we're here at all. That it could happen again is unfathomable." Saying it out loud didn't make him feel any better, and a sense of foreboding encased him. "Let's make haste, Nortia. We must ready ourselves and the baby."

Nortia cried freely now and hugged Ati tightly. "Mother, I don't want to leave you here. I'm so afraid for you."

"And I for you." Ati returned her daughter's embrace. "But we must trust Hemisatres. We are but small parts of a grand story—and we must play our parts well." Ati was also crying as she finished hugging her. "Go now, my daughter, and get ready. I feel that there isn't much time left."

Antoni followed Ati and Nortia into the house, and Nortia ran upstairs to get the baby. Patrizia lay still on her pallet downstairs. She'd never looked closer to death. Ati gave Antoni a desperate, hopeless look, then went to Patrizia and patted her brow with a cloth.

When the cool cloth touched Patrizia's head, she opened her eyes, reached up, and grabbed Ati's tunic.

It surprised Antoni that she had any strength left.

"Remember this, Ati—there's always time."

Her voice had only been a hoarse whisper, but Antoni heard it.

She lay her head back down, released Ati, and closed her eyes. That one sentence had used up everything she had left.

Somehow Antoni knew she didn't mean that they should take their time leaving. She'd said it in a more prophetic way. He would never understand all that was going on, and he didn't want to. He'd tried—but the idea of tiny thinking machines and whole civilizations being destroyed was too much for him. He was a warrior, and his job was to protect the women. Regretfully, he couldn't protect all of them, and that tore him apart.

He agonized over leaving the two older women behind. They were completely defenseless. But maybe because they were defenseless, they would still be safe. It wouldn't be honorable to hurt helpless women. Antoni shuddered as he remembered that day on the beach. Those eyes had been so void of compassion, and they were intent on their deaths. There had been no honor in those sinister eyes.

Making sure Nortia and the baby were safe was what he had been instructed to do. He abhorred splitting up, but he was out of options and had to obey.

Outside, there was the echoing sound of approaching hoofbeats and commotion.

Ati's eyes darted to his. "They're here," she said.

A chill ran down his back. How could he not have heard them coming? He'd grown soft from months on the farm. The noises outside grew closer—squeals from the horses, metal scraping on metal.

The dark riders were upon them. Hemisatres had been right—and now it was too late.

"*Nortia!*" Ati shrieked up the stairs. "You must get the baby and come now. *Hurry!*"

Patrizia lay unmoving, past all worry.

Antoni drew his sword, readied his shield, and walked outside to meet their attackers. Their horse's hooves were churning up the ground. After one look at the twelve riders hurtling toward him, he knew he would die. They would all be killed. There was only enough time for a moment of regret before he looked into the glowing, violet eyes of the demon once more.

She smiled down at him, her huge horse viciously snapping the air, inches from his face. "We meet again," she hissed. "And this time, you *will* die."

He raised his sword and stood, unflinching.

"No!" Ati screamed. "It must not happen this way."

In the span of a heartbeat, Antoni's head turned, ever so slightly. He saw Nortia standing behind Ati, with the baby in her arms. She was strangely calm, like a woman waiting to be asked to dance. Her long brown curls were floating in the air.

The demon raised her sword. Horse and rider plunged toward him.

"Nortia, now!" Ati shouted.

Before Antoni could stop her, Ati moved between him and his attacker. The demon woman's sword came down, making a hideous cut on Ati's arm. Blood spurted from the wound.

Nortia wrapped one arm around him.

He couldn't stop the attack—his sword would slice Ati. In horror, he looked down at the tiny baby between them. "Nortia, no! Not now! Your mother needs—"

The words he shouted were ripped from his mouth as his body jerked upward. A roaring sound filled his ears, crushing him with its deafening volume. Then there was nothing.

~~~

"They have escaped again!" Vanth screamed.

Charontes knew she would be crazed by this failure. She raised her sword to strike a killing blow to the old woman, the only person who still stood before her. The others had vanished.

He leaped forward, swinging his sword to deflect Vanth's blow—but her sword still partially reached its mark. The old woman staggered from the second blow to her arm and fell to the ground. Charontes had managed to save her from death by mere inches.

What is Vanth thinking? This woman is the only person who could possibly lead them to the other half of the stone, and she's going to kill her. "Stop at once!" he bellowed.

"I will kill her for her deception. How dare she interfere!" Vanth's rage looked to be at its zenith, only fueled to greater heights by the effects of using the stone. Vanth stopped what she was doing and held her head in agony.

Charontes hoped her screaming had created as much pain for her as it did for him right now. His head ached—even the sunlight hurt his eyes.

Ignoring his discomfort, he took the opportunity to place his horse in front of the felled woman. "Stop, don't be foolish," he said, looking into Vanth's sadistic eyes. "She is the one person who may be able to tell us where they've gone."

"*Do I care?*" Vanth screamed at the top of her lungs. "No! I want her dead!" She turned her horse, cruelly pulling the reins in her anger. Her horse reared up, screaming out a savage squeal. Then it came down hard, planting its front hooves firmly on the ground. "Fine, question her," she said finally, backing down. "*Then* I will kill her. Secure the house, then take her in."

Charontes warily watched Vanth dismount. He didn't trust her. Once on the ground, she motioned for the two nursemaids, who were sitting on the ground by the outer perimeter of the yard, looking generally unwell. Charontes grimaced as one relinquished her last meal onto the ground after she stood up. He knew they shouldn't have come.

He signaled to the other Riders, who all looked haggard but still followed their orders. At his command, some dismounted and went into the house, while others rode around the back to secure the property. Charontes picked up the bleeding old woman, and carried her inside.

Inside, the Riders had hold of a young girl, who cried and struggled to get away.

"Do not hurt any of them—we will need them to answer questions," Charontes said as he laid the old woman on a pallet, next to another old woman who appeared to be dead. The dead-looking woman's raspy breathing was the only evidence that she was still alive.

"Ati!" the young woman called out in anguish, sobbing and trying to pull away from her captors.

The Riders released her, and she ran to Ati. Charontes pointed to the woman's bleeding arm and told her to take care of it. The young girl looked terrified, but seemed to understand. She tore several pieces from her underdress, then pressed them to the wound, staunching the blood flow.

Vanth stormed back into the house, followed by her nursemaids. The small space amplified the ever-incessant sounds of Aidyl's cries. The wailing of the child seemed to push Vanth over the edge of sanity that she usually balanced so precariously on.

Charontes saw something inside her give way. Years of waiting coupled with the loss of the stone a second time must have been more than she could take. She had had it so close to her possession not just once, but twice—only to have it slip away again.

Aidyl's piteous cries provided the perfect backdrop for Vanth to perform her usual macabre actions. Short sword drawn in the blink of an eye, Vanth rushed forward. At that very moment, Charontes knew she was about to kill the woman the girl had called "Ati." He tried to cover the five steps between himself and the old woman, but he proved to be too slow.

Vanth was so unpredictable and so blindingly fast. Eyes glassy and blinded by the haze of her own blood lust, Vanth plunged her short sword into the old woman's chest.

But it wasn't Ati that Vanth stabbed—it was the other old woman.

The servant girl let out a heart-rending wail, adding to the cacophony of sounds in the small house.

Vanth stood there, her diabolical smile forming a crevasse in her glacial beauty. Her sword was now dripping with the old woman's blood. "She was too weak to talk, anyway," she said icily.

Charontes grabbed her sword arm and lifted Vanth bodily into the air. He must get her from the house and away from all the people. No one was safe around her. "You are a crazed woman!" he shouted in his disbelief and frustration. "You never think first—you just kill."

He carried her outside to the front of the house and set her down, still holding firmly onto her sword arm.

"I told you she wasn't doing much talking, anyway," Vanth said as she twisted around behind him with viper-like agility, until she had her sword to his neck poised for the kill.

She didn't scare him like she did the others, and he just laughed a deep, forced laugh. "You killed the wrong old woman."

His statement was enough to make her lose her concentration for a moment. Charontes moved, one step to the side and one step back, grabbing her from behind. Her own sword was now gleaming across her white neck. "Not doing much talking now yourself, are you?" He whispered mockingly into her ear. "Maybe I ought to kill you."

He knew he really shouldn't goad her. She was already so furious that he doubted she could get any more enraged. But he couldn't help it. She'd completely sapped his patience. Vanth didn't have one redeeming quality—and being in such close proximity to her for so many months had finally pushed him to his limit.

"Enough of this...release me," Vanth said with conviction, but in a surprisingly calm tone. "I don't care which old woman I killed—I just want to get that stone. Get the Riders together, and we will go now. Our stone should allow us to follow them. We all must be together, touching, and we must leave quickly."

"What about Nortia's mother?" Charontes asked.

"What about her?" Vanth spat back.

"She's too badly injured to go with us, but we should still question her before we go," Charontes said. "Also, someone should watch her, since Nortia may be back for her."

"Why would Nortia come back for her?" Vanth asked, trying to wipe blood off the back of one of her hands.

Charontes shook his head, "She's her mother, her family—you know, she *cares* about her."

"Well, that makes it sound like she's coming back for sure. We'd better have someone really good watching over her, a very skilled warrior." Vanth's eyes narrowed and an insincere smile twisted her lips. "Since you seem to like old women so much, *you* can stay!" she shouted, then stomped toward her horse.

Charontes truly hated Vanth. Her demeanor was rotten as a bloated battlefield corpse. She wanted to punish and demean him in front of his men, and he'd had his fill of her. Truthfully, he thought it would be a relief to be away from her vile conduct.

All those months waiting for the stone had given him time to contemplate. He suspected Vanth may be too far gone and too demented to handle all the power the joining of the stones would bring.

Vanth chuckled to herself as she signaled for the riders to assemble. She let out an ungodly holler for the nursemaids. The women scurried outside with Aidyl, who, of course, was still crying.

What an unlucky child, Charontes thought. *In her short life, she's probably cried more than she's been content.*

He could hear the young servant girl still sobbing inside the house. He resented being left with such a mess. He didn't know what time they were in—only that this wasn't *his* time. Vanth's decisions kept getting progressively worse. Her half of the stone must be sickening her, or her greed for power was corrupting her mind.

He'd always thought of the Riders of the Reunity as warriors with a purpose. But to kill a dying woman? She'd been completely defenseless. Ashamed of Vanth's actions, he'd be glad when she was gone. She'd turned evil. It wasn't the first time he'd thought that maybe Vanth wasn't fit to have the other half of the stone. The stone belonged to Aidyl, the chosen child—not Vanth.

Charontes watched the Riders gather together, knee-to-knee. The nursemaids were also in the lineup. Vanth's black hair floated in the air like it had done last time. Charontes took a deep breath. The air smelled like it did before a thunderstorm.

"Charontes," Vanth called out to get his attention. "I held true to the prophecy. The stone showed me who the father of the chosen child should be. It showed me that it should be you, so I made sure that you were the only one that I'd been with. Aidyl is your child." She smirked cruelly. "Once I get my hands on the other half of the stone, I hope nothing harms her."

An unfamiliar sick feeling, one that could only be fear, washed coldly up and down his body. Then rage took its place. Charontes leaped at the line of riders, aiming his body at the nursemaid with Aidyl, but Vanth had caught him off guard.

They vanished.

He fell to the ground grabbing only air where Aidyl had been.

"I'll kill you!" he called after Vanth into the nothingness. "You hurt her, and you will die!" His shouts of fury and frustration echoed into the empty air.

He *would* kill her. She had taken his child.

Chapter 20

September 1986 AD

Buffalo, New York

They were souls lost in time.

Antoni awoke clutching his sword, his left hand wrapped in Nortia's curls. As his eyes adjusted, he could see clouds blanketing the sky above him. Awareness rushed back. He breathed in deeply, as you would after a long sleep. The tang of wet leaves and earth filled his nostrils. Cool grass poked at the back of his head and around his ears.

Reality seeped back, and he rolled up onto his knees with a groan, anxiously looking around for dark riders. He didn't see any immediate danger, so he stood up on his unsteady legs. His left leg almost gave way, still stiff from his old injury. He shook his head hard to clear it, then was immediately sorry that he had. It throbbed with a searing pain and his stomach flipped in rebellion. He forced his nauseous insides to calm down—he would not disgrace himself.

Looking down, he found Nortia lying on her side, fast asleep. Her arms were tightly wrapped around a kicking, squirming bundle. Antoni tipped back the blankets, and the baby gave him a huge smile. He couldn't help but smile back. *That's odd,* he thought. *The journey hasn't affected the child at all.*

Antoni took a quick survey of his person. Except for the horrible pounding in his head, he was whole. He hoped Nortia could be easily roused. He would never get used to these journeys through time. He would just try to take Nortia and the baby somewhere safe.

He knew they must immediately get away from their arrival spot—the faster the better. The riders would try to follow them using their half of the stone. *Give chase before the trail goes cold. That's what I would have done.*

Looking around, he didn't recognize any of their surroundings. They had arrived in a small clearing. Trees and bushes were scattered about the edges, blocking most of his view. As he took a few shaky steps to see though the trees better, he saw a giant naked man. It only took him a moment to realize the man was a statue. It was about fifty feet away, and except for its size and persistent immobility, it looked very real. Antoni couldn't help but stare at the very lifelike sculpture. Sending a silent prayer to the gods that people of this time weren't the same size as the statue, he continued his exploration.

Turning back the other way, he saw what looked to be a bridge. The construction was unbelievable. It started from the ground, and snaked around into a spiral, then arched up and out. Each space for the rails was exactly the same. It was perfect.

The bridge's sides were covered with a rigid net that had identical, small, circular shapes all over it. He could only see the beginning of the bridge, but not the end of it. There wasn't any water under it, either. He decided that he wouldn't take Nortia and the baby over that bridge—it just didn't look right.

There was a lake in the opposite direction of the bridge, very close to where they were. A bridge *away* from a lake didn't make sense to him. They must have gone forward in time, which would explain the precision of the bridge's construction.

Patrizia had explained to him about some *future inventions*, as she called them. Although she'd been happy to share the information, he'd just laughed at her, stubbornly unwilling to believe much of anything she'd said. Future inventions aside, it didn't matter what time they were in— they must to get to safety.

If they headed toward the lake, they could walk around it and look for somewhere safe to hide. The lake was large enough that it would provide a recognizable point that they could return to, if necessary. It would also supply their other obvious and immediate need—water to drink.

Antoni shook Nortia. "Awaken, Nortia."

Nortia groaned.

Antoni felt a twinge of sympathy for her, knowing all too well how she felt. He saw Nortia reflexively tighten her already-snug hold on the baby.

The baby began to cry.

Nortia immediately opened her eyes and began cooing to the baby. Carefully, Antoni pulled on Nortia's arm to loosen her hold on the baby.

"No, you cannot have her!" Nortia yelled. "She's mine. Stay away from her, you demons!"

The baby cried louder.

"Nortia, calm down. It's just me, Antoni. Loosen your hold on the child—we are safe for the moment."

Nortia relaxed her hold and looked up at Antoni. His heart hurt for her. The look in her eyes made him want to take her into his arms and never let her go. It made him wish he could promise her that she would always be safe. And even though he would slay anyone or anything that tried to hurt her or the child, he knew he couldn't promise her that. He was only one man, and he couldn't keep all the Riders of the Reunity at bay forever. The thought made him feel like raging to the gods for being so unfair.

He remembered how it felt when the Riders were upon them at the farmhouse. How ridiculously defenseless they really were. Oh, he would have fought them, of course, and would have gladly died defending Nortia and the child—but by the gods, they *would* have died. There were just too many of them.

Nortia groaned again. Antoni helped her into a sitting position as she began to comfort the child.

I have to get them out of here as soon as possible, Antoni thought nervously.

"Where are we?" Nortia asked, squinting from the sunlight. "Where are the dark riders?"

"I don't know where we are—there isn't anything I recognize. We may have advanced through the years again. I have seen very little since awakening, but it's unlike anything I've ever seen before. I'm sure it was the work of Hemisatres. It has helped us escape the Riders and a certain fate once again—at least for the moment."

Nortia regarded him with a look Antoni had grown used to since their time at the farmhouse. It was the look of someone lost, who was closed down to almost everything—as if what they couldn't bear to think about, or even fathom, wasn't actually happening. All the finer details were lost to Nortia—she only seemed to be hearing parts of what he said.

"Oh, my mother!" she cried. "What about my mother?"

Looking at his feet, Antoni didn't know what to tell Nortia. He just wasn't good at that sort of thing. Comforting women hadn't been part of his warrior training. He wouldn't give Nortia false hopes—and he feared it did not bode well for Ati. His last memory before they jumped was the demon woman's sword striking Ati's arm with a cruel blow.

Tears made tracks down either side of Nortia's face, evidence that she was cognizant, at least on some level. Somewhere deep inside, Nortia knew that her mother had been gravely injured or worse.

"Hemisatres knows what is best for us all," Antoni said, unable to believe he consoled Nortia with platitudes he didn't believe in himself.

She hugged the baby, who was blissfully unaware. "I just don't understand why this has happened to us. Somehow, we must have angered the gods."

Antoni didn't have an answer to that. Anyway, Nortia may be right—maybe they *had* angered the gods. He forced himself back to what he knew—being a guard, just like his fathers before him.

He helped her to her feet, carefully supporting her until she became steady. "Are you able to walk? We must go. We need to stay ahead of the Riders. If what Patrizia said is true, they may be able to follow us anywhere we go in time."

"Yes, the magnets will find one another easily, now that the chosen children are born." Nortia looked down at the pin on her tunic.

Antoni groaned. He didn't like the misted-over look in Nortia's eyes. This whole prophecy was so beyond his comprehension—and why them? They seemed to be the least equipped to deal with what was happening. Look at what they'd lost already: Ati, Patrizia, their home, and all their possessions. Next it would be their lives. All they had with them were his weapons and their clothes.

Antoni became distracted from his thoughts when Nortia raised her hand to touch Hemisatres. His hand shot out and grabbed hers. "No, please don't touch the magnet. We are safe for the moment, so let's try to get away from here in case the Riders follow."

"Yes, Antoni." Nortia rearranged the blankets around the baby.

The cool air nipped his face as they started their journey. It seemed to be just after dawn. Antoni shook his head. He would never get used to "riding the four quarters of the sky." It made him helpless to protect ones he was sworn to protect. He wouldn't wish the choices he'd made over the past few months on any warrior.

Gripping his sword, he used his other arm to support Nortia and the baby. "Come, we will go this way." He steered her toward the small lake. It took less than a minute to reach the edge of the water, where they found a smooth path of black stone.

The path was flat and perfect, and it lent shape to a winding walkway. Antoni tapped his sandal onto the stone. It was definitely placed there by man—it was too precise to have occurred naturally. He stepped onto the path, guiding Nortia alongside him. Then he turned to walk toward the rising sun. *Why not? One direction is as good as another for all I know.*

"Come, Nortia—we'll go this way." He tried to sound confident, and even make a small jest to cheer her up. "Look, at least we will have water to—"

A cataclysmic crashing noise reverberated, and the ground vibrated under their feet. Light flashed blue, then white. The water on the lake roiled and swelled, splashing up over the bank.

Antoni pulled Nortia and the baby down under a shrub, behind a large tree. He could hear horses squealing and thrashing. Daring to look around the tree, he already knew what he would see.

The Riders and their horses seemed disoriented. Some lay on the ground with their prone riders, barely moving. Others flailed their legs to get up. They created a horrible din.

Antoni saw their evil leader lying beside her horse.

He grabbed Nortia and the baby and ran with them. Now was their chance to get away, while the riders were still recovering from their ride through time. Nortia kept up with him, matching him stride for stride, terror lending speed to her feet. They rounded the edge of the lake and headed east into the rising sun.

He could hear Nortia breathing heavily. Slowing down, he moved off to the side and around another tree to let her catch her breath. Looking back, he could see that they weren't being followed yet.

After an all-too-brief rest, he urged Nortia on. He followed the path around the lake, then veered sharply off it, so they weren't such easy targets. He headed up the side of a broad hill.

Nortia needed help carrying the baby, but he knew he must keep his sword arm free. Besides, she would never let go of the baby when she was this frightened. Instead, he held Nortia by the arm, supporting her as best as he could, half pulling her up the hill. They stopped at the top, desperately trying to catch their breath.

Antoni saw it first. A large chariot, unlike any he'd ever seen before, was coming right at them. No horses were pulling it, yet it was approaching at full speed, wheels turning and turning.

It was one of the future creations Patrizia had tried to warn him about. How he'd laughed at her, not believing a word she said. He wasn't laughing now.

"By the gods, where are we?" Nortia shouted out.

The chariot made a loud sound as it bore down upon them. He looked down. They were on another black path, but this one was larger than the last. Even though there were no ruts from chariot wheels, it seemed to be a road of some sort.

Antoni pulled Nortia and the baby back onto the grass as the chariot went by, growling. It sped by at an unbelievable speed, never slowing down, never stopping. The sun glinted off its armored sides and top.

"Antoni, where are we?" Nortia asked, panicked. "Are we even alive? That must be a chariot of the gods. They sounded angry." She was still out of breath and panting. The baby made a happy noise from inside of her blankets.

"I know not. Patrizia spoke of such things, though. It must be something rare and beautiful in this time. We are most likely blessed to have even seen one of them." Antoni had just finished saying those words when two more chariots became visible, heading down the road at them.

"Nortia, we must run." Antoni took her arm and ran from the chariots, careful not to step on the black road. Terrified, he could hear them gaining ground with impossible speed. When they were almost upon them, he shoved Nortia roughly behind him and stopped, turning to fight the chariots with his sword. The huge, horseless monstrosities just went by them, even faster than the first one.

Antoni could see drivers in the chariots holding onto something as they raced by. Music came out of one of the rolling nightmares.

"It is safe, Nortia. They seem to have no quarrel with us. The horses must be hidden under the chariot's armor." Even as he said that, he knew it wasn't true. The chariots were moving too fast, and he hadn't heard any horses—just loud growling and music.

Patrizia *had* tried to explain to him about the chariots that moved by themselves. He wished now that he'd listened to her.

Chariots or not, they must keep moving and hide themselves. "Let's go, Nortia." He started running again, pulling Nortia along with him.

Nortia remained quiet in her terror. Clutching her baby close to her, she did just as Antoni said.

They made it around the lake and stepped onto a lighter-colored stone path. Since they were higher than the lake, Antoni could still see the Riders in the distance. Some were milling about, trying to catch their horses, but not all of them were off the ground yet.

If he pushed on just a bit farther, they would be out of the Riders' sight. Then he could cover their trail and find a place to hide. But he had to find a hiding place soon. Pain streaked through his leg, and Nortia was nearing the end of her endurance.

They continued up the path at a slower pace than Antoni would have liked, but one that Nortia could manage. He kept alert for any possible hiding places. Over the road and to the left, Antoni could see statues of all different shapes and sizes dotting the landscape. Rectangles, winged women, and small tomblike structures jutted out from what looked like a burial ground.

Expecting the sound of hooves at any moment, Antoni kept glancing back behind them. He urged Nortia on, and she increased her speed without complaint. Just ahead of them on the right were houses—but they were different from anything he'd ever seen before. Their roofs were tall and pointed sharply on top, and many unused chariots were abandoned along the road in front of them.

We must hide, he thought, forcing himself to pass all the future wonders without slowing down. He had little doubt now that they had advanced forward many years. Everything they passed looked strange, and their symmetry was almost *too* perfect. *The craftsmen in this time must be highly skilled.*

He heard the ominous thunder of hooves—but when he turned, he didn't see anyone coming. They would have to find a temporary place to hide, *now*. He couldn't risk being seen by the Riders of the Reunity—they could never outdistance them on foot. He hoped the new, astounding surroundings would help slow them down.

"They mustn't capture us, Antoni," Nortia said between gasps for air.

"They will have to go through my sword first." He put his free arm around Nortia again. "Come, we must hide." He angled them behind some shrubs, out of the line of sight, and peeked out. His blood froze.

There were thirteen black horses at the far edge of the lake, plunging up toward the road, twisting under their rider's tight rein.

They had to keep running, but the terrifying scene rooted him to the spot.

"What's happening, Antoni?" Nortia asked anxiously. "Have they seen us?"

"No, but they are close." His eyes were still glued to the horrifying sight, which only got worse.

A chariot came up fast, right behind the dark riders. From his experience earlier with the chariots, he didn't think this one would slow down.

A horse's scream cut through the early morning dawn, sending chills down the back of his neck. He watched the horse and rider, fly up and over the top of the chariot. The horse's legs flailed wildly, its light underbelly flashing as it rolled. The chariot careened sideways, slamming into a second horse's hind end. The huge horse went down onto its side, and its rider was thrown under a back wheel of the chariot.

He didn't need to see any more. "Hurry, Nortia—this is our chance!" he shouted in panic. "Do you know which way to go? Because *I* don't. Can you ask the magnet?"

"I can't—it will just be the right way," she said in a shaky voice.

"How can it 'just be the right way?' Nortia, please, I need guidance. I don't know where to go."

Nortia remained silent.

"Then I will go this way!" he yelled, desperate for action.

"Then that is our desti—"

Antoni pulled her sharply into a run, the last word ripped from her mouth. If it didn't matter, then they would take the easiest route, straight down the lighter path. He had to put as much distance as possible between them and that nightmare back there.

He heard the angry, confused yells of the Riders in the distance. Not knowing what else to do, he followed the path, which led them around a circle with a spraying fountain in the center. He remained alert for signs of attack from animals or other people, but no one else was about.

Huge palaces loomed overhead, threatening to overwhelm them. Nortia said nothing, but continued to keep up. He saw some people on the other side of the chariot road, but he just pressed on. A few of the people laughed and pointed at them. One youth, empty handed, pretended to fight with a sword. Antoni anticipated an attack, but none of the people were armed.

Nortia began to tire.

Suddenly, he heard hoofbeats again. The people they had passed began shouting.

Nortia couldn't keep up at this pace much longer. Across the road, he saw a large structure that looked like a temple of some type. Patrizia had told him stories of future times and people taking refuge from evil in temples. She had been wise indeed—and somehow, she knew precisely what things about the future they would need to know. Silently, he thanked her.

Antoni saw no other choice. They would have to go into the temple and find a place to hide or someone to help.

He took care crossing the road and looked for chariots. Still early in the morning, the village, except for a few people, didn't seem to be stirring yet. He crossed the road, dragging the exhausted Nortia with him.

The temple doors were large and heavy. He pulled one door open and helped Nortia and the baby through. Taking care to keep his body hidden behind the partially open door, he chanced a look back toward where the noise was coming from.

There were less Riders now, but they were coming. Far down the road, he could see the long, black hair of the rider in front, streaming behind her lithe form. Even from that far away, he could see her evil head turn in his direction. She was relentless.

There was too much distance between them for him to see her eyes, but her horse pivoted, midstride, and began galloping directly toward him.

She had seen him.

He ducked his head back through the door, hugging Nortia to him as she quaked with fear.

Pushing her back, he looked at her face. As his eyes adjusted to the interior's dimness, her facial features came into focus. Terror lit her eyes.

"Nortia, I must hide you and the baby. Will you be able to keep the baby quiet?"

"No, that isn't what's ahead of us," she said.

"What do you mean? Has Hemisatres told you what to do?" His voice took on a hopeful edge.

"The dark riders will not stop until they have the other half of the magnet, and my child is dead. They want all of Satres's power to themselves. Our only hope is to give them Hemisatres while we run."

"No, we will *not* give them the other half. Then they would have all the power. They would have ultimate control of time and would slay us easily, anyway. Think, Nortia. They could even go back to the beach and slay us there—then your child would have never even been born. We have no time to argue about this. Patrizia told us to never relinquish Hemisatres, no matter how hopeless the situation—or we will lose its protection."

"I don't care if I die!" Nortia wailed. "But my child…I *must* save her!"

They were running out of time, and they both knew it.

Antoni heard the soft footsteps of someone approaching and put his hand on the hilt of his sword. A man wearing a black robe entered the room. Antoni recognized him to be a holy man. They had to act now.

"We will see if the holy man will aid us," he whispered to Nortia, in a not-so-soft whisper. "Maybe there are secret passageways underground. I will leave you and the baby hidden with him, then lead the Riders to follow me."

"They know I have the pin and the baby, Antoni. Why would they follow you?"

"We must decide now. What would you have me do? I will fight them, but there are too many. I can detain them for only a few moments."

The holy man spoke. Antoni didn't understand a word of what he said, but it had the ring of a friendly greeting.

Nortia looked at Antoni. As she closed her eyes, tears leaked out. She looked down tenderly at the babe in her arms. "We must leave her with the holy man. I will take the bundle of blankets, folded to look as if I'm still carrying her. Then they will follow us. I won't let my child die. When we have eluded them, we can come back for my baby."

Antoni felt a pang in his chest when he realized that he couldn't protect the woman he loved so dearly. He would gladly die a hundred times for her, but they were out of time and choices. Nortia's solution, in one of her rare moments of clarity, was perfect. He didn't have the heart to tell her that they both would almost certainly die—but at least they could save the baby.

Nortia walked up to the holy man, took the baby out of all the blankets except one, and handed her to him.

He looked confused, but took the child into his arms. Antoni saw comprehension dawn in his eyes, and the holy man shook his head. He tried to hand the child back, pushing the bundle back toward Nortia.

Nortia looked pleadingly up into his eyes, "Please, holy man, save my child. Run and hide her. You are our only hope. Please, I beg you."

Something crashed just outside the doors, and there was the sound of many hooves on marble. Antoni drew his sword.

The holy man stood there, mouth open, holding the child out and away from his body. He looked at Antoni's sword, and Antoni motioned for him to run away. There were deafening crashing sounds outside the entrance of the church.

The holy man pulled the child close to his body, looking around wildly.

"Come, Nortia, we must run now, or all will be for naught!" Antoni shouted, tugging at her arm.

"Wait." Nortia pulled free of his grasp and approached the frightened holy man. She leaned in and pressed her cheek to the baby's cheek. "I love you, my little girl. I love you more than life."

The holy man pushed the bundle toward her, but she only pushed the baby back, turning her tear-soaked face toward him. "Thank you…thank you." She kissed his hand and pointed to the baby. "Her name is Lydia."

The uproar outside the doors grew louder. Antoni grabbed Nortia by the hand, and gestured the holy man away with his sword. The holy man stumbled backwards, looked toward the noise, then ran with the baby to a side wall. Antoni watched him disappear through a door hidden behind a lattice panel.

They had a small chance, and he would make the best of it. He ran toward the back of the temple, Nortia in tow, frantically looking for a way out. He heard the doors boom as they smashed open. The sound reverberated off the walls of the temple. Then there was the clatter of hooves on the marble floor.

He couldn't believe it. The Riders were taking their mounts right through the temple. *This might just buy us some extra time*, he thought, thrusting open a small door. Sunlight hit his face. The Riders would never fit through the opening. They would have to turn their mounts around, go back out the temple's front entrance, then come around back.

Antoni forced Nortia along. "Try to run faster—we must hide. If we don't keep ahead of them, they will catch us."

She wasn't even trying to keep up. "I don't care!" Nortia screamed hysterically. "I have nothing left to live for now!"

"Do you want them to know we tricked them?" Antoni asked. "We must get as far away as possible, then try to hide. They will think the magnet has made us travel through time. Nortia, it's Lydia's only chance—and ours." He pulled her with a sharp jerk to make her listen.

Nortia began to run in earnest now.

Antoni realized that they hadn't fallen into this plan by chance. It must have been Hemisatres's influence on Nortia—and with any luck, it just might work.

He had no idea where to run. They just needed distance between themselves and the Reunity Riders. As they ran, he tried not to make too many turns, as he had to remember how to get back to the temple to get Lydia.

The sound of hoofbeats behind him made his heart lurch. They weren't going to make it. He could hardly breathe anymore because of all the running they'd done. Suddenly, Nortia planted her feet, pulling him to a stop.

"Don't stop now, Nortia! Please run!" He yanked her hard.

She stumbled but held her ground.

Antoni turned. For the second time in one day, he looked into the enraged eyes of the Rider's leader. They'd lost the fight, and they would now be cut down and killed. With only moments to live, bile rose into his mouth, and dread closed his throat. He tasted the bitterness of failure.

The Riders bore down upon them, their horses flanking out from either side of their she-demon leader. He pulled at Nortia's arm, a hopeless endeavor. She was immovable, and he didn't have time to carry her. Frantic, he moved her out of the way of the death that now bore down on them.

Nortia still clutched the blankets, and her hair floated in the air. "Antoni, the pin is burning me." She reached her hand up to it, and turned toward him. Her eyes were wide and desolate. She looked so anguished that it stayed his frenzied efforts to move her.

"My baby," she whispered. "I've lost my baby!"

Antoni's ears rang with Vanth's enraged scream.

Chapter 21

1717 AD

Liverpool, England

Two souls lost in time, bound only to each other.

Antoni awoke before Nortia. Eyes still closed, he smelled a familiar heavy marine scent. The cool air was so humid, it seemed thick. He was home again, at the villa in Populonia. It had all just been a horrible dream. His arms were around Nortia, and her scent was delicate and feminine. A gentle breeze carried the intoxicating smell of her skin up to his nose.

Breathing in deeply, he opened his eyes. Nothing looked familiar except for Nortia. In his stupor, he thought about how accustomed he was getting to waking up and not knowing where he was. He waited, knowing his head would begin to pound, and grim reality would descend once again.

Nortia lay there, clutching the empty bundle of baby blankets. Her eyes were closed, and her face was stained with tears.

Instantly, it all came back to him. They'd left Lydia in another time. It hadn't been their fault. It was either that, or they would have all been dead.

Antoni shook Nortia. They had to get moving. These days, they were always running—and he was so tired.

Nortia's eyes opened, focused on him, then closed again. Perhaps she needed one more moment to herself before facing the agony of having lost her child. Placing Nortia to the side, he stood up. He'd had better days; two time jumps in one day did not exactly put him in the best of moods. In addition to his head pounding, his stomach felt ill, and his bad leg throbbed.

He wouldn't have thought it possible to get even slightly used to time jumping and treat it so casually. Well, he wasn't really used to it—he just had no control over when they jumped. That was the doing of their half of the magnet in Nortia's pin. It had protected them so far. Except for Lydia.

Why had he ever agreed to leave the baby with the holy man? What had they done? They thought their decision would save the baby from imminent death, but now, Nortia might not be able to live with that choice. He would encourage her to make the best of it and try to survive—that much he knew. He was her bodyguard and lived to ensure her survival. It was why he existed.

At least they still had the magnet, Hemisatres. They would just go back for Lydia. Looking around, he saw that they were under a tree, on a large hill. Past the hill, he could see the ocean. His view of what was below the hill was cut off by the incline.

He shook Nortia again and lifted her to her feet. He needed to get a better idea of where they were. Staying in the open this way wasn't safe. What if the dark riders came? They must find cover.

He pulled the groggy Nortia along with him to the edge of the rise. The sight below took his breath away.

Huge wooden ships with giant masts and white sails floated by in the water, their flags fluttering in the wind. Most were making their way either toward or away from a narrow opening which was secured by great wooden gates. The massive gates opened to a vast, water-filled holding area for the docked ships. It created a large bay and a safe harbor for dozens of boats, big and small.

On the brick-lined shore, men teemed around the ships, pulling ropes and carrying things on and off the vessels. Horse-drawn carts, as well as hundreds of people and animals, created a noise and smell that left Antoni speechless. The backdrop of the dock came into focus next. It was a thriving city, crowded competitively around the waterfront with impressive, tall buildings with long streaks of smoke that stretched toward the sky.

Antoni stood there, mouth agape, taking in the sights.

"My baby," Nortia said, barely looking at the foreign landscape. "Oh, Antoni, we are in another time, and my baby is back at the temple. We must go back for her."

"Yes, we will try to go back," he said, giving her a reassuring squeeze.

A hopeful smile appeared as she touched the pin on her chest. "The magnet is warm—it's going to work. Hold me tightly." Nortia beamed with joy.

The wind picked up, and the sun hid behind the clouds. Antoni closed his eyes, preparing himself for the gut-wrenching upward surge the time jump would wreak.

Nothing happened.

Antoni stared at the pin.

Nortia also looked down at it. It shook and strained upward on her tunic, then ripped from the front of the garment, flying straight up into the air.

"*No!*" Nortia screamed, clawing the air. "It's gone! Why is this happening? I'll *never* get back to my child," she sobbed.

Antoni felt like sobbing himself. This day had been nightmarish beyond all imagination.

Chapter 22

May 1481 AD

Firenze

Time wasted need not be spent.

Charontes walked back into the house. So unused to feelings, he hadn't recognized the ones Aidyl had stirred within him. He hated Vanth. She'd taken his child. Now it was too late. They'd launched into time with his helpless baby, who was completely vulnerable to that creature's vileness.

He entered the house, and stark reality hit him. The warm, pungent smell of blood assaulted his nostrils.

The servant girl, crying in earnest, tended to Nortia's mother. As soon as she saw him, she scurried behind a chair.

"I won't hurt you," he said, knowing she couldn't understand him. She'd seen him trying to save the old woman, but he couldn't blame her for being afraid. She'd get over it. He didn't care about a servant girl, anyway.

The body of the other woman needed to be removed—he couldn't leave it in the house. He stooped to pick it up, and the girl came at him yelling and waving her arms.

Her audacity was unbelievable, but commendably brave. He briefly thought about just killing her, but he didn't have the stomach for murdering a woman.

The girl positioned herself between the two women's bodies, one arm over each. Uninterested in dealing with girlish outbursts, he decided to wait on taking the body. Instead, he would look around the farm, and make sure everything was secure. If sufficient time passed, the girl might calm down.

He stepped out the front door and checked each side of the house. Circling around to the back, he saw a small, wooden stable, about ten yards behind the main house. In the distance, geese and ducks slipped in and out of a small pond.

He followed a narrow path that led to the stables. Inside, there was a cow, a few goats, and a horse that looked like it had seen better days. Everything looked secure, so he decided to put his horse up in the stable. He led his horse in and began unsaddling it, rubbing it down with handfuls of straw.

The horse lashed out at him twice, in fast succession. He easily dodged the kicks, then chuckled. Mean to the core, his mighty equine's temperament clashed with the quiet serenity of the barn. The stallion snapped viciously at a curious goat that got too close, and Charontes grabbed his head, just in time. He'd put him in the empty stall. It looked sturdy enough to keep him out of trouble.

As he led the horse to the stall, he saw a young man of around twenty, tied up and gagged, lying on the straw. At least now he had a solution for getting rid of the old woman's body. Unarmed and obviously not a warrior, the young man posed no threat. He took off the trembling boy's gag and untied him.

Aware that he may not understand what he said, Charontes pointed toward the house and told him to get rid of the woman's body. Surprisingly, the young man did as he was told, stumbling off in the direction Charontes had indicated. After putting his horse in the stall, he reluctantly made his way back to the house, as well.

When he stepped into the main room, he became furious with Vanth all over again. The servant girl was sobbing loudly in the young man's arms. He gave Charontes an incredulous look, as if he couldn't believe he would kill a defenseless old woman.

The girl saw the look, then shook her head and went into what sounded like an emotional explanation of what had transpired. Charontes didn't understand a word of it, but he didn't care—he knew that the youth wouldn't dare challenge him. Anger seethed through him. If anyone thought he owed them excuses for Vanth's heinous behavior, they were sorely mistaken.

He'd had his fill of womanly tears for one day, and still fumed about Vanth taking his child. *How dare she*. That was one woman he *would* be able to kill. Caring about someone else made him tread through unexplored territory, which was loaded down with responsibility and made him feel vulnerable. Hopefully, that part would go away soon.

The thought of Vanth hurting Aidyl fueled an inner rage that pulsed just below the surface of his skin. He had to find them. He *would* find them. What time had they gone to?

He didn't know how he could find out, unless the old woman knew. He would question her, if she was strong enough. He wondered where he had arrived in time. Not that it really mattered—he'd always be a warrior, in any time period.

First things first—the body. He motioned to the young man by pointing to the dead woman and making a sweeping movement toward the door.

The young man talked with the girl, then made an exaggerated nod to him to show he understood. The youth bent down and picked up the body. The girl cried and fussed at his side as he carried it outside.

Charontes didn't like to see that. He could tell they both cared deeply for the old woman. Was she their mother? The woman seemed a bit old to be their mother, and the two of them hadn't really been acting like brother and sister when he'd walked into the house. He couldn't worry much about it. He had to keep a close watch on the only link to his daughter—Nortia's mother. If Nortia came back for her mother, Vanth would follow. Wherever Vanth was, hopefully, his child would be, too.

It wasn't exactly a plan, but it was all he had at the moment. His stomach rumbled.

~~~

Three boring days passed. The old woman woke the day after her injury, too weak to rise. Blood stained through her bandages every four or five hours, and the girl dutifully changed them.

Charontes tried to question the stubborn old woman, but she refused to answer. He wasn't sure if she understood him, but she looked at him as if she could see into his soul. This made him feel extremely uncomfortable. Surprisingly, however, her eyes held no malice toward him and were as deep as a bottomless lake. They held his gaze and made him feel that they could see more than most people could. He wanted to tell her about his child being the other chosen child, and to explain why he asked her so many questions, but he couldn't—he didn't speak her language. Eventually, he gave up and left her alone.

On the morning of the fourth day, Nortia's mother grew hot from the poisons in the wound. Since she was already so weak, Charontes thought she might die. As he watched the girl changing a bandage on her arm, the old woman opened her eyes and looked at him.

It startled him that she had the energy to open her eyes. She wore the strangest look, like she knew something he didn't or was holding some kind of a secret. The back of his neck prickled, and he had to look away. Those piercing eyes were able to frighten a warrior.

He tried to shake the feeling that she was saving her energy for something. *Is she waiting?* He shrugged it off. Of course she was. She probably just wanted to escape. He would also want that if he were lying there in her stead.

When night fell, the old woman began to shake and moan, heat pouring from her tiny body. At that moment, Charontes knew she would die. He didn't like to see her suffer, but he had to watch her closely, as she was the last connection to his daughter. He sat alone in a chair at the edge of the room.

The servant girl, who had been diligently trying to cool the old woman with damp cloths all evening, had finally dozed off in a chair beside the pallet.

Unable to relax his vigilance, he grew tired from a lack of sleep, and his eyes burned. As he rubbed them, he thought for a moment that the old woman had smiled at him. He rubbed his eyes again.

She *was* smiling—and her silver hair began to float off the pallet.

By the time he saw the glimmer of gold in her right hand, it was too late. He'd been tricked. As she disappeared, he heard her say a single word.

"Lydia."

He leaped for her. "No!" Enraged that he had been deceived a second time by the stones, he landed with a crashing thud on the empty, blood-spattered pallet.

The young girl, awakened by all the noise, stared down at him on the empty pallet with a look of terror. Then she let loose an ungodly, high-pitched shriek as she ran through the kitchen.

Charontes heard the back door slam, and the sound of her small feet running toward the stable. He cursed loudly. The old woman had known—he'd seen it in her eyes. She'd known all along that the stone would come back for her.

Chapter 23

September 2016 AD

Buffalo, New York

Drift freely for all time.

Ati felt strong arms lift her up, people shouting, then a loud wailing sound. She drifted back off into a dream world.

When she opened her eyes again, she looked straight into eyes identical to hers. Violet specks flickered in their brown depths. She knew then that she'd made it. Her vision had been true, and her part of the story was now over. She'd brought their half of the magnet to Lydia.

There *was* always time. Patrizia had been right. She smiled into the beautiful eyes of her granddaughter and felt herself rise from her battered body. At last, she was free from the pain.

Chapter 24

July 1481 AD

Firenze

To everything – turn, turn, turn

There is a season – turn, turn, turn

And a time for every purpose under heaven.

—The Byrds (from Ecclesiastes 3)

My eyelids hurt. I blinked a couple times just to reassure myself that I was still alive. *Ouch. My body hurts so bad.* What had I done to deserve this retribution from God? *Hang on—where am I?* I felt around—touching what I could with my fingers, then tentatively opened my eyes.

I rubbed my hand along something hard, but silky-soft at the same time. My eyes focused on it. He was beautiful, and his arm felt heavenly. That was it—I must be in heaven. There could be no other explanation.

A man was sleeping by my side, his head lying on my arm. I touched his hair, and it was feather-soft, like it belonged to Adonis or some other Greek god. It was dark brown and shiny, and it flowed gracefully down the back of his neck. *He must be very tired*, I thought, *he's sleeping so soundly*. His skin had a healthy sheen, bronzed from the outdoors, and he was huge.

Who was this man? I could see the definition of his muscles, toned and taut under his shirt, even as he slept. He looked like the Hulk, except that his niceness hadn't shrunk him down yet. *The Hulk? Hmm.* Something nibbled at my memory.

Should I poke him?

Where am I? Why does every part of my body hurt? Maybe I could just sleep a little longer.

He radiated warmth. If I could touch him and snuggle up to him a bit, I would be able to sleep better. I tried to scoot closer to him, twisting my upper body in his direction.

He stirred. His arms were up on either side of where I lay, bent at the elbow. *What a gorgeous armband. It must have cost a fortune.* It looked like solid gold. *What a gorgeous everything,* I thought. *Well, what I can see of him, anyway.* Although he was nice, my head would probably explode from pain long before he ever woke up.

Although I tried to fully open my eyes, I could only manage to open them into little slits. I couldn't remember where I was or what happened. I was disoriented, like when you wake up from a nap and don't know if it's day or night.

My arms would barely move, but I could close my fists. With a lot of effort, I managed to lift my arms up the smallest bit. That reassured me that I must still be alive. There was no harp music in the air, and I could move. I tried my legs next, but only the right one responded. I looked down at the thin cover over me.

He was a handsome man and all, but why couldn't I move my leg? I tried to feel my leg with my fingers, but it felt numb. A little at a time, I pulled the sheet off and tried to move my leg again, straining with effort. Finally, I managed to turn my left leg to the side. Pain shot up the length of it, confirming it was still attached. My vision swam for a moment and a wave of nausea hit me. I swallowed and breathed in deeply, then looked down at my leg. Cloth bandages and sticks were wrapped around it, holding it in place. It was a rudimentary splint around what appeared to be a badly broken leg.

I closed my eyes and opened them wide again—then reality slammed into me like a bus. *That man next to me is the one who had chased me.*

I should run, I thought. *He kidnapped me. Held me against my will.* I needed help.

So why is he sleeping?

My head hurt, and I couldn't bear to stay awake. I squeezed my eyes shut since the daylight was hurting them. *If I could just move to the side and get him off my arm*, I thought. His touch repulsed me. My leg ached and tiny lights danced underneath my eyelids. I swallowed. My throat burned, and thirst overwhelmed me.

Why wouldn't anyone help? Was there no one?

Maybe if I sleep for one more minute, someone will come and save me.

~~~

Charontes felt her stir. He rose, took a wet cloth, and wrung it out. Using two big fingers under the cloth, he wiped Lydia's face. The cool cloth startled her, and her eyes flew open. She looked at him, her eyes crossed a bit, then her eyelids slowly lowered.

"What's your name?" she whispered in a strange Greek dialect.

"Charontes."

"Does that mean something special in Cro-Magnon?" She yawned wide and long.

She's talking nonsense, he thought. *Clearly, she is still suffering the after effects of the wound poison.* "Rest and close your eyes," he said.

Her eyelids fluttered for a moment, as if she fought his suggestion. Then she slept.

As he covered her legs, he felt a twinge of happiness, realizing that she was going to live. He struggled to convince himself that the only reason he felt relieved was because she knew the secrets of the stone. Hope surged within him that she would be able to help him. He didn't know how she fit into everything, but if she used the stone once, she could use it again. After she had healed some, he would ask her about it.

Suddenly he realized that her injury was partially his fault, since he'd taken too long to decide what to do. If he had asked her for help as soon as he found her, maybe she wouldn't have run away and hurt herself. He hated seeing her like this. For now, though, his questions would have to wait.

Why had he not recognized Vanth's treachery sooner? He was angry with himself and needed some time to think everything over. Ideals he'd believed in for so long now seemed tainted and tarnished, and it had taken a while for him to sort through it all. His life had been so uncomplicated before—but he wasn't that man any longer.

When he saw the pin in Nortia's mother's hand, he was furious. Although he tried to stop her, he had been unable to do so. *Where did she go?* Five weeks had passed since she'd tricked him. Then Lydia had shown up with the very same pin in her hand.

He couldn't figure it all out. Vanth had said each half of the stone protected its own chosen child. So why had the stone returned *without* Nortia's child to a place he was guarding? It didn't make sense. *Where are Nortia and the child? Where is Vanth?* He sighed with worry. *Where is my child?*

Vanth would still have Aidyl's half of the stone with her. His head hurt from trying to figure out who was where and why Lydia was here. However, there was one thing he did know for certain: Vanth wouldn't quit searching until she had both halves of the stone—or had died trying.

He stopped himself short of wishing Vanth a terrible death, only because it would leave his daughter unprotected. Once he had Aidyl, he'd happily watch Vanth die on the end of his sword.

He'd devoted his whole life to the Riders of the Reunity, as had generations of his forefathers before him. But he couldn't be sure of the Reunity's causes anymore. The thought of them being strengthened to near invincibility when the stones were united terrified him. Vanth was already maniacally corrupted, and she didn't even have both halves of the stone yet. Just thinking about the mayhem she would create if the power to ride the four quarters of the sky were hers alone made him shudder. If she controlled the joined halves of the stone and was able to choose what times she went to, the shrew would distort all history.

If Aidyl was the only one who could use the stone's power, Vanth would make her life a living misery. She would turn his child into something evil. Aidyl would be merely her pawn.

Charontes couldn't let that happen. He'd been given a second chance to right the wrong he'd helped create. If he had to destroy the stones, he would—anything to make his daughter safe again.

Vanth would be back. She would have to—he possessed the other half of the stone. He stroked Lydia's hair. It was a simple plan, but still only a plan. As a warrior, he knew all about strategy. Simple plans were often successful precisely *because* of their simplicity. Uncomplicated plans were quick to execute and left little room for error. The opponent could easily be caught unaware.

"Oh, she'll be back, and she'll bring my daughter with her," he whispered into Lydia's ear. "It will be perfect—by then, you and I will be friends." She was well beyond hearing him, but it still felt good to talk to her. "We'll be friends, my beautiful one—and when Vanth comes back, it will be *our* turn to do the deceiving."

The servant girl came down the stairs and gave him a timid greeting. She felt Lydia's head, nodded, and even smiled. The girl looked relieved and rested, so he would leave her to care for Lydia. Right now, he needed to check on the stone.

He walked out toward the stables while the early morning air was still cool. By afternoon, it would be unbearable. The only respite at those times was a prevalent breeze, which he greatly appreciated. The squealing of his horse echoed from the stable.

When he entered the barn, he saw the young man trying to throw straw into his horse's stall. Ears back, the beast lunged and snapped menacingly at the man. He motioned for him to hand over the straw and then leave.

Charontes watched him walk out, shaking straw out of his curly black hair.

He approached the stall, easily dodging the snapping white teeth. Throwing the straw into the stall, he grabbed the distracted stallion's head, gripping onto the leather halter straps. The horse tried to back away into the stall, but Charontes effortlessly held him in place.

Once the animal calmed down, he reached up to an inconspicuous narrow tube attached to the top of the halter, the same black color as his horse's coat. It lay hidden under the thick locks of its mane.

For years, it was his hiding place for small, valuable items he didn't want to have stolen. No one had ever discovered it. He pushed aside the bushy tangle of hair, opened the tube, and pulled out the pin.

Charontes turned the pin over in his hand, inspecting it. It was just one little stone, half of a whole. It wasn't even pretty. *All the trouble it's caused,* he thought. How many people had died, and how many more would cease to exist because of it? Was the stone itself evil? Or just the people who possessed it?

His horse snorted, and a hefty amount of horse snot splattered over the lower half of him. Cursing the horse, he put the pin back into the tube and secured it. The pin would stay safely hidden from sight under all the hair. His horse wouldn't let anyone, except himself, get near it.

The morning heat neared its zenith. *A swim at the pond would be perfect.* Especially considering the mess his horse had made of him. He was a good swimmer, unlike some of the other Riders, and he liked to keep his body washed. Bathing rejuvenated him, and his body and mind benefitted from being cleansed of the sweat from toil or battle. It also smelled a lot nicer.

Behind the stables and past the small duck pond, Charontes followed a narrow trail made by deer which cut through the surrounding brush. As he walked to the larger, hidden pond, he remembered how he had first come upon it one day during a hunting excursion. Since the farmhouse managed to be surprisingly self-sufficient due to the bounty from the gardens, he'd only needed to hunt for fresh game a few times since he'd arrived. During one of these hunting excursions, he'd stumbled onto the lovely pond, deep in the woods—and it had instantly become a favorite spot.

He plunged deeper into the woods, until the trees opened into a natural clearing. A fairly good-sized pond appeared before him, sheltered on three sides by tall trees that bent lazily over the water. Branch tips tickled the surface in some spots, their shelter making the pond enchanting and private. A small, gradually sloping beach on one edge which was not blocked by trees made a perfect place to ease himself into the water.

Opposite the beach, between two enormous trees, a deliciously cold stream flowed into the pond, forming a waterfall. The water cascaded over a mound of huge stones then dropped off sharply into the pond. Scattered here and there on the shore and in the shallows were large, flat rocks which now basked in the late morning sun.

He stripped off his clothes and dove into the refreshingly cold water. He'd wash his clothes out after his swim and let them dry on the rocks. Floating on his back, he watched a dragonfly buzz and dart about, skipping across the water. Its wings reflected the sun like green jewels.

Failing to clear his mind, thoughts of Lydia kept creeping into his head. *What a fair face*, he thought, remembering the way her brown hair curled into tight circles that spiraled down from her head. He loved the brave, intelligent set of her chin and those eyes—a man could get lost in them.

He remembered his mouth on hers—it had felt so right. He stopped his thoughts there, stood up, and splashed his face with the soft, cool water. What possessed him to act like a lovestruck boy? It must be because he hadn't lain with a woman in so long. As hard as he tried, he couldn't shake off the feeling. His unquenchable need for this woman coiled up inside him, as well as a longing for her to want him, too.

It didn't matter—she hated him. *Being her captor would prove to be a huge obstacle to befriending and earning her trust*, he thought with a half-smile. He'd never had a friend, and he really didn't have any idea where to start. Maybe when she woke up, he would try talking to her, explaining why he was holding her there. At least they seemed to understand each other's language.

After explaining things to her, maybe she would grow to trust him. How much time did he have before Vanth returned in search of the other half of the stone? Gliding out of the water, he stood there dripping as the sun warmed his bare skin. Hopefully there would be enough time to gain Lydia's trust—his daughter's life depended on it.

Chapter 25

July 1481 AD

Firenze

Time has a way of granting wishes.

I opened my eyes to find myself lying flat on my back. The sunlight from an uncovered window made me squint. I lifted a leaden arm to cover my eyes. Groaning, I tried to roll onto my side—but pain shot up my left leg and straight into my brain. "Ow, what's wrong with my leg?" I said aloud. "It's killing me."

A blurry form swam around in my line of sight. My eyes uncrossed and the angelic form of Amelia began to take shape. I smiled. "Hi, Amelia. How are you and why does my leg hurt so damned bad?"

"I don't understand what you're saying," she answered. "Speak Italian, please." Her soft brown curls hid the side of her face as she leaned forward to smooth my cover.

Okay, once again, but in Italian, I thought. "Why does my leg hurt so damned bad?" I said in her language. I noticed a slur when I talked.

Amelia giggled.

"I just woke up. What do you expect—perfection?"

"No…no, my lady, I'm sorry. I shouldn't be laughing—it isn't funny at all. You have broken your leg quite badly. The bone came through the skin, and you had a fever. You're talking funny because the medicine for pain I've been giving you makes people say and do funny things."

"I broke my leg." Alarmed, I tried to sit up and pain surged through my leg again.

"No, please lay back." Amelia put a gentle hand on my shoulder. "It was only yesterday that the fever left you. You must rest and be at ease."

I lay back, not in compliance, but because my head was spinning and I felt too weak to sit up. "I'm very thirsty. Can I please have something to drink?"

"Of course. Right away, my lady." Amelia helped me sit back up a bit and held a metal cup to my mouth.

I gulped down three or four mouthfuls then lay back down, exhausted. "It hurts for me to think. Will you tell me what's happened?"

"I don't wish to frighten you, my lady."

"Too late—I'm already frightened and apparently hideously injured. So please, tell me what's happened."

"You ran away from this house twice. The second time, I think, you went into the city. When Sir brought you back, you were injured. Your leg was broken, and you had hit your head."

Again, no wonder my head hurt so badly. I closed my eyes, and it all came rushing back to me. I'd been kidnapped from a hospital by some huge, muscle-bound lunatic and somehow magically time traveled to 1481 Florence. Yep, those were pretty much the basics.

I remembered running through narrow streets of the city, and the men attacking me. "Three men attacked me," I said, still half dazed.

"I wondered how you'd broken your leg," Amelia said. "Sir was very angry when he went after you, but he's never hurt any of us. That explains it. You were attacked, and he must have rescued you," Amelia added, looking pleased with herself.

"*Rescued* me? How do you rescue your own prisoner? Is that like some new rule in the kidnapper code of ethics?"

"Begging your pardon, my lady, but I don't quite understand what you are saying all the time."

"Don't worry, neither do I." I took a deep breath and closed my eyes.

Amelia giggled.

"I'm tired—haven't I slept at all?"

"You've been with the fever for seven days."

I couldn't believe it. My whole world turned upside down. A burning lump rose in my throat, and I held back tears. My leg began to throb in earnest now. I'd lost seven whole days of my life. *What am I thinking?* I thought, stifling a bitter laugh. It was 1481, and I wasn't even born yet. I had all the time in the world.

"You know, Sir has been very worried about you," Amelia said. "I think he likes you. He has even taken care of you when I've tried to sleep."

"Please don't leave me alone with him," I said. I felt panicked and tears began to roll down my cheeks. "He's a bad man."

"Here—have some more water to drink and a little medicine. You must be in a lot of pain. Rest now so that you can get better." Amelia put the water cup to my lips again.

"You must promise me that you won't leave me alone with him," I begged between sips, becoming increasingly more agitated and loud. The memory of him kissing me went through my head. I'd loved it. He kissed me twice and said I was beautiful. What really worried me was that I loved it a little *too* much. *Well, he did call me "beautiful,"* I thought.

What would happen if I was alone with him for more than 6.2 minutes? Would I be married to him? What kind of floozy hostage throws herself into her captor's arms? Not *just* my captor, either—he was my re-captor and re-re-captor. He'd definitely established his intent.

I had to keep away from him—he was just too handsome. He had some kind of inner strength that drew me to him—and outer strength, for that matter.

That's it. I have that psychosis where you fall in love with your abductor. The medicine blurred my memory, making it hard to recall such details. *What is it called again? Oh, I know—Hostage Abductor Nymphomania Disorder Syndrome, more commonly referred to in psychiatric journals as H.A.N.D.S.* The final verdict was in, I was definitely losing it.

"Drink some of the medicine and then we will talk about it," Amelia said.

I took a big gulp of the bitter medicine. I recognized the flavor—it tasted like the paregoric my mom used to give me when I was little and had the stomach flu. That made sense. I thought they had opium in 1481, but I wasn't sure. *Have I confused it with laudanum?*

My brain started to fuzz, and the pain in my leg lessened considerably. *There are lots of poppies in Italy,* I thought with a giggle. *Fields of poppies, just like in* The Wizard of Oz.

Toto, we're definitely not in Kansas anymore.

I looked up at Amelia. She looked worn out, and dark circles ringed her eyes. Caring for me this whole time had taken its toll on her. Suddenly, I felt very selfish.

"Amelia, thank you for taking care of me. I don't know what I would have done without you. I owe you my life."

"You are welcome—but Sir came almost every night and cared for you so I could sleep."

"Yeah, but he's my *kidnapper*. The bad guy, you know? It's not like I can tell *him* 'thank you.'" My tongue tripped badly on the Italian word for "thank you," and it came out sounding a lot like "grizzly."

"But he did save you in the city, and I've seen him do other things that were good," Amelia said, defending him. "I don't speak his language, so I can't talk to him. My mistress, Patrizia, told me about a few things that were going to happen. I wish I had listened to her more closely. I just always thought she would be here with me. I think she tried to get me ready for something. She always told me that I would know 'when the time was right.'"

I didn't have the energy to say anything to comfort Amelia. My eyes refused to cooperate, and I couldn't keep them open.

~~~

"You're awake again—twice in the same day. That's good." Amelia greeted me with a sip of water and a brilliant smile.

I noticed that my eyes didn't hurt so much. The softer candlelight was much easier on my eyes than the sunlight. Amelia struggled to prop me up in bed, then rolled up blankets behind my back.

I tried my best to help her, but the position hurt my leg. I wanted to sit up for a while, so I gritted my teeth and didn't tell her how badly it hurt. "Is it the same day then?" I asked, trying not to wince.

"Yes, my lady. It's the same day."

"Good. I'm afraid to fall asleep and then wake up ten days from now."

I wasn't making complete sense, but Amelia laughed, anyway. The sound of her laughter perked my spirits up.

"Do you think you could eat a little bread dipped in broth?" Amelia asked. "You're getting so thin, and I need to fatten you up a little."

"I would love some."

My stomach picked that very moment to make a loud rumbling sound, and the noise made both of us laugh.

Amelia disappeared into the kitchen for a couple of minutes, then came out with big hunks of bread and some steaming broth. She put them in front of me and patiently broke off some small pieces of the bread. My hand shook when I picked up a piece of bread and dipped it into the rich broth. It smelled heavenly. I chewed the delicious bread slowly, which was softened just enough by the fragrant broth. I ate with hardly any effort.

I managed three more bites before stopping. The pain in my leg reached an excruciating level, and I needed to change my position. "Amelia, the pain in my leg is becoming worse when I sit up. Could you help me move onto one side?"

"Sure, let me give you more medicine first. It has been hours since you've had any, and it has probably worn off." Amelia hurried to get the medicine.

I had a fleeting thought that I was becoming some kind of primitive drug addict—like the village dope head, or a Renaissance junkie. My leg really *did* hurt, though. I drank a couple mouthfuls of the medicine Amelia gave me, wondering how she measured the strength of it. After a few minutes, the drug's warm fingers started to relax me. I nodded to Amelia that I was ready.

Amelia, a tiny, little thing, tried with all her might to roll my uncooperative, drugged body onto its right side. Unhelpful, I just groaned, the pain preoccupying my world. A deep, low voice cut through my haze.

"Stop, let me help you," it rumbled in a deep bass.

At the sound of his voice, Amelia immediately stopped straining and froze where she stood.

I felt myself being lifted up and turned onto my side as if I weighed no more than a child. *What a relief to be off my back*, I thought. The pressure was almost completely off my broken leg.

Amelia rushed to and fro, bracing my leg up with the remaining blankets.

I looked up to see what cast such a large shadow over me. I had the feeling that I already knew. *Let's see—really huge, blots out the sun. Can lift people with the greatest of ease. Speaks some sort of ancient Greek that no one but me understands and dresses like a gladiator. Well, now...that makes it easy. It must be my kidnapper.*

I looked up into his eyes and felt my heart skip a beat. *He* must *be a criminal,* I thought. It had to be against quite a few laws to be that good-looking. I must have looked afraid, because he took one of my hands into his and got down on one knee in an absurd attempt to make himself seem smaller and less intimidating. It didn't work, and as soon as I could breathe again, I would tell him so.

"I won't hurt you, Lydia." His voice came out in a soothing growl, like a lion with a full belly.

My head swam from the effects of the medicine. I couldn't take my eyes away from his. They were so black, I could look at them forever—just trying to see where his irises ended and his pupils began. *Good family fun*, I thought, and a giggle slipped out.

The giant man looked bewildered and turned toward Amelia with a questioning look.

Amelia held up and wiggled the bottle of medicine while shrugging her shoulders.

Then something strange happened. He smiled. I could tell he didn't smile often, since there was a distinct lack of laugh lines on his face. His countenance garnered a fresh new look when the smile bloomed, and I just knew it was probably only the fifth time in his entire life he'd genuinely smiled. Worry and compassion shone in his bottomless eyes.

Then I heard Amelia leave, and I felt strangely safe being alone with him. *Surely it's the opium.*

He took a dampened cloth and wiped my forehead and cheeks, then dabbed it gently around my neck and shoulders. Flushed from the medicine, the house suddenly felt stifling, but the cool cloth relaxed me. A slight breeze came in and caressed over the parts he'd dampened, making the little hairs on my skin stand on end. It felt heavenly.

My arms and legs were leaden from the medicine, and I just lay there. I didn't want to move, anyway. If I stayed really still like this, I could barely feel any pain in my leg. Charontes took the cloth and smoothed it under my shirt and down over my left shoulder. He pulled up the back of my shirt and wiped slowly down the length of the tense muscles in my back.

My eyes were barely open, and the room spun just a little bit each time I closed them. *I wish I'd always known how truly great it is to be a hostage.* Taking a deep breath, I closed my eyes while a small, contented sigh escaped my lips.

He ran his fingers over my scalp and through my hair, over and over again. His touch was soothing and gentle, and it felt strangely familiar to me—he must have touched me like this during the last few days. My memory was too patchy to remember. I felt his warm breath in my ear, then his lips on my cheek and my forehead.

In a low voice, he whispered softly into my ear, "You are so beautiful, my Lydia. I try each night not to touch you, but I fail. Your skin is tender like the softest petals of a new flower. My hands are big, scarred, and unworthy of your beauty—and yet, I cannot still them.

"These lips are undeserving of your taste. They have shouted vile curses and cried out in battle, and now they refuse to obey my will. Your essence is slowly possessing me. I am your captor, yet you are the one who has imprisoned me."

I'd heard him, every single word—but I kept my eyes closed, afraid of what I might do. His words were like raindrops, hissing as they soaked into the dry, cracked ground—or the first bite of food, bursting with flavor and sustenance, after days without. I was ravenous for his words—and I was ravenous for *him*.

I hadn't always been starving for love. Growing up, I'd felt secure and loved—but ever since I left home, I knew what it was like to be lonely. The love of a man was different. There had been my fiancé, but I'd eventually realized he'd never really loved me. That time I'd spent with him seemed empty, like I'd never been with anyone at all.

It's wrong to feel this way, I chided myself. *I should be afraid of this man.*

The drug kept weighing me down—I wanted to get up and ask him questions, but I couldn't. He just kept running his feather-light fingers through my hair. Gently, he turned me onto my back. I felt his warm breath by my mouth, then his lips on mine.

He gently nipped the edge of my lip, then ran his tongue over it, soothing the spot he'd just nipped. Then his mouth softly covered mine. It made me want to kiss him back. He smelled like sunshine, leather, and straw—exactly how a man should smell.

I began to respond to his kisses, and my heart fluttered. *This must be wrong*, I thought. *But it feels so right.* I heard him moan with a deep rumbling in his throat as he moved his mouth over mine for a better position. *This has to be right.* My two years with Scott had never felt anything like this.

I was quickly losing control. Anything he asked for he would probably get. It felt like he knew it, too. I breathed faster, and Charontes began kissing down my chin and neck. Not just kissing, but with each kiss, the tip of his tongue touched my skin. He was tasting me, savoring the flavor of my skin—and it was driving me wild. Sensual and primal, he was completely natural in his movements as he enjoyed me. He breathed hard now, too—and a low, frustrated growl came out of his throat. I felt the growl vibrate onto my newly sensitized skin. Then he stopped.

I couldn't breathe and didn't want to open my eyes, but I had to find out why he'd stopped. He had a hand on each of my shoulders when I opened my eyes. Dark hair fell in waves just above his shoulders, and his eyes smoldered with longing. I studied the perfect, full lips that had been kissing my body just moments before. His arm muscles strained under his arm band. He was both erotically barbaric and entirely gorgeous.

I realized I was holding my breath and exhaled slowly. *How can a man look so brutish—yet be so gentle and speak so tenderly?*

"Lydia, you are beautiful, and I want you in every way a man could want a woman—but you are injured too badly. I don't ever want to hurt you. It is my solemn vow that I will *never* hurt you. You will be mine—you and I will someday be one. With every touch and every kiss, I feel it is our destiny. You have been brought here to me."

Wow, it must be nice to have everything all figured out, I thought. But I remained speechless, as I was still reeling from the medicine—and the kisses. Even if I did speak, my tongue would only betray me.

Then to make matters worse, he lifted me onto his lap, careful that my legs remained supported on the bed. Too weak to object, I laid my head against his chest.

"Rest, my beauty. Over the days, your strength will return, and I will be here for you. When you are stronger, we will talk. You will also see that our destinies are one, and your heart will learn to trust me. We *will* become as one, neither of us a prisoner any longer." He kissed the top of my head and settled back into the chair, still holding me.

His arms around me felt warm and secure, and I faded toward sleep. Deep in my heart, I wished it could be this simple—but I was Lydia from Buffalo. Girls like me don't meet barbarians that look like Greek gods. I was just a regular girl—boring, single, and a nurse at a hospital. Homesickness washed over me. I had to get home. I couldn't stay in 1481—this couldn't be *my* destiny.

~~~

Lydia belonged in his arms. Charontes didn't know what came over him when he kissed and touched her—he'd just known she had to be his. More than just for the taking. For *life*.

Everything he'd said to her he'd meant. Instead of being terrified with the realization, he felt strengthened and resolute. His life seemed so meaningless before he knew he had a daughter and before he met Lydia. He brushed a curl from Lydia's face and shut his eyes tightly. Had all those lonely and unfeeling years with the Riders been a waste?

For good or ill, they'd made him what he was today. He chose not to fear this transformation. Such a sudden change could only be because it was long overdue and meant to be. He'd never been an indecisive man, anyway.

Layers, years in the building, felt like they'd been suddenly shed. He'd spent all his life fighting the battles of others. Now, he'd fight his own. He'd make it all right again by stopping Vanth and getting Aidyl away from her. Something told him that Lydia was the key.

He gently stroked her face with one finger as a gentle breeze came in through the window. Putting his head back, he pulled Lydia closer and closed his eyes. She was his destiny—he was sure of it.

Chapter 26

July 1481 AD

Firenze

Rewarding is the time spent making friends.

"Lydia, wake up."

I could hear Amelia's voice, but I didn't want to open my eyes. Memories of last night drifted through my quasi-wakefulness—Charontes touching and kissing me, then whispering sweet nothings in my ear. Had he meant what he'd said? He didn't even know me. If my groggy calculations were right, I'd only been here eight or nine days. That certainly wasn't long enough to know that someone was your destiny, pledging yourself to them, as he'd done.

"My lady, wake up." Amelia sounded more insistent.

I opened my eyes and tried to smile at her. "You don't hate me, do you?"

"Hate you? Why would I?"

"I've given you such a hard time, running away and what not. You've also waited on me hand and foot for days."

Amelia cast her eyes downward and smiled. "Pardon me for saying so, but it doesn't look like you're going to be running away again. At least, not for a while."

I looked down at my leg, frowning, "Yeah, you've got that right."

"Is it hurting you much, my lady?"

"Please, Amelia…just call me Lydia. It makes me feel like I'm ninety years old when you say 'my lady.'"

"If that's what you'd like…Lydia." Amelia enunciated her name as if she were trying it out for the first time.

"And no, my leg actually feels okay today. A little stiff and sore, but I haven't moved it yet."

"I'll help you sit up for breakfast. If it pains you a great deal, I can give you more medicine."

"I would really like to try taking *less* medicine. I can't think straight after I've taken it."

As I looked up at her, her brown eyes twinkled and a knowing smile played on her lips.

"What?" I asked. "Why are you smiling like that?"

"Oh nothing...nothing at all." Amelia busied herself, straightening the light coverlet over my legs.

"Well, now you're going to have to tell me." I smiled, too. "You can't just say nothing and keep grinning like that."

"It's just...well, when I went to bed last night, I just wondered...did Sir take good care of you?"

I blushed furiously, instantly giving myself away. "What do you mean, 'take good care of me?'"

"He is very handsome and strong," she said. "He seems to really like you."

"He doesn't even *know* me!" My voice was two octaves higher than it should have been. "And if he cared so much, he wouldn't have kidnapped me, now would he?"

The more I thought about it, the more irritated I got. What right did he have to hold me here? And look what happened because of it—my leg got broken, and it was all his fault. What was it he'd said? 'I don't want to hurt you?' Well, too late. I was already hurt, and he couldn't take that back.

"And his name isn't Sir—it's Charontes," I said, trying not to take it out on Amelia. However, the earlier levity had vanished from my voice.

"Oh, he told you his name? He's been here for over a month, and he's never told *me* what it was. See…he *must* like you."

Amelia walked into the kitchen while she talked, and I took a moment to look around. I lay in a bed about the size of a double bed. It was pushed against the far wall of the living room, on the first floor. I could see the front door across the room and just off to the right. To my left was a cold hearth without a fire. A few chairs were set about, and rushes covered the wood-planked floor.

There were two chests, one on each side of a window that was large enough to let quite a bit of sunlight in. The window was adorned with metal bars, similar to the ones upstairs. The walls themselves held few decorations: a small but magnificent painting of a woman, a delicately crafted metal cross, and wall sconces made of metal and glass, one candle per sconce—each waiting patiently for nightfall.

Amelia set a dull silver plate which appeared to be made of pewter in front of me. She'd filled it with an assortment of fruit and cheese.

"He's still holding me against my will," I said, briefly wondering if I should confide in Amelia about being from a different time. I decided not to, realizing that it was too big of a bomb to drop on a person that you didn't know—and I really needed her as an ally. If I told her I came from five hundred years plus in the future, she wouldn't understand. She would think I was certifiable and not talk to me anymore—or worse, disregard everything I'd ever said as the rantings of a sick person. I couldn't deal with that kind of isolation right now.

Charontes owed me an explanation. I needed to talk to him right away and ask him about getting home. My family would be worried sick about me.

"Thank you for bringing me this meal," I said. "It's very kind of you to take such good care of me. I know you're just teasing me to make me feel less frightened and I appreciate it—but this has gone far past anything we can joke about. I have a lot of questions for Charontes and need to talk to him as soon as possible."

"I'm sorry, Lydia, I didn't mean to make light of your situation," Amelia said. "You're right—you should not be kept here against your will. It's just that over the last month and a half, I've had a lot of time to watch Sir and can see he is not the enemy. When he first came here, he terrified me—but that has changed. So will you talk to him then?"

"Yes, he has some explaining to do. Don't you think?"

"You are a brave woman," Amelia said. "You talk different than other women do and act much bolder. I wouldn't dream of displeasing Sir for fear of being beaten and cast from the house. You act as if you are his equal— some of the things you say and do remind me so much of my mistress." Amelia's eyes misted over, and she sat down beside my bed.

I pointed to the wall. "Is that a painting of your mistress?"

"Yes, that's her," Amelia said. "My mistress's friend painted that for her when he was a student of Verrocchio."

"Do you mean 'Leonardo da Vinci?'" I asked, my head about to explode.

"Yes. You know him, too? He's only visited once or twice since I started working here, but my mistress said he used to come often. They were friends."

"No, I don't know him," I sputtered. "Well, not personally. I've heard of him, though. He's quite famous, isn't he?"

She looked proudly at the painting. "Somewhat now. Years ago, my mistress commissioned him to paint that for her. It's lovely, isn't it? His painting is masterful."

I couldn't believe it. A real Leonardo da Vinci, hanging in the living room. He'd actually *been* there—in that house, in that room. *Incredible.* What had they talked about? *What would you talk to Leonardo da Vinci about, anyway? "Hey, Leo…how's the inventing coming along?"*

Amelia smiled as she noticed my appreciation of the painting.

"What happened to your mistress?" I asked. "Are you able to talk about it now? You were telling me about some evil woman." I needed to find out as much as I could, and Amelia seemed to be opening up.

"I do get sad when I talk about her—she was very good to Franco and me. I will tell you what I can, but I still don't know exactly what happened. Her name was Patrizia. She lived here at this house for many years. I grew up as an only child at a neighboring farm with my parents.

"About two years ago, I lost my mother and then my father, each dying within a month of the other. Patrizia had come to help when they were sick, but there wasn't anything anyone could do. They both died, anyway."

Amelia looked so young and helpless as she told her story. My heart ached for the girl's losses. To have so much grief in her short number of years was unthinkable.

I touched her arm, trying to be supportive. "I'm sorry your parents died," I said softly.

She looked at me, tears filling her big, brown eyes. "Thank you, Lydia. It's nice to talk to another woman. I've been lonely since my mistress died. I only have Franco to talk to, but it's never quite the same."

Amelia took a deep breath and went on. "When my parents died, Patrizia knew I wouldn't have a place to live any longer and offered to take me in. She said she could use the help around the house.

"I accepted, of course. I knew her to be a kind woman with knowledge of the healing arts. It was too good to be true for a girl in my circumstances—a room and a small wage in exchange for help around the house. She even promised to teach me healing methods so I would have a useful skill.

"True to her word, she gave me a wonderful place to live and taught me many things. I worked, but never too hard. Franco had already been here when I came to live. He helps in the gardens and manages the livestock. A year went by, and I grew to love Patrizia like a grandmother. Then things began to change.

"One day in the fall of last year, three strangers arrived. They came without forewarning, but my mistress welcomed them into her home. She even spoke their language. I didn't know she could speak in other languages, but she knew theirs. It sounded similar to Sir's. The three who came were a mother and daughter, Ati and Nortia, and their guard, Antoni." She paused, studying me. "You aren't too tired, are you, Lydia? Does your leg pain you?"

"No, no, go on, please. It's so nice to talk to you, and your story is fascinating." Eager to learn all that I could from her, I encouraged her to continue. But so far, nothing she'd said clicked into place.

Reassured, Amelia continued, telling me more about Nortia, Antoni, and Ati's arrival and extended stay there. She also gave a vague description of a later attack, after the arrival of Charontes, the dark woman, and the dark riders.

"Nortia was pregnant through all this?" I said. "Poor thing, she must have been terrified." Amelia's story was so riveting. Finally I was getting somewhere. I had a hundred questions—but I didn't know what part to focus on. I didn't want to scare her and stop her from talking.

Amelia blushed. "Yes, she was with child when they arrived at the farm, and the baby was born in April of this year. The new baby lifted all our spirits, since we were so distressed and downhearted over my mistress's sickness. She was an adorable baby girl. Funny, the baby's name was

Lydia…just like yours." Amelia smiled and seemed to be thinking of the little babe.

"Well, that explains it—*that's* why she was so adorable." I clowned, tipping my head a little to one side.

We both laughed, but Amelia didn't relax any. She was holding something back.

"What exactly happened that last day?" I asked. "Can you tell me in more detail?"

"I hope you won't mind, my la—I mean, Lydia, if I have a sip of your wine. My throat has grown dry, and my hands are shaking."

"No, of course. Whatever you'd like—and I'll have some too, please." I was sitting up in bed, but my leg ached enough that I wanted to fidget around and change positions. I fought to remain still. Too much movement might distract Amelia from answering my last question.

Amelia poured two cups of my watered-down breakfast wine and handed one to me. "That day, my mistress seemed agitated. From her sick bed in the room here, she talked to Ati for a while. I only remember it because she hadn't spoken much at all in the previous few weeks. I didn't even think she was well enough to talk for that long. Afterwards, Ati looked extremely upset. I became frightened and asked my mistress if all was well.

"She told me all would be fine and that I would know when the time was right. Then I was to share the things that she'd shown me, months earlier. I figured the medicine had affected her thinking, because over those last few weeks, she would always repeat the same thing: 'You will know when the time is right.'

"She kept saying that, but would never tell me how. How am I to know when the time is right? I still don't know what I'm supposed to do—only that I'm supposed to do *something*."

"That day…what happened on that day, Amelia? Maybe we can figure this out together." I had to keep her on track, as she was starting to unravel before my eyes. "Come on, take another sip of the wine and try to calm yourself. I'm sure you did everything that you could."

"That's what really pains me—I was helpless to do *anything*. I just watched. Watched while *she* stuck a sword through the mistress I loved." Amelia took another long sip of wine and leaned back in her chair. A single tear rolled down her cheek.

"She…she *who?*" I asked in a ghost-story-by-a-campfire kind of whisper.

"She led them all. Her hair was long and black, and she shrieked out orders to nearly a dozen, evil-looking men, all on huge black horses. Her eyes looked like the eyes of a devil."

The hair crawled on the back of my neck. The look of despair on Amelia's face as she relived that horrible day was painful to witness.

"Charontes was with them, too. I was inside the house by my mistress's side. I looked through that window," she pointed to the window, "to see what was happening. It all happened so fast—I still think my eyes deceived me. I will tell you, but you must promise not to think me mad."

"Believe me, I won't think you're mad," I reassured her. "Nothing you could tell me could seem any more outlandish than what I've seen in the last two weeks."

"From where I stood, it was difficult to see." Amelia looked down, as if deciding to go on, then looked right at me and started talking quickly, as if purging herself. "The evil woman charged Antoni and Nortia. She paid no regard to the babe in Nortia's arms. Ati jumped in front of the evil one's sword and was cruelly cut down. When I looked up, Nortia and Antoni were…*gone*. They were there one moment and then vanished the next.

"At first, I thought my mind had played a trick on me, but then the evil woman started yelling and shrieking. I knew then that Nortia and Antoni had somehow escaped her. Poor Ati, though—the evil woman tried to kill her, then and there, with a second blow—but Charontes stopped her sword. He carried Ati in and laid her down beside my mistress.

"I was terrified. Some of the men had come into the house during the attack and were grabbing me and hurting me. I just wanted to get to my mistress's side. Charontes stopped the men from hurting me. He protected me, I know that now. We would have all been dead that day if it hadn't been for him. That's how great the evil one's wrath is. Then she came into the house, and even brought her child with her."

"Who? The evil one?" I asked. "She had a child, too?"

"Yes, and two nursemaids, for all the good that did. The child cried loudly the whole time. Men were yelling, the baby wailed, and the evil one screamed at everyone. I kept trying to stop the blood that poured freely from Ati's arm.

"Then, before anyone could stop her, the evil one walked up to my mistress and put her sword through her heart. Just like that. She didn't have a care for her life at all. It meant nothing for her to end it."

"Oh, Amelia…that's *horrible*," I said. "I can't believe that all happened here. It must have been terrible for you. You said Charontes came with them, but he also tried to help all of you?"

"Yes. After that woman killed my mistress, he picked the evil one up, kicking and screaming, and carried her from the house. She cursed him and shouted for her riders, then all of them were gone…well, all of them but Sir.

"My poor mistress never took another breath." Amelia put her head into her hands. "They haven't been back since. If they do come back, I'll not stay here for another minute. Franco promised me he would take me away from here if they ever return."

"I think that would be a very smart idea, Amelia. If you two leave, I want to come with you."

Amelia gave me a pained look. "I will try to take you with us if they come back, but I can't promise that it will work. Franco and I grew up around here, and we both know places to hide—but it would be difficult to take you with your injury." Amelia kept her eyes down and didn't look at me.

"Of course, I didn't even think about that. I would slow you down too much. Don't worry about me then—I'll be fine. Besides, we don't even know if they *will* be back."

Who was I kidding? With the way the last two weeks had gone, I felt genuine surprise that the killers hadn't shown up already and lopped my head off—a couple of times.

She'd recounted an awful story. I couldn't believe Amelia still trusted anyone. Why did she stay at the same farmhouse where all those horrible things had happened? Then again, I'd seen firsthand how cruel this time period could be to a woman who was alone. Amelia hadn't been raised with the independent mindset of a twenty-first century girl, so how could I expect her behave like one?

"I hope you're right, Lydia. Maybe they won't be back. How is your leg? Is it paining you again?"

"Yeah, it's hurting me. Can you help me lie down on my side?"

"Yes. Would you like more medicine?"

"No, I'd like to see if I can just take it at nighttime." I hoped I could hold out until then—I wanted my head to be clear when I saw Charontes. *I must talk to him.* I refocused on Amelia. "Hey, Amelia, what happened to Ati? Did she die? I haven't seen her at all."

"No—well, I don't know for sure what happened to her," Amelia said hesitantly.

"What do you mean 'you don't know what happened to her?'"

"After she was injured, her arm wounds gave her a sickness. She became hot and lay still for days. I cared for her as best as I could, but it seemed hopeless. One night, I went upstairs to get some sleep while Sir was watching over her. I'd only been asleep for a couple of hours when I heard Sir downstairs, in a rage. I was afraid, but I had to see if Ati had remained unharmed. When I went downstairs, she was gone."

"Gone?" I asked. "Where?" The story kept getting stranger and Amelia looked really nervous to tell this part of it.

"I don't know…just *gone*. There wasn't any way she could have run away, because she was too weak. Sir had been sitting there watching her. That's all I know. I told you that you'd think I was crazy." Amelia had that jumpy look of someone who wasn't telling the truth.

"I don't think you're crazy," I assured her. "There was no one else in the house?"

"No. It was nighttime. I slept upstairs, and Franco slept outside. I should have been with her." She had a guilty look on her face.

I could tell she'd left something out, but I still felt sorry for her. "Don't think it's your fault. There must be an explanation for this—and I think I know exactly who to ask."

It all came back to Charontes. *He* knew what was happening. I had a sinking feeling that I had a pretty good idea how all these people were just *disappearing*. That meant that he must somehow be at the bottom of all this. I had to talk to him, so I hoped he was in a conversational mood when I next saw him.

"Here, Lydia—let me help you lie down now," Amelia said.

"Yes, let me help you," said a deep male voice out of nowhere.

Amelia jumped, but she said nothing.

How could he have walked in so quietly? "It's nice to see that you could take a little time away from your cave drawings to spend some quality time with us," I joked.

Chapter 27

July 1481 AD

Firenze

A time to be loved…

Charontes lifted me up and a riot of butterflies took flight in my stomach. His hands were large and warm where they touched me. He gently turned me onto my side.

"I have a few questions for you," I said. *Might as well get this over with.*

He turned his gaze toward Amelia, who curtsied and left without another word. Charontes pulled a chair up beside my bed and took my hand in his. For such a large man, he moved with a deliberate grace.

I looked up into his eyes and felt my heart skip a beat. That happened every time I looked at him. He was just one of those people that were so good-looking, you couldn't help but stare at them. The contours of his cheekbones and jawline softened in all the right places. Instead of being harsh and angular, they were pleasing to the eye. My gaze lowered, drawn down over his cheek and toward his full lips. A few hours' growth darkened his face where his beard grew. His face was the perfect combination of masculinity and handsomeness.

A twinkle of amusement danced across his eyes, making me suddenly realize that I was staring at him like a dunce. I pulled my hand away from his.

"Look, I think it's time you answered some of my questions," I said, trying to sound irate—but it came out more breathless than anything else. All I wanted to do was smell his skin and lay my head on his chest while he held me.

He just looked at me, not saying a word—but his eyes did. They held a fondness that seemed to welcome my questions.

"Why are you holding me here?" It was such a simple question, but one I burned to have answered.

"You are not my prisoner, beauty." The timbre of his voice was bottomless, and it melted me from the inside. "Not yet."

"What do you mean, 'not yet?' I've been locked in a room and chased. I've been thrown onto charging steeds, kissed without permission, and now my leg is broken." Simply hearing myself put it that concisely raised my hackles.

"For all those things, except the kisses, you have my deepest and most sincere apology," he answered. "They will never happen again." He looked at me with a sexy, self-assured look.

I couldn't believe him. *Is he actually flirting with me?* "If this is your fossilized approach to courting a girl, it's not really working out so well. In case you haven't noticed, you don't get women by kidnapping them. At this rate, I'll never survive the whole dating process, anyway. What *do* you do for first dates? Sacrifice your partner to pagan gods? I don't want any part of it, or you, and I don't think any of this is very funny."

"Nor do I," he said. "I cannot understand all your words, but I promise you one thing—you are not my prisoner. What you spoke of will never happen again—except for the kisses. For them, I am not sorry, and it *will* happen again." He leaned forward, looking into my eyes.

"You're a real piece of work. How can you say that I'm not a prisoner? If I'm not, can I leave now?" I waited for the negative answer that I knew would follow.

"Yes, if you must. I will not keep you here. Although, if you do leave, I will follow you. Not because you are my prisoner, but because I am yours—in more ways than you know."

"What is *that* supposed to mean?" I asked incredulously. "I'm not your prisoner, but you're *mine?* Why are you trying to confuse me? I don't understand you."

He took a deep breath, "We need to talk, you and I."

"You're kidding me, right? I thought that's what we were doing right now—*talking*." I felt like we were going in circles.

"We need to talk about the pin," he said.

That instantly got my attention. "What pin?"

"The pin you had when I found you. You were holding it in your hand."

"I...I *was?*" I tried to reconstruct exactly what had happened that day. I'd touched the pin, and it electrocuted me. My hair had floated up, and the next thing I knew, I'd woken up in Renaissance Florence. Now I didn't know what to say, or who to confide in.

I weighed the pros and cons of confessing to being a time traveler, but I wasn't sure it was a good idea. I didn't have the pin anymore and didn't even know where it had gone. In fact, I'd forgotten all about it until he'd mentioned it. *Maybe I shouldn't admit to knowing about it.*

He waited, looking at me intently.

I have to say something, I thought nervously.

He hadn't even blinked. His black eyes were still boring into me. "Yes, you were. You were clutching it in your hand. How did you come to find the stone?"

"You mean, the *pin?*" I asked, stalling.

"Yes, the stone is set in the pin."

It was no use. I would have to tell him some things about myself, or I would never be able to solve this puzzle. I needed to know how to get home. "You found me? You didn't take me and bring me here? Why did you lock me up then?"

"I have my reasons and will share them with you once you have answered my question," Charontes replied. "How did you come to have the stone?" He didn't sound angry and looked as pleasant as he did when he'd first sat down. He just waited patiently for my answer.

"I found it," I said, hedging.

"Where?"

I'd have to confide in him—there was no other choice. He may already know how I'd gotten there and how I could get home. From the sounds of it, he'd already known about the pin. Also, he'd found me, not abducted me. Wasn't that sort of like rescuing someone? I almost laughed out loud. *If this guy was as ugly as a troll, I wouldn't be making these excuses for him,* I thought. *I'm so weak.*

"A lady had it," I finally blurted out. "I was caring for her when she died. I tried to pack up her things, and when I touched the pin, it made me come here." *There. I answered him without giving too much away.*

He didn't look very happy with my answer—almost disappointed. He sat back in his chair and ran his fingers once through his brown hair. "So…you don't know how to make the stone work?"

"What are you, some kind of wizard or something? Don't worry, I don't know how the stone works. I won't steal any of your trade secrets. I don't even have it anymore, anyway."

"I have the stone."

"Well, there you go—*you* have the stone. That should make you happy."

"Lydia, you don't understand." He paused. "Are you from this time?"

There, he'd asked me point blank. No squirming around his answer this time. Still, I felt unsure. I imagined I could smell smoke—the smoke from the burning sticks they would pile at my feet, right after they'd decided to burn me for being a witch. Why would he ask a question like that?

"Are *you* from this time?" I asked, quite proud of my momentary reprieve from the pyre.

"No, I'm not."

He astonished me with that admission. That meant he might know how I could get home and back to my time. "Well, when *are* you from?" I couldn't believe I was having this conversation.

"From many saecula in the past. I don't know when we are now, so I can't tell you how many. But it must be a large number."

I didn't know what a saecula was, but it sounded really old. Looking at him, I had no problem believing he came from the past. He looked like a gladiator. No, more than that—an *antique* gladiator.

"Well, you seem to be just fine and dandy being from another epoch," I sassed. "Personally, that discovery leaves me with a few unanswered questions of my own, like…can you tell me what in the hell is going on?"

The edges of his mouth curved up into what could have been the ancestor of a smile. "Again, some of your words elude me, but it's similar to when a battle begins to turn for the worse. I have the same uneasy feeling as you do—the feeling I no longer have the upper hand."

I flashed him a quick smile. *This guy's actually okay when he isn't galloping after me in full battle regalia.*

"Lydia, we need to learn to trust one another. I need your help, and I am fairly certain you need mine. I ask you again—are you from this time?" He tipped his head down and looked at me, raising his eyebrows a bit.

"No, I'm not," I admitted in a low voice.

"When are you from?" His voice was low, gentle, and soothing.

"I'm from the future. If I told you the year, I don't think it would make any sense to you, anyway. Let's see…from now, if we were to have around five hundred more winters, that's when I'd be from. So, five hundred more years."

"I see." He looked a little dazed and at a loss for words.

"This is all so crazy," I said. "You said the pin is what made us move through time?"

"Yes."

"Would you care to expound on that a bit? I'm sorry, but personally, I'm not used to traveling through time and all these 'when are *you* from' chats. In fact, I can safely say that this one would be my first."

I paused, catching my breath. Then a horrible thought occurred to me. "Oh no, wait a minute. Don't tell me you're *not* a wizard. You don't know how to use the pin either, do you?"

"I hoped that *you* did," he said.

"Perfect, absolutely perfect." I felt as if someone had punched me in the stomach.

"It is? Why?"

I groaned, realizing he didn't understand the concept of sarcasm. "You said you still have the pin, right?"

"Yes."

"Okay, my talkative barbarian…we need to figure out what's going on. You tell me what you know, and I'll tell you what I know. Does that sound like a strategy to you?"

"Yes, but first, we will eat," Charontes said. "You need to regain your strength."

I'd only been up for a few hours, but felt as weak as a kitten. I couldn't argue. I *did* need to build my strength back up.

"Amelia!" he bellowed, but not in an unfriendly way.

She came in from the kitchen. Charontes pointed to his mouth, then to me and himself again.

"I think that's 'I'm hungry' in giant talk, Amelia," I said in Italian.

Amelia curtsied quickly and ran from the room, trying to unsuccessfully hold back a giggle.

Charontes stood up, squinting his eyes. Black as a moonless night, they gave away no hint of emotion. Bending over me, he put one hand under my right shoulder and the other on my left hip. "It's nice to see you're feeling so much better." He lifted me a few inches off the bed and into a sitting position.

My leg had been aching, but I didn't feel any sharp pain when he repositioned me.

Charontes smirked. "Maybe when you're well enough, I will think of some way to tame your treacherous tongue." He put one finger under my chin and tilted my head up.

I looked up into his eyes. Unable to stop the impulse, I licked my lips.

"Or maybe I should start taming it right away," he said, covering my lips with his.

A brief, warm moment, I closed my eyes. He tasted so good. I couldn't believe this god of a man was kissing me.

He pulled back and sat down, never taking his eyes from mine. "Tonight, I will continue with your training." His accent was mind-bendingly sensual.

I fanned my flaming cheeks.

Amelia came in from the kitchen, carrying two plates loaded with food which she set on the small table by my bedside. She made two more trips, bringing out wine, cups, and napkins.

Charontes nodded at Amelia, and she left the room. He pulled the table toward him and poured the wine.

I could see that one plate held fruit and cheese, and the other held roasted meat and hunks of bread. The meat looked like pork and smelled slow-roasted and delicious, falling apart into pieces off the edge. The rich scent of the browned and roasted meat stimulated my hunger.

Charontes handed me a cup of wine.

"Please put the table where I can reach it, too," I said. "You *do* share, don't you?"

"I will feed you what you need to eat," he said, looking at me with a sexy and arrogant expression. Then he pulled off his shirt.

Oh God, I'm not going to survive lunch.

He took a grape and pulled it from the bunch. When his hand got close to my lips, I could actually feel the heat from his fingers. He touched the grape to my lips, and I took it into my mouth. The crisp skin and juicy sweetness danced over my taste buds as I crunched down.

Oh Lord, I've forgotten how good grapes taste, and these are the best grapes ever. I chewed in rhythm with the thumping of my heart. I felt aroused. Aroused from lunch. Well, actually, from just one grape. If I didn't cool it, I'd be moaning and panting before he got to the figs. Why did he have to take off his shirt? Merely to torment me, or to keep from doing too much laundry? The industrial age was highly overrated.

He came at me with another grape, then at the last minute, he put it into his own mouth.

Good. At least I'll be able to catch my breath.

I tried to drink the wine, but my hands were shaking. He picked up my cup and put it to my mouth, tipping it while holding a napkin under my chin.

The tangy bite of the wine swirled around with the sweetness of the grape in my mouth. He leaned over, holding my face in his hands and kissed me, tasting my wine.

Oh good god, soon I'll be begging him for some meat. I let out an audible moan. He was driving me absolutely crazy.

"You are so hungry, my beauty," he whispered lightly, his lips brushing mine with each word. "So very hungry."

His blatant teasing was making me molten hot.

He picked up a fig and bit it in two, then fed me the other half. The fig, although sweet, wasn't as juicy as the grape. I could feel the soft fur of the fig's skin and the tiny seeds sliding against my tongue. It was sensual to know he was tasting the same thing as I was. If he did this at every meal, I could easily see myself ballooning out to a couple thousand pounds.

He pulled off a piece of meat and slowly lowered it, dripping, into my mouth—never taking his eyes off mine.

I took the opportunity to hold the end of his finger in my mouth for an extra second, then suck on it as he pulled it from my mouth. *Ha! Take that barbarian boy. Two can play your game.*

His eyes closed, and a slight flush crept up the sides of his neck. Taking a deep, stabilizing breath, he reached for the cheese.

I was hungry. He brought out every primal urge in me, and I'd only just met him. When he spoke to me, his voice melted away every last barrier of resistance. My heart beat so hard that I could feel it just below my ears. I felt breathless whenever he was near.

Looking at my cup, I silently communicated that I wanted more wine. He picked it up and put it to my lips. If he got me any hotter, I would spontaneously combust.

Who knew being fed could be so erotic? Anyway, not just any man could have pulled it off.

So intent on what he was doing, all else seemed to take backstage. I was his primary focus, and he never stopped watching me. I could tell how badly he wanted me, and I liked it. He didn't try to hide the want at all. The tension made my heart race.

He kissed me again, then stopped himself. "At this rate, we will starve to death," he said. After straightening my long tunic, he brushed back an errant curl behind my ear. Pulling his long hair back, he stretched and leaned back into his chair. "Have some more meat. It's very tender."

How could he even think about eating right now? I waited until my breathing slowed down a little. "You're a very good kisser," I said. *Stupid, stupid. Why did I say that? Duh...you're a very good kisser. How idiotic.*

"We are meant for each other," he said. "Soon we will be as one, neither of us a prisoner any longer. We will be set free, because our destinies lie together."

Again, I was so glad he had it all figured out. I chewed another bite of meat, which was crispy on the outside, warm and soft on the inside.

"You like boar?" he asked. It sounded more like a statement than a question.

"My first guess wouldn't have been boar, but now that you mention it, yes, it's very tasty. Caught this little guy yourself, I suppose? Chased him down with only a loin cloth, battleaxe, and a mace or two, huh?"

"No, I used a spear." He looked at me for telltale signs that I was joking with him.

I gave nothing away.

He shrugged, "Anyway, you do not chase wild boar, they chase *you*. And, unless you want to be caught, it's best to use a spear."

I groaned. *Great—Hunting and Gathering 101, taught by Professor I-Use-Clubs-A-Lot.* Suddenly, I found myself attracted to a man who nonchalantly killed huge wild animals with only a spear. How did this happen? Is it because life isn't challenging enough on its own, so we're naturally attracted to bad boy types? Even I had to admit, Charontes might be a little extreme. He woke up one morning, stretched, splashed water on his face and said, "Gee, what a beautiful day. I think I'll go out and hunt wild boar. Yes, that's what I'll do—

confront a six-hundred-pound, enraged wild animal with gleaming, razor-sharp tusks. I'll barely escape with my life, because I'll impale it from mere feet away with only a spear. *Yawn.*

There wasn't too much I could do about it. I couldn't get up and leave. I'd just have to make the best of a dilemma unlike anything I'd ever dealt with before. Taking that into consideration, I needed to try not to be too hard on myself.

The meal was incredible, and I'd finally started to get full. I also wanted to hurry up and finish eating so I could hear what Charontes had to say about the pin.

He dipped a piece of bread into the juice from the meat, and let me bite off what I wanted. Some of the juice ran down his arm.

My eyes met his.

"You are beautiful," he said.

My gaze followed his arm up and across his impossibly wide shoulder, then over his bare chest. Mechanically, I chewed the bite of bread and continued my stimulating perusal down toward his stomach. I just couldn't help myself.

My eyes drank in his magnificent physique. His thick body was offset by a flat stomach, rippled with muscle. My eyes were drawn to the line of dark brown hair just below his navel. How invitingly it disappeared into the top of his skirt. His thighs, each about as big around as my waist, were dusted with hair and tapered down to long, perfectly proportioned legs.

"*I'm* beautiful?" I asked. "Have you seen yourself lately?" I entertained the idea that I was actually in a dream. "You may want to put your shirt back on." I grabbed the front of my tunic and tugged it as a visual aid. The Greek word I used for "shirt" most likely wasn't what he was used to. "Otherwise, I don't think I'll hear a word you're saying."

He raised an eyebrow at me and got up to put his shirt on. I studied him from the side. His tanned muscles flexed as he tugged his shirt over his head, giving a whole new meaning to the words "Bronze Age."

I needed to get a grip on myself and focus. Although these were wonderful distractions, they didn't take away from the very real fact that we were in the middle of a precarious situation—one that could endanger all our lives at any moment.

"Would you mind telling your story first?" I asked. "I'm feeling tired and wouldn't mind just lying still for a moment and listening."

"I will. My story is a simple and short one. Does your leg hurt? Would you like to lie down?" He didn't wait for my answer and stepped toward me to move me.

"It can't be overly simple," I said. "Why were you with those bad people?" I was so relaxed, I'd inadvertently let slip something Amelia had said to me.

Charontes's eyes momentarily clouded over. He picked me up and turned me onto my uninjured side. Sitting down, he began to speak. His deep voice was now a familiar and reassuring sound.

Chapter 28

July 1481 AD

Firenze

A time to gain and a time to lose.

Charontes told Lydia about the two stones that made time travel possible—and how, with their joining, they would become even more powerful. He explained that the holder of the single, united stone would have the ability to choose what time they traveled to. Contrary to his usual nature, he kept talking, desperate to keep his mind away from touching her.

Thoughts of her enchanted and consumed him, but it felt wonderful. She possessed qualities he'd never valued or even noticed in a woman before, such as intelligence and wit.

During his story, he began to both cherish and dread these attributes in Lydia. He tried valiantly to avoid exposing any of his newly acquired feelings, but her direct questions became more difficult to reply to unemotionally. He sorely lacked experience with matters of the heart.

Since he'd been unable to answer Lydia's questions about the intricate workings of the stones, she suddenly brought up Vanth's betrayal and his change of heart regarding the Riders of the Reunity.

"So, let me get this right," Lydia said. "All your life, you were part of a group called the 'Riders of the Reunity?'" She sounded disappointed.

"Yes. Of late, I served second in command, only answering to Vanth. Like my ancestors before me, we were trained when we were young to find the other half of the stone. The irony of it being, now that I've found the other half of the stone, I no longer believe their cause to be just. Vanth is malevolence incarnate."

"So, you switched sides, just like that?" Lydia asked. "You expect me to believe that, after generations of your forefathers dedicated their lives to these Riders of the

Reunity? I don't understand, and I'm not sure if I believe you. What could possibly make you change your mind so suddenly?"

Charontes called on every bit of patience he possessed not to get angry with her. He could tell by the way she spoke so freely that she must be used to a different set of rules than he was. No man would dare speak to him that way without drawing his sword, and now a woman accused him of being untruthful.

"Lydia, you come from a different time than I do, so I will try to take that into consideration when I talk with you." No longer soothing, his voice took on a menacing tone. "But you may not accuse me of speaking less than the truth. I tolerate that from no one, and I will not tolerate it from you."

"Oh…well, thank you *so much* for being patient with me," Lydia shot back. "When you've finally carved your way out of the Stone Age, maybe you'll see that when it comes to patience, I've been the patient one here. I'm not your child, you know, and I won't be spoken to like one." Lydia looked unsure when she said that to him, and her perfect little chin trembled as she stuck it up at him in defiance.

She was impossible, but so brave. Of all her wonderful qualities, he admired her bravery the most. Even while she was lying before him, wounded and completely vulnerable, she still had the courage to challenge him. Nonetheless, it infuriated him when she dared to insinuate that he wasn't telling the truth.

What he'd learned today frustrated him. Frustration because he couldn't have her. Frustration because he'd waited so long already, unable to take any action toward rescuing his daughter. How could he find Aidyl if neither of them knew how to use the stone?

Charontes rose up to his full height with his arms folded and his feet apart. His face was flushed with emotion. "I know full well you're not my child. Vanth has taken my only child," he said in an anguished voice. "I am the father of Vanth's baby. She's torn her from me and has taken the other half of the stone. My failure to recognize the truth soon enough, although it was vivid and directly in front of me, caused this. It was a direct result of my own stupidity.

"At first, I didn't know what to do with you, Lydia, so I locked you up. Then you seemed to be my only hope of finding my daughter. Now...now you have me bewitched. I am like a man reborn. Reborn, and as a result, my life's direction has changed. I cannot account for its suddenness other than to say that before my daughter and before you, I was a man. But *only* a man. Now I have seen that love may have a chance for the first time in my dark, desolate life. That knowledge has given me a soul."

Tears glistened in Lydia's eyes.

He had to walk away. If he had stayed, he wasn't sure if he would hurt her or make love to her. He walked out toward the stable. None of this was Lydia's fault, but all that troubled him had surfaced at the same time. Not used to this depth of feeling for others, he was worried for his daughter and had taken it out on Lydia.

~~~

A small hand rubbed my shoulder, but I just buried my face farther into the blanket I'd been using as a pillow. I couldn't stop my tears. Why did everything have to be so confusing?

I'd listened silently, up until he'd said he no longer was a Rider of the Reunity. I shouldn't have asked him about it the way I did, but it had sounded so incredible. Right or wrong, he'd grown up believing in time travel and the power of the

stones—but I hadn't. I had difficulty digesting all that in one afternoon.

I felt like a terrible wretch. If I hadn't been so distrustful, he wouldn't have stomped off before finishing his story. Now all I had were disjointed pieces of it, and I couldn't fit them all together. My heart wrenched thinking of that awful woman stealing his child. I wished I'd known about that before I shot off my mouth. I would have trodden much more carefully.

Still, I felt jealous. I shouldn't be so selfish, but I wondered what type of relationship he'd had with that evil lady. They'd had a child together. He'd made love to her. *Are they married? How could he have slept with a murderer?*

What did I have to do with the stone, anyway? *Lucky me, I touched an old woman's pin and, of course, it happened to be a magic, time-traveling pin.* Now I'd become ensnared in the whole mess. But I wasn't so sure I regretted touching the pin in the first place. If I hadn't, I would have never met Charontes.

It took a while, but gradually my tears stopped flowing. The small, comforting hand never left my shoulder. The last things he'd said swirled around in my head. He claimed that I had bewitched him, and he had become a man reborn. That love had given him a soul. Did that mean he was falling in love with me? How could he do that if he was married to Vanth? Maybe I'd misunderstood his pattern of speech. It was quite different from my own.

"Please don't cry anymore, Lydia." Amelia's sweet voice soothed. "Let me give you a little medicine. When it takes effect, I will wash you."

"I couldn't possibly let you wash me," I said, mortified.

Amelia giggled. "Who do you think has been cleaning you up until now? Remember, you've been sick for days. Don't worry—I cared for my mistress when she was sick."

I wanted to crawl in a hole. *How embarrassing.* I guess it didn't differ much from the bed baths I gave my patients, though. "You're right, I'm thankful you've kept me washed. I will wash what I can and you can help me with my back, okay?"

Amelia handed me a little bit of the bitter medicine, and I pulled myself into a sitting position. I only sipped half of it and made a mental note to begin dramatically tapering myself off the potent drug.

"You've done a wonderful job taking care of me," I said. "Where I come from, they call me a 'nurse,' but I guess you can say I'm a healer of sorts, just like you."

Amelia beamed at my compliment. "Where *are* you from?"

I hated to be untruthful to Amelia after she'd been so nice to me. *Let's see, we're in 1481, and in 1492, Columbus sailed the ocean blue.* I had nothing to lose by telling the truth. "I'm from a place called 'Buffalo.'"

"Oh, I don't recognize the name, but I've never been out of Firenze, either." She gave a lighthearted little laugh. "Is your home far from here?"

"Yes, very far." A wave of homesickness washed over me.

Amelia intuitively changed the subject. "Here are some clean clothes for you." She laid out a thin, slip-like white dress, a long brown linen skirt, and a light tan tunic. "They belonged to my mistress. I hope you don't mind. I know they will fit you, because I've already put you in some of her clothes."

"Of course I don't mind," I said. "It would be my privilege." I pulled the slip over my head, followed by the tunic. Amelia then helped me pull the slip down and put the skirt on.

"I've left everything in my mistress's room untouched. I cannot bring myself to change anything because I miss her so much. Since your arrival and injury, I've been caring for you, and I haven't had much time to think about her. Now that you're awake, you remind me so much of her that she's on my mind again."

I reached my hand out to Amelia. "I'm sorry…I don't mean to make you sad."

She took my hand and sat by the bed. "No, it's not your fault. I miss her in a *good* way. You remind me of her independent ways, that's all." Amelia looked at me with a sad smile.

Then a puzzled expression came over her. She put her face right up into mine and stared hard into my eyes. She broke into a huge smile of relief.

"What? What's the matter?" I didn't know what had come over her.

She made the sign of the cross and looked up toward the heavens. "Thank you, God...I knew you would show me what to do."

"What are you talking about?" I hoped Amelia hadn't started dipping into the medicine herself.

"Your eyes," she said, as if that were enough of an explanation.

"What about my eyes?"

"They have purple in them."

"I know."

"I have only seen that on two other people," she said.

"You have? I've never seen anyone else with it," I said. Then the memory of the dying woman in the hospital flashed through my mind.

"Ati and Nortia," she said. "They both had the same purple specks in their eyes. I hadn't noticed them in yours until today."

"Okay, well…that's really weird, I guess. Why the praying and thanking God?"

"My mistress told me I'd know what to do when the time was right. *You* must be what she was talking about. She showed me where all her manuscripts were, then told me I'd know what to do when the time was right." Amelia's voice trembled with excitement. "Lydia, can you read?"

"Yes."

"I *knew* it! I knew it. I'm right." Amelia kissed me so hard it hurt all the way down to my leg.

"Ow! Okay, all right! What kind of manuscripts are they?"

"Why, my mistress's, of course."

"I know that—but what are they about?"

"I wouldn't know, I cannot read, not a word," Amelia said, smiling. "I will get them right now. I am sure they are meant for you, Lydia. You are so much like my mistress, and those eyes—I should have known."

She leaned in and looked into my eyes again. Then she backed up and just stared at me. "Come to think of it, your eyes are the same color, and you actually look a lot like Nortia. Your hair is curly like hers and is almost the same color. Your face, too, favors hers. Anyway, I will be right back. They are in the chest in my mistress's room." She hurried out.

I leaned my head back, and my eyes drooped. My head spun a little from the medicine. It felt wonderful to be clean, and the clothes Amelia had given me were light and airy. She'd seemed so excited all of a sudden. I wondered what had gotten into her.

She bounced down the stairs with an armful of large, leather-bound notebooks, and set them on the table beside me. "Here's three of them, and there are many more in her room. These are the ones my mistress pointed to when she gave me those talks, so I brought them first."

"Oh, I don't know if I can read them right now."

"I thought you said you could read." Amelia sounded crestfallen.

"I can. It's just I don't know if I can *right now* because of the medicine." I closed my eyes again, just for a second.

"Oh. Please try…I want to see if they truly are meant for you."

"Okay, let me see one of them," I said.

Her eager face was difficult to disappoint. Amelia handed me the manuscript on top. I put it in my lap and gingerly opened it. The first page was unattached and slid out at an odd angle. I picked it up and began reading.

My eyes flew over the first three or four sentences. Then my stomach fluttered and blood pounded in my ears. The whole world turned a little bit. The room suddenly seemed stifling hot. I was going to pass out.

"What?" Amelia asked. "What's wrong? Lydia, are you unwell? What does it say?"

Amelia's voice seemed to be coming from far away. She shook my shoulder hard. I looked down at the paper again. I must be confused. It was the medicine—I was hallucinating. I concentrated, trying to make my eyes and mind cooperate.

I held the paper up where I could see it better, refocused my eyes, and forced myself to read.

I don't want to frighten you, but I'm afraid there is no way other than to just say what must be said. If you are reading this note, Lydia, it means the magnet has found you. I must be dead, and my sweet Amelia has figured out exactly what to do.

There is no gentle way to tell you this, and no matter how I put it, it will come as a shock. You, my dear, are the Chosen One. Yours is one of the DNA sequences programmed into the magnet. At first, you may try to deny it, but eventually, you will realize that what I'm telling you is true. All the pieces of the puzzle fit. What you once did not understand will suddenly become perfectly clear.

The manuscripts contain detailed information on all I know about our family and the magnet. There are thirty years of research chronicled into multiple manuscripts. Three of them are vital to you, so please read them first. They contain the core of what you need to know in order to survive and find the other half of Hemisatres.

Lydia, the magnet set in your mother's pin—keep it with you always. It will protect you. It is imperative that you find its other half. When the two magnets are joined, its united power will save the future of mankind. You must not let it fall into the hands of evil. I know you can do it, since you are the Chosen One. You are Nortia's child, Lydia.

Tell Amelia that I love her. I have papers in the chest upstairs that bequeath all my belongings to her, including the house. Please make sure she gets them. You can trust her with your life. Now may be the time to share some of what is happening with her.

I will see you again soon,
Patrizia

"What's the matter with you?" Amelia cried. "Lydia, you look terrible. I am afraid to ask what the paper says."

"She…she knew my name," I said. "Okay, okay, just give me a second." Finding it hard to breathe, I placed the paper down gently on top of the manuscript, then put my face into my hands so I wouldn't hyperventilate. Nortia was my biological mother?

"Oh dear. This is bad, very bad," Amelia said, sitting beside the bed in an attempt to comfort me.

Yes, this was very bad. Ridiculously bad. Just because things couldn't get any crazier, now somehow, they did. *I am the Chosen One.* They had my DNA and programmed it into the pin? Who even did that in Renaissance Italy? I knew one thing—I didn't want to be the chosen *anything*.

I picked up the paper, scanning it for a word I'd forgotten. *Hemisatres.* What magnet was she talking about? She must mean that the stone in the pin is really a magnet. Suddenly I realized that my coming here had already been planned out.

Oh Lord, I'm going to be sick for sure.

Chapter 29

Jurassic Age

Man's entire existence is but a tiny speck in time.

Vanth opened her eyes and immediately wished she hadn't. Her head felt like a herd of horses had run over it. The bright sunlight and hot, steamy air sent a wave of nausea coursing through her. She waited for the sick feeling to pass.

Her memory rushed back. They'd moved through time after she'd almost had the other stone. Familiar rage coursed through her. She tried to sit up, but fell back hard into the sand, jarring her aching head. She stayed down after that, turning her neck only slightly to look for the rest of her group.

Riders and horses lay nearby, unmoving, strewn about in haphazard black mounds on the sand.

She heard Aidyl begin to cry. *Of course the baby is awake and crying,* she thought angrily. Vanth's head pounded. *Those useless nursemaids had better wake up and take care of the noise coming from that baby.*

She turned onto her side and propped herself up on one elbow. They were on a small strip of beach, sandwiched between a large, still lake, and a lush forest, swathed in a myriad of brilliant greens.

The plant life here was so densely packed, it appeared to be impenetrable. Strange leaves, taller than a man and shaped like bird feathers, spiked out of the ground. Trees as thick as two horses, end to end, soared to impossible heights. The tree tops were connected by snakelike vines, the thickness of a man's arm, crisscrossing everywhere. Vanth had never seen anything like this place before.

"Wake up, you useless slugs!" she screamed from her spot on the ground. "Get up now, I command it."

She heard a few moans from her Riders as they started to rouse. The baby cried louder.

"Get up!" she yelled. "Damn you all!"

More moans ensued and a few of the Riders sat up, and held their heads. The horses also stirred and began to heave themselves up, one by one.

Vanth pulled herself up to a standing position, using her horse for balance. "Do I have to kick you two?" she bellowed at the nursemaids' inert forms. One sat up slowly and began an inching crawl inland toward the crying baby. The plumper of the two still lay motionless beside the water's edge.

"Shut that baby up now, woman, or I will run you through with my sword." The volume of her own voice brought tears of pain to Vanth's eyes. She looked down at her bracelet, "Where have you brought us now?" She rubbed the stone over and over. "Get on with it, damn you—we need to find Nortia. Don't waste any more of my time. Take me to her now!" she shrieked through the water-laden air.

Vanth swayed, pulling hard on her mount's reins in order to stay upright. The horse jerked its head up and whinnied in pain. "Shut up, you stupid animal," she said, savagely smacking its neck.

"All of you, come close and stay together. If the stone begins to work again, I want you nearby. Nortia's stone isn't here—I can sense it. I don't know what this useless rock is doing to us, but I don't like it. Hurry up, you fools!" she shouted, stamping her foot.

The Riders began collecting their dazed horses.

She turned her malevolent glare toward the nursemaids. One had managed to reach the baby and now cradled her in her arms. The other still lay unconscious.

Leading her horse behind her, Vanth began walking in the direction of the prone nursemaid. "A good kick will wake her from her lazy stupo—"

Vanth suddenly stopped dead in her tracks. The blue-green water rippled and heaved from movement beneath. She saw the shadow of something large under the water, moving rapidly toward the motionless nursemaid.

Vanth drew her sword.

Her horse squealed and reared, pulling her back sharply as a huge, dark green, serpent-like monster broke the surface of the water. It was terrifyingly ugly and had a long, pointed snout. Its jaws gaped open, and the water from within ran out in rivulets over rows of gleaming, dagger-sharp teeth.

Vanth froze where she stood, her reins dropping to the ground. What sort of demon-place had the bracelet taken them to?

She heard several shouts from the other Riders, but the rasp of swords being drawn spurred her into action.

The beast, immense in size, hugged low to the ground as it emerged from the water on crooked legs that were bent out like elbows. Its impossibly long, scaly body ended in a tapering tail.

"I will kill the demon!" Vanth yelled, lunging forward, straight for the beast. The monster's jaws clamped down on the nursemaid's leg with a resounding snap as it crunched down through the bone. Her piercing yell of pain ripped through the air.

Vanth's sword plunged into the beast's back.

The demon bellowed in pain, viciously lashing at Vanth with its massive tail.

Using only warrior instinct, she immediately put her head down and pushed herself up into a headstand, balancing over her sword. Arms trembling with the strain, her hands clenched the hilt of her sword as the lethal tail hissed harmlessly by. The added weight of her entire body drove her blade deeper into the leviathan's back.

The thrashing, screaming nursemaid's small fists bounced off the beast's giant head in a desperate effort to free herself.

"Oh, you're awake now, aren't you?" Vanth shouted pitilessly at the nursemaid as she came down from her headstand, pulling her weapon from the creature.

Vanth raised her sword, then moved back in to renew her assault.

The beast began rolling violently. The nursemaid flopped over and over in its jaws, slapping the water with each revolution.

Amazed and left without an opening, Vanth just stood there, impotently poised for attack. The creature receded, spinning into the water and dragging the now-soundless woman along with it.

"What sort of demon-hell are we in?" she cried out toward the sky.

A huge bird that looked like a long-tailed lizard with wings flew overhead, screeching down at her from its long, pointed beak. The creature tipped its wings and began to circle, calling out again and again.

As close now as she'd ever come to experiencing fear, Vanth channeled that fear into anger. "A group of warriors, and not *one* of you assisted me! You are all useless! Mount up and get into a group. We must leave this place at once."

The men began to move.

Vanth turned toward the surviving nursemaid, who sat there sobbing hysterically back near the tree line. Vanth noted that she had moved as far away from the water as possible.

"You're an easy one to find," Vanth spit out at her. "All I have to do is follow your sniveling and the wails of the child you are supposed to be caring for."

The trembling woman began trying to soothe the baby with small, comforting sounds. She kept her eyes down as Vanth approached.

"You think you are safe away from the water?" Vanth asked in a low, malicious tone. "If the water holds that demon, and the sky holds the other one, I can only imagine what is lurking in the forest."

The nursemaid's gaze darted to the brush line. She stood unsteadily with the baby in her arms, then began walking toward the men.

The Riders had grouped together. Uneasy, their swords were drawn, all watchful for signs of an attack.

"I don't know what games the stone plays with me now," Vanth addressed the entire group, "but my patience is at an end, and murder is in my heart. Give the child to me." Vanth reached out her arms toward Aidyl.

To her credit, the nursemaid hesitated.

"Woman, give me my child now, or I will throw you into the water to join your inept friend."

She handed Vanth the crying baby.

"Mount your horses now," she barked, vaulting into her saddle and holding Aidyl in the crook of her arm. "Everyone move together until we are all touching."

All did as they were told.

Vanth drew her sword and pointed the tip directly at her baby's heart.

"I don't know what game you're playing with us, or why you waste my time," she shouted into the rising wind, "but I swear to you, I will drive this sword through your Chosen One's heart if you don't do as I say.

"Remove us, at once, from this nest of demons. Think on it for but a moment, for that is all you have. Look into my heart if you must, and you will know that I speak only the truth. Take us to Nortia, now."

The water began to roil and the wind whipped at the blackness of her cloak, but the point of her sword never wavered.

Her hair began to float in the air. In her evil heart, she knew she'd won.

Chapter 30

July 1481 AD

Firenze

A time of discovery.

Amelia jumped to help me. "Please, Lydia…are you going to be all right? What can I do to help you?"

"I'm fine. I just need to lie here for a while. That note was from your mistress, and you were right—it certainly *was* for me." I eased into a lying position.

"I knew it. What did she say? Did she mention me at all? Was it really bad? Are we in danger from the evil one?"

I didn't blame Amelia for being upset. My head whirled with the new information, and my heart raced thinking of the implications. "Yes, it was really bad, but your mistress left instructions and information in the note that may help us. Oh, on the bright side of the news, she did say that she was giving you all her possessions. The papers for that are in one of the chests in her room."

"All her possessions?" Amelia's voice croaked out, barely above a whisper.

"Yes, including this house. The bad news is, apparently I have to save the world with a brooch."

"There must be some kind of a mistake," Amelia said, the breath taken out of her.

"There absolutely has been a mistake. A really *huge* mistake. And I don't mean about you getting the house, that part is good. Also, Patrizia said to tell you that she loved you."

Amelia started crying. "Now we are both upset—I'll be back," she said and ran upstairs.

My mind raced. *Nortia was my mother? How could that even be possible? This must be a dream.* Things kept getting more and more bizarre, but all the pieces in the puzzle fit. According to Amelia, Nortia had disappeared, or as I supposed, time traveled, from here with Antoni and a baby named—Lydia. They were being chased. It all fit. Goosebumps ran down the back of my neck.

I couldn't believe it. I was over five hundred years old.

When Amelia returned, I didn't know how long I'd been sitting there with my thoughts spinning, trying to put everything together. She, however, looked a little more composed.

"Could we talk about the note now, Lydia? I am longing to hear the words of my mistress again."

"Yes, sure. Are you okay?"

"Yes, I'm better. I went into my mistress's room. It makes me feel like I'm near her when I lay on her bed. I also looked to see if I could find the papers you said she mentioned in the note. There are many manuscripts, and it was silly of me to try to find them because I can't read. Once you're feeling better, you can help me find them." Her sadness seemed to have given way to a rising excitement.

"Of course I will, especially after how much you've helped me. I'll read it to you, but first, I have to explain some things to you that may not seem possible. When I heard them initially, I thought that they weren't possible, either. I hope you don't think that I'm crazy.

"I'm scared, Amelia, and I can hardly believe these incredible things are happening around me. Your mistress said in the note that you may be ready to hear the truth. She knew all along—the truth, that is. I hope her words in the note make what I'm about to say more believable. Don't judge me too harshly, and keep in mind that you trusted your mistress."

I didn't know where to start. Any opening sentence would be either frightening or sound absolutely insane to a girl from the fourteen hundreds. "What if I told you that there was a stone that had special powers?" I said tentatively.

"What kind of powers? You mean like magical powers?"

"I'm not sure what kind they are or how they work, only that they *do* work." I wanted to take this really slowly.

"I know they would often all talk about a stone," Amelia said. "It was one of the few words in their language that I understood." Amelia didn't seem too upset, and she even seemed to be trying to be helpful.

So far, so good. "Well, there is a stone like that," I said. "Actually, there are *two* stones like that."

"Where are they?"

"One of them is here. Charontes says that he has it. The other is with the evil woman, Vanth." I waited. I'd purposely led her down this trail in order for her to discover what was going on instead of outright dumping all the information on the poor girl.

"Oh no, we won't have to see that evil woman again, will we?"

"Honestly, Amelia, I don't know. What's happening is that the two stones used to be one stone, but they were separated. Now Vanth is trying to get the stone back together."

"Why?"

"What I've learned in the past few days is that when the stone is whole, it's much more powerful."

"Who told you that?" Amelia asked.

"Charontes. It was also written in the note from your mistress."

"Does the stone have something to do with why you are here?"

"I'm not sure why I'm here. I didn't try to come, it just happened when I accidentally touched one of the stones."

"Maybe you should read the note to me. I believe you, but I'd like to hear what my mistress wrote. There have been a lot of strange things happening here. People showing up out of nowhere, then disappearing—strangely dressed people, ones with ancient armor, killers, and demons. I want to know what is going on. I'm tired of being afraid and thinking that I'm losing my mind."

I grabbed the note, sending a silent prayer to the heavens that I wouldn't lose Amelia as a friend. As I read it, her face changed expression several times, ranging from surprise, to shock, and finally to fear.

"Are you well, Amelia?" I knew it was a lot for anyone to take in, much less someone from Renaissance times.

"Yes…no. I just don't understand. It's not possible for you to be Nortia's child. That child was born this spring," Amelia said quietly.

It was the moment of truth, literally. I hoped I was doing the right thing by telling her everything. "That is the power of the stone, or magnet, as your mistress explained. It makes a person move through time faster than everyone else.

"I don't know how it's possible that I am grown up already—I'm just trying to figure it all out myself. The only thing that I can think of is that Nortia and Antoni disappeared from here in...when was it?"

"The end of May," she answered, eyes the size of saucers. "But their baby was only five or six weeks old."

"Yes...and I really don't know how to say this without confusing or scaring you even more." I paused, collecting my courage before speaking. "Amelia, I come from the future."

Amelia scooted her chair a few inches away from me.

"But you're old," Amelia said softly, fear creeping into her voice.

"Please, Amelia, don't be afraid. I'm not going to hurt you. Just look at me. I can't walk or chase you. Not that I would, anyway. Oh, it's just no use. This is all too crazy. If it weren't happening to me, I'd never believe it, either. I don't blame

you…never mind."

"Lydia, I'm frightened, that's for sure. What you're saying is unbelievable. It's even heresy. But if I didn't believe you, I wouldn't be so frightened."

"Thank you," I said. "I appreciate that more than you know. I really need a friend right now, and I'm probably going to need your help to get out of this mess."

"You *are* my friend," Amelia replied. "Please finish— I will try to be a better listener."

I told her about being left with Father Tom as a baby, my adoption, and my birth year.

"*Nineteen eighty-six?*" Amelia asked incredulously. "Lydia, that's not possible."

I'm telling you that I grew up in the nineteen hundreds. Before I came here, I was at work, and it was the year of our Lord two-thousand-sixteen. Yes, I know it's unbelievable, but what's inconceivable to me is that I'm suddenly five hundred years in the past."

"Yes, it's strange for both of us. I just saw Nortia's baby not long ago. I held her in my arms. That baby was *you?*"

"According to your mistress, yes. I'd like to discount everything she wrote in that note, but I can't. I'm faced with the real truth—I'm here in the fourteen hundreds. I can't explain it other than it must have been something the stone or magnet did."

"It must be in the pin that Nortia always wore," Amelia said.

"You're right. I was caring for an old lady, and she had the pin in her belongings. When I touched the stone in the pin, everything went crazy. The next thing I knew, I was here."

"What was wrong with the old lady?" Amelia asked.

Lydia noticed a strange light in her eyes, like she knew something. "She was sick with infected cuts," I answered, tipping my head questioningly.

"Was she about this high?" Amelia held her arm out to about five feet.

"I don't know, I guess. I never saw her standing. Why?"

"Did she have silver hair that came down like this?" With her hands, Amelia indicated straight hair that ended at the shoulders.

"Well…yes, but most old people have silver hair." I got a creepy feeling and tried to remember exactly what the old woman had looked like. I should have thought of this before. She'd had the pin. Come to think of it, all her clothes had been old-looking. I distinctly remembered thinking that they looked medieval or something. "Why Amelia? What are you thinking?"

"You said the stone in the pin makes you move through time, right?"

"Yes, the magnet does, according to your mistress."

"What kind of cuts did the old woman have?"

"She had two huge cuts on her arm." I pointed to my own arm where the cuts had been.

"Her *left* arm?" Amelia's voice came out slow and very quiet, as if she didn't want to ask the question.

"Yes, why?" I had a sinking feeling in the pit of my stomach. Something tugged at my memory, someone else who had had an arm injury.

"That woman was Ati, Lydia…that's why she had the pin," Amelia said. When I told you about what happened here, I left a part out. I was afraid you would think that I was not in my right mind if I told you the whole truth."

"It's okay, Amelia, I understand. It's been difficult for all of us. We've all just met and didn't know who we could trust. I don't blame you. What were you going to say?"

"The night Ati disappeared, she was near death. She just lay there, moaning from the pain. I tried to give her the medicine, but she wouldn't take it. No matter what I did, she kept refusing. I even tried to dribble it into her mouth when she slept, but she would wake and spit it out.

"I didn't really go upstairs to bed that night." Amelia recounted the events of that evening up until she'd fallen asleep. "When I opened my eyes, everything was happening at once. I looked down at Ati, and she was awake and smiling. She held something gold in her hand and her hair floated in the air. Sir yelled very loudly and leaped for her, but she just vanished."

"She had the pin in her hand," I said.

"Yes…and the last thing Ati said before she disappeared was 'Lydia.' She must have known what was going on."

"Tomorrow, I'll start reading the manuscripts," I said. "Hopefully, they will answer a lot of the questions we have. Would you like to be there?"

"Yes. We need to quickly find out all we can in case that evil woman comes here. I have a feeling she will come back for the pin."

"Unfortunately, I think you're right, Amelia."

"In the meantime, we have to go on living. I'm hungry." She smiled. "How about you? I made some stew."

"Mmm, is that what I've been smelling? I'd love some, thank you." I realized she was trying to change the subject, but I didn't mind. We'd discovered a lot of frightening things today and absorbing it in small doses might help to keep us both sane.

Amelia smiled a worried smile, then hurried off toward the kitchen.

Left alone with my thoughts, I reflected on the irony of the situation. All those times I'd dreamed about my real mom, and here she had been, so completely out of my reach. I not only didn't know *where* my birth mother was, I also didn't know *when* she was. I didn't even know if she existed at all anymore, for that matter.

Then Ati had shown up in the ICU. I'd watched my own grandmother die, and I hadn't even known it. How brave she must have been. She refused the medicine just so she would be alert enough to give me the pin. *Me, the Chosen One.* Somehow, it didn't seem very likely.

I wished Charontes would come back from wherever he had gone, and I hoped he wasn't still angry. I needed to tell him what we'd found out today. We were in serious danger. Vanth could be back at any time, and we all needed to be on the same page.

I tried to read the manuscripts Amelia had brought down, but I couldn't make out the words in the candlelight. I knew I should be doing more to figure out a plan that would protect us, or get us all out of there, but I couldn't. Frustrated and anxious, I just sat there and waited for my supper.

Two little birds on the window ledge watched me and sang prettily. "Shouldn't you two go find a cozy tree to sleep in before dark?" I asked the birds absently.

The birds became excited when I spoke to them. One flew over and landed on my bent knee.

"Hello, little guy. You Renaissance birds sure are tame." The bird chirped back at me as if we were having an in-depth conversation.

My stomach rumbled, and the little bird flew back to the ledge. I should have eaten more during lunch, but I'd been distracted by a gorgeous barbarian. I closed my eyes and smiled, thinking about him. I heard scrabbling on the ledge as the frightened birds flew away.

I opened my eyes and there he stood, leaning against the door frame, head almost touching the top of it. He wore a loose, short-sleeved, off-white shirt, which had a rough "V" torn into it for a neck line. His chest and shoulders looked even bigger in the confined space of the doorway. The wide golden arm band was his only adornment.

Below his waist hung a short leather skirt, divided into vertical sections, like tags. I didn't know what they were called, but the skirt certainly didn't look girlish on him. His impressive thighs could be seen through some of the pleated linen, which hung almost to the knee. It may have been all one piece, but I couldn't tell. The long shirt was held in place by the leather skirt.

"You seem to like my pteruges more than most," Charontes said.

I realized that once again, I'd been caught staring below the belt. "Is that what you call it? Where's all your armor?"

"I don't wear it in the house when times are peaceable. Times *are* peaceable, are they not?"

"Yes, I apologize for not believing you. I realize now that you were telling the truth."

I truly was sorry and hoped he wouldn't still be angry, but still felt jealous of Vanth. Strange, she terrified me, but the girl in me felt jealous. He probably didn't even care what I thought. I had no right to be jealous anyway—I had no claims to him. But why would he have said all those things to me, about being destined for each other? Maybe he was a player, just like the rest of them.

"I accept your apology," he said. "How did you finally realize I spoke the truth?"

I accept your apology. Argh. Thanks, pal. He didn't get it. By telling me he and Vanth had a child together, he'd admitted to sleeping with that witch. Either that, or he didn't care.

I pushed those thoughts aside, as there were more important things to worry about than my love life. Mainly, *my* life and the fact that I apparently had a death squad coming after me. I needed to take it seriously, but I felt like I was dreaming it all.

"Amelia found a note from her mistress," I explained. "The note actually addressed me by name. Somehow her mistress knew I would be here at the house. There are manuscripts, too, filled with information about the stone. The note said I must read those three manuscripts first." I pointed to them.

Charontes looked excited. "This is good news then. We will be able to learn how to use the stone. That is strange, though—how did she know your name?"

"I think we may have figured that out, too."

"Good, what else have you learned?" He sat beside me on the bed, his perfect eyebrows raised expectantly.

"Well, according to the note, I guess...well, from what she says..." I couldn't seem to bring myself to say it.

"Well, what is it?" His voice boomed around the small space of the room.

"I'm the Chosen One," I whispered, hoping he would just ignore that part and go right on to the next part—like maybe a "kissing me" part. I was hopeless. He had literally slept with the devil, and I still wanted him.

"What did you say?" His voice rolled across me like the growing rumble of thunder.

I raised my voice competitively. "The note said...I am the Chosen One."

Chapter 31

1481 AD

Firenze

Flowers wilt with time, but love grows.

"You're *what?*" Charontes couldn't believe what he'd just heard.

"Do you have rocks in your ears?" Lydia said, snapping at him. "I'm the Chosen One. At least, according to Patrizia." There was a jealous light in her eyes.

Charontes ignored her rock comment. "Who's Patrizia?"

"Amelia's mistress, the lady that Vanth killed," Lydia said, nearly spitting out the word *Vanth.* He knew Lydia was provoking him again, but it seemed like she couldn't help herself. He struggled to maintain his composure.

"You should start at the beginning, and tell me what you have learned today. It's highly unlikely that you are the Chosen One. The Chosen One is my daughter, and she's just a baby."

"Your daughter is the Chosen One?" Lydia sounded baffled.

Charontes groaned. He was so tired of being confused. He never seemed to know what was going on. None of them did. It made him feel vulnerable. "Yes, my daughter is the Chosen One. Vanth told me Nortia's child is also the Chosen One, but that didn't make much sense to me. She said she would kill that child and then there would be only one Chosen One—Aidyl."

"I can't believe it. That witch wanted to kill me, and I was just an innocent baby. And you…you were helping her? You slept with her, had a child with her, and then tried to kill me. Are you two married?"

Lydia looked very upset, and he had no idea what she was talking about. "Vanth tried to kill you? When?"

"Are you trying to be funny? *When*? I'm so mixed up now." There were tears in her eyes. "I'm angry and scared."

"You have no need to be scared. I won't let anything hurt you, ever." He smoothed down one of her dark, brown curls that spiraled out from the top of her head. "Calm down and try to answer me. When did Vanth try to kill you?" He sat down on the edge of the bed and took her hand. She pulled away.

"No. *You* answer *me*." She imitated his deep voice. "'Lydia, we're destined for each other, and we will become as one.' You said all those things to me, and all along, you're married to a demon."

"Now I see the problem," Charontes said. "You're jealous. That's a good sign, my beauty. Yes, Vanth is a demon. I can assure you that one night was the extent of my whole relationship with Vanth. One night of weakness that, except for my daughter, I regret."

Charontes didn't want Lydia to be upset, but he couldn't help being happy that she was jealous. That meant she cared for him.

"One night?" she asked.

"Yes, she tricked me. Later, she said the stone told her who the father of the Chosen One should be. She went to me on that night on purpose. I should have known better, but she was very convincing, and I was weak. But it meant nothing to me.

"You will see that you alone are the only one for me. As time passes and we get to know each other, you will never question my feelings for you again. You won't have to. Now, please tell me when Vanth tried to kill you. I have fought by her side for years."

"According to Patrizia's note, I'm the Chosen One— because I *am* Nortia's baby."

Charontes felt like he'd had the wind knocked out of him. "How is that possible? You are a grown woman."

"Yes, but you are forgetting about time travel. It opens up all sorts of possibilities. When Nortia and Antoni left here with a baby, that baby must have been me."

He listened as Lydia told him everything she'd learned that day. When she finished, he knew she was right. He hadn't been able to figure out where Lydia fit in before, or why she'd been lying there in the woods. Now it all made sense.

Lydia read him the note, and he felt sad. What if his daughter was already grown and he'd missed it? What if she'd learned to be evil like her mother? She could have already lived out her whole life span in some other time and already be dead. It all seemed so hopeless. They were dealing with powers that were beyond them. How could he fight these problems with strength and a sword?

He felt her small hand on his forearm. At least he had Lydia. At that moment, he vowed to never let her leave him—and never let her go to another time without him.

"I know you must be upset," she said. "We both are. We must figure out a plan, but tonight, let's eat and rest. Please, try not to worry. We need to stay calm so our judgment isn't clouded. Can you smell the stew? It smells wonderful. Tomorrow, we'll look at the manuscripts, and things will seem much clearer.

"Patrizia said the three notebooks contain years of research and vital information. I think we should be hopeful that there may be a way to beat Vanth. Those books are our advantage over her. Maybe they'll have instructions on how to use the magnet. You have the pin with the magnet, right?"

"Magnet?" he asked. "I have the pin."

"A magnet is a certain kind of stone—it's okay, I'll explain tomorrow. As long as you still have the pin, we're fine. Patrizia said I must keep it with me always for protection."

"No!" he shouted. "I won't give it to you!"

"Wow, calm down. I'm just trying to remind you about what *she* said. I don't want to steal your stupid pin."

He could tell from her tone that he'd hurt her feelings. *She must think that I don't trust her with the pin.* "I care too much for you to give it to you. Everyone who has it disappears. I'm not going to take the chance of losing you, too."

"Oh." She gave him a small smile. "Well, we must read the notebooks tomorrow and figure out what to do. I have a feeling that we may not be safe here for long. Let's not fight about things we don't understand, especially when the answers may be so close at hand."

"You are right, my beauty. We will wait until tomorrow. We've fought enough for one day—it's time to stop fighting." He put her hand to his mouth and started kissing his way up the length of her arm. He thought she might pull away, but she didn't.

He heard Amelia clear her throat. Slowly, he put Lydia's hand down and leaned out of Amelia's way. She set down a steaming bowl of stew for each of them and a large loaf of bread.

It smelled intoxicating, but hardly distracted him from his thoughts of kissing Lydia again. He'd been out riding for hours, trying to sort things out in his head, and he'd built up a healthy appetite. Giving into his other hunger, he picked up a hunk of bread and dipped it into his bowl of stew.

Lydia picked up her bowl. "Thank you, Amelia…this smells excellent. You're such a good cook. I appreciate the time you take to make these meals."

"You are most welcome, Lydia." Amelia curtsied and left the room.

"You know, you're going to have to start treating Amelia like a little more than a serving girl," Lydia said.

"Why should I?"

"This is her house, her land, and everything in it belongs to her." Lydia smiled sweetly, then took a big bite of stew-sopped bread.

"It is? Oh yes, the note. I remember," he grumbled between mouthfuls.

"She's become a friend of mine, and I trust her," Lydia said. "When I read her the note, I had to explain things to her."

"What things?" He felt a drop of juice trickle down his chin.

"I told her that I wasn't from this time. I explained what I could about the stone, but I didn't tell her much about you. I wanted to ask you first. I think we can trust her, though." Lydia's eyes never left his face.

He wiped his mouth. He liked the way she used the word "we" as if they were truly together. "Yes, that's fine with me, if you trust her. I see no harm in it. I will have to figure out how to begin treating her like the lady of the house. I don't think that will come easily. I can't converse with her, since she doesn't speak my language."

"I'm sure we'll figure it out," Lydia said.

Lydia talked strangely, too. Sometimes he couldn't understand what she meant, although he thought he got pretty close most of the time. Right now, though, it didn't matter. They ate in companionable silence for the rest of the meal.

Amelia came in and picked up their dishes.

"Thank you again—it was delicious," Lydia said. "As soon as my leg is better, I'm going to help you with the dishes and cooking. I feel bad you have to do everything."

"I don't mind at all," Amelia said in a soft voice.

Charontes felt he should say something, too. She had worked hard over the weeks, and she'd never caused him any trouble. "Amelia, the meal was hearty." He saw the girl startle when he spoke.

Lydia laughed. "That's giant talk for 'thank you,' and 'I liked your cooking,'" she translated.

Amelia looked down, trying to hide a smile. She said something that could have been 'you're welcome' in her language. Then she left the room.

Eager for tomorrow, Charontes hoped the manuscripts would shed more light and help them in their dilemma. He had been on edge, feeling an overwhelming, impending sense of doom. *Vanth will be back.* He found it hard to believe that it had taken her this long. They had to be ready for her when she got here, or all of them would be dead.

"I'm going to ride out and make sure everything is secure. I will be back." He got up, kissed the sleepy-looking Lydia on the forehead, and left. He would come back and hold Lydia while she slept. It made him feel calm inside.

~~~

Morning came with brilliant rays of sunlight streaming in, illuminating objects around the room where I lay. I felt dreamy and warm, as if I could still feel his arms around me.

Amelia bustled into the room with an excited gleam in her eyes. She startled five birds that lined the window ledge into flight. "Good morning, Lydia. Are you well this morning? I see your friends were visiting."

"Yeah, they're always here. Yes, I'm feeling good, thanks." A chipmunk pulled its body up onto the ledge, then shrieked when it saw Amelia and ran.

We laughed.

"It's the strangest thing," I said. "Animals keep jumping onto the ledge. It's as if they're interested in me. Maybe it's the lingering effects of the medicine, but I think I can almost feel what they're feeling, like when they're happy, scared, or curious."

"They do really seem to like you," Amelia said, setting a tray down in front of me. "I am so nervous about the manuscripts. I can hardly wait until you read them."

"I'll hurry and eat, then we'll get started. Have you seen Charontes?"

"He is just outside. Do you want me to get him?"

"Yeah, just give me a couple minutes." I hurried and finished my breakfast. Amelia helped me with a quick toilet, then ran to get Charontes.

I liked the shirt Amelia had given me to wear after I'd washed. I could definitely get used to Renaissance fashions. A gorgeous burgundy color, the shirt fit loosely, going down past my waist. The sleeves were roomy and got wider toward the wrists. Over my shirt, I wore a thin, white overshirt. It was sleeveless, beautifully edged with different colored strips of cloth, and intricately embroidered with birds. I actually felt pretty.

Charontes came in, with Amelia behind him. He stood there, openly admiring me.

"What? You seem to like my tunic more than most," I teased, throwing his own words back at him.

Charontes smiled one of his rare, barely-there smiles and went into the next room. He came back with a chair for Amelia. "We are all very excited to see what the manuscripts contain," he said. "Shall we get started?" He looked at me expectantly.

Amelia smoothed the back of her skirt and sat down on the chair he had brought.

He handed me the top manuscript. I could feel butterflies in my stomach as I opened the notebook. It felt thick, probably about 150 pages long.

"How do you want me to do this?" I asked Charontes in Greek. "You both speak different languages."

"Are the writings in Amelia's language?" he asked.

"Yes."

"Then read it in the language it is written in, and translate for me each half page or so."

"That will work," I replied.

I began to read, and the tale unfolded into an amazing story. Amelia sat quietly while I spoke. Occasionally, when I paused to look up at her, her eyes were misted with tears. It was her mistress's life story.

Charontes sat in stony silence. I couldn't decipher his expression, but he waited patiently for me to translate each piece to him. At about page fifty, he leaned back in his chair and let out a long sigh.

"We're in the middle of something bigger than all of us," he said. "This has been going on for many lifetimes. I never realized how many people's lives this magnet has changed."

I translated to Amelia what he'd said.

Amelia nodded her head, her eyes wide. "What are we supposed to do?" she asked. "I'm scared."

"Me, too," I agreed. "Maybe this *is* too big for us."

I translated for Charontes and prepared to read on.

"We have to know more than Vanth," Charontes said. "That's the only way we will have a chance to beat her. Can you keep reading?"

"Yes, I'm fine. I want to keep reading."

"Good." Charontes crossed his legs at the ankles and scooted a bit farther down into his chair. It creaked and groaned, but held.

I began to read.

It was some time past noon when I shut the notebook. I'd finished 145 handwritten pages. We'd learned so much about the magnet, or Satres, and how Patrizia had come to be in the farmhouse. I wanted to start right into the second notebook.

"That's enough for now," Charontes said. "We will eat and talk about what you've read."

"Maybe I should keep reading," I said to Charontes.

"I am going to make something for us to eat," Amelia said, as if she understood what Charontes had said. "It has been many hours since we broke our fast."

"I guess I'm outnumbered then," I said in both languages. It made me feel at home to switch back and forth between Italian and Greek. It was almost like I was talking to my parents again.

Amelia went into the kitchen. Plates and dishes clanged as she began to prepare the meal.

"What do you think?" I asked Charontes.

"I want to hear what the other two manuscripts contain. If I hadn't gone through time myself, what you just read would be completely unbelievable."

Amelia came into the room, "Lydia, can you sit at the kitchen table?"

"If someone helped me get there, I think I could." I looked over at Charontes. "Amelia is asking if I could sit at the table to eat. If there's any way you could help me, I would love to. I'm tired and sore from being in bed all the time."

He stood and picked me up. He held me so that my face was near his and said, "If it pleases you, my beauty, you have only to ask me once." He headed toward the kitchen with me, sheet and all.

I thought I would faint. To think I had to time travel to meet this guy. They just didn't make them like this anymore. I wondered if Charontes, like my dream man, would remain true—even with bamboo splinters being shoved under his nails.

He sat me ever so gently into a chair. I knew there were more important things I should be thinking about, but I found myself staring stupidly at his large, flat nails. Even *they* looked manly. I was definitely falling hard.

I tried to imagine what it would be like to always be with him, in my own time. To be able to call him *my* man. My very own statue, come to life. When my friends came over to the apartment, at first they would mistake him for an exceptionally tasteful piece of artwork. Then he would move, and they would all gasp, realizing he wasn't fine art at all. I would proudly introduce him as my new boyfriend.

Amelia started serving the food, breaking me out of my fantasy. "You are a genius with food, Amelia…who taught you to cook?" I asked, crunching down on a juicy grape.

"My mom was an excellent cook, and I really enjoy it," she said.

"Did you hear that, Charontes? Amelia's mother taught her to cook, and she really enjoys it."

"That's good, because I really enjoy eating." He grabbed a huge hunk of bread. "Ask her if the stew is ready."

"If it weren't for bad manners, you'd have none at all," I said sarcastically. "Amelia, Charontes says that he enjoys your cooking so much, he can hardly wait for the stew to be ready." I squinted my eyes at him.

He squinted back at me. "I know you tell her different things than what I say. As long as you make me sound better, I don't mind."

"I usually make you sound whiny, almost like a girl," I said with raised eyebrows.

For what was probably the first time in his life, Charontes actually laughed out loud. An explosive, deep, and genuinely mirthful laugh. The unexpectedness of my comment made him choke on his bread. A rogue bite flew out onto the table.

"I don't think I'm going to have to translate *that* one," I said.

Amelia and I were already laughing at him.

"Don't worry, I never make the same mistake twice," he said, trying desperately to hold onto some of his lost dignity.

"Thank goodness, because then we'd need more napkins," I said, unable to resist one last tease.

"It's definitely love," Amelia said with an exaggerated sigh of longing.

"We need to let you rest briefly," Charontes said, sobering the mood. "Then you have to continue reading. We must not relax our vigilance—our lives depend on it."

I translated to Amelia, who heartily agreed.

"I will clean up while you rest," she said.

Charontes picked me up and carried me back to my bed. "It can get dangerous to laugh at a warrior," Charontes said, setting me into bed. "Didn't your father teach you that?"

"Where I come from, they don't have warriors like you—believe me when I tell you that."

"What are your warriors like?" he asked, looking very interested.

"You would be unique among them, let's just put it that way." I didn't want to answer him cryptically, but I didn't know how detailed of an answer he was looking for.

"Unique? Do you mean I would be inferior?" he asked, puffing up a bit.

"Oh no. No, you would not be inferior. Nope, not one little hair on your body would be or could be considered mediocre where I come from." Smiling, I looked him up and down. "Relax, you can put away the plumage."

"I don't understand every word you say, and your choice of words can be quite puzzling. But it's reassuring to hear I would not be considered inferior—I don't ever want to disappoint you."

As if he ever could, I thought.

"Do men in your time have more hair than I do?" he asked suddenly. "You know, I have a lot of hair you haven't seen yet. I'm sure as much as other men."

I had to giggle at him. He was hopelessly sweet in an oversized sort of way. I couldn't help but wonder what other sayings of mine he'd misinterpreted. "You do *not* disappoint me, not in the least, and I will try to speak more clearly. What

I meant to say was that there isn't a single part of you, not even the smallest hair, that I would consider inferior."

He stood up, looking immensely pleased. "You rest now. Then you must read some more."

Amelia came into the room. "Before you rest, I would ask something of you both. I would like to have Franco inside for meals, but I am unsure if it would be permissible."

I repeated what she'd said to Charontes. He nodded and shrugged.

"Of course," I said. "It's *your* house."

The radiance of Amelia's smile almost blinded me.

Chapter 32

August 1481 AD

Firenze

What if it were perfect every time?

A week had passed since I started reading the manuscripts. It had been a week of terrifying revelations, but also one of splendor and ecstasy. Every day, we learned more about the magnet. We'd become acutely aware of the tremendous danger and obstacles in our way.

In order to relieve our stress after spending hours reading, Charontes had begun taking me to his special pond. My fear of water kept me on a rock near the edge. He would swim and try, unsuccessfully, to coax me into the water. He knew I was afraid, but he let me blame it all on my splint, which I was supposed to keep dry.

Our love blossomed in the paradise-like surroundings. Still, it felt tarnished by the continual anxiety of being unable to take action. It seemed like we were just waiting for something bad to happen.

I'd finished reading the manuscripts that day, and now sat in the kitchen, not hearing a word Amelia said to me. I would just nod and say "yes" or "really" every time I heard a long pause. I couldn't help being so distracted—my mind kept going over and over the details in the manuscripts.

Patrizia's notes had been filled with intricate details on how Satres worked. How they had discovered the magnet contained nanotechnology and I.N. Her writings about the science of implanting tiny machines and computers into the human body amazed me.

Although the notebooks were packed with information, most of the nanotechnology and I.N. specifics had been way over my head. With only one year of physics in college, when Patrizia began plugging the magnet's time-travel capabilities into a time-dilation formula and calculating it using the magnetic forces surrounding the earth, the concepts had simply become too difficult for me to grasp.

Charontes and Amelia had just stared at me when I read those parts. I'd done my best to explain what I could, but they weren't alone in their incomprehension. Patrizia had been a mathematical genius from an advanced civilization. Satres itself was from an even more advanced time. The three of us did the best we could to learn what we could from her notes.

We found out that once the chosen children were conceived, each half of the magnet would keep trying to find its other half until they were joined. Individually, the magnets would continue to work independently.

It was in the magnets' programming to calculate outcomes and discern what was best for their Chosen Ones, then always function to ensure their safety. Once the two halves were united and Satres was whole, a Chosen One could use it at will.

We learned that the Chosen One was merely a programmed receiver. Since I had the right DNA sequence, that meant a two-way, actual conversation would be possible with the whole magnet, Satres.

I thought that would be an important feature, seeing that the magnet had been sent from the future, for me to save the future, and I didn't have any idea how to go about doing that. In fact, I didn't want to have *anything* to do with it.

How was I supposed to harness this nanotechnology I knew next to nothing about? Then save the future, which I knew even less about, from a deadly virus I definitely knew nothing about.

Apparently, I could use Satres, the united magnet, to travel through time and go to any time period I chose, except for repeating times. Her notes made it sound like the Chosen One would have almost limitless power to control time. Except for one small hypothesis she'd mentioned only once— even the Chosen One would not be able to repeat time.

This rule had intrigued me. Since I'd already lived from 1986 through all the years leading up to 2016, I could not go back into those years again. Still, it seemed to be the only rule Patrizia hadn't been entirely sure about.

It made Charontes furious when I read that part to him. He shouted that it would be advantageous to go back and correct your mistakes.

I agreed with him and asked him to give me the magnet so we could try it. He just became angrier, then stormed out of the house. I didn't know why he'd gotten so angry, but I knew I'd find out sooner or later.

After he'd left, I kept reading. The reading became so technical that even Amelia wandered off to do chores, leaving me to read in silence. I wasn't an expert like Patrizia, and I'd never even heard of a closed timeline curve before—but I tried my best.

Everything I knew about crossing a time paradox, I'd learned from the movies. One thing was for sure, though—crossing one never led the movie stars to a happy ending. Usually it resulted in end-of-the-world-as-we-know-it kind of situations.

It was unnatural to go through time, but repeating it did seem really wrong to me. How many times would you be willing to go back until you got it right? How would you ever know *if* you got it right? It seemed like too big a burden to put onto any one person.

Would that person then be expected to keep going back, fixing any and every mistake they or others made? Would alternate timelines be created each time they went back, leading to multiple existences and multiple universes?

With the whole magnet, the user would be tempted to go back and fix things. They could go back to times they hadn't lived in. If Patrizia's hypothesis held true, then they would only get one shot at it.

This felt right to me. No one person should be saddled with the monstrous task of fixing the mistakes of everyone else—especially when that person could very well be me.

I hoped her theory about not being able to repeat time was true.

It boggled my mind that I was conceived in 384 BC, born in 1481 AD, and lived in 2016 AD. That made my maximum age, counting from conception, 2,400 years old. If I counted just from my actual birth date, I was only four months old right now. I liked the sound of that one better.

If I never got back to my own time, I would have to just keep adding onto my age now to keep track of it. It felt strange to put time and its relevance into perspective this way. It *was* only relative to the individual. That must have been what Einstein was talking about. Funny, it took actual time travel for me to finally grasp his most basic concept.

"So you agree with me then, Lydia?" Amelia asked.

"Huh? Oh yes, uh-huh."

"So goats *can* fly?" she asked. "I knew you weren't listening to me." She didn't sound angry, though—she just smiled at me. "I know what you're feeling—it's love."

"I'm so sorry, Amelia. I was just daydreaming."

"Daydreaming…I like the way that sounds. It's fine, Lydia. I, too, am in love." Amelia had a shy smile on her face.

"You are?" I had a pretty good idea who she was in love with. I'd seen her around him, and it wasn't too difficult to tell. Also, the choices here were a tad limited.

"Franco and I…we want to get married, now that we have the house and a way to support ourselves. It's what we want. Franco has stayed by my side through the bad, and now he will be there through the good. I feel so happy, I could shout, sing, and dance."

"Wow, I'm so glad for both of you!" I said. "It's very important to have someone who cares for you." I couldn't help but smile back at her. The pretty wisp of a girl grinned from ear to ear. One big smile seemed to be all she was made up of.

A bird flitted up to the window ledge, joined by two others that were already sitting there, staring at me adoringly. It chirped a repetitive warning while doing a busy little dance. I was becoming accustomed to using their miniature alerts like a sixth sense. I turned toward the door just as it opened.

Now that I understood why the animals were attracted to me, I felt a little more at ease with it. Patrizia's notes explained in detail her theory on the women in our family and their "gifts." Since we were rewritten, so to speak, we had different gifts.

At first, when the animals began appearing, I thought that maybe woodland creatures from the fourteen hundreds were more tame. It made sense—less contact with humans meant less fear of them. Then I began to realize that the animal's attentions were devoted *specifically* to me.

Not only that, like faithful dogs, all the animals would try to anticipate my every move. Everywhere I turned, there was a little squirrel, bird, or something, trying to stay as close to me as possible—yet still steering clear of anyone I was with.

Days ago, when my mind completely cleared from the effects of the medicine, I realized that I knew what the animals were thinking. They weren't verbally coherent thoughts, just more or less what they were feeling. I could sense when an animal felt fear, happiness, or contentedness sitting in the sunshine on the window ledge.

I could also sense their devotion. I didn't want it, but the animals were subtle. They didn't thrust their adoration on me, it just *was*—as if it had always been that way. I tried to ignore it at first. What else could I do about it, anyway?

Then gradually, possibly because everything else was so different, I'd started to accept it. It was a gift, so I would respect it. I didn't know who it came from, but it certainly wasn't a burden to bear.

I felt that my closeness to the magnet must have activated my gift. I definitely would have noticed previous animal devotion on a scale like this. Now I would smile, because every time I looked down, there was usually something soft, furry, and totally adorable standing there and admiring me.

Now when I looked *up*, there was also something soft, furry, and totally adorable standing there admiring me— Charontes was in the doorway.

"Are you coming back to yell again?" I asked. "We really need to talk about what we're going to do. I'm not going to just sit here and wait for Vanth to come back and kill us all."

"Yes, we need to talk—but first, there's something else."

He just stood there looking like a little boy who had done something wrong.

"What is it? Are you okay?"

"I'm fine." His voice was deep and almost coy. "Why do you ask?"

"Well, let's see—you're standing there like a big lump with your hands behind your back."

"I am merely resting them. I do not have lumps—I am in perfect health. Why do you ask so many questions?"

"Amelia, can you see what he has behind his back?" I slyly switched languages.

Charontes noticed Amelia leaning around to peek at what he had hidden behind him. "I would like a moment alone with you, woman." He looked at me with anticipation.

"Big man says respectfully that you have to go so he can harass me in private," I said to Amelia, who giggled her way to the kitchen.

"One day, your translations will get you in trouble." He bent down and kissed me. "You are my love, and I want you to know that."

My stomach flip-flopped, and my head spun. I just couldn't believe this perfect man called me "his love." *Fine, I'll do my best to put up with it,* I thought. *If a bronzed Adonis insists on loving me, who am I to question it?*

"I would like to gift you with something. It's not crafted well, since I'm not used to using my hands to create.

Mostly they have been used to destroy." His head hung down as he talked, and he scuffed his foot on the floor boards, scattering the rushes.

"A gift for me? What is it? Show me…Come on. Why are you teasing me?" I wondered what on earth he could have made.

He pulled a walking stick out from behind his back and shoved it at me. "Here, it's nothing. Just a simple tool for you to use," he added in a gruff voice.

I took the walking stick and turned it over in my hands. It was beautiful. The handle sported an elegantly carved yellow bird taking flight. The detail of the beak and each individual feather must have taken hours to carve.

The whole stick had probably taken him several days to make. It was beautifully balanced and burnished from hours of rubbing it to a glossy shine. I looked up at him with tears in my eyes. "You *made* this for me?"

"Give it back, and I will throw it away. I'm sorry it makes you unhappy. It's the work of a child. Carvings from your time must be much more advanced. Hand it to me, and I will put it in the fire."

"You will *not!* I love this—it's absolutely gorgeous! I'm crying because I'm so happy. I'll keep it forever, and by the way, wood carvings from my time aren't any more beautiful than this one is. You must have spent hours making it for me. Thank you so much."

"In truth, you are fond of the gift?" He began to puff up a little from his previously deflated state.

"Yes, in truth I am. How did you know about the yellow bird, though?"

"What about yellow birds? You don't like them? Here, give me the stick."

"No, let go of it. Yellow birds are my favorite." I said. "It makes me very happy, and I will always cherish it. I won't be able to use it right away, though. It's been almost three weeks, so maybe in a few more days, I'll try to stand while using the stick."

"I do not know this word, 'weeks.' But I will not burn the stick if you like it. When you believe you are able, I will help you to stand."

"Thank you, I'm sure I'll need all the help I can get. I was wondering if you'd like me to teach you some words from my time. I would enjoy spending the time with you, and maybe you'll be interested in some of the future things you can learn."

I knew I wasn't being entirely forthcoming with my reasons for teaching him about the future, and maybe even a little bit devious. Anyway, I didn't even know if we'd be able to get back to my time. Patrizia's manuscripts had been quite clear—we would need both halves of the magnet to be able to pick which time we'd go to.

"I would like that," Charontes answered, oblivious to my scheming. "I have been told I learn quickly, and I've always done well learning words from other languages."

His trusting ways made me feel a little uncomfortable, like I was lying to him. *Should I just ask him if he wants to come to my time with me?* He said he loved me, but maybe ancient guys told everybody that. I was scared to ask. *I'll ask another time.*

"Lydia, did you hear me?"

"Oh yeah, sorry. I was just wondering what made you so angry before. At the risk of getting you mad again, I need to know what you're thinking. We have to be on the same page. You know, the same team. Was it because I asked for the magnet, or because Patrizia said we wouldn't be able to repeat time?

"Both."

"Are you going to talk to me about it?" I asked, hoping he wouldn't stomp off again.

He hesitated.

"Listen, Charontes, I'm scared. I have no idea what I'm supposed to do, or if I even really am this chosen person. I've been ripped away from everything and everyone I know, and I'm pretty sure people are coming to kill me for a magnet I don't even have—*you* do."

"That is exactly it. I know Patrizia said you are to have the magnet, but I don't want you hunted down because you possess it. I'm also afraid you will disappear once I've given it to you. If we could repeat time," his voice rose to a booming level, "it would all be so simple. We would know exactly where and when to go to get my daughter. It makes me so angry that I have no other choice but to drag my woman into battle with me."

I began to see his frustrations in another light. "Okay, okay, calm down. Take it easy. It seems like you've already given this a lot of thought. Do you have some sort of a plan then, if you refuse to give me the magnet? You said we would talk about it. Now that we've finished reading Patrizia's manuscripts, we have to figure out how to stay one step ahead of Vanth and the Riders."

"Yes, I have a plan. I don't like it for reasons I've already told you, but I do have one."

"Good. What is it?" I felt an excited sort of relief that he may have come up with a way to help ourselves.

"Once you are almost healed, we will find the other half of the magnet…and my daughter." The tone of his response implied that any fool should have thought of that.

"Great—but exactly *how* do you plan to do that?" I tried to stay calm and let him talk.

"I don't want to, but I will give you the pin. You must allow me to hold you in my arms when you take possession of it, though. I will not lose you, Lydia. Then if Patrizia's notes are correct, the magnet will find its other half for us."

I thought about what he'd said and realized that, although simple, it was a great plan. We had to find his daughter, and one way or another, I wanted to get back home. Hemisatres automatically sought its other half, so that part was taken care of.

"Better to hunt than be hunted," Charontes said.

Wow, that must be a really old saying. "Okay, it sounds like a plan. Now all I have to do is get better and pray in the meantime that they don't show up. I hope we're doing the right thing."

"We have no other choice," he said in a patient voice. "I cannot take you into battle with an injury. It seems to me that the magnet may be protecting us now. In fact, I believe it has protected Nortia, and thus you, all along. It has kept you just out of reach of danger every time. I only hope it continues to do so for a little longer, at least until you are healed."

For an ancient guy, he was really quite logical. "I hope so, too. I feel better just knowing we have a plan."

"Yes, try not to worry. I will protect you. In the meantime, while you mend, you will tell me about where you come from. I want to know all about the warriors in your time."

"I may have to give you a little background information first." I smiled at his seriousness. I could tell he felt a little jealous.

Chapter 33

September 1481 AD

Firenze

These were the best of times.

Six weeks had passed since I ran away and broke my leg. But now, I was head-over-heels in love. I spent nearly the entirety of every day with Charontes, laughing, kissing, touching, and talking. In my eyes, he was magnificent.

We'd spent this last week talking about where I came from and many of the modern wonders. Once he got past his initial disbelief of a new concept, he learned quickly. I attempted the daunting task of filling him in on what had transpired between ancient times and 2016. Each time I thought I was on the right track, I would realize that a gaping hole in history had been left out. Usually one of his astute questions would bring the oversight to my attention.

Not being a historian, what I knew about history tended to be blurry and almost certainly flawed. I tried to explain that to him, but he just told me to do the best that I could.

I liked hearing him using modern words when he asked me questions. His accent when he said words like "electricity" was mouthwateringly sexy. I continued to speak to him in Greek but used English for most of the modern words he learned.

I dreamed of bringing him back with me to 2016. If that ever became a reality, he would need to learn English. It was marvelous how he could hear a word once or twice, then use it correctly and remember it. He hadn't been kidding when he said he learned languages fast.

He doted on me regularly. When I stood up for the first time, ten days ago, he'd been right there at my side. I'd proudly used my walking stick and stood for nearly a full minute. Now I could take limping steps. Enough to get from the bed to the chair or take care of my personal needs. For anything else, he was right there.

It seemed silly to think of my life now as ideal. I was displaced in time, unsure of how or if I would ever get home. My leg was broken. A murdering cult was tracking us and could show up, literally, at any time—but life just couldn't be any better. I had to admit that it was a little ironic.

I didn't know what I was going to do about being the Chosen One. I'd reread Patrizia's manuscripts and started to read the others in her room. So far, I'd found no instructions on how to be the Chosen One. Deep down inside, I felt there must be some kind of a mistake.

Why me, anyway? I knew about the whole descendant-DNA thing, but still…why *me?* It just didn't make sense. I didn't want that kind of responsibility and this undefined role. It was crazy. I had a million unanswered questions after reading the notebooks.

Who exactly in my future family had made the magnet? What kind of technology could make time travel possible? Why a magnet, and what kind of I.N. technology did it have? What horrible fate did the virus hold in store for my future ancestors, and how could I possibly prevent it? I hoped they knew what they were doing, or would be doing, when they'd picked me.

I'd have to take things one day at a time. Since I didn't understand the full picture, it made the future, if I could call it that, seem ominous. At least for now, I only had half of the magnet to worry about. Thank heavens that my half seemed to function without any guidance, because I certainly didn't know how to use it.

Amelia's voice rang out, calling for Charontes. I smiled at how confident she had become as the new mistress of the house. She still couldn't converse with Charontes because of the language barrier, but she would now boldly call his name whenever she needed his help.

Sitting on the edge of my bed, I hurried to finish washing and dressing. Amelia was calling for Charontes to carry me to the table, and I wanted to be ready.

I recalled an ugly scene from last week. Amelia had called for Charontes numerous times, just like today—but there was no response. Then I'd heard her asking Franco if he would carry me to the table, because she couldn't find

Charontes. It had been strange for him not to be right there. He usually hovered over me, and he was certainly never late to a meal.

Franco seemed a bit uneasy about carrying me, but strength-wise, he managed to lift me well enough. While carrying me, he just kept apologizing, and his face kept getting redder and redder. I thought he might be nervous about touching me. I remembered thinking how much I hated being a burden to everyone.

We were almost to the kitchen when Franco tripped, and I felt myself falling. I'd thought, *Perfect, with my luck, I'll break the other leg.* Franco made a small cry of dismay when I started slipping from his grasp.

It had all happened so fast.

Suddenly, Charontes plucked me out of Franco's hands just before I hit the ground.

"Tell him never to touch you again," Charontes roared out to me, "or he will know what it is like to die from my sword." He fixed a deadly stare down onto poor Franco, sprawled on his butt on the floor.

"I won't tell him that!" I said. "He was just trying to help."

Charontes hadn't even shifted his gaze off Franco as he growled murderously, "Tell him now."

For that second, I'd actually felt afraid of him. Seeing his nice side every day made it easy to forget how lethal he could be when crossed.

"He says to be more careful," I loosely translated to Franco, "and next time only *he* will move me." I'd felt like a wretch even saying that much to him and tried to wear an "I'm sorry" look on my face when I'd said it.

Franco had been defensively returning Charontes's glare, but thankfully, he finally dropped his gaze with a nod of ascension. I knew Franco was smart enough to figure out what Charontes had really said. Even with the language difference, there had been no mistaking his deadly tone.

When that had happened, I couldn't help but wonder if it would be a tragically bad idea to bring Charontes back to my time. That is, if we ever made it there, anyway. *What would he do, skewer my father for kissing me hello? Behead a*

grocery clerk for having an attitude? Slay the neighbor's
dogs for barking?

It would definitely be interesting. He might have to
tone the armor down some. I tried to imagine him in jeans and
a loose-fitting, white button-down shirt, with two or three
buttons undone. Not enough undone buttons to make him
look like a silly disco dancer, but enough to look casual and
sexy.

Amelia's voice rang out again for Charontes. Amelia
wouldn't be asking poor Franco for help anytime soon. I
sighed and looked at the squirrel curled up on my bed. I was
starting to feel like Snow White. While I couldn't bring
myself to touch the wild animals, I could tell that they really
wanted me to.

On our walks, whenever Charontes would put me
down and step back, the animals that had been following at a
safe distance would get closer and closer. Deer ate out of my
hand. The funny thing was, I'd begun to get used to it.

Using my mind, I would experiment and call certain
animals to my window ledge. I wouldn't use a name, but
would just imagine what they looked like in my mind. I

would ask them to come by thinking of them moving toward me and they would show up.

They were always overjoyed to be called and were excited to see me. I hoped I would always have this connection with the animals, because it was actually kind of neat.

The squirrel woke with a start, and scrambled for my ledge, as if he were in fast-forward mode. That was my cue that someone was approaching.

"You look beautiful, as always," Charontes said as he came through the doorway. He bent forward and gave me a kiss.

It came so naturally now to share affection with him. He truly was becoming a part of me. "Why, thank you, and so do you," I said.

This made him emit a grunt, which may have been a Paleolithic chuckle. "Are you hungry?"

"I'm starved," I said truthfully. The extra effort it took standing and trying to walk honed my appetite. The buttery smell of roasting chicken had been wafting through the house for hours now, tempting me.

Charontes started forward to pick me up and carry me to the table, but I stopped him. "Wait, I have a surprise for you." Using my walking stick, I started limping slowly. "I can make it all the way to the kitchen—now there won't be even the smallest chance of losing any helpful-but-innocent bystanders." I looked at him reproachfully, remembering the incident with Franco.

"I'm glad you're getting better, but I will miss carrying you," he said, completely ignoring my jab.

"Oh, I wouldn't worry about that. I can only make it ten or fifteen feet. I'm far from being out of your arms. You're my warrior taxi. Besides, I don't think I'll mind letting you carry me around, even when I'm well. Maybe I'll let you carry me everywhere and just forget how to walk," I teased.

"I will make you keep at least part of that promise," he said, following me into the kitchen.

Amelia beamed at my progress. "I'm so happy for you," she said. "You are walking well, Lydia."

"Thank you, thank you very much," I said, using my best Elvis voice, which went completely unappreciated by my current audience. My leg felt like it was filled with water as I lowered myself into the chair, trying not to wince.

I wasn't sure, but maybe my splint that looked like it was from the *Clan of the Cave Bear* could come off today. I had been wearing it for six weeks, and I needed to start bending the joints. *But first, lunch,* I thought.

Meals were my favorite times here—okay, *second* favorite. Talking with Amelia and Franco at each meal brought us all closer. Since the incident last week, Franco treated Charontes with a healthy respect, but they still got along.

If that had happened between two women, they would have hated each other forever, I mused. Minutes after an altercation like that, they would have been plotting out the other's demise, not stopping until the other was dead. Bringing an all-new feminine light to the term "burying the hatchet."

Men were different.

They must have an unwritten universal code of behavior about claiming women, one which was virulent enough to have endured centuries. *She's mine. That one's yours. Don't make me kill you. Okay, let's eat.*

I was just happy the men were getting along. Mostly, Charontes preferred to listen and let everyone else do the talking. I translated for him, but I could tell he was picking up on Italian. Lately, I'd noticed him smiling when something funny was said, even before I'd translated it.

After lunch, we planned to go to the pond. I couldn't wait. I planned to take my splint off and have Charontes bring me into the shallow water. He knew how terrified I was of the water, but if he held onto me, I would try to control it long enough for the glory of having a bath. I hoped I could manage. To be even partially submerged would be heaven.

The entire time we ate, Charontes watched me closely, and I could easily tell where his thoughts were. Then he abruptly stood up from the table. "We are going now," he said in a clipped, strangled sort of way.

I laughed. He must have known what I was thinking— I could see the big vein on the side of his neck sticking out a bit. It felt good to know I could get his blood pressure up. He was a muscle-bound Goliath, but could be really adorable sometimes.

"Charontes said, 'Pardon us, my fair Amelia,'" I translated. "'May I take the pleasure of reminding you that your meals get better each time we eat them? It was heavenly dining with you, and you also, Franco. Regrettably though, we must leave your bountiful table and go for a walk.'"

Charontes already had me in his arms and was heading out the door, growling at my subterfuge. I continued on, "'But, worry not, fair lady and brave sir—we shall return. While we are gone, I will try to teach this maiden manners that are as impeccable as mine.'" I had to shout the last part, and I could hear the fading sounds of Amelia's giggles as we went down the path. He was so much fun to tease.

"I will teach you something today, Lydia, and believe me, it will not be manners," he said in Greek.

I laughed and melted into his arms. I knew he was understanding more Italian than he let on. I closed my eyes and concentrated on how I was going to be a good student.

When we reached the pond, Charontes put me onto the rock I always sat on. I felt safe on it, even with so much water near. I hiked up my skirt and began to untie my splint. "This thing is coming off," I said. "I think it's been on long enough. And, fear or no fear, I desperately need to wash myself."

"Yes, you are most likely right," he teased. "I will be happy to see you washed, too."

"That's not nice! You know how afraid I am, and you're making me feel bad." I had the splint half untied already. Charontes walked back to the shore and began quickly stripping off his clothes while I tried to focus on the splint ties. I didn't think I'd ever get used to him whipping his clothes off like that. Already, I could feel my pulse racing.

There was a quiet splash, and he swam to the far side of my rock where the water was the deepest. "I want to make you feel good, Lydia, not bad," he said. His big black eyes looked up at me sincerely. Wet from the swim, his long brown hair was now slicked back from his face.

He was so handsome. *Oh boy, why won't these ties come apart?* I made a bumbling mess of taking my splint off. My hands shook. "It's because I'm afraid of the water, you know that," I said, not entirely lying.

He took his hand and covered both of mine with it. "Let me help you," he whispered, then ripped away each tie until my leg was free.

The leg looked weird without all its wrappings. I bent it to test it. My knee felt stiff, but it wasn't painful to move.

"Are you ready to come in here with me?" Charontes asked. "Do not fear, I will hold you. No harm will come to you. Take off your clothes."

"I—I," I stuttered, partially afraid of the water—and partially embarrassed about stripping down outside, right there in front of him.

I knew he'd already seen me naked when I had the high fever, but it was at times like these when it became vividly apparent that my warrior was a free-spirited, non-constrained toga type. The chastely covered Renaissance people would have been thoroughly scandalized with his casual, naked behavior. I felt like I fell somewhere between the two mindsets.

"I will not," I said, at a loss for what to do next.

"Why? Your clothes will be wet." He sounded confused.

I knew I was probably making some sort of ancient bathing blunder or prehistoric swimming faux pas. We were from different times, and it seemed like instead of things getting simpler, they were only going to get more confusing.

At the risk of treading on his primordial toes, I had my own set of values and I decided to stick to them.

He reached up and put his hand behind my neck, pulling me down for a kiss. Then he kissed my neck and down one arm. My tunic had come undone. *Pesky antique ties.*

After two minutes of kissing, I felt the tunic glide over my head. He kissed me in earnest, touching me through my chemise, which was wet now and plastered to my upper body—and completely transparent.

Okay, now where am I? That's it, my own set of values. No matter if we traveled through time or what, I would keep them intact. Yes, intact, because they defined who I was. It would be similar to losing my identity if I didn't hold on to them.

I slipped farther into the mists of passion. I felt him pull my skirt off. Well, I still had on my chemise. It wasn't like I was entirely naked. He lifted me down into the pond, holding me tight. Since I was so distracted, I didn't feel the usual terror when the cool water closed over my body.

"Your underdress will be wet now. How will you remedy that?" He had a sly smile as he held me, letting me float on my back.

I looked down at my front and had to stifle a gasp. My chemise was completely see-through. I might as well not have worn anything at all.

"You are beautiful, Lydia. Why do you worry?"

"Just an old habit of mine. The whole wearing-clothes-so-you're-not-naked thing. Where I come from, we wear more clothes than what you seem used to."

"I love every part of you. Why would you think to cover it? Would you want me to cover myself?"

"You do have a point there. But if I were muscled like you, I would be parading down Main Street, too."

"I know not what you mean," he answered. "I don't like my women overly muscled."

I looked at him in disbelief. I couldn't believe he was serious. His face was set, but I could see a glimmer of amusement in his eyes.

"It's nice to know that you can have so much fun at my expense," I said, trying to sound hurt.

"You are enticing to look at, with your clothes on or off. Although, I prefer you with them *off*."

He pulled me down through the water so I faced him. I couldn't reach the bottom, but I still felt safe. He held me, pressing me gently but firmly against his body. Every inch of him could be felt within that tight embrace.

~~~

Charontes held Lydia tightly to him. He never wanted this moment to end. They were as one. "Lydia, we are meant to be," he said, wading back out of the water with her.

He put her onto the stone where her clothes lay, and pushed off the rock to swim while she dressed. He wanted to give her the privacy that she seemed to need. Their stolen moments here at the pond gave him only the briefest respite from the thoughts that plagued him.

Time grew short. The warrior in him could feel it.

Lydia was much improved—but she was still unable to run or even walk for more than a few steps. They were in a very vulnerable position here, and it chafed him that he could do nothing about it.

Try as he may to figure out a better strategy, it was all contingent on Lydia's being able to get around better.

What then? Give her the pin? What if the magnet only moves her *through time?* Even if he held onto her, there were no guarantees. The magnets appeared to do as they pleased. He could lose her, as well as any chance he had of finding his daughter.

This problem seemed unsolvable. Give Lydia the pin and risk losing her, or don't give her the pin and possibly never see his daughter again. Worse still, take no action and risk Lydia being cut down by his own men. He knew Vanth would never stop. He was one man against all of them. None of this seemed fair.

Every sensible thought he had screamed out for him to hurry up and give Lydia the pin. With the element of surprise on their side, they could find the Riders. Then, one by one, he would cut them down. The enemy would be eliminated, and he would be able to rescue his daughter.

Even now, his fears stopped him from giving Lydia the pin. She hadn't fought him about it, but they both knew what Patrizia's note had said: *Lydia should wear the pin at all times for protection.*

He just couldn't bring himself to give it to her. He couldn't lose her.

Chapter 34

September 1481 AD

Firenze

Uniquely, time can grow short.

Limping a bit, I approached the stable. I needed a distraction. I would see what animals were housed there. I sensed them inside, yearning to get to me, but unable to because of their confines.

My leg felt strong today, almost as strong as my good leg. Pulling open the stable door, I went inside. Enveloped in darkness, I waited for my eyes to adjust. The smell of straw and leather filled my nostrils.

Two weeks had passed since I'd removed the splint. I was so in love with Charontes that I'd felt as if I were floating on a big, fat, fluffy cumulonimbus cloud. Unfortunately, all good things come to an end. I just hated that it was all because of me.

Earlier this week, when the haze of passion cleared the tiniest bit, I noticed Charontes's behavior growing increasingly strange. His temper flared at the slightest provocation.

Before, small things hadn't bothered him. Now, a dropped stick of firewood or a slammed door would elicit a foul curse on his part. He seemed jumpy and would change the subject when I wanted talk about the plan or the manuscripts. If I pressed on with it, he would get up and stomp out. Only when he held me in his arms would he relax again and turn into the man I had fallen in love with.

Later this week, even that ended. It all came to a head today when he'd grabbed my arm and randomly said, "I don't care if I ever go back to the time I came from. I would never blame you, Lydia. I love you too much to give you the pin and risk losing you. If I never find my daughter again, I alone will be to blame. I must learn to live with that."

Instead of falling into his arms, cooing, as he must have anticipated I would, I lost it. "You mean you want to jeopardize all our lives and the life of an innocent child because of *me?* How can you say that and expect me not to blame myself?"

Then the guilt had set in. Feeling suffocated, I had to get out of the house and away from him. That's when I'd set out for the stable. My heart felt like it had an iron shackle around it, dragging me down.

I fought back the tears. *Stupid girl*, I thought. Here I was, happily making plans to bring Charontes back to my time. *Perfect.* I could just see him in the express lane at a supermarket. *No, Charontes dear, there's not a lot of room in Aisle Eight. You'll have to use your short sword or your dagger, not the long sword.*

Never once had I considered the ramifications to everyone else. His daughter left alone with that murdering, crazy woman. Charontes ripped away from everything he'd ever known.

I loved him so much. I knew I should only want what was the best for him, not what was best for me. I was a liability to be around. *The Chosen One.*

When push came to shove, no one wanted to kill Charontes, Amelia, or Franco. They wanted to kill *me*. I was the threat, and anyone around me would suffer the consequences.

My heart was breaking. I'd found the love of my life, only to figure out that I was hazardous to his health. Amelia and Franco were also in dire jeopardy, if what Patrizia said was true.

I'd thought that Charontes had been waiting for my leg to mend. Then, like we'd planned, they would take Hemisatres and try to find his daughter. Now, because he cared for me so much, he couldn't risk losing me.

It had to be tearing him apart inside. No wonder he'd been acting strangely. It would be horrible to have to make that choice—being forced to choose between love and what is right.

I felt the anguish build up inside. Charontes had made his choice. He chose love. Life could be so unfair. By loving me, he unwittingly left me with only one choice. If I really loved him, I must give up that love for what was right.

Somehow, I had to get the pin and use Hemisatres to find his daughter. Even if I was unsuccessful in rescuing Aidyl, I had to try. I'd take the pin and leave, leading the dark riders away from the people I cared about.

That decision set loose tears which ran freely down my cheeks. Death loomed in the horizon. Too much time had already been wasted because of me. I loved him too much to stay. Charontes would fight to the death for me. Outnumbered as he would be, my staying only condemned him to certain death.

I looked down and saw two goats, busily chewing on my skirt hem. One of them was thinking about flowers. Then I heard a soft whicker. It was Charontes's horse. He'd told me stories about his stallion and warned us all to stay away from him. Franco had described the horse as a "vicious black devil." He said the animal nearly took his hand off every time he threw him hay.

Gently shooing the goats away, I thought about the horse as I moved toward him. I sensed his intentions toward me weren't malicious. Still, being fairly new at this Dr. Doolittle stuff, I inched just a bit closer. I took care to leave myself room enough to pull back out of reach of the stallion's teeth, if need be.

Towering over my head, he stretched his velvety nose out toward me from over the stall door. He was enormous. I didn't dare hold my hand out to him, but let him snuffle my arm for a minute. He behaved in a perfectly docile manner toward me, and I could tell that he didn't want to hurt me. In fact, he was happy to see me—and he also wanted some food and to be let out to run.

I couldn't believe how much I could gather from his thoughts when I really tried. They were like picture thoughts or suggestions, not sentences or anything with words. I didn't send him any thoughts back other than a feeling that I wouldn't hurt him. Somehow, he had already known that.

Stepping in closer, I let him rub his head up and down on the front of me. What a magnificent animal. I reached way up and patted either side of his face. The stallion's long mane was in tangles on the top. Without thinking, I stepped on an overturned bucket so I could it reach better, then started trying to pull the tangles apart.

Then I felt a small, cylinder-shaped compartment attached to the top of his halter.

It felt warm. Warmer than just the heat from the horse's neck. *Odd place for a compartment.* Curious, I continued to struggle with the clumps of hair so I could get a look at it. The stallion wasn't being cooperative at all. He was too busy using me as a scratching post.

I thought about the stallion being very still—and then he was. Then I pictured him lowering his head—and he did. It was nothing short of amazing, this communication with animals, and now it came effortlessly to me. I just imagined something, and they complied. Intuitively, I knew that more complex thoughts would be lost on animals of lesser intelligence, but the stallion was smart.

I had perfect access to the cylinder, and I opened the leather thong that held it shut. It got even warmer under my hand, and I felt compelled to open it. The stallion remained perfectly still. He was thinking that he wanted to help me. Gingerly pulling the top open, I saw the pin lying there inside.

What a perfect hiding spot.

Well—almost perfect.

"Lydia, please…I beg you," said a familiar male voice behind me. "Do not touch it." Charontes's face was pleading.

I didn't turn around, because if I did, he would have time to grab me. I couldn't let that happen. The noble horse still hadn't moved an inch and still stood frozen in one spot.

I hadn't thought my decision would come to fruition this quickly. I hesitated, feeling unsure. My hand was outstretched, directly above the pin. My hair floated in the air, and my heart raced in my chest.

"I love you more than life," Charontes beseeched. "Now that I've found you, I couldn't bear losing you. Please, Lydia." His voice cracked, laden with pain, but he didn't advance.

If I heard him take even one step, I would grab it. I just needed to think for a second. The pin called out to me to touch it.

A horrible commotion erupted outside. There was yelling and loud, grinding noises.

I knew it was now or never.

I grabbed the pin and shouted, "I'm doing this to save you. I love you with all—"

As the words were ripped from my throat, all my air was sucked away. I felt the sensation of being propelled up into the air at an unbelievable speed. Then, everything went black.

~~~

"Lydia!" Protracted and infinitely sad, Charontes heard his own disembodied shout as he fell to his knees.

Lifting his head up, he roared to the four quarters of the sky, shouting out his rage and anguish. His stallion began going crazy, kicking the sides of his stall and rearing up.

The noises outside got louder.

Charontes knew he should see what was going on out there, but he really didn't care. Unable to move or think, he just knelt there, staring at the last spot she'd been. He couldn't believe she'd left him. She'd gone back to her time, a time of incredible things he could never offer her. How could she do this to him? His first and only love. The one person he trusted enough to care about.

It hurt. His chest felt like a spear had pierced it. He ground his teeth together and tried to breathe. On each exhale, his chest felt crushed, the air unwilling to return. *Why? Why did she do this?* She'd heard him telling her to stop and saying how much he loved her, but she'd touched the pin, anyway.

Maybe she didn't love him. She'd never once told him that she loved him. But it seemed as if he'd told her that, over and over again. He thought back and couldn't remember one time she'd actually said that she cared for him.

A horrible realization dawned on him: she *didn't* love him. For weeks now, she'd acted so loving, he hadn't questioned it. His gaze dropped to the floor. For the first time in his life, he felt utterly defeated.

She didn't love him. He was such a fool. How could he have been so blind? Of course she didn't love him; she had all the warriors from her time to choose from. Why would she want him?

He got to his feet slowly, and his body felt heavy. Every old wound and scar complained as he rose. He felt old.

He *was* old. Ancient, in fact.

Like an old plaything, she'd used him because nothing better had been around. Discarded now, she was finished with him.

His anger seethed.

He felt a familiar fury and fought hard against it. He hated it. He'd felt that way for so long, and it was such a lonely feeling. He loved Lydia, and he couldn't make that go away.

Why did the Gods have to be so unfair?

"Where are they?" Vanth shrieked at him.

Drawing his short sword, Charontes whirled around. *What's happening? Vanth is here?* He'd been so caught up with his own despair, he hadn't even heard the warriors approaching. Where had the warrior in him gone? All those ingrained instincts, dulled by just one woman.

"I *said*, 'Where are they?'" Vanth yelled loudly. His horse kicked the side of the stall, punctuating her screaming.

Mounted on her horse, Vanth filled the doorway. Cloaked and armored, all paleness and evil. Her long, black hair contrasted her skin and fell into disheveled tousles. She looked sick and insanely angry. Long sword drawn, veins stood out vividly on her thin neck as she glared down at him.

"Who?" Charontes knew that answer would infuriate her more, but he didn't care. He didn't care about anything anymore. It hurt too badly. He didn't fear Vanth, anyway.

"Who do you *think* I mean?" she shouted. "Nortia, her guard, and the baby. The bracelet brought us back here. They must be here!"

He knew something must be askew. Why would Vanth ask for Nortia and a baby? Maybe she didn't know Lydia was grown. He needed to think fast and stall for time to figure out what had happened to Vanth and the Riders while they were gone.

"Why should I tell you anything?" he shot back. "You just left me here!"

Riders of the Reunity began slowly assembling behind Vanth. Charontes was cornered and hopelessly outnumbered. With regular warriors, he could have held his own, but these Riders were trained the same way as he had been, and he couldn't defeat them all.

"It's really very simple," Vanth said in a low, viperous tone. "You should tell me, because otherwise, we will kill you. You are not mounted and are but one man against eight warriors."

"Eight? What happened to the other two?" he asked, purposely being obtuse to buy time.

"Who cares? We are eight and myself." Vanth shrugged. She grabbed her head, as if in pain. "Answer my question, Charontes," she said, visibly trying to suppress her fury.

"If you attack me, how many of you will I take down before I fall? Even now, your numbers dwindle. Can you afford to lose more Riders? Why would you attack me, anyway? Do you think I hold ill will toward you because of the child? I don't believe the child to be mine as you claim. You, Vanth, are not known for your truthfulness."

He laughed a short indifferent laugh and waved his hand dismissively, "Anyway, who cares—it is but a child. I'm sure I have many about. It matters not to me. Finding the stone is what I've been trained for, and what I've dedicated my life to."

Vanth squinted her eyes. "Then if you are this dedicated, why is it so difficult to answer my question? I am your high priestess. You are to do my bidding." She swayed a bit in her saddle but caught herself from falling.

"I am merely angry at having been left here," he lied. "You humiliated me. The task was without challenge or honor for a warrior. One old lady was already dead, and the other one died shortly thereafter. Both are now buried. I have been here for days with naught but two servants to stare at."

He hoped he wasn't making things worse. He didn't want Vanth to know how much time had really passed while he was at the farmhouse. His only hope of finding and saving Lydia now lay in convincing Vanth that he was still anxious to get the other half of the magnet. Even if Lydia didn't want him, he loved her and would make sure of her safety.

He had to get to Lydia first and take the pin away from her. She would never be safe as long as she had it. He wasn't very good at being untruthful, but he wouldn't really have to be. He really *did* want to get the other half of the magnet.

Pretending he didn't want his daughter came from years of knowing Vanth. If he didn't care about the child, she wouldn't use her to get to him. Eventually, Vanth would relax her guard. He would wait—and when the time was right, he would find a way to rescue Aidyl and Lydia from her.

"That's a lie," Vanth said, yelling again. "We've only been gone for hours." She pressed her hand to her temple.

"Then your hours have been days here," Charontes growled back, slipping easily back into his old self.

"How is that possible?" Vanth's pallid skin began to splotch red from her screaming wrath. She looked a fright. "We grow farther and farther behind them."

"Could the stones have done this?" He wanted to lead her in the right direction, without letting her know how much he'd learned about the magnet's capabilities. He had to get her to use the magnet again…soon.

I must find Lydia before Vanth does.

Vanth seemed to be weighing the possibilities. Then she gave a weak order for everyone to line up to follow Nortia and the other half of the stone again.

Charontes hurried to saddle his horse and equip himself. Just minutes later, he came out of the stable. Looking at the group, he noticed that the Riders seemed dazed and not completely well. Even the horses looked sick—their heads were hanging down, and pink froth formed in the corners of their mouths.

He remembered all too well how he'd felt after advancing in time—it was akin to having been hit in the head with a round rock. That was what all the Riders looked like now. Some were swaying in their saddles, just like Vanth.

Everyone looked ill except for the baby. He stole a glance at Aidyl as they lined up. The child seemed perfectly fine, like she enjoyed jumping through time. The nursemaid, however, looked horrible, like she'd just wretched. Her swollen face had a greenish cast to it, and her eyes were barely open. A strong wind could have easily blown the bright-eyed, wriggling baby from her arms.

And where's the other nursemaid? Another loss that Vanth gives no credence to.

This would be the Riders' fourth time jump, in, as far as he could ascertain, the same day. No wonder they looked so ill. He was glad the baby didn't seem to be affected by it. She was too young to have withstood that kind of punishment to her tiny body. She *was* the Chosen One—maybe that was why it didn't hurt her.

As they lined up to jump, he saw Franco move behind a tree in the distance. Charontes looked around carefully to see if anyone else had noticed him, but no one was looking in that direction. He caught Franco's eye and gave him a small, curt, negative shake of his head. Hopefully that would be enough to warn the young man to keep his distance.

Charontes looked over and noticed Vanth staring at him with red-rimmed, bloodshot eyes. She looked toward the tree where Franco hid. Nothing was there. Even unwell, she was a cunning demon of a woman.

"Everyone line up, touching legs." Vanth's shout was hoarse.

Everyone seemed almost too ill to obey.

"Hurry up, you fools!" she screamed. "Push together— we're already days behind."

Charontes let out the breath he'd been holding. It seemed that Amelia and Franco would live to see another day.

Vanth's hair floated in the air.

He couldn't believe his good fortune. Just a short time before, he'd been in despair. Now, it seemed like he would have a chance to get everything he wanted—he was reunited once more with his daughter, and now hopefully on the way to finding Lydia.

He only wished it could be what Lydia wanted, too—but that was not to be.

He pulled his cloak over his head in a cowl. He knew he must hide his countenance. If Lydia saw him, she would give away his ruse. Already, he wasn't too sure Vanth believed him.

As the air ripped from his body, it sounded like thousands of bees. Oh, how it hurt. Lightning crackled, and he hurtled upward.

Chapter 35

September 2016 AD

Buffalo, New York

A time to cast away stones,

And a time to gather stones together.

—Ecclesiastes 3

Something tickled my nose, and my eyes fluttered open. I lay on my back, outside. A squirrel scampered toward some woods as a large golden retriever ran up to me, dragging his leash behind him. The dog worried for me and sat by my side. I sat up in the cool grass and pulled my skirt over my knees.

It looked to be about noon, because the sun was at its zenith. A slight chill gripped the air, even though the temperature must have been around sixty degrees. I tried to get my bearings. I could see a small lake with a bridge, as well as woods and paths. The retriever's leash was bright red and made of nylon, which was a good sign. I'd arrived at a park of some sort, and it looked exactly like Delaware Park in Buffalo.

A man of about fifty jogged toward me with a worried look on his face. "There you are, Buster. Come here, boy. I'm sorry...he just pulled the leash right out of my hands. He never does that. Are you okay, miss?"

As the dog turned toward me, he worried that something really bad was coming. He didn't picture what it was, but wanted everyone to leave there *now*.

I got up and brushed off the seat of my skirt, smiling at the man. "Yeah, I'm fine. Just enjoying the beautiful day. Buster didn't bother me at all." I pictured myself walking away from the dog and sending it feelings of gratitude for the timely warning.

"Well, have a nice day. Thanks for grabbing him." The man and dog headed away from me. The dog pulled his master along as fast as he could.

Sit back down and cry. That's what I wanted to do. I should be jumping up and down for joy right now, for it seemed like I might be back in my own time. Instead, all I could think about was Charontes. To think I'd never see him again was agonizing. Tears spilled down my cheeks.

I open my clenched hand and looked at the pin. I didn't know if I hated it or loved it. Without Hemisatres, I would have never met Charontes—but because of it, I'd also lost him. *Some Chosen One.* I didn't want any part of it. I should just throw the stupid pin into the lake and be done with it.

My hand closed reflexively back around the pin.

The decision to find the pin and rescue Aidyl seemed so logical only a short time ago. Now, when faced with the reality of actually doing it, I wasn't so sure. It seemed like such a monumental task for only one person. Where did I start?

The manuscripts said I was the Chosen One, but what did that feel like? I didn't feel any braver or stronger—I was still just plain, old Lydia. How did this magnet propose I fight mounted warriors and a demon woman? Rescue a child? The only thing I'd ever rescued was a kitten when I was twelve.

I began walking toward what I thought would be Elmwood Avenue, one of the main roads through the heart of Buffalo. My leg barely complained. My apartment was on Elmwood, just after Forest Avenue. I loved the neighborhood—it had an artsy flair and a college pulse that kept it fresh.

Many of the large, turn-of-the-century homes along Elmwood had been beautifully restored, and the two- and three-story dwellings had been divided into multiple apartments. Their owners chose to paint the decorative woodwork on the outsides of the dignified homes in unique, bright colors. My home was one of three apartments in one of these buildings—I rented the entire top floor.

After recognizing some familiar landmarks, like the Albright-Knox Art Gallery, I knew I'd landed in Buffalo. Heading down Elmwood, I stopped at a newspaper dispenser.

Looking through the small, scratched-up window, I saw the date—September 29, 2016—the day after I'd left.

I'd only been gone for a day, as if nothing had even happened. I just wanted to get home. My heart hurt.

Mom and Dad wouldn't even know I'd been gone unless work had called them. *What would I tell them at work?* Hopefully, Erin and Paula had covered for me. My shift had almost been over, and one of my two patients were deceased.

Yeah, I reminded myself, *my grandmother from the past.*

I couldn't even think about it now. I began to walk faster. My leg complained, sending a sharp pain up the outside with each step. *Only one block to go.*

A few people looked at my ribbon-laced tunic and my unusual skirt, but the way I was dressed was entirely possible, thanks to the area's "anything goes" attitude. One woman, dubbed the "White Lady," had been walking around Elmwood for years, swathed from head to toe entirely in white. White gloves, white head wrap, and even white sunglasses. Only a small part of her face peeked out. No one knew why she dressed like this, well, at least I didn't. At this point, I could care less what anyone thought—I just hoped the spare key to my apartment was still in its hiding spot. Fortunately for me, it was.

Relieved, I entered my apartment. Everything seemed strange, like when you go on a long vacation and see your home again for the first time. You see everything around you again with fresh eyes—and you also notice smells which you might have normally ignored.

Completely drained, I belly-flopped onto my bed, pin still in my hand.

My message machine flashed, but I couldn't bring myself to check it. Touching the technology would only make the realization that I'd returned to my own time more concrete. If I just lay there and closed my eyes, I could pretend I was still at the farmhouse. Any minute now, Charontes would come and take me to the pond.

Hot, angry tears landed on the quilt.

~~~

Five of the horses couldn't get up. It had been a big mistake on Vanth's part to time jump again so soon after the last time. Charontes looked around at the moaning, sprawled heaps of people and horses, flailing their legs to stand. It was his first time jump in months. He felt like he'd been bludgeoned in the head, but other than that, he could function.

The rest of the group had not fared so well.

He went from one person to another, trying to reposition their bodies for comfort. Then he saw Aidyl, safe in the crook of her nursemaid's arm. The nursemaid looked ghastly. She was alive, but she wasn't moving. He thought that now would be a perfect time for him to grab his child and leave.

Unfortunately, he didn't know what time they were in. Once Vanth figured out where his loyalties lay, there would be no turning back. Best if he continued his ruse until he knew for sure that he was in Lydia's time. For the moment, he left the child where she was.

They were at the edge of a clearing. A few hundred trees formed a small wood nearby. Charontes took the horses that could walk, and one by one, tied them to trees, out of sight. He remembered Lydia telling him that in her time, they didn't ride horses anymore, except in very few places— usually for fun.

Lydia had told him that there were hardly any horses around where she lived, and she'd laughed when he'd mentioned riding with her in her time. Apparently, even one horse would draw a lot of attention where she lived.

Yes, I must have been a great source of amusement for her, he thought.

He had to get everyone to the cover of the woods so they wouldn't draw attention to themselves. He wasn't sure what kind of danger they had to look forward to here. He began rousing the Riders and urged them to stagger toward the woods. A few of them even crawled.

With the greatest care, he lifted the nursemaid and began to carry her, his child still in her arms. Aidyl looked right into his eyes, and he felt the black ice around his heart melt. She was flawless. Her eyes were the same onyx as his, but they had tiny flecks of purple in them. Her hair was a poof of jet black fluff, and her skin was the palest of whites, just like her mother's. When she smiled at him, he felt a fierce feeling of protectiveness well up inside him.

He would die for this child—for *his* child.

Suddenly, he felt eyes on him. Forcing himself to set the nursemaid down, he turned away from his little girl.

Vanth stared over at him. She'd managed to crawl to a rock and pull herself into a sitting position. Breathing hard from the exertion, she propped her back up against the rock. As she turned her face up toward his, a thin stream of blood ran from one nostril.

When he saw her like that, he knew she wouldn't stop until she had the other half of the stone. She was absolutely unrelenting.

"What happened?" she asked angrily, wincing from pain.

"It seems all of you are growing weary and sick from using the stone so many times."

"Of course," she minced. "*You* are fine and uninjured."

"Aidyl also seems to be fine, in case you were worried for her safety," he growled. *She doesn't deserve the honor of being a mother.*

"Oh, *now* you call her by name, when before it was—*the child,*" Vanth said, raising her perfect ebony eyebrows.

"Do not bait me, woman. I care not for your petty suspicions and even less for your accusatory tone. I merely called the child by its name. Her name *is* Aidyl, is it not? Or need I remind you?"

"Any other time I would embrace fighting with you, Charontes, but I fear I am not well," Vanth panted out, letting her head fall back against the rock.

He wished she were dead as he eyed her bracelet covetously, but that would not serve him well. He didn't know how the stone worked, or if they were even in Lydia's time. Otherwise, all the Riders and Vanth would already be dead.

At least this would gain him some trust with Vanth, however undeserved it may be. She knew they'd been at his mercy, and he'd helped instead of betraying them.

He stooped to pick her up, but her icy stare stopped him.

"Don't touch me. I will get to the trees on my own. I don't want the men to see me as weak. I just need to rest for a moment."

"You will need more than a moment's rest," Charontes answered. "When one Rider is able to stand guard, I will scout ahead to see if Nortia and the other stone can be found. It would be best if you and the other Riders stay out of sight for now. None of you are able to defend yourselves for long." He hated the thought of leaving Aidyl with them, but for now, he could see no other solution. He had to find Lydia.

As long as Lydia possessed the pin, she was in mortal danger. Vanth could never know that Nortia's baby was really the now-grown Lydia.

The fact that all of the Riders and Vanth were unwell was actually a stroke of good fortune. If he found Lydia first, he could take the pin from her and warn her not to reveal her origins to anyone. Without the pin, she would be indistinguishable from everyone else. He couldn't make Lydia love him, but he could save her life.

He knew he must get to her first without Vanth's watchful eye on them. If Lydia saw him, she would certainly reveal that she knew him. It wouldn't take long for Vanth to figure out that Lydia was a pivotal piece in what was transpiring. And when Vanth was unsure, she never hesitated to kill.

When one warrior felt well enough to fight, Charontes struck off in a random direction. He'd waited just long enough to be sure that Aidyl would be protected. Even though he left, it probably still looked good to the others. His waiting until there was someone able-bodied enough to defend the group served to further prove his dedication to the Riders of the Reunity.

Not wanting to draw attention to himself with his horse, he set out on foot, his black cloak billowing out behind him. He kept his short sword drawn, his long sword at his side, and his shield on his left arm. *At least the weather isn't an issue*, Charontes thought as the sun glinted off his armor.

~~~

He came to the edge of the clearing and saw a road made of smooth black stone. Lydia had told him about the streets that the horseless chariots, or "cars," rode on. He felt elated when a car rode by him. This must be Lydia's time— for there were cars. He took care to stay out of their path.

Soon he came to a large building made of marble. As he climbed the stairs, a few people passed him, but they were unarmed. The people stared at him and laughed, but didn't challenge him. He went through the doors the people had used and found himself in a large room. Pottery, sculpture, and some small weapons were on display.

People walked about inside looking at the wares. With excitement, he realized that he must have found the indoor marketplace. Surely someone would know Lydia here. *Maybe she's even here now.*

"Lydia! Lydia!" he shouted at the top of his voice.

Everyone grew quiet and stared at him.

"Do you know where I might find Lydia? It's a matter of great importance. Her life may be in danger."

A few people laughed nervously and whispered to each other in a language he didn't recognize.

This could prove to be a problem. He'd called out in Greek, but that wasn't what they were speaking. Lydia had taught him a few words in her tongue, but not enough that he could converse in it. *Surely someone knows Greek,* he thought.

"Does anyone here speak Greek?" he called out into the crowd. "Greetings. Can anyone understand this tongue? Does anyone know where I can find Lydia?" he bellowed loudly, wanting to make sure people in adjacent rooms could hear him.

"Are you for real or what?" asked a tall, slim, blond man in his early twenties as he entered from the next room.

"I am real," Charontes said, relieved he'd found someone who understood him. "You speak Greek? Do you know Lydia?"

"My mother is Greek. Lydia...*who?*" he asked.

"Lydia, the one I seek," Charontes answered. "Why? Are there many Lydias? I will see them all then."

"What planet are you from?" the man asked. "Do you work for the museum or something? Why are you dressed like that and carrying swords?" The light-haired man had a natural athletic build, which fell short next to Charontes, but he straightened to his full six-foot-one height, anyway.

"I do not work. I am a warrior. I will be indebted to you if you bring me to these Lydias." Charontes noted that the man didn't wear armor or any weapons.

"No, I won't bring you to these...*Lydias*. I don't know any Lydias."

"That is unfortunate. Then you cannot help me." Charontes began to bellow out Lydia's name again. "Lydia!"

Two men came toward him from across the room. Charontes slung his cloak behind his shoulder and raised his sword menacingly. They were armed and wore similar clothing to each other. *These two attackers must be warriors in the same army*, he thought.

"Whoa, whoa, big guy," the young, blond man said in Greek. "You can't do that. You're going to get yourself arrested."

He lowered his sword a few inches, feeling unsure. *Arrested?* He didn't know what that was, but it sounded unsavory.

"I would be indebted to you for your help," he said, addressing the young man at his side, still facing the approaching attackers. "I am not from this time, and I don't speak their language. I give you my word of honor that I will not harm you. I will kill these two warriors, then you can help me find Lydia."

"Stop," the light-haired man said, putting a tentative hand on his arm. "I'll help you, but you must not kill those men."

Charontes shrugged off his hand, raising his sword again. "Fear not. I can slay them easily. They don't even have their swords out."

"I get it—you're like some kind of terminator, but from the past." The young man hissed his words out in a loud, forced whisper. "I'm telling you, though, if you kill them or anyone else, I won't be able to help you. I'll be out of here, then who will help you? I can't believe you. Put your sword down…*now*."

Charontes remained poised for a defensive attack, feeling unsure again. But he was sure of one thing—he would *not* take orders from an unarmed man who could barely grow a beard.

The light-haired man stepped in front of him when the two warriors neared. The two attackers yelled and pointed toward him, but the young man talked and laughed, shaking his head.

The two visibly relaxed and issued what sounded like orders to the young man, pointing toward the door.

Charontes didn't relax his fighting stance. *It could be a trick,* he thought.

The blond man turned to him and began speaking in a faked, laughing voice which Charontes understood must be for the benefit of the two other men. "I think they're going to let us go. I told them you didn't speak English and were part of a film for my humanities class project. I said you were just practicing. Be cool. Come when I tell you, and for God's sake, don't kill anyone."

Charontes didn't understand most of what the light-haired man said, but deciphered enough that he knew he most likely wouldn't have to fight the two warriors. "I am not warm—it is most suitable in here. Tell them if they advance no further, I shall let them live."

The young man rolled his eyes, but turned and addressed the two warriors. Then, after a minute, both men laughed, and the young man laughed along with them.

He would never smile at a moment like this. It is unwise to show any sign of weakness to your opponents. He growled at them, leaning in.

The two looked a little nervous, but laughed again.

One warrior roughly patted the young man on the shoulder, pointed toward the door again, laughed, and shook his head.

"Come on, let's go," the light-haired man said. "They said you're huge, and you scared them to death. The only problems they ever have in the museum are people touching the artwork. When they saw those swords, they thought you were seriously going to start trouble. They were very relieved by the excuse I gave them."

"I am large and serious with my swords. What kind of puny warriors fear a good challenge? I should kill them for their cowardice."

"Listen, mister, I don't know who you are or what you want. But if I were you, I'd walk out of here with me. They're letting us go, so don't do or say anything else until we get outside."

"Many thanks for your help," Charontes said.

The blond man had saved him considerable time. Killing the two might have taken longer if others in their army had come to their aid.

The young man led the way out. Charontes backed out of the room, sword ready. The light-haired man foolishly turned his back on the enemy.

Once outside, he turned to Charontes and stared. "Let's start from the beginning. My name is Nicholas. What's yours?"

"Charontes."

"Okay, now where are the cameras? This is some kind of a gag show, right?"

"I do not know the words you are saying." Charontes started to get annoyed. The young man had helped him, but now, he was beginning to slow him down. "I thank you again for your help, and I will fight by your side if need be as I am in your debt. I must find Lydia now."

"You're serious, right?" Nicholas asked. "You're just going to stroll down Elmwood Avenue with two swords and a skirt?"

"I must find Lydia!" He tried to be nice to the man because he felt indebted, but it was becoming difficult to do so. He tried to remember his promise not to hurt him.

"Listen, Charontes. If you walk down the street like that, caped and swinging your swords, you're going to get thrown in jail."

Charontes tipped his head, not understanding his meaning.

"You know, captured? No freedom? You'd be breaking all kinds of laws." Nicholas sounded exasperated.

He leaned down toward Nicholas and gave him one of his fiercest faces. "I have *never* been captured, and I will *not* be captured," he hissed through clenched teeth. "Death is preferable."

"Okay, don't get mad at me. I'm just trying to help. If you really are from the past, you have to admit that there are things about this time you don't know. Right?"

"Yes…" he answered, ever alert for trickery.

"Let me help you then. If you are for real, you're the answer to my prayers. I've been bored out of my mind all summer, ever since graduation. But you'll have to trust me."

"I *must* find Lydia," Charontes said. "There is little time left. She's in danger."

"Okay, who is this Lydia?" Nicholas asked. "What's her last name?"

"The last name she had was Lydia. She lives in a time like this, with…cars," Charontes answered, distracted by the lines of cars driving by.

"Well, that really narrows it down. Look, you're going to have to come to my place with me, and I will help you there. I can try looking her up on the computer if you know anything else about her. We have to get you off the street since you're dressed this way. You're going to have to lose the swords and shields and stuff. They're drawing too much attention."

As if to prove Nicholas's point, a small crowd of people nearby began pointing at them. Charontes could hear the young women giggling. *What is so funny?* He looked at the blond man. "I will not lose my weapons. How can I? They are right here with me."

One of the girls in the crowd pushed to the forefront and asked Nicholas a question. Then she turned in

Charontes's direction and looked coy, blinking her eyelashes. The other girls laughed.

"I think they like you, Charontes," Nicholas said. "They are asking if you're part of a gladiator show, then asked where they can buy tickets. The blonde one said you're *gorgeous*." Nicholas waggled his eyebrows.

"That is enough laughter!" Charontes bellowed toward the crowd. He would not tolerate their insolence.

A man yelled something out, and the crowd broke into peals of laughter. Even Nicholas laughed. "I'm sorry," Nicholas translated to Charontes, "I didn't mean to laugh. No disrespect, it's just a line from a movie. In the movie, the main character yells out, 'This is Sparta!' really loudly, in a voice a lot like yours."

That's it, I will kill him. How dare they mock me. He wasn't entirely clear on what the man had said, but everyone had laughed.

Charontes parted the crowd with just one hand, then lifted the man up into the air by the throat. "Your puny life is worthless, and you are in the final moments of it!" Charontes screamed into the terrified man's face. "Tell me how it feels to die." He began squeezing the man's neck.

Nicholas yelled and jumped at the side of Charontes's elbow in an attempt to pull his arm down. Although he was tall, Nicholas still needed to jump *up* to reach it. Even though it wasn't Charontes's sword arm, it still wouldn't budge.

"Charontes, please…think of Lydia," Nicholas pleaded. "Put him down—now."

Charontes didn't move.

"Listen to me. Don't hurt him, or we'll never get out of here. They were just saying how *good* you look. I swear it. Oh God, he just imitated a movie where the guy was dressed like you. They *like* you. Really. Now…put him down."

Charontes lowered the man to the ground and released him.

The attacked man croaked something out, then stumbled around, gasping for air and grabbing his injured throat. Nicholas patted the injured man on the back, talking to him the whole time in a soothing voice, trying to help him stand.

The man finally stood on his own. Suddenly, he looked very surprised at something that Nicholas said. In a cracked voice, he said something that sounded like an apology in Charontes's direction.

"Let's get the hell out of here before he changes his mind," Nick said. "I told him you were my Greek cousin, and what he shouted out translated to one of the highest insults in Greece. Thank God he believed me."

"He still deserves to die," Charontes grunted. It seemed like the foolish people from this time welcomed injury.

As if afraid touching him would provoke him further, Nicholas used his fingers to motion for Charontes to follow. "Look, you can't do that, *ever*. In our society, the only time you can hurt or even touch someone is if you feel your life is in imminent danger. Do you get that? *Imminent danger*. In your case, this would mean them riding at you on a bulldozer or something. That guy didn't have any swords or daggers or shields. What were you thinking? You have to promise me you won't attack just because you're mad. We'll discuss it *before* you attack. Okay?"

"No." He was tired of Nicholas talking to him like he was a child.

"No? What do you mean, *no?* Look, do you want me to help you or not? I don't *have* to help you."

Charontes thought about it. A guide from this time who spoke the language was a wise thing to have. He had much at stake, and Nicholas had already helped him out of two different situations. "Yes, you are right. I attacked an unarmed man, and there is no honor in that. I would be grateful if you would help me, Nicholas."

"Okay, because I could walk away right now. God knows that would be the smart thing to do. But I just can't pass this up if you are for real. But no killing, maiming, or decapitations, *please*. Hey, is that real gold?" Nicholas reached out to touch Charontes's armband.

Charontes smacked his hand away. "Don't touch me."

"Why? Do you pop back into your own time again or something, like that Christopher Reeve movie? Do you know how to time travel? Can you do it again? Can I go with you?" Nicholas sounded very excited.

Charontes groaned. All the questions were making his head hurt. "We must find Lydia now. She can answer all your questions. I'm a warrior, and I'm not used to answering questions."

"Okay. Hey, are you sick? You look like you're in pain. Does your head hurt?"

"I am feeling temporarily unwell from time jumping, but soon I will be right again." Charontes hated admitting any weakness, but he didn't feel threatened in the least by the man. Unless it was possible to be talked to death.

"Time jumping, cool. Is that what you call it?

"A wise woman from the future has dubbed it that," Charontes said, trying to be vague to discourage any more questions.

"From the future? Like *my* future or *your* future? Cause your future is way different from my future. If it were my future, that would be totally cool. Where is this woman? Can I talk to her? What's her name?" Nicholas prattled on, undeterred.

"Patrizia. And no, she is dead," he said, hoping to finally silence the man. His head hurt. He hated being vulnerable, but he had to lie down. He must close his eyes for a short while—they had stopped working correctly. When he looked at Nicholas, two people formed in his vision, as if he'd drunk too much wine.

"That's too bad—I would have liked to have talked with her. Wait a second—is she dead in the past or in the future? It could make a difference, you know. Wow, if you can time travel, then I guess it *wouldn't* make a difference. Or would it?"

Thankfully, Nicholas had momentarily confused himself into silence.

"Okay, here we are at my apartment," Nicholas said. "You know…my *home*." Nicholas enunciated as he took out metal pieces and opened the door with them. He started up a flight of stairs. Charontes tried to follow but stumbled on the narrow stairs.

"Are you okay?" Nicholas asked. "Listen, you need to buck it up and climb these stairs yourself. There is no way on God's green earth I'll be able to drag your big, bulky, muscled self up them. Come on, it's only a little bit further."

"I will climb the stairs," Charontes growled out. "I am fine."

"Okay, okay, I *know* you're fine. When you get up here, you can lay down for a while. Hopefully, you'll feel better then."

"Yes, I will close my eyes for a short time. I will be in good health after that. I am usually of a hale and hardy constitution." Charontes held onto the wall on one side, but he finally made it the rest of the way up the stairs.

"You don't need to tell me you're hale and hardy. You look like you eat small children for snacks."

"I do not eat children, Nicholas," Charontes said, disgusted he would think that of him.

This only made Nicholas laugh more. "I'm *joking*. You know, kidding? Having fun? Playing?"

Charontes just shrugged.

"Okay, let's get you to bed," Nicholas said. "This is my humble abode." He swept his arm out in an all-encompassing gesture.

It was a tiny place with only a few small rooms. Charontes looked around but really couldn't focus on anything other than the fact that it looked safe. He desperately needed to lie down. "Thank you, Nicholas. Show me where I might rest."

"Right here. It's my bed, but you're welcome to it." He showed Charontes into one of the small rooms, which was darkened from the window coverings. "I'm going to get you something to wear while you're asleep, because you can't go out again in that get-up."

Charontes was past arguing. "Is it safe here?" he asked, sitting down heavily onto the bed. "Will I be able to sleep unmolested while you are away?"

"Yeah, are you kidding? Believe me, no one will bother you. I live alone, and I'll lock the doors when I leave. Charontes, please stay here until I get back with your new clothes. Hey, how big are your feet?" Nicholas asked, looking down at Charontes's feet. "Wow, those are more like pontoons. I'll tell you what—just keep the boots or whatever those are. They'll look fine under pants." Nicholas visually assessed Charontes one last time, then left.

Charontes grunted and fell back onto the bed. Too weary to take anything off, he left his cloak, armor, and even his greaves on. Holding his sword over his chest, he closed his eyes. He must rest. If Nicholas said it was safe, he would believe him.

Chapter 36

September 2016

Buffalo, New York

Sometimes things are meant to be.

Charontes woke. He hadn't moved from the spot where he lay down. He could hear someone outside the door, trying to get into Nicholas's home. Silently, he moved toward the door. He could run his sword straight through it and skewer the person trying to enter.

The door flew open, and Nicholas stood there, laden down with bags. His eyes widened as he stared at Charontes, poised to strike.

"I can't believe it! You were actually going to stab me, weren't you? You seriously need to relax. You're going to hurt someone—namely *me*."

"I did not stab you," Charontes said. "I merely made sure that it was indeed you entering."

"Uh-huh. Okay, I can see where a secret knock, or better yet, a whistle, might come in handy when dealing with you. Anyway, I went to AMVETS and bought a few different things to make sure I got something that fit you." Nicholas put the bags on the couch and began rummaging through them.

"Nicholas, I do not want clothes. I *have* clothes. I want to find Lydia."

"I know. While I shopped, I thought about it. I have a plan. You're hungry, right?"

"Yes." He hadn't eaten since the night before.

"Okay, we need to go and get something to eat. My parents own the Greek restaurant down the street. My dad's Egyptian, but my Mom is Greek. She runs the place. Not a big call for Egyptian food here in Buffalo, so they went for Greek cuisine."

Charontes listened to every word Nicholas said, managing to get most of his meanings—but there were many words he didn't understand. Nicholas talked too fast to ask him each unknown word's meaning. He would just have to do his best.

"Anyway, if I bring you there—they'll flip. Their absolute favorite thing in the world is feeding people, and you look like you can eat. The more someone can eat, the happier they are with them. It's tradition or something. Who knows? But I say we go there, and while we're eating, you tell me everything you know about Lydia. I guarantee you there is some detail you don't even know you remember that could help me. When we figure out what it is, I'll plug it into my computer and find her."

"Lydia told me of these computers. You think they can find her?"

"If anything can, they can. It's just a matter of asking it the right questions from knowledge or details we have of Lydia."

"I agree then," Charontes conceded.

Nicholas switched on the light in the living room and began pulling out the clothes.

"How did you do that?" Charontes asked.

"You are in for a lot of surprises, my mammoth friend. Technology has advanced a bit since…uh, when did you say you're from?"

Charontes just shook his head and began turning the amazing light on and off. Lydia and he had been through this before. Since his calendar was different from hers, they hadn't been able to determine an exact date he had come from. "I don't know how to explain it in relation to your calendar. Lydia and I also had this problem."

"Ever heard of Jesus?" Nicholas asked.

"No. Should I know him?"

"Let's see, Jesus Christ, from Jerusalem. Son of Mary and Joseph?" Nicholas pressed on. "No clue? Okay, stop it with the light."

"No, I do not know him." Charontes flipped the light switch on and off four more times before he stopped. He would not take orders from this boy.

"Well, that alone tells me you're from a hell of a long time ago. You look like you're an ancient Greek or a gladiator or something. Ever heard of the Coliseum in Rome?"

Charontes looked at him blankly. He really only understood about half of what Nicholas said. *Good thing he talks a lot.*

"Never mind, even that was built after Jesus. I just graduated with a bachelor's degree in history, but I definitely don't specialize in ancient history. Listen to *me—just* graduated. It was months ago. Not that it matters. There aren't any jobs around here, and that makes for either a move or being completely bored out of your mind.

"Anyway, enough about me. Try this on." Nicholas threw him an extremely large black button-down shirt. "You're going to have to take your armor off."

"No. What if we're attacked and we have to protect ourselves?" Charontes didn't like Nicholas's idea.

"Have you *seen* yourself lately?" Nicholas asked. "You're huge. You look like the Incredible Hulk. No one is going to touch you—they'd have to be stupid."

"Hulk? Who is this 'Hulk?' Lydia would call me this name." Charontes felt reassured that this time, Nicholas viewed him as a formidable warrior. He took off his cloak and began unfastening his cuirass.

"He's just this really big, monster-like guy on television and movies," Nicholas said, pulling a huge pair of jeans out of the bag.

Fascinated, Charontes remembered Lydia telling him about the boxes people watched with moving people in them. "What of this television, do you have a box?"

"Yes, I have one, but I'm afraid if I show it to you, we'll never get out of here."

"Why? Will it trap us here?" Charontes began reaching for his armor again.

"No, and will you stop with the armor? All I mean is, if the light switch occupied you for that long, how long will you want to watch TV for? Here, put on these jeans."

Charontes tried pulling the pants up over his greaves.

"Maybe I've been unclear, Charontes. You are going to have to take off the shin guards and the swords, and you'll *definitely* have to lose the skirt."

"Then I will be unarmed," Charontes said, stunned at Nicholas's ridiculous suggestion. "Only doomed men walk around unarmed."

"Then, true to your ancient quote, we're *all* doomed here. No one is armed in this time. Well, except maybe the police or bad guys."

"*Bad guys?* You see, what I say is true. Why would they let the *bad guys* carry weapons?" Charontes struggled with his greaves.

"Okay, point taken. I'll tell you what—take the dagger you have in your boot, and keep that. There, then you'll be armed. Your weapons will be safe here. If you feel like you need more than your dagger where were going, I'll take you back to rearm. How does that sound?"

"Nicholas, I find myself in a time that I know very little about. I feel that you are to be trusted. I will defer to your greater knowledge regarding the customs of your people."

"Hallelujah, that's great. Look, if you want to fit in around here, you're going to have to start talking a little more like we do. So when you agree with me or want to say yes, instead of all those words, just say 'okay.' Okay?"

"Okay," Charontes said in his deeply accented and still ancient-sounding voice.

Nicholas laughed, "All right, it's a start. Let's have a look at you. Here, I'll help you with the buttons." He noticed that Charontes had managed to dress himself, but without fastening any of the clothing.

Nicholas kept his hands up in front of him, where Charontes could see them. "I'm just going to show you how to close your shirt and pants. Do not twist or lop off any of my appendages when I do." Nicholas fastened a few on the shirt, showing him. "Just be careful with the buttons—they're not very strong, and you can't pull very hard on them."

"I know of buttons. I can do the rest." He finished buttoning his shirt, and tried to do his pants.

Nicholas laughed. "I'm just going to talk you through this one, as it seems like it would be more conducive to helping me stay alive. There's a button at the top, but below that, there's a zipper. Just pull it up by the little metal piece— it's aligned so it will go into the same spot, every time."

Charontes followed Nicholas's instructions, surprised that the device worked. He was fascinated.

Nicholas stood back and looked at Charontes. "You look great. The pants are a little tight, but the shirt fits perfect."

Charontes just stood there. The clothes felt awful around the tops of his legs. He hated them, but he didn't want to stand out or be laughed at, like he had been before.

"One more thing, and it's probably best if I just show you. We do not relieve ourselves where others can see us." Nicholas pointed at the crotch of his pants. "There are special places for that here, and they're called 'bathrooms.'"

He felt insulted that Nicholas thought he might relieve himself in the open. Curious though, he remained silent.

Nicholas led him to the smallest room in the house and proceeded to relieve himself in a marble basin filled with water. Then he pushed down on something and the water swirled and disappeared downward. New, clean water filled the basin again.   *Impressive*, Charontes thought.

"It takes care of it all, any way you have to go—you know, even the other way. If you have to do that, then you sit on the toilet here to relieve yourself. The water and waste will go away every time. Got it? Go ahead and try."

"Yes. Toilet, okay." Charontes didn't know if he would be able to get used to relieving himself in the house—it was disgusting. Nicholas shut him in the bathroom, and he imitated exactly what Nicholas had done. He liked making the water swirl down.

"You only have to flush it once," Nicholas said from outside the door.

Charontes stopped swirling the water and came out.

"You're a quick learner," Nicholas laughed and tried to pat his shoulder.

He nimbly leaned out of reach and gave him a mean look for trying to touch his person again.

"Come on, big guy. Let's go get someone—I mean, *something* to eat," Nicholas said in a teasing tone. He laughed.

Charontes was famished. "Okay." It was a great word. He found he didn't have to talk much—just use "okay" instead.

Nicholas chuckled when he said the word.

"Am I saying it correctly?" Charontes asked, unsure.

"Boy, being laughed at is not high up on your favorites list, is it? Yes, you're using the word perfectly. I'm laughing because I'm happy you learned it, and I guess I feel proud I taught it to you."

They walked out of the home and headed away from the direction they had originally come. He hoped Aidyl was still safe. Vanth would be feeling better by now, and was probably already beginning to fester.

Hopefully, she didn't recover too quickly. If he returned to the Riders by morning, he felt confident they would wait for him. Any longer and they would most likely set out on their own.

It was dusk. Cars drove down the road with what looked like glowing eyes on their fronts. The sight of them unnerved him. He repeatedly reached for his absent sword. He felt naked without his weapons. Thankfully, Lydia had explained a lot of modern things to him. Otherwise, he would not have remained this calm.

People still stared at him when they walked by, but they didn't look for long. It was mostly the women whose glances would linger.

"Wow, I thought *I* was a ladies' man. Women really like you," Nicholas said, teasing again.

"I love Lydia—she and I are meant to be one," Charontes said, very matter-of-factly.

"I can see you have that all decided on. I take it the little lady had a different idea?"

"Do not provoke me," Charontes rumbled out.

"All right, but we *are* going to have to talk about Lydia, remember?"

A motorcycle came down the street, revving its engine loudly. Reaching for his dagger, Charontes crouched down.

"Relax, calm down," Nicholas said. "Leave the dagger there. It's okay, it won't hurt you. They're like cars, just smaller and louder."

"They sound like thunder. What type of demon rides on them?" Charontes stood up, and they continued walking.

"No demons. Just regular people ride them. Even women," Nicholas added.

Charontes gave him a disbelieving look. "I'm glad Lydia told me stories of her time. Seeing the inventions, as she called them, makes me realize she spoke the truth."

"She's very special to you?" Nicholas asked.

"Yes. Lydia is in danger now. The Riders of the Reunity are here to get the other half of the magnet. I must get to her first, or she will be killed."

"Wow, and I thought being unemployed was tough. Listen, the whole Riders of the Reunity and magnet thing brings about a million more questions to mind, but it will have to wait. Here we are. This is my parents' place."

They approached a one-story building, which was painted white and blue. There were tables outside, but no one sat at them. The smells coming from inside the building told Charontes that someone inside was cooking.

"In case you didn't know, my parents sell food here. That ought to make you happy. I think we're a little early. I work here to help my mom and dad out every now and then. It's not dinner hour yet, so our timing is perfect."

As they walked in, two women who were dressed alike smiled at them, then said something that sounded like a greeting.

"Let's sit over here." Nicholas pointed to a table toward the back right.

A middle-aged, smiling couple came out from the back of the restaurant. The woman was a little plump, with gray curly hair that had small vestiges of its once-blonde color. The man was also graying, but dark-complected and slim. He was almost as tall as Nicholas.

"That's my mom and dad," Nicholas said.

His mother wiped her hands on her apron and gave Nicholas a big hug. "Hello, Nicky. Who's your friend? Is he hungry?"

"Mom, he only speaks Greek." Nicholas said to his mom in Greek. He leaned over toward Charontes. "Now she's *definitely* going to feed you to death," he whispered out the side of his mouth.

"Greek?" she nearly shrieked out, "Oh, it's so nice to meet you. You just call me Bess. Where in Greece are you from?"

Before Charontes could answer the question—for which he didn't have an answer anyway—Nicholas's mother ushered him toward a table.

"You are such a handsome Greek boy," she said. "Are you hungry? Sit down." She took no breaths between her sentences. "We will bring you food. Nicholas, say hello to your father."

Charontes sat. He could definitely tell where Nicholas got his fondness for speaking.

Nicholas hugged his father, who hadn't said a word yet.

"A friend from school, I presume?" his father finally asked. "He looks a little old."

"Dad, you know I graduated already. But yes, this is Charontes. He was a foreign exchange student my last year at school. He's decided to stay in the States a little longer."

Charontes couldn't understand everything Nicholas was telling his dad, but he could tell by the sound of his voice that he was lying. Then Nicholas switched to another language to talk with his father, one Charontes had never heard before.

Nicholas's father looked skeptical but shrugged his shoulders. "Oh, okay. Well, nice to meet you, Charontes," he said in Greek. "My name is Omar."

Charontes stood and gripped his hand. He held Omar's elbow with his other hand. "It is good to meet you both. We are hungry." Charontes even attempted a smile.

Nicholas and his parents burst into laughter.

"Now you've done it," Nicholas said. "You've signed your own death warrant. Death by food. Oh boy, I can't believe you said that."

"I do not understand. I did not mean to offend. They are mad now? They seem very accommodating." He was bewildered.

"No, you're fine. You haven't offended anyone. Worse, you've *encouraged* them. Remember, I warned you— they like to feed people. I hope you can eat, big guy."

"I can eat, and I am hungry." Charontes stomach felt pinched.

True to Nicholas's word, his parents brought out plate after plate of food. Not much of it looked familiar, but all of it tasted exquisite. After their initial pangs of hunger were sated, Nicholas opened the conversation.

"So, start at the beginning. I don't know how much you want to tell me, but I am a trustworthy person, and I certainly don't know any of the same people you know. It's up to you, Charontes. I'd like to help."

Charontes struggled with the decision to trust him. In the end, though, he realized that he desperately needed his help. Nicholas had already assisted him immensely and had proven his reliability. Over the next hour, he gave Nicholas an outline of what had happened and why Lydia now faced such great danger.

"So there are eight other guys like you and one really horrible warrior woman in Delaware Park right now?" Nicholas asked. "Armed to the teeth, waiting for you to get back there?" He leaned back in his chair, running his hand through his unruly blond hair.

"Yes, I must return by the morning, or they will not wait any longer for me."

"This is really bad. I hate to burst your bubble, but Lydia could be anywhere. Although, it seems like these magnets conveniently put you where you're supposed to be. Let's get back to my place, and I'll do a search on her. It sounds like she's a nurse, either an LPN or RN, from how you described her work. We'll start there.

"I see adventure on the horizon," Nicholas said. "I want to talk to my dad before we go. Can you wait for me for a couple minutes? Dessert is on the way. That should keep you occupied. You know, sweets, more food? By the way, my parents love you. I can't believe you can eat that much. Most people turn away fourth helpings."

"Nicholas, before you go, I want to tell you how grateful I am for your help," Charontes said. "My child and Lydia mean everything to me. You have undoubtedly saved me from many indignities and hardships. I will forever be in your debt." Charontes reached out and touched his arm. The joy of making a friend was a new and strange feeling.

"You're welcome. I just hope we can get to Lydia before Vanth does. Then we have to rescue Aidyl, too. Well, *you* do—I can't use a sword or fight. They don't teach that at college." He paused. "You know how you were saying that it seemed like everything was meant to be, fated to happen a certain way? It may be nothing, but did you ever notice that 'Aidyl' is 'Lydia' spelled backwards? They have exactly the same letters."

"No," Charontes said. "I do not spell or read."

"I know. You're a warrior. I'm sure that being a warrior is much handier where you come from than knowing how to read. Look, I'll be right back."

"Okay," Charontes said. *Unbelievable, Lydia and Aidyl are almost the same word.* They were the Chosen Ones, and that must be why. Now he knew he was not mistaken—it all *was* meant to be.

Chapter 37

September 2016

Buffalo, New York

A time to mourn and a time to dance.

—Ecclesiastes 3

The rumbling in my stomach woke me. It reminded me I hadn't eaten in—what was it? Five hundred years? Tears started to well up in my eyes again, and I wiped my face hard with the back of my hand. *No, I'm not going to just lie around my apartment and sob. Get over it.*

Rolling over in bed, I set the pin on my bedside table. I'd made a choice and I would stick to it. I splashed my face with cold water, stuck my chin out, and stared into the mirror.

I didn't look brave—I just looked like a regular person. Well, except for the red-rimmed eyes, wild brown curls, and clothes from Leonardo da Vinci's time. Other than that, I looked perfectly normal.

Showering felt glorious, and it tamed my hair. I dressed slowly in jeans and a blouse. My jeans strangely constricted the tops of my legs since I had become so used to wearing skirts. I stretched out my hurt leg as a test. It felt good as new. *Just to be safe, I should probably have it looked at and get an x-ray,* I thought.

I checked my messages. There were two voicemails, one from Erin and one from Paula. They both said they were worried about me and asked me to call them back. They assured me they'd covered for me at work and told me not to worry—losing a patient got to all of us now and then.

My next problem was my stomach. I eyed the pin on my nightstand. *Should I take it with me?* Putting on my sneakers and a light jacket only delayed the inevitable decision of whether to take the pin or not.

The time I'd spent in the fourteen hundreds already only felt like a very real dream. I didn't want to let it become only memories. Somehow, I had to rescue Aidyl. *Who am I kidding? Like I'm some kind of hero or something.* Even after reading as many of the manuscripts as I could, I still didn't know how to make the pin work. In fact, Patrizia had hypothesized that as long as I only had half of the magnet, it would do whatever *it* wanted.

The pin had brought me here. Patrizia's notes said to have it with me at all times, and it would keep me safe. Maybe that's how it worked. Why else would it bring me back to my own time and my own town? Possibly, the pin had not only protected me, but also helped me spare Charontes, Amelia, and Franco's lives. I didn't know what the truth was since I still hadn't seen any directions on how to be the Chosen One. I would leave the pin right here, on my nightstand. It had already caused enough trouble. I'd put on some lipstick, then I was out of here.

Looking at myself in the mirror again, I wondered what Charontes had seen in me. I wasn't beautiful—cute, maybe. Tiny flecks of purple flashed as I looked at my eyes. Was I the person they claimed me to be?

Whirling from the mirror, I found that my mind wasn't made up about anything. At the last minute, I walked over, grabbed the pin, shut off the lights, and locked the door. I pinned the magnet to my blouse, out of sight under my jacket, and set off down Elmwood Avenue.

I pulled my jacket around me tighter. The sun had set, and the street lights were on. A cool breeze chilled the tip of my nose. Sidewalks were already beginning to fill up. There were college kids laughing outside of Cole's, and the alien smell of cigarette smoke wafted up to my nose as I passed by. Familiar sights like cars, electric lights, and people on cell phones only made me more depressed. I would just get something to eat, then go home and try to figure everything out.

"Hey, cutie, you're too pretty to be walking by yourself," a man said. "Would you like a little company? Where are you off to?"

Great, some guy is hitting on me, I thought. *I really don't feel like dealing with this right now.* "Listen, I just want to be left alone, okay?" I told him as I walked, not wanting to even look at him.

"What's the matter? Why are you so sad?" The man was slurring his words, and I could smell alcohol on his breath.

When I turned to look at him, he definitely looked intoxicated. "Look, buddy," I said, "either you go away *right now*, or I'm going to kick you in the shins."

The man laughed at me, then reached out and grabbed my arm.

I looked up for help.

Then a monster of a man in jeans and a black shirt appeared in my line of sight. He looked so familiar. *Wait a minute…no, it can't be him. His clothes are too modern. It's not possible—I must be hallucinating.*

Then I froze on the spot.

The man loomed toward me, a head above the rest of the crowd, wearing a wounded expression on his face. I watched that expression change from wronged to murderous. Strains of "Yellow Bird" started soft and low in my ears. I felt faint.

"Charontes!" I screamed, kicking the man holding onto my arm.

~~~

Charontes saw Lydia, but she was walking with another man. His heart lurched in his chest. She replaced him that easily? It hadn't even been one day. She must have had someone all along. What other lies had he been told?

Lydia turned to the man and said something. The man laughed and touched her arm. She looked away from the man and saw him.

Dead. The man had maybe three or four breaths left to take before becoming a corpse.

Charontes couldn't believe he'd let Nicholas talk him into going out without his weapons. Now he would have to kill with his bare hands, and that was messy. Sprinting toward them, he heard Lydia shout his name. She turned to fight the man holding her. *He's holding her?*

Suddenly he realized that she was being attacked.

Relief flooded through him. He grabbed the man.

"Charontes, *stop!*" Nicholas yelled.

This time, he would *not* stop. How dare someone touch his woman. He heard the man's arm snap. He yanked him hard and hit him full in the mouth with his elbow.

"Charontes, please—listen to me!" Lydia cried. "You *must* stop! You're killing him. Please!"

Charontes looked at her as he stood over the man, his foot pressed into the man's throat. "You are very observant, Lydia." He pressed his foot in slightly. "Do you love this man?" he roared, shaking with rage. "Is *that* why you want his life to be spared?"

"Holy shit!" Nicholas yelled desperately. "Charontes, what are you doing? You have to stop!"

"*Silence!*" Charontes shouted at the top of his lungs. "Answer me, Lydia. Do you love him?"

"*Love him?*" Lydia half shouted, half cried back at him. "I don't even *know* him! He just walked up to me, and I told him to go away. He laughed at me and sounded drunk. I saw you and kicked him. Please stop. Please!" She sobbed. "I love *you*—just you."

Charontes felt some of the rage leave him. "You have a different way of showing your love than most people do. Leaving the one you love is not usually a sign of affection."

"I did that for *you!*" Lydia shouted defensively through her tears. "To *save* you!"

Charontes heard a strange, loud, high-pitched wailing.

Nicholas grabbed Charontes's arm. "Look, you two can have your little quarrel somewhere else. The police are coming, and if we don't get out of here now, we're all going to jail. Take your boot off his neck so he can breathe, then let's go."

Charontes removed his foot, and held his arms out to Lydia. Her throat made a strangled noise when she jumped into his arms. Charontes ran after Nicholas, carrying Lydia out of habit.

"You are one crazy dude, Charontes." Nicholas shouted back to them as they ran. "And please, for the love of God, don't ever get mad at me." Nicholas was breathing hard as he yelled over his shoulder to Lydia, "I hope you know how much he loves you, lady."

Charontes and Lydia didn't answer him.

"Come on, turn this way," Nicholas panted. "I grew up around here and know all the side streets. We'll double back to my place."

Five minutes later, they were safely inside Nicholas's apartment.

"I have to use the bathroom," Nicholas said, "You two make yourselves comfortable."

Charontes put Lydia down and she hugged his middle. "I never thought I'd see you again. How on earth did you get here?" Her voice came out in a high pitch.

"When you left the farmhouse, Vanth appeared soon after," Charontes said. "She had the bracelet and used it again, almost right away. She thinks that I am part of the Riders, and like her, that I still seek Nortia and the other half of the magnet."

"You mean, as soon as I left, she showed up?" Lydia asked, looking up into his eyes.

"Yes. Possibly Hemisatres left a mark or made itself known to the other. I do not know what happened, only that Vanth appeared."

"Good thing I left when I did then," Lydia said, not sounding very sure of herself.

"Lydia, you are in great danger. Vanth still seeks Nortia and the baby. When her magnet leads her to you, it will not take her much to realize what has happened. Even if she is unable to fully comprehend what is taking place, she'll just kill you for possessing the other half of the magnet."

"Yes, I know," Lydia said.

"Then why did you leave me?" He shook her gently to make his words sink in. "That was the worst possible decision you could have made. I could not protect you anymore. If you do not love me, I will try to live with that—but I cannot let Vanth kill you."

"I *do* love you," Lydia said. "I only left to protect you. You've got to believe that. When you told me you would never give me the pin, I couldn't live with that kind of guilt. It would have been my fault if you never found your daughter. And if I had stayed at the farmhouse, the Riders would have come there. Then you, Amelia, and Franco would all have been killed while being forced to defend me. It would have been all of the Riders against you. I would have died inside if something had happened to you because of me."

She tried to hug him, but Charontes kept her at arm's length, still hurt and angry.

"I took the pin to try and find Aidyl," Lydia said in a low voice. "I didn't know how I would do it, but as stupid as it sounds, that was the plan."

"Then you would have perished on the point of Vanth's sword." He crushed her into his arms. "Lydia, we will do this together. Never leave me again." He held her tightly to him. It felt good to have her in his arms again. He thought he'd lost her forever.

"So…who is he?" Lydia asked, peeking out from under his arm at Nicholas.

"This is my friend, Nicholas," Charontes said proudly. He liked the novel ring the word "friend" had to it.

"Pleased to make your acquaintance, Lydia," Nicholas said with a mock bow. "I've heard a lot about you…believe me," he said, smiling.

"You have?" Lydia asked. She looked at Charontes. "He's your friend? How long have you been here?"

"I came with Vanth this morning. But Nicholas and I have been through much together in a short time."

"A very *exciting* short time, I might add," Nicholas said happily.

"Oh, I almost forgot," Lydia said. "Where's Vanth?"

"Waiting for me where we arrived, too ill to proceed any farther. The time jumps have sickened her and the other Riders. There are only eight left, plus Vanth. She waits for news of Nortia and the other half of the magnet. It was all I could do not to kill them while they were weak and take Aidyl—but I had to find you first. Vanth will only wait until morning for me."

"She has Aidyl? Charontes, I'm so sorry. You could have saved her if it weren't for me." Lydia bit her lip and sat down on the couch. "You know, this could be good. As scary as it is, everyone is in the same time now."

Nicholas's eyes widened as he tried to take everything in.

"Somehow, we have to figure out a way to get Aidyl," Lydia continued. I don't really care about the other half of the magnet, but if we took it from Vanth, she would be powerless to leave this time period." There was hope flooding into her voice.

"Now that you two lovebirds are reunited, we definitely need a plan," Nicholas chimed in.

Chapter 38

September 2016

Buffalo, New York

Sometimes the blackbirds

Must be chased away

So the yellow birds may play.

Flocks of blackbirds made dark patches on the already-gray sky. A thick mist rose two feet up from the ground, giving the field an ethereal look. Dew glistened on the grass as the first rays of the sun burnt through the cold dawn.

I shivered. *Our plan has to work.*

Charontes walked beside me, wearing metal armor and swords. He was silent and lethal. Wading through the mist, cloak billowing, he looked every bit the ancient warrior that he truly was. Brought forth by time, then forgotten.

He grabbed my arm and pulled me roughly toward the trees. The magnet's warmth radiated through my shirt. Its temperature was increasing, and it began to burn into my skin—but I ignored it.

We neared where Vanth hid. It was the only logical plan we could agree on. It made sense since I looked so much like Nortia—but Charontes had protested vehemently against using me as bait.

My hand closed around the small dagger Charontes had given me.

"Make some noise, Lydia, but not too much. I want only some of the Riders to hear us." He pushed me to the ground in front of him and drew his weapons.

"Leave me alone you idiot, that hurt," I cried out. It *did* hurt, being shoved onto the hard, wet ground like that.

What had we gotten ourselves into? Charontes may be used to fighting battles, but I could safely say that this was my first.

Hidden on the sidelines, Nicholas's presence did little to reassure me. He was just a regular guy, not even a warrior. Charontes had insisted Nicholas stay out of the fray, stating that he would be of no use to us if he were dead. Nicholas had looked relieved. I couldn't blame him. My heart was racing with terror.

Three Riders emerged on foot from the tree line with swords drawn.

"I have captured someone." Charontes motioned down to my prone form, almost hidden in the mist at his feet. "Come, look. Vanth will be pleased."

It's working, I thought. *Lure them out, then Charontes will try to kill as many as possible before they all descend on him at once.*

"She is a pretty one," the closest Rider said, leering down at me. He nudged me with his toe. With a *swoosh*, his head suddenly rolled to his feet. Time went into slow motion.

The man began to crumple onto me, blood spraying from the top of his neck.

I scrambled to get out of the way.

The deadly *swoosh* of Charontes's long sword whistled overhead again, mortally wounding the second Rider before the first one had even hit the ground. The cry of the third Rider changed from a warning howl to a death gurgle.

Five left, plus Vanth. Now what? My heart pounded in my chest. Charontes had killed the guards in one fell swoop. Surprise was on our side.

The plaintive wail of a child rose out of the trees. Riders poured forth, a few half-dressed and hastily armed.

"Run, Lydia!" Charontes shouted. "You cannot help me any longer." He leaped toward the lead Rider to engage him before the others. "Get out of harm's way!"

Flattening myself to the ground, I refused to leave him to die alone. My trembling fingers blanched white from squeezing the hilt of the dagger. The raucous calls of the alarmed blackbirds echoed in my head. Another Rider, under Charontes's brutal assault, fell near me.

The detached, rational part of my mind just counted. *Four Riders left plus Vanth.*

Charontes staggered from a crushing blow to his arm guard, and he roared out in pain. Blood oozed down his arm. He renewed his attack with a murderous frenzy, using both swords at once, blocking and rending.

Three to go plus Vanth. Yellow bird, up high in banana tree. I clung to this happy song from my childhood so I could stay brave in the face of death.

The three remaining Riders encircled Charontes. Sweating and bloody, he gulped in large mouthfuls of air. I realized the Riders were now acting as one unit, and Charontes's original advantage was gone. *Yellow bird, you sit all alone like me…*

Vanth's sinister laugh floated over the mist, her horse dancing nervously under her. "Truly, Charontes, did you think you could win against us all?" She urged her horse forward, the adornments on its chest plate tinkling as it walked.

Static electricity crackled in the air.

"My bracelet is warm. You must have brought me something *very* special." Looking at her for the first time sent a chill down my spine. Her eyes glowed, emanating an evil excitement. Small wisps of her jet-black hair did a demented dance as she stared at me. "Too bad I will have to kill you for your trouble." The accent that sounded so charming coming from Charontes lent a wicked lilt to Vanth's speech.

She sat astride her horse, only ten feet away. I had to do something now, or both Charontes and I would die this morning.

You can fly away, in the sky away. You more lucky dan me.

A blackbird screeched when the answer dawned on me. *That's it—the birds!* They were upset because I was in trouble, and they wanted to help. This morning, I decided I would take them up on their offer.

I closed my eyes and imagined hundreds of birds pecking at the three warriors' heads and eyes. I let the birds feel my desperation. Opening my eyes, I pictured the warriors exactly, and thought of the birds flapping, swooping in and diving at them.

Like a dark swarm, the birds descended on them. Charontes used the distraction to skewer another Rider.

There were two left.

Charontes battled on with renewed vigor. Birds were everywhere, and they even flew at Charontes. The poor, sweet things wanted to help, but just weren't that smart.

Then there was one.

Vanth yanked me to my feet by my hair. "Ahhh, you bitch! That hurts—let go of me!" I yelled, struggling. My legs flailed as I bounced off her horse's side. I tried to mentally connect with Vanth's horse, but its mouth was in too much pain, so it wouldn't listen.

Vanth dragged me toward Charontes.

The scorching heat of the pin seared into my chest. How it burned. I grabbed it with one hand and ripped that part of my shirt away. I had to get it off me.

The birds swooped in at Vanth. Now lacking the element of surprise, they had become nothing more than a nuisance.

I had to find the courage somewhere within to do what I must do. *I am the Chosen One.* Dagger in one hand, pin in the other, I blindly reached up and stabbed into Vanth's arm. I prayed it was the arm with the bracelet.

I had pierced straight through her arm with my unexpected assault. Vanth's shriek echoed through the mist while I pulled down on my dagger with all my might. Vanth began to topple down toward me.

She hit the ground hard on her back, and the air whooshed out of her. Releasing the dagger, I grabbed frantically at the bracelet and pried it off Vanth's wrist.

As if guided by someone else, I knew exactly what to do. Quickly, pin in one hand and bracelet in the other, I narrowed the distance between the two magnets. Suddenly, the two pieces snapped together. I watched as the magnets fused together seamlessly, and the pin melted and wrapped itself into the bracelet.

A white light flashed and enveloped me as I stepped onto Vanth's throat, trying desperately to hold her down. Vanth grabbed my leg and clawed maniacally, reaching toward the bracelet. I looked desperately over at Charontes—I needed his help.

Either the shriek or the light caused Charontes to turn, mid-swing, for the briefest of instants to look at me. It had proven to be a fatal mistake.

The last remaining Rider's sword pierced between his shoulder blades.

A mortal blow.

Charontes didn't turn back. Already a dead man, he shoved his sword backward, clean through his killer.

And then there were none.

"*Charontes!*" My scream echoed in my head along with the police sirens.

He had been an almost-indestructible warrior—completely invulnerable—except he'd never fought when someone he loved was at stake. That had been his one fatal flaw.

Charontes fell heavily to his knees, looking up into my eyes. Blood welled up and streamed over his bottom lip. Unable to speak, his mouth moved in his final words to me:

"I never make the same mistake twice."

Then everything happened at once. Nicholas rushed up and began stomping on Vanth's hands, kicking the short sword she'd managed to draw. Vanth kept screaming. Nicholas yelled something about the police being on their way.

Then, my beloved Charontes died.

"I never make the same mistake twice" had been his last words—not "I love you." Why would he say that to me? Uncomprehending, I stood frozen in that spot. He'd meant *something* by those strange words. I blocked everything out.

Then all was silent. The breeze ruffled my hair.

Satres is whole again. I will go back in time, back to when we were together.

"Lydia," a voice in my head said, a voice as deep as time itself, *"don't do this. Even the Chosen One cannot repeat time."* I knew it was Satres. Somehow, the magnet knew my thoughts.

"I don't care," I shouted my grief to an indifferent sky. "I'm going back…not for long…just a few minutes." Surely that wouldn't harm the space-time continuum that much.

Staring at my beautiful warrior, face-first in the grass, I didn't care what would happen, anyway. He'd just saved them against impossible odds—eight warriors plus Vanth. I sobbed as my hair floated in the air.

Unsure how Satres worked, I focused hard.

"Don't do it, Lydia. You may fail to rejoin the two halves this time. Even if you do, it may damage the programming permanently, and then I'll never get out."

"Please, whoever you are—I need to try. Five minutes is all I need."

"I have no choice, you override me now."

I heard a rending sound. I felt myself being pulled swiftly up, then being placed immediately back down.

~~~

Vanth had me by the hair, dragging me toward Charontes. Dagger in one hand, pin still in the other, I reached up and stabbed Vanth's arm, hearing the gratifying sound of Vanth's shriek for the second time today. I silently thanked whoever gave me this second chance.

I seemed to be the only one aware that the scene was being repeated. I had to think fast. As I pulled down on the dagger, Vanth toppled and hit the ground on her back. Everything was playing out exactly the same as last time.

An idea ignited a sliver of hope in my mind. I grabbed the bracelet, and let it slide off Vanth's hand. I watched as the two pieces of magnet fused together. Their joining was not seamless as before, and a small crack remained at the top. *One small difference.*

The white light enveloped me as I stepped on Vanth's throat. Desperate to do everything exactly the same. I only wanted to change one outcome. Looking over at Charontes— he was about to turn.

I yelled with all my might, *"Don't turn! I'm fine!"*

As simple as that, it worked. This time, Charontes *didn't* turn. Instead, he shoved his short sword forward, right through the last Rider.

Just time separates life and hope from death.

I managed a grim smile as Satres's voice resonated in my head.

"And then there was one…and he's all yours. Wielded by one of the Chosen Ones, such a small time deviation worked once, but not without dire consequences to the magnet's integrity.

"You must never repeat time again, Lydia, or the I.N. programming will be irreparably damaged. Then we won't be able to accomplish our ultimate goal. As it is, what you've done could take me years to fix."

Whose voice is that? I wondered. It was a man's voice that I didn't recognize. Or were those my own thoughts? I couldn't be sure. I wanted to ask it, but there was too much going on around me.

"I'm Victor. You're busy, so we can talk later. I'll be here if you need me."

Charontes pulled his sword from the dead Rider and bounded toward me. He reached me at about the same time as Nicholas did.

After a short struggle between Vanth and Charontes, Vanth was crudely trussed in her own cloak, still shrieking. Nicholas had stopped Charontes from killing her, saying she would be a good piece of evidence.

When he finally turned to me, I fell into his arms. He was relatively unharmed and very alive. My heart felt like it would burst with joy.

"My beauty, we did it." His deep voice caressed the top of my head as he held me tightly to his chest. His armor bit into my cheek, but I didn't care. I closed my eyes and thanked the unknown force that had saved him.

A baby's wail rose over the ungodly noise Vanth made. *The baby.* They must act now.

"My child," Charontes said, pushing me from him. "I must get my child." "Nicholas," I said, "the police will be here any second. Get the baby, and take her and Charontes back to your place. I'll meet you there."

"No, you will come with me now," Charontes said. "We will stay together, Lydia."

"I have to be here when the police get here. Someone has to make sure they take Vanth to jail for this. I want to make sure she's held responsible and is put behind bars. Otherwise, we'll always be looking over our shoulder for her." She looked at Nicholas. "I'm not sure what I'll say yet, but I'd never be able to explain him, dressed in armor and all covered with blood," I pointed to Charontes. "He needs to get out of here—I'll figure something out. Hurry...you must go now. Wait for me for as long as it takes. Don't let him out of your sight, Nicholas."

Charontes looked like he would balk.

"Charontes, please," I pleaded. "Think of your baby. Take her from that nursemaid, and make sure she's safe. The police won't hurt me—they'll be happy to have a witness. You have to listen to me. This is *my* time—trust me on this." One more minute, and it would be too late.

Without another word, Charontes turned toward the wood, pulling Nicholas with him. Then they vanished into the tree line.

The police sirens grew louder. The sound of Aidyl's cries had faded to nothing, right when the police cars screeched to a stop near the field.

Guns drawn, the officers came at Lydia. Vanth screamed and kicked to free herself of her bonds.

"I am unarmed…please help me!" I yelled at the approaching swarm of police, my shaking arms raised over my head. "I've been attacked by a crazed madwoman. She's killing everyone. Help me! I barely managed to defend myself from her. She was going to kill me!"

I began sobbing, and it wasn't all an act. Emotion poured out of me. The enormity of all that had happened hit me like a ton of bricks. I'd barely managed to hold it together the whole time.

"It was j-just a walk. Then I was attacked. It's not safe to go anywhere anymore!" I wailed. A policeman pulled me a safe distance away from the now-surrounded Vanth.

Another officer kicked Vanth's sword even farther from her, placed a not-so-gentle knee in her back, and cuffed her. He pulled the cloak down, uncovering her head. Her murderous eyes blazed with an insane violet light, a more damning piece of evidence than any testimony.

Her eyes locked onto mine. "You just wait. I will *never* give up. I will find you and have the *stone!*" she screamed out, hitting an extremely painful octave. The language was unintelligible, of course, to anyone but me.

"Good God—do you know that woman?" A policeman asked me.

"I...I've never seen her b-before in my life, I stammered out, sounding thoroughly terrified.

Unable to smile for fear of giving myself away, I could only think about what I really wanted to say.

Take that, you crazy bitch!

Chapter 39
September 2016
Buffalo, New York

Dream of having grand adventures in your time.

I opened my eyes to the sound of Aidyl, cooing in a small crib beside my bed. Morning light streamed in through the window of my apartment. I turned to my other side and saw Charontes smiling at me, elbow on the bed, head propped on one hand. Who knew how long he'd been lying there, watching me sleep.

"Good morning, my beauty. Now both my girls are awake." His tone was deep and sexy.

"Mmmm," I said, stretching and languishing in the last few moments of sleep. "How's your arm?"

"It's fine," he answered. "The wound remains closed."

Afraid of arousing suspicion with a hospital visit, I had disinfected the ugly cut and put some butterfly stitches on it, doctoring it up the best I could. I couldn't believe everything had happened only three days ago.

I'd spent all the first day at the police station, then arrived late at Nicholas's apartment that evening, where we'd slept that night. Early the next morning, Charontes, the baby, and I went back to my apartment since it was more spacious. The police requested that I be available by phone in case they had more questions.

I clumsily changed Aidyl's diaper and placed her on the bed between the two of us. "She's so beautiful, Charontes," I said, stroking one of her perfect little hands. It's hard to believe who her mother is."

"Her father made up for all that was lacking in the mother," he said with pride in his voice.

I laughed at his arrogance. "Your daddy is so full of himself. Isn't he?" I tickled the baby's belly, and she rewarded me with a brilliant smile. Aidyl's hair was black and already promising to curl. I wasn't surprised to see black-on-black eyes. "Look, she's got your eyes…almost exactly."

He looked closely at Aidyl's eyes. "She does, except for the little bits of purple, just like her mother's and yours," he said.

"You know, Aidyl and I are related. Aren't we, little one?" I wiggled her toes until I got another sweet smile from her.

There was a knock at the door. I jumped up and threw on my robe. "Who is it?" I asked, mouth to the doorjamb.

"Nicholas."

I opened the door and gave him a big hug. He'd been such a big help. He'd spent half of yesterday shopping for baby supplies, thoughtfully including a few books on how to take care of a baby—because none of us had a clue.

"Did you hear from the police yet?" Nicholas asked.

"Yep, they called yesterday evening after you left."

"Come on, you're killing me." Nicholas returned my smile. "It must be good news."

"Yes. One of the senior officers remembered a similar incident that happened back in the eighties, where two people died. They compared photos taken from the bodies years ago and eyewitness accounts.

"In the end, they concluded that it must be the same 'cult,' at least that's what the police are calling the Riders. The horses, swords, and the way they were dressed all those years ago was identical to the bodies in the park.

"I was excused as just a passerby who was in the wrong place at the wrong time." I smiled even wider at my little joke. "One of the officers told me the case remained unsolved because none of the cult members had ever resurfaced until now.

"Vanth, they're assuming, was raised by the cult. To quote one officer, 'She's crazier than a loon. She'll probably be judged insane, but either way, she will be going away for a long time.'"

"That's it, then?" Nicholas asked. "You're off the hook?"

"Well, I have to testify in court in two weeks, but then yes, I'm off the hook." I turned toward the baby's squeal of delight. Charontes was lying on the bed and had her up over his head with her little belly in his palm. Two big fingers supported her head. The baby looked elated, happily kicking and squirming.

"So what now?" Nicholas asked.

"Come in and sit down—I was just going to make some coffee."

"Lydia…" Charontes's voice had a quavering edge to it, like something was wrong.

I looked over and he still had his arm extended, but the baby was free-floating in the air, an inch over his palm. She was squealing and making baby gurgles.

"I know exactly whose side of the family she gets *that* from," I said. "She's so happy, she's floating!"

"Hey, uh, guys?" Nick said, "Your baby is flying. Is that normal?"

"It's not *normal*-normal," I said, "but for us, I guess it *is* kind of normal. If that makes any sense at all. Because of the closed timeline curve, all of us girls have been rewritten and have certain gifts. Only I don't think they usually show up this soon."

I knew that would initiate a volley of questions from Nick, so I tried to distract him. "Don't drop her, Charontes. Please be careful."

"I am. She just went up into the air on her own. And how could I drop her, anyway? She's floating." He focused his attention to the baby above him. "Now listen here, little girl, there will absolutely be no flying. I don't want you to get hurt."

He continued trying to coax her down, but Aidyl didn't understand him. He ended up just grabbing her shirt and holding onto her that way.

She just cooed, oblivious to what was happening.

"That is going to put a whole new twist on babysitting," I joked.

"I can safely say," Nick said, "you all are the most interesting people I've ever met. I would love some coffee. Thank you, Chosen One." Nick sat down at the table. "Now, what were you saying before we were so rudely interrupted by your flying baby?"

I laughed at Nick's silliness. It felt good to laugh again. "We were up late last night, trying to figure out what to do. Charontes and I have decided that, after the trial, we want to go back to fourteen eighty-one. That is, of course, if Satres still works the way we suspect, and if our friend Amelia will have us."

I left out the part where Charontes and I had pledged our love to each other, and promised that, no matter what happened, we would always stay in the same time together.

"We'd like to make that time our home base. With Satres, we can pretty much do anything we want, whenever we want."

"Why don't you try it out now?" Nicholas asked.

"Not without me and the baby, she will not," Charontes growled out. He'd laid the baby on his chest. The deep rumble from his voice made her coo happily again. Charontes kept a hand on her back, I presumed, so she wouldn't float up again.

I rummaged through the cabinets for coffee. "You can see what I'm up against," I said to Nicholas. "He won't let me try it until we can all go at the same time. The time jumps don't affect me or the baby, but they seem to knock everyone else for a loop. So we'll wait until we're both ready to go, then try it at the same time."

"Why fourteen eighty-one? What about your family and friends—and your job?" Nicholas asked.

"We loved our time together in fourteen eighty-one, and Charontes will definitely get in trouble if we stay in this time too long. I think he blended much better into Renaissance times." I smiled fondly at Charontes. "We're going to see my parents tomorrow. I called them last night and said I had a surprise for them."

"I'd say that's kind of an understatement," Nicholas said, laughing.

"I'm going to tell them the truth. I think between the two of us, we can convince them. Can you bring us a few smaller pieces of his armor from wherever it is you hid them? Between Charontes's pattern of speech, and showing them ancient armor in new condition, I think that should do the trick.

"My parents are very knowledgeable about Greek and Roman history, and I'm certain they'll believe me. Then there are my sisters—they know I wouldn't make something like this up."

"Sure, I'll bring the armor tonight, no problem. I'll even bring a pizza." Nicholas looked in Charontes's direction. "Well, maybe *four* pizzas. Hey, what about your work?"

"Lydia, can I come into your thoughts?" said a foreign voice in my head.

Sure, I thought. *Good morning, Victor.*

"Good morning."

Setting the mugs out on the table, I said to Nicholas, "Well, once I've convinced my parents, I'll enlist their help. When and if we successfully time jump, my parents will obviously know. Then, they'll have instructions to call my work. They can tell them that I've suddenly eloped and that I've moved to my new husband's country. I'm not sure where yet, but somewhere far away. Most of my friends are from work and will find out that way. The rest of them know my parents, and they'll probably call them when they notice I'm not around."

"Wow, Lydia—you *do* have it all figured out."

"Well, all except for Charontes's horse. The police, with the help of the humane society, took him and the other horses. That day at the park, when they took them, I was still there and managed to tell the horse to behave until we can come for him. He fought so hard before that, I thought they would shoot him, right there in the park. He seemed to understand me. He's quite smart, you know?"

"Oh, of course—using that animal-mind-meld thing you told me about," Nick said. "I just don't know how I'm ever going to get used to you people."

"I hate to say it, Nick, but it doesn't look like you're going to have to. We're not staying for long." I felt a tug of homesickness already.

"Well, while we're on that subject, there's something I'd like to ask you both." Nick looked nervous, but hopeful.

I poured out the coffees.

"Is my coffee ready?" Charontes asked.

"One day of drinking coffee, and he's already a coffeeholic," I said.

Charontes came up to the table, holding Aidyl. Her diaper looked clean, but the tape clung dangerously off to one side—evidence of our inexperience.

"What is it?" Charontes asked. "You need only ask, and it shall be yours, Nicholas, my friend."

"I want to go with you," Nicholas said in a serious voice. "And, hear me out before you say no. I feel somehow that this was meant to be. I'm supposed to meet both of you, and go with you. Since I've finished college, there's been a void in my life.

"Whenever I've imagined my future, I just come up with a blank. I realize now that's because I was trying to imagine a future in this time. I think I can't, because I'm not meant to have one *here*. I know it sounds crazy, but that's why I'm supposed to go with both of you."

"Oh...but Nick, what about your parents?" I asked, stopping the coffee mug inches away from my lips, the fragrant aroma wafting into my nose.

"Please take a sip of your coffee, Lydia," Victor said. *"I promise to be quiet and not pester."*

"I already talked with my father," Nick said. "I didn't tell him about the time travel or anything, but he already suspected something was going on. I wasn't sure if you two would be time traveling, but if you did, I wasn't going to miss the opportunity of a lifetime.

"I told my dad something important was going on in my life, and that I thought an amazing opportunity was going to happen for me. I said I might have to go away, but it wouldn't be forever. Would you both ever plan to come back to this time?"

"Yes, I'm pretty sure we can count on Satres to work the way it's supposed to. So, if we could, we'd like to come back for visits, as well as other creature comforts and supplies when we need them," I said, taking a big sip of my coffee.

"Oh, that's really good," Victor said. *"Mmmm, I've missed coffee so much."*

Victor, it's really hard to concentrate when you're oohing and aahing in my head.

"Sorry, Lydia."

"Great," Nick said. "So, what say the two of you? Can I go with you? I really need this adventure. If you're worried about changing the future, don't—because I believe this *is* my future." Nicholas looked excited.

I glanced at Charontes. I would defer the decision to him. I was more than happy to take Nick along. Having someone from my time that I could talk to would help immensely with the homesickness.

"Nicholas, it would gladden our hearts to bring a friend like you along," Charontes said. "We'd welcome you anywhere we go. You and I can train and hunt together."

"Wait a minute, Charontes. You know I don't know anything about fighting or hunting, right?"

"I will teach you," Charontes said. "Aidyl will learn, too, when she is old enough," He held Aidyl in one arm as he thumped Nicholas on the back with his other.

"Okay, okay. Ow. Easy, big guy. Yeah, then once I'm trained, you can take me on your next adventure." Nick laughed.

"Don't laugh," I said. "That adventure may happen sooner than you expect. Since the magnet became a whole, I'm able to talk to it. I haven't had a lot of time with it yet, but I'm learning more every day. The magnet was completed in the year twenty-five-fifty-nine, and went live, so to speak, in twenty-five-sixty.

"I know we've been faced with some really hard-to-believe concepts, but wait until you hear this one. It's incredible. There is someone encoded into the magnet whose name is Victor Pirata. He's the son of Satres's inventor and is a distant, future relative of Aidyl's and mine.

"Victor said that when the magnet is rubbed, microscopic pieces of I.N. are imbedded and absorbed through the skin. That's how he's able to communicate with me."

"So he actually talks to you with the…what is it…implantable nanotechnology?" Nick asked. "That's awesome—like a genie in a bottle. Can I rub it, too?" He was as unflappable as ever.

"No. That's why Aidyl and I are the Chosen Ones. Our DNA is programmed into Satres. We're really just glorified receivers. Somehow the magnet is set up to only be able to talk to people whose DNA is already programmed into it. All we have to do is rub Satres once, and the I.N. goes inside us.

"That's why it's called S.A.T.R.E.S. It's an acronym for 'Self Aware Time Travel Receiver Encoding Supercomputer.'" Something in the tone of my voice gave my thoughts away.

"So, you're infected with this I.N. stuff now?" Nick asked. "What about Aidyl?"

"She hasn't touched Satres yet, and I'm trying to look at it as a good thing," I said. "Not a contagion."

I closed my eyes and took another big sip of my coffee. I had to admit, it was starting to sound like something from that movie, *Invasion of the Body Snatchers*. I couldn't believe I was just calmly sitting here, casually explaining all this over coffee.

"So, this Victor…he's Satres?" Nick asked. "Is he sorta like that computer, HAL?" As usual, he was not even close to running out of questions.

I didn't mind. I was happy to have someone to talk with about it. Charontes didn't understand the technology yet, and was jealous of the *other man* inside my head.

Men.

"I'm still a little fuzzy on specific details," I said, "but I think Satres is the magnet and all its programming. So basically, it's a supercomputer. Victor is an actual person whose thoughts and complete nonphysical being were encoded into the computer."

"Why would anyone want to do that? It's not going to suck us into it, too, is it?" Nick sounded leery.

"Honestly, I'm not an expert on it, but from what Victor told me, his father, John Pirata, put him into the magnet to save his life. A virus had become an epidemic and casualties were rising exponentially. It was only a matter of days before the virus would breach their laboratory compound.

"His father, a genius with I.N., had been working for years on Satres. He'd just finished programming the magnet when they ran out of time. The I.N. hadn't found an antibody for the virus yet. His father told Victor he could save him by encoding him into Satres. His physical body, however, would have to stay in the lab in a suspended animation, run completely by I.N."

"Wow, that is so weird," Nick said. "It must have been really hard for him to leave his dad to die. He did die, didn't he?"

"Lydia, does this guy ever stop asking questions?" Victor asked. *"I don't know if my dad died or not. Besides, we're in the past now, so it's really not relevant."*

"He says he doesn't know if his dad died or not," Lydia said to Nick.

"You're talking to Victor right now? Nick asked incredulously. "You must not get any privacy. Tell him I said hi."

"He heard you. I can call out to him when I have a question, or I can ask him to give me privacy. Other than that, he's like another person in the room, except he's forced to experience the world as I experience it through my senses. And he says, 'Hello, Nick. Nice to meet you.'"

"Hey, Vic. Lydia, that's unbelievable. It's going to make you go bonkers, though."

"No, but she's going to be asking for *lots* of privacy," Charontes said, sounding indignant.

"Thanks for your vote of confidence, guys," I said.

"I promise, Lydia, I won't take your privacy away
from you," Victor said. *"It's just been good to be able to*
sense things more realistically again. It's been almost three
millennia since I've been able to see, hear, taste, smell, and
feel things in a way that isn't a computer simulation. Thank
you for allowing me to do that."

You're welcome, I thought. *Three millennia...that must*
have been horrible. I'm so sorry for you.

"Don't be, it's no one's fault," Victor said. *"I chose*
this, but without fully understanding what kind of sacrifice I
was making. But still, I chose it freely. Even now, I welcome
the challenge."

You're very brave, I thought.

"What about his body?" Nick asked. "Why'd they put
it in suspended animation? Is he going to get it back?" He
cleared his throat to speak once more. "Victor, hey, buddy.
How are you going to get your body back?" Nick asked in a
raised voice, unnecessarily vying for Victor's attention.

My exchanges with Victor took only a fraction of a
second. Compared to speech, thoughts traveled the neural

pathways at phenomenal speeds. There could even be multiple layers of thoughts.

"You don't need to ask every question twice, Nick," I said. "Victor says his father stayed behind to continue working on finding an antibody using I.N.. If he isolated it before he succumbed to the virus, he would inject it into Victor's body. Then Victor's body would be a vessel to hold the cure to the virus. His father was very close to isolating an antibody—a week or even just days away."

"So now what?" Nick asked. "Do we have to get his body or something?"

"No, we are not," Charontes said. "I will not risk my girls' lives to retrieve a dead body."

"Wow, you've got your work cut out for you, Lydia," Victor said.

Be nice, Victor.

"His body may *not* be dead," I said. "I'm not sure what we're going to do yet. If it means the survival of the human race in the future, Charontes, we may have to take a few risks.

"Victor says he has a lot to repair, anyway, because of the crack I made in the magnet. We can do simple time jumps now, but the repairs must be done before we go to the future and do something as important as, oh, *save all mankind.* First though, we need to regroup—and I would rather do that in fourteen eighty-one, where I think we'll all be safe."

"I'm in," said Victor.

Ha, ha. You're a regular comedian. "Victor says that he's in."

"I'm in, too." Nick replied without hesitation.

I looked at Charontes.

"What?" Charontes said. "As long as I am with you and Aidyl, I will be happy. I don't care where we are."

"Okay, Nick, we're going to take you up on your offer," I said. "I don't know what our next adventure will be. This is going to sound crazy, but I'm just going to go ahead and say it. In addition to saving the world, I would like to find my biological mother. She's out there, and I don't know where or when—but I owe it to her to find her.

"The police found only two bodies all those years ago. They were both men. That means my real mother is out there somewhere. I have a feeling that there's a wise, old lady named Patrizia, somewhere in time, who's expecting us. She might have some ideas on what we should do."

I heard Nicholas gulp. Then Victor began to speak.

"Lydia, I can help you locate Nortia and Antoni. I'm not sure exactly when they are, because Satres was in two pieces at the time, but I'll start searching all the files that were made when the magnet was separated.

"I know you're aware of this, but we need to complete the original mission and eradicate the virus. I have a lot of repairs to do— so many that it could take years. I've become a very patient man, and we have time on our side now. I won't pressure you, but when the time comes, I'll let you know. I want you to know that I'm eternally grateful for everything you went through to make Satres whole again."

I smiled. *Thank you for telling me that, Victor. And you're most welcome.*

~~~

Later that evening, Charontes held Lydia in his arms. He could never get enough of her. He thanked the Gods for sending him Aidyl and Lydia.

He whispered into Lydia's ear, ever so softly, "You are perfect, my beauty. Perfect…*every time.*"

END

I hope you've enjoyed reading *Paradox I.N. Time* as much as I did writing it.

Thank you for reading! The response from readers has been wonderful and one of the best parts about writing this series.

If you enjoyed the book and would like to share that with others, please consider leaving a review.

Paradox I.N. Time is book one, in the *It's About Time Series*. I look forward to publishing book two, *Pirates and Paradoxes* in late 2017.

I always enjoy hearing from readers feel free to email me at Lauren.duchateau@yahoo.com or visit my website at www.lduchateau.com

Thanks again,

Lauren DuChateau

Made in the USA
Middletown, DE
21 August 2017